Before embarking on her writing career, Cecelia Ahern completed a degree in Journalism. In addition to her bestselling novels, all of which have reached number one, Cecelia co-created the ABC Emmy Award-winning TV comedy, *Samantha Who?*, Hallmark's *Three Wise Women*, and adapted her own novella, *Mrs Whippy*, for the stage. She lives in Dublin with her family.

Cecelia's books are available in print, audio and ebook form and are published in forty countries around the world.

Acclaim for
P.S. I Love You

'A wonderfully warm and witty debut from a terrific new writer … This exceptional novel about bereavement, friendship and lost love is both heartbreaking and uplifting'
Daily Express

'A sensational debut novel that proves true love never dies'
Cosmopolitan

'A wonderfully life-affirming, witty debut'
Company

'Like an Irish *Sleepless in Seattle*'
InStyle

'A fun, fresh read'
Marie Claire

'Wild humour and heartbreak tangled up in one great read'
Cathy Kelly

'Heartwarmingly good'
Heat

'Everything she writes comes from the heart'
Sunday Tribune

'Insightful and true'
Irish Independent

Acclaim for Cecelia's previous bestsellers

'Cecelia Ahern is queen of the modern fairytale.
Ahern has given her readers exactly what they want:
love, magic, happy endings. And most of all, hope'
Irish Times

'A sweet moral tale lifted by Ahern's special brand
of magical twist'
Daily Telegraph

'An absorbing heart-warming story'
Glamour

'The key to Ahern's success is her ability to not just tell
a good story, but sprinkle it with plenty of laughs,
tears, and a little bit of magic'
Mirror

'Unputdownable'
Grazia

'Heart-warming, emotional, funny and filled
with unexpected twists'
RTE Guide

'Utterly irresistible … I devoured it in one sitting'
Marian Keyes

Also by Cecelia

Cecelia Ahern

P.S. I Love You

HARPER

HARPER

An imprint of HarperCollinsPublishers
77–85 Fulham Palace Road,
Hammersmith, London W6 8JB
www.harpercollins.co.uk

This paperback edition 2013
1

First published by HarperCollinsPublishers 2004

A catalogue record for this book
is available from the British Library

ISBN: 978-0-00-751860-9

This novel is entirely a work of fiction.
The names, characters and incidents portrayed in it are
the work of the author's imagination. Any resemblance to
actual persons, living or dead, events or localities is
entirely coincidental.

Typeset in Sabon by Palimpsest Book Production Limited,
Falkirk, Stirlingshire

Printed and bound in Great Britain by
Clays Ltd, St Ives plc

MIX
Paper from
responsible sources
FSC™ C007454

FSC is a non-profit international organisation established to promote
the responsible management of the world's forests. Products carrying the
FSC label are independently certified to assure consumers that they come
from forests that are managed to meet the social, economic and
ecological needs of present and future generations,
and other controlled sources.

Find out more about HarperCollins and the environment at
www.harpercollins.co.uk/green

For David

Writing this book was a labour of love and there are so many people I owe thanks to for allowing me to share it with the world.

I owe huge gratitude to my family for their love and support, without which this book would most definitely never have been born. The ever patient and encouraging clan, the big engine that is such a motivation to this little train; Mimmie, Dad, Georgina, Nicky and David. Welcome to the world Rocco and Jay.

Thank you to my agent Marianne Gunn O'Connor who goes far beyond the call of duty to encourage, inspire and help make the magic happen. Thanks also to Vicki Satlow and Pat Lynch for such hard work and belief in my work.

Thank you to the HarperCollins team for their endless support. Thanks to Lynne Drew, Maxine Hitchcock, Amanda Ridout, Moira Reilly (who was there before it even started), Fiona Mcintosh, Claire Bord and the many many other people involved.

Thank you to all the readers and booksellers for getting behind this book in such an overwhelming way. I am eternally grateful.

But most importantly, thank you to Holly and Gerry for visiting my imagination that night with their story. You made an impact and have never left my mind.

CHAPTER ONE

Holly held the blue cotton sweater to her face and the familiar smell immediately struck her, an overwhelming grief knotting her stomach and pulling at her heart. Pins and needles ran up the back of her neck and a lump in her throat threatened to choke her. Panic took over. Apart from the low hum of the fridge and the occasional moaning of the pipes, the house was quiet. She was alone. Bile rose in her throat and she ran to the bathroom, where she collapsed to her knees before the toilet.

Gerry was gone and he would never be back. That was the reality. She would never again run her fingers through his soft hair, never share a secret joke across the table at a dinner party, never cry to him when she got home from a hard day at work and just needed a hug, she would never share a bed with him again, never be woken up by his fits of sneezes each morning, never laugh with him so much her stomach would ache, never fight with him about whose turn it was to get up and turn the bedroom light off. All that was left was a bundle of memories, and an image of his face that became more and more vague each day.

Their plan had been very simple: to stay together for the rest of their lives. A plan that anyone within their circle would agree was accomplishable. They were best friends, lovers and soul mates, destined to be together, everyone thought. But as it happened, one day destiny greedily changed its mind.

The end had come all too soon. After complaining of a migraine for a few days, Gerry had agreed to Holly's advice to see his doctor. This was done one Wednesday on a lunch break from work. They thought the migraine was due to stress or tiredness, and agreed that at the very worst he might need glasses. Gerry had been upset that he might need glasses. He needn't have worried, since it turned out it wasn't his eyes that were the problem. It was the tumour growing inside his brain.

Holly flushed the toilet and, shivering from the coldness of the tiled floor, she shakily steadied herself to her feet. He was thirty years old. By no means was he the healthiest man on the earth, but he was healthy enough to . . . well, to live a normal life. When he became very sick he would bravely joke about how he shouldn't have lived life so safely. Should have taken drugs, should have drunk more, should have travelled more, should have jumped out of aeroplanes while waxing his legs . . . his list went on. Even as he laughed about it Holly could see the regret in his eyes. Regret for the things he'd never made time to do, places he'd never seen and sorrow for the loss of future experiences. Did he regret the life he had had with her? Holly never

2

doubted that he loved her, but feared he felt he had wasted precious time.

Growing older became something he wanted desperately to accomplish rather than merely a dreaded inevitability. How presumptuous they both were never to consider growing old as an achievement and a challenge. Ageing was something they wanted so much to avoid.

Holly drifted from room to room while she sobbed fat, salty tears. Her eyes were red and sore, and there seemed to be no end to this night. None of the rooms in the house provided her with any solace, just unwelcoming silences as she stared around at the furniture. She longed for the couch to hold out its arms to her but even it ignored her.

Gerry would not be happy with this, she thought. She took a deep breath, dried her eyes and tried to shake some sense into herself. No, Gerry would not be pleased at all.

Holly's eyes were tender and puffy from crying all through the night. Just as she had every other night for the past few weeks, she had fallen into fitful sleep in the early hours of the morning. Each day she woke to find herself sprawled uncomfortably across some piece of furniture – today it was the couch. Once again it was the phone call from a concerned friend or family member that roused her. They probably thought that all she did was sleep. Where were their phone calls when she listlessly roamed the house like a zombie, searching the rooms for . . . for what? What was she expecting to find?

'Hello,' she answered groggily. Her voice was hoarse from all the tears but she had long stopped caring about maintaining a brave face. Her best friend was gone and nobody understood that no amount of make-up, fresh air or shopping was going to fill the hole in her heart.

'Oh, sorry, love, did I wake you?' the concerned voice of Holly's mother came across the line. Every morning her mother called to see if she had survived the night alone, always afraid of waking her, yet always relieved to hear her speak; safe in the knowledge her daughter had braved the ghosts of the night.

'No, I was just dozing, it's OK.' Always the same answer.

'Your dad and Declan have gone out and I was thinking of you, pet.'

Why did that soothing sympathetic voice always send tears to Holly's eyes? She could picture her mother's face, eyebrows furrowed, forehead wrinkled with worry. But it didn't soothe Holly. It made her remember why they were worried and that they shouldn't have to be. Everything should be normal. Gerry should be here beside her, rolling his eyes up to heaven and trying to make her laugh while her mother yapped on. So many times Holly would have to hand the phone over to Gerry as her fit of giggles took over. Then he would chat away, ignoring Holly as she jumped around the bed, pulling her silliest faces and doing her funniest dances just to get back at him. It seldom worked.

She 'ummed' and 'aahed' throughout the conversation, listening but not hearing a word.

'It's a lovely day, Holly. It would do you the world of good to go out for a walk. Get some fresh air.'

'Um, I suppose.' There it was again – fresh air, the alleged answer to all her problems.

4

'Maybe I'll call round later and we can have a chat.'

'No thanks, Mum. I'm OK.'

Silence.

'Well, all right . . . give me a ring if you change your mind. I'm free all day.'

'OK.' Another silence. 'Thanks, though.'

'Right then . . . take care, love.'

'I will.' Holly was about to replace the phone when she heard her mother's voice again.

'Oh, Holly, I almost forgot. That envelope is still here for you – you know, the one I told you about. It's on the kitchen table. You might want to collect it. It's been here for weeks now and it might be important.'

'I doubt it. It's probably just another card.'

'No, I don't think it is, love. It's addressed to you and above your name it says . . . oh, hold on while I get it . . .'

The phone was put down, the sound of heels on the tiles toward the table, chairs screeched against the floor, footsteps getting louder, phone being picked up . . .

'You still there?'

'Yeah.'

'OK, it says at the top "The List". Maybe it's from work or something, love. It's worth just taking a . . .'

Holly dropped the phone.

CHAPTER TWO

'Gerry, turn off the light!' Holly giggled as she watched her husband undress before her. He danced around the room performing a striptease, slowly unbuttoning his white cotton shirt with his long slender fingers. He raised his left eyebrow towards Holly and allowed the shirt to slide from his shoulders, caught it in his right hand and swung it around over his head.

Holly giggled again.

'Turn off the light? What, and miss all this?' he grinned cheekily while flexing his muscles. He wasn't a vain man but had much to be vain about, thought Holly. His body was strong and perfectly toned. His long legs were muscular from hours spent working out in the gym. At almost six foot he was tall enough to make Holly feel safe when he stood protectively beside her five foot five. Most of all she loved that when she hugged him her head would rest neatly just below his chin, where she could feel his breath lightly blowing her hair and tickling her head.

Her heart leaped as he lowered his boxers, caught them on the tip of his toes and flung them at her where they landed on her head.

'Well, at least it's darker under here, anyway,' she laughed. He always managed to make her laugh. When she came home tired and angry after work he was invariably sympathetic and listened to her complaining. They seldom fought, and when they did it was over stupid things that amused them after, like who had left the porch light on all day or who had forgotten to set the alarm at night.

Gerry finished his striptease and dived into the bed. He snuggled up beside her tucking his freezing cold feet underneath her legs to warm himself.

'Aaaagh! Gerry, your feet are like ice cubes!' Holly knew that this position meant he had no intention of budging an inch. 'Gerry,' Holly's voice warned.

'Holly,' he mimicked.

'Didn't you forget something?'

'No, not that I know of,' he answered.

'The light?'

'Ah yes, the light,' he said sleepily, and pretended to snore loudly.

'Gerry!'

'I had to get out of bed and do it last night, as I remember.'

'Yeah, but you were just standing right beside the switch a second ago!'

'Yes . . . just a second ago,' he repeated.

Holly sighed. She hated having to get back out of bed when she was nice and snug, step onto the cold wooden floor, and then fumble around in the darkness on the way back to the bed. She tutted.

'I can't do it all the time, you know, Hol. Someday I might not be here and then what will you do?'

'Get my new husband to do it,' Holly huffed, trying her best to kick his cold feet away from hers.

'Ha!'

'Or just remember to do it myself before I get into bed.'

Gerry snorted. 'Fat chance of that happening, my dear. I'll have to leave a message on the light switch for you before I go, just so you'll remember.'

'How thoughtful of you but I would rather you just leave me your money.'

'And a note on the immersion,' he continued on.

'Ha-ha.'

'And on the milk carton.'

'You're a very funny man, Gerry.'

'Oh, and on the windows so you don't open them and set the alarm off in the mornings.'

'Hey, why don't you just leave me a list of things for me to do in your will if you think I'll be so incompetent without you?'

'Not a bad idea,' he laughed.

'Fine then, I'll turn off the bloody light.' Holly grudgingly got out of bed, grimaced as she stepped onto the ice-cold floor and switched off the light. She held out her arms in the darkness and slowly began to find her way back to the bed.

'Hello? Holly, did you get lost? Is there anybody out there, there, there, there?' Gerry shouted out to the black room.

'Yes, I'm hhhhowwwwwwcch!' she yelped as she stubbed her toe against the bedpost. 'Shit, shit, shit, fuck, bastard, shit, crap!'

Gerry snorted and sniggered underneath the duvet. 'Number two on my list: watch out for bedpost . . .'

'Oh, shut up, Gerry, and stop being so morbid,' Holly snapped back at him, cradling her poor foot in her hand.

'Want me to kiss it better?' he asked.

'No, it's OK,' Holly replied sadly, 'if I could just put them here so I can warm . . .'

'Aaaaah! Jesus Christ, they're freezing!!'

Which made her laugh again.

So that was how the joke about the list came about. It was a silly and simple idea that was soon shared with their closest friends, Sharon and John McCarthy.

It was John who had approached Holly in the school corridor when they were just fourteen and muttered the famous words, 'Me mate wants to know if you'll go out with him.' After days of endless discussion and emergency meetings with her friends, Holly eventually agreed.

'Aah, go on, Holly,' Sharon had urged. 'He's such a ride, and at least he doesn't have spots all over his face like John.'

How Holly envied Sharon right now. Sharon and John had married the same year as Holly and Gerry. Holly was the baby of the bunch at twenty-three, the others were twenty-four. Some said she was too young and lectured her about how, at her age, she should be travelling the world and enjoying herself. Instead, Gerry and Holly travelled the world together. It made far more sense that way because when they weren't together . . . well, Holly just felt as though she was missing a vital organ from her body.

Her wedding day was far from the best day of her

life. Like most little girls, she had dreamed of a fairy-tale wedding with a princess dress and beautiful, sunny weather, in a romantic location surrounded by all who were near and dear to her. She imagined the reception would be the best night of her life, pictured herself dancing with all of her friends, being admired by everyone and feeling special. The reality was quite different.

She woke up in her family home to screams of, 'I can't find my tie!' (her father), or, 'My hair looks shite' (her mother), and the best one of all was, 'I look like a bloody whale! There's no way I'm going to this bleeding wedding looking like this. I'll be scarlet! Mum, look at the state of me! Holly can find another bridesmaid 'cos I'm not bleedin goin. Oi! Jack, give me back that feckin hair dryer, I'm not finished!' That unforgettable statement was made by her younger sister, Ciara, who very regularly threw tantrums and refused to leave the house on the basis of having nothing to wear, regardless of her bursting wardrobe. She was currently living somewhere in Australia with strangers, and the only communication the family had with her was an email from her every few weeks. Holly's family spent the rest of the morning trying to convince Ciara how she was the most beautiful woman in the world. All the while Holly silently dressed herself feeling like shite. Ciara eventually agreed to leave the house when Holly's usually calm dad screamed at the top of his voice, and to everyone's amazement, 'Ciara, this is Holly's bloody day, NOT YOURS! And you WILL go to the wedding and enjoy yourself AND when Holly walks downstairs you WILL tell her how beautiful she looks and I don't wanna hear a peep out of you FOR THE REST OF THE DAY!'

So when Holly walked downstairs everyone oohed and aahed while Ciara, looking like a ten-year-old who had just been spanked, tearfully gazed at her with a trembling lip and said, 'You look beautiful, Holly.' All seven of them squashed into the limo – Holly, her parents, three brothers and Ciara, and sat in terrified silence all the way to the church.

The whole day just seemed a blur to her now. She barely had time to speak to Gerry, as they were both being pulled in opposite directions to meet Great-aunt Betty from the back arse of nowhere, whom Holly hadn't seen since she was born, and Grand-uncle Toby from America, who had never been mentioned before but was suddenly a very important member of the family.

And nobody told her it would be so tiring either. By the end of the night Holly's jaw was sore from smiling for photographs, and her feet were killing her from running around all day in very silly little shoes. She desperately wanted to join the large table of her friends who had been howling with laughter all night, obviously enjoying themselves. Well for some, she thought. But as soon as Holly stepped into the honeymoon suite with Gerry her worries of the day faded and the point of it all became clear.

Tears once again rolled down Holly's face and she realised she had been daydreaming again. She sat frozen on the couch with the phone still off the hook beside her. The hours just seemed to pass her by these days without her knowing what time or even what day it was. She seemed to be living outside of her body, numb to everything but the pain in her heart, in her bones, in her head. She was just so tired . . . Her stomach grumbled and she realised she couldn't remember the last time she had eaten. Had it been yesterday?

She shuffled into the kitchen, dressed in Gerry's dressing gown and her favourite pink 'disco diva' slippers that Gerry had bought her the previous Christmas. She was his disco diva, he used to say. Always the first on the dance floor, always the last out of the club. Huh, where was that girl now? She opened the fridge and stared in at the empty shelves. Just vegetables and yogurt long past its sell-by date leaving a horrible stench in the fridge. She smiled weakly as she shook the milk carton. Empty. Third on his list . . .

Christmas two years ago Holly had gone shopping with Sharon for a dress for the annual ball they attended at the Burlington Hotel. Shopping with Sharon was always a dangerous outing, and John and Gerry had joked about how they would once again suffer through Christmas without any presents as a result of the girls' sprees. They weren't far wrong. Poor neglected husbands, the girls always called them.

Holly had spent a disgraceful amount of money in Brown Thomas on the most beautiful white dress she had ever seen.

'Shit, Sharon, this will burn a huge hole in my pocket,' she said guiltily, biting her lip and running her fingers over the soft material.

'Aah, don't worry, Gerry can stitch it up for you,' Sharon replied with her infamous cackle. 'And stop calling me "shit Sharon". Every time we go shopping you address me as that. If you're not careful I might start taking offence. Buy the damn thing, Holly. It's Christmas, after all, the season of giving and all that.'

'God, you are so evil, Sharon. I'm never shopping with you again. This is like half my month's wages. What am I going to do for the rest of the month?'

'Holly, would you rather eat or look fab?'

'I'll take it,' Holly said excitedly to the sales assistant.

The dress was low cut, which showed off Holly's neat little chest perfectly, and it was split to the thigh, displaying her slim legs. Gerry hadn't been able to take his eyes off her. It wasn't because she looked so beautiful, however. He just couldn't understand how on earth such a little slip of material had cost that much. Once at the ball, Ms Disco Diva once again overindulged in the alcoholic beverages and succeeded in destroying her dress by spilling red wine down her front. Holly tried but failed to hold back her tears while the men at the table drunkenly informed their partners that number fifty-four on the list prevented you from drinking red wine while wearing an expensive white dress. It was then decided that milk was the preferred beverage, as it wouldn't be visible if spilt on expensive white dresses.

Later, when Gerry knocked his pint over causing it to dribble off the edge of the table into Holly's lap, she tearfully yet seriously announced to the table (and some of the surrounding tables), 'Rule fitty-fife ov the list: NEFFER EFFER buy a spensive white dress.' So it was agreed, and Sharon awoke from her coma from somewhere underneath the table to applaud and offer moral support. A toast was made (after a startled waiter had delivered a tray full of glasses of milk) to Holly and to her profound addition to the list.

'I'm sorry bout your spensive white dress, Holly,' John had hiccuped to Holly, before falling out of the taxi and dragging Sharon alongside him into their house.

Was it possible that Gerry had kept his word and had written a list for her before he died? She had spent every minute of every day with him up until his death and he had never even mentioned it, nor had she noticed any signs of him writing it. No, Holly, pull yourself together and don't be stupid, she told herself. She so desperately wanted him back that she was imagining all kinds of crazy things. He wouldn't have. Would he?

CHAPTER THREE

Holly was walking through an entire field of pretty tiger lilies; the wind was blowing gently, causing the silky petals to tickle the tips of her fingers as she pushed through long strands of bright green grass. The ground was soft and bouncy beneath her bare feet and her body felt so light she was almost floating just above the spongy earth. All around her, birds whistled their happy tune as they went about their business. The sun was so bright in the cloudless sky she had to shield her eyes, and with each brush of wind that passed her face the sweet scent of the tiger lilies filled her nostrils. She felt so . . . happy, so free.

Suddenly the sky darkened as the Caribbean sun disappeared behind a looming grey cloud. The wind picked up and the air chilled. Around her all the petals of the tiger lilies were racing through the air wildly, blurring her vision. The once spongy ground was replaced with sharp stones that cut and scraped her feet with every step. The birds had stopped singing and instead perched on their branches and stared. Something was wrong, and she felt afraid. Ahead of her in the distance a grey stone was visible amidst the tall grass. She wanted to run back to her pretty flowers, but she needed to find out what was ahead.

As she crept closer she heard BANG! BANG! BANG! She quickened her pace and raced over the sharp stones and jagged-edged grass that tore at her arms and legs. She collapsed to her knees in front of the grey slab and let out a scream of pain as she realised what it was. Gerry's grave. BANG! BANG! BANG!

He was trying to get out. He was calling her name; she could hear him!

Holly jumped from her sleep to a loud banging on the front door.

'Holly! Holly! I know you're there! Please let me in!' BANG! BANG! BANG!

Confused and half asleep, she made her way to the door to a frantic-looking Sharon.

'Christ! What were you doing? I've been banging on the door for ages!'

Holly looked around outside, still not fully alert. It was bright and slightly chilly – must be morning.

'Well, aren't you going to let me in?'

'Yeah, Sharon, sorry. I was just dozing on the couch.'

'God, you look terrible, Hol.' Sharon studied her face before giving her a big hug.

'Wow, thanks.' Holly rolled her eyes and turned to shut the door. Sharon was never one to beat about the bush, but that's why she loved her so much. That's also why Holly hadn't been around to see Sharon for the past month. She didn't want to hear the truth. She didn't want

16

to hear how she had to get on with her life; she just wanted . . . oh, she didn't know what she wanted. She was content to be miserable. It somehow felt right.

'God, it's so stuffy in here. When's the last time you opened a window?' Sharon marched around the house, opening windows and picking up empty cups and plates. She brought them into the kitchen where she placed them in the dishwasher and then proceeded to tidy up.

'Oh, you don't have to do it, Sharon,' Holly protested weakly. 'I'll do it . . .'

'When? Next year? I don't want you slumming it while the rest of us pretend not to notice. Why don't you go upstairs and shower, and we'll have a cup of tea when you come down?'

A shower. When was the last time she had even washed? Sharon was right, she must have looked disgusting, with her greasy hair, her dark roots and dirty robe. Gerry's robe. But that was something she never intended to wash. She wanted it exactly as Gerry had left it. Unfortunately, his smell was beginning to fade, replaced by the unmistakable stink of her own skin.

'OK, but there's no milk. I haven't got around to . . .' Holly felt embarrassed by her lack of care for the house and for herself. There was no way she was letting Sharon look inside that fridge or she would definitely have her committed.

'Ta-da!' Sharon sang, holding up a bag Holly hadn't noticed her carry in. 'Don't worry, I took care of that. By the looks of it you haven't eaten in weeks.'

'Thanks, Sharon.' A lump formed in Holly's throat and tears welled in her eyes. She was being so good to her.

'Hold it! There will be no tears today! Just fun and

17

laughter and general happiness, my dear friend. Now shower, quick!'

Holly felt almost human when she came back downstairs. She was dressed in a blue tracksuit and allowed her long blonde (and brown at the roots) hair to fall down on her shoulders. All the windows downstairs were wide open and the cool breeze rushed through Holly's head. It felt as though it was eliminating all her bad thoughts and fears. She laughed at the possibility of her mother being right after all. Holly snapped out of her trance and gasped as she looked around the house. She can't have been any longer than a half an hour but Sharon had tidied and polished, vacuumed and plumped, washed, and sprayed air freshener in every room. She followed the humming noise she could hear to the kitchen where Sharon was scrubbing the hobs. The counters were gleaming; the chrome taps and draining board sparkling.

'Sharon, you absolute angel! I can't believe you did all this. And in such a short time!'

'Ha! You were gone for over an hour. I was beginning to think you'd fallen down the plughole. You would and all, the size of you.' She looked Holly up and down.

An hour? Once again Holly's daydreaming had taken over her mind.

'OK, so I just bought some vegetables and fruit, there's cheese and yogurts in there, and milk, of course. I don't know where you keep the pasta and tinned foods so I just put them over there. Oh, and there's a few microwave dinners in the freezer. That should do you for a while, but by the looks of you it'll last you the year. How much weight have you lost?'

Holly looked down at her body. Her tracksuit was sagging at the bum and the waist tie was pulled to its tightest, yet still drooped to her hips. She hadn't noticed the weight loss at all.

She was brought back to reality by Sharon's voice again: 'There's a few biscuits there to go with your tea. Jammie Dodgers, your favourite.'

That did it. This was all too much for Holly. The Jammie Dodgers were the icing on the cake. She felt the tears run down her face. 'Oh, Sharon,' she wailed, 'thank you so much. You've been so good to me and I've been such a horrible, horrible bitch of a friend.' She sat at the table and grabbed Sharon's hand. 'I don't know what I'd do without you.' Sharon sat opposite her in silence, allowing her to continue. This is what Holly had been dreading, breaking down in front of people at every possible occasion. But she didn't feel embarrassed. Sharon was just patiently sipping her tea and holding her hand like it was normal. Eventually the tears stopped falling.

'Thanks.'

'I'm your best friend, Hol; if I don't help you then who will?' Sharon said, squeezing her hand and giving her an encouraging smile.

'Suppose I should be helping myself.'

'Pah!' Sharon spat, waving her hand dismissively. 'Whenever you're ready. Don't mind all those people who say that you should be back to normal in a month. Grieving is all part of helping yourself, anyway.'

She always said the right things.

'Yeah, well, I've been doing a lot of that. I'm all grieved out.'

19

'You can't be!' said Sharon, mock disgusted. 'And only a month after your husband is cold in his grave.'

'Oh, stop! There'll be plenty of that from people, though, won't there?'

'Probably, but screw them. There are worse sins in the world than learning to be happy again.'

'Suppose.'

'Promise me you'll eat.'

'Promise.'

'Thanks for coming round, Sharon. I really enjoyed the chat,' Holly said, gratefully hugging her friend. 'I feel a lot better already.'

'You know it's good to be around people, Hol. Friends and family can help you. Well, actually, on second thoughts, maybe not your family,' she joked, 'but at least the rest of us can.'

'Oh, I realise that now. I just thought I could handle it on my own at first.'

'Promise me you'll call round. Or at least get out of the house once in a while.'

'Promise.' Holly rolled her eyes. 'You're beginning to sound like my mum.'

'We're all just looking out for you. OK, see you soon,' Sharon said, kissing her on the cheek, 'and EAT!' she added, poking her in the ribs.

Holly waved to Sharon as she pulled away in her car. It was nearly dark. They had spent the day laughing and joking about old times, then crying, followed by some more laughing, then more crying again. Sharon had given her perspective too. Holly hadn't even thought about the fact that Sharon and John had lost their best friend, that her parents had lost their son-in-law and Gerry's parents had lost their only son. She had just been so busy thinking about herself. It had been good being with the living again, instead of moping around with the ghosts of her past. Tomorrow was a new day and she intended on beginning it by collecting that envelope.

CHAPTER FOUR

Holly started her Friday morning well by getting up early. However, although she had gone to bed full of optimism, and excited about the prospects that lay ahead of her, she was struck afresh by the harsh reality of how difficult every moment would be. Once again she awoke in an empty bed to a silent house, but there was one small breakthrough. For the first time in over a month, she had woken up without the aid of a telephone call. She adjusted her mind, as she did every morning, to the fact that the dreams of her and Gerry being together, which had lived in her mind for the past ten hours, were just that: dreams.

She showered and dressed comfortably in her favourite blue jeans, trainers and a baby-pink T-shirt. Sharon had been right about her weight: her once-tight jeans were just about staying up with the aid of a belt. She made a face at her reflection in the mirror. She looked ugly. She had black circles under her eyes, her lips were chapped and chewed and her hair was a disaster. First thing to do was to go down to her local hairdressers and pray they could squeeze her in.

'Jaysus, Holly!' her stylist, Leo, exclaimed. 'Would ya look at the state of ya! People, make way! Make way! I have a woman here in a critical condition!' He winked at her and proceeded to push people from his path. He pulled out the chair for her and pushed her into it.

'Thanks, Leo. I feel really attractive now,' Holly muttered, trying to hide her beetroot-coloured face.

'Well, don't, 'cos you're in bits. Sandra, mix me up the usual, Colin get the foil, Tania get me my little bag of tricks from upstairs – oh, and tell Will not to bother getting his lunch, he's doing my twelve o'clock.' Leo ordered everyone around, his hands flailing wildly as though he was about to perform emergency surgery. Perhaps he was.

'Oh sorry, Leo, I didn't mean to mess up your day.'

'Of course you did, love. Why else would you come rushing in here at lunchtime on a Friday without an appointment? To help world peace?'

Holly guiltily bit her lip.

'Ah, but I wouldn't do it for anyone else but you, love.'

'Thanks.'

'How have you been?' He rested his skinny little behind on the counter facing Holly. Leo must have been fifty years old yet he didn't look a day over thirty. His honey-coloured hair matched his honey-coloured skin, and he always dressed so perfectly. He was enough to make any woman feel like crap.

'Terrible.'

'Yeah, you look it.'

'Thanks.'

23

'Ah well, at least by the time you walk out of here you'll have one thing sorted. I do hair, not hearts.'

Holly smiled gratefully at his odd little way of showing he understood.

'But, Jaysus, Holly, when you were coming in the door did you see the word "magician" or "hairdresser" on the front of the salon? You should have seen the state of the woman who came in here today. Mutton dressed as lamb. Not far off sixty, I'd say. Handed me a magazine with Jennifer Aniston on the cover. "I want to look like that," she says.'

Holly laughed at his impression. He had the facial expression and the hand movements all going at the same time.

'"Jaysus," I says, "I'm a hairdresser, not a plastic surgeon. The only way you'll look like that is if you cut out the picture and staple it to your head."'

'No! Leo, you didn't tell her that?' Holly's jaw dropped in surprise.

'Of course I did! The woman needed to be told – sure, wasn't I helping her? Swanning in here dressed like a teenager. The state of her!'

'But what did she say?' Holly wiped the tears of laughter from her eyes. She hadn't laughed like this for months.

'I flicked the pages of the mag for her and came across a lovely picture of Joan Collins. Told her it was right up her street. She seemed happy enough with that.'

'Leo, she was probably too terrified to tell you she hated it.'

'Ah, who cares? I have enough friends.'

'Don't know why,' Holly laughed.

'Don't move,' Leo ordered. Suddenly he had become awfully serious and his lips were pursed together in concentration as he separated Holly's hair ready for colouring. That was enough to send Holly into stitches again.

'Ah, come on, Holly,' Leo said in exasperation.

'I can't help it, Leo. You got me started and now I can't stop . . .'

Leo paused in what he was doing and watched her with amusement. 'I always thought you were for the madhouse. No one ever listens to me.'

She laughed even harder. 'Oh, I'm sorry, Leo. I don't know what's wrong with me, I just can't stop.' Holly's stomach ached from laughing so hard and she was aware of all the curious glances she was attracting but she just couldn't help it. It was as if all the missed mirth from the past couple of months were tumbling out at once.

Leo propped himself back on the counter and watched her. 'You don't need to apologise, Holly. Laugh all you like. You know they say it's good for the heart.'

'Oh, I haven't laughed like this for ages,' she chortled.

'Well, you haven't had much to laugh about, I suppose,' he smiled sadly. Leo had loved Gerry too. They'd teased each other whenever they'd met, but they'd both known it was all in fun. Leo snapped himself out of his thoughts, tousled Holly's hair playfully and planted a kiss on the top of her head. 'But you'll be all right, Holly Kennedy,' he assured her.

'Thanks, Leo,' she said, calming herself down, touched by his concern. He went back to work on her hair, putting on his funny little concentrating face, which started Holly off again.

'Oh, you laugh now, Holly, but wait till I accidentally give you a stripy head of colour. We'll see who's laughing then.'

'How's Joe?' Holly asked, keen to change the subject before she embarrassed herself again.

'He dumped me,' Leo said, pushing aggressively with his foot on the chair's pump, sending Holly higher into the air and causing her to jerk wildly in her chair.

'O-oh, Le-eo, I-I-I-'m soooo sor-reeee. Yo-ooou twooo we-eerree soooo gree-aat togeeeeth-eer.'

'Yeah, well, we're not so gree-aat together now, missy. I think he's seeing someone else. Right. I'm going to put two shades of blonde in: a golden colour and the blonde you had before. Otherwise it'll go that brassy colour that's reserved for my prostitute clientele only.'

'Oh, Leo, I'm sorry. If he has any sense at all he'll realise what he's missing.'

'He mustn't have any sense so. We split up two months ago and he hasn't realised it yet. Or else he has and he's delighted. I'm fed up; I've had enough of men. I'm just going to turn straight.'

'Now *that's* the stupidest thing I've ever heard . . .'

Holly bounced out of the salon with delight. Without Gerry beside her, a few men looked her way, something that was alien to her and made her feel uncomfortable, so she ran to the safety of her car and prepared herself for her parents' house. So far, today was going well. It had been a good move to visit Leo. Even in his heart-break he worked hard to make her laugh. Holly took note of it.

She pulled up to the kerb outside her parents' house

in Portmarnock and took a deep breath. To her mother's surprise Holly had called her first thing in the morning to arrange a time to meet up. It was three thirty now, and Holly sat outside in the car with butterflies in her tummy. Apart from the visits her parents had paid to her over the past month Holly had barely spent any proper time with her family. She didn't want all the attention directed at her, the intrusive questions about how she was feeling and what she was going to do next being fired at her all day. However, it was time to put that fear aside. They were her family.

Her parents' house was situated directly across the road from Portmarnock beach, the blue flag baring testament to its cleanliness. She parked the car and stared across the road to the sea. She had lived here from the day she was born till the day she moved out to live with Gerry. She had loved waking up to the sound of the sea lapping against the rocks, and the excited call of the seagulls. It was wonderful having the beach as your front garden, especially during the summer. Sharon had lived around the corner, and on the hottest days of the year the girls would venture across the road in their summer best and keep an eye out for the best-looking boys. Holly and Sharon were the complete opposite of each other: Sharon with her brown hair, fair skin, and huge bosom; Holly with her blonde hair, sallow skin, and small chest. Sharon would be loud, shouting to the boys and calling them over. Holly would just stay quiet and flirt with her eyes, fixing them on her favourite boy and not moving them till he noticed. Holly and Sharon really hadn't changed all that much since.

She didn't intend staying long, just have a little chat

and collect the envelope. She was determined to end her silent self-torture about what could be inside. She took a deep breath, rang the doorbell and placed a smile on her face for all to see.

'Hi, love! Come in, come in!' said her mother with her usual welcoming, loving face that Holly just wanted to kiss every time she saw her.

'Hi, Mum. How are you?' Holly stepped into the house and was comforted by the familiar smell of home. 'You on your own?'

'Yes, your father's out with Declan, buying paint for his room.'

'Don't tell me you and Dad are still paying for everything for him?'

'Well, your father might be, but I'm certainly not. He's working at nights now so at least he has a bit of pocket money these days. Although we don't see a penny of it being spent on anything for here,' she chuckled, and brought Holly to the kitchen where she put the kettle on.

Declan was Holly's youngest brother and the baby of the family, so her mum and dad still felt they had to spoil him. But their 'baby' was now a twenty-two-year-old, studying film production at college and he constantly had a video camera in his hand.

'What job has he got now?'

Her mother rolled her eyes to heaven. 'He's joined some band. The Orgasmic Fish, I think they call themselves, or something like that. I'm sick to death of hearing about it, Holly. If he goes on one more time about who was there at the gigs promising to sign them up and how famous they're going to be I'll go mad.'

'Ah, poor Deco. Don't worry, he'll find something eventually.'

'I know, and it's funny because, of all you darling children, he's the least I worry about. He'll find his way.'

They brought their mugs into the sitting room and settled down in front of the television. 'You look great, pet. I love the hair. Do you think Leo would ever do mine for me, or am I too old for his styles?'

'Well, as long as you don't want Jennifer Aniston's hairstyle, you'll have no problems.' Holly explained about the woman in the salon and they both rolled around laughing.

'I don't want the Joan Collins look, so I'll just stay clear of him.'

'That might be wise.'

'Any luck with a job yet?' Her mother's voice was casual but Holly knew she was just dying to find out.

'No, not yet, Mum. To be honest, I haven't even started looking. I don't quite know what I want to do.'

'You're right,' her mother nodded. 'Take your time and think about what you like or else you'll end up rushing into a job you hate, like the last time.' Holly was surprised to hear this. In fact, everyone was surprising her these days. Perhaps it was herself with the problem and not the rest of the world after all.

The last job Holly had was working as a secretary for an unforgiving little slimeball in a solicitor's office. She had been forced to leave her job when the creep failed to understand that she needed time off work to be with her dying husband. Now she had to go looking for a new one. For a new job that was. But at the moment it seemed unimaginable to go to work in the morning.

29

Holly and her mother sat in a relaxed atmosphere, falling in and out of conversation for a few hours until Holly finally built up the courage to ask for the envelope.

'Oh, of course, love, I completely forgot about it. I hope it's nothing important. It's been there for a long time.'

'I'll find out soon enough.'

They said their goodbyes and Holly couldn't get out of the house quickly enough.

Perching herself on the grass overlooking the golden sand, Holly ran the envelope over her hands. Her mother hadn't described it very well, for it was not an envelope at all but a thick brown package. The address had been typed onto a plain sticker so she couldn't even guess the origin. But most importantly, above the address were two words, thick and bold: 'THE LIST'.

Her stomach did a little dance. If it wasn't from Gerry, then Holly finally had to accept the fact that he was gone completely from her life and she had to start thinking about existing without him. But if it *was* from him, though she would be faced with the same future, at least she could hold on to some fresh memory. A memory that would have to last her a lifetime.

Her trembling fingers gently tore at the seal of the package. She turned it upside down and shook the contents out. Out fell ten separate tiny envelopes of the kind you would expect to find on a bouquet of flowers, each with a different month written on them. Her heart missed a few beats as she saw the familiar handwriting on a loose page underneath the pile of envelopes.

It was from Gerry.

CHAPTER FIVE

Holly held her breath and with tears in her eyes and a pounding heart, she read the words, aware all the time that the person who had sat down to write to her would never be able to do so again. She ran her fingers over Gerry's handwriting, knowing that the last person to have touched the page was him.

My darling Holly,

I don't know where you are or when exactly you are reading this. I just hope that my letter has found you safe and healthy. You whispered to me not long ago that you couldn't go on alone. You can, Holly.

You are strong and brave and you can get through this. We shared some beautiful times together and you made my life . . . you made my life. I have no regrets.

But I am just a chapter in your life – there will be many more. Remember our wonderful

*memories, but please don't be afraid to make
some more.*

*Thank you for doing me the honour of being
my wife. For everything, I am eternally grateful.*

*Whenever you need me, know that I am with
you.*

*Love for ever,
Your husband and best friend,
Gerry.*

*PS. I promised a list, so here it is. The
following envelopes must be opened exactly when
labelled and <u>must be obeyed</u>. And remember, I'm
looking out for you, so I will know . . .*

Holly broke down, sadness sweeping over her. Yet she
felt relief at the same time; relief that Gerry would
somehow continue to be with her for another little while.
She leafed through the small white envelopes and
searched through the months. It was April now. She had
missed March so she delicately picked out the envelope.
She opened it slowly, wanting to savour every moment.
Inside was a small card with Gerry's handwriting on it.
It read:

*Save yourself the bruises and buy a bedside lamp!
PS. I love you . . .*

Her tears turned to laughter as she realised her Gerry
was back!

Holly read and reread his letter over and over again
in an attempt to summon him back to life. Eventually,

when she could no longer see the words through her tears, she looked out to sea. She had always found the sea so calming, and even as a child she would run across the road to the beach if she was upset and needed to think. Her parents knew that when she went missing from the house they would find her here by the sea.

She closed her eyes and breathed in and out along with the gentle sighing of the waves. It was as though the sea was taking big deep breaths; pulling the water in while it inhaled and pushing it all back up onto the sand as it exhaled. She continued to breathe along with it and felt her pulse rate slow down as she became calmer. She thought about how she used to lie by Gerry's side during his final days and listen to the sound of his breathing. She had been terrified to leave him, even to answer the door, to fix him some food or to go to the toilet, just in case that was the time he chose to leave her. When she would return to his bedside she would sit frozen in a terrified silence while she listened for his breathing and watched his chest for any movement.

But he'd always managed to hang on. He had baffled the doctors with his strength and determination to live; Gerry wasn't prepared to go without a fight. He kept his good humour right up until the end. He was so weak and his voice so quiet, but Holly had learned to understand his new language as a mother does her babbling child just learning to talk. They would giggle together late into the night and other nights they would hold each other and cry. Holly remained strong for him. Throughout, her new job was to be there for him whenever he needed her. Looking back on it, she knew that she really needed him more than he needed her. She needed to be needed so she could feel that she wasn't just standing idly by, utterly helpless.

On the second of February at four o'clock in the morning, Holly held Gerry's hand tightly and smiled at him encouragingly as he took his last breath and closed his eyes. She didn't want him to be afraid, and she didn't want him to feel that she was afraid, because at that moment she wasn't. She felt relief – relief that his pain was gone, and relief that she had been there with him to witness the peace of his passing. She felt relieved to have known him, to have loved him and to be loved by him, and relief that the last thing he saw was her face smiling down on him, encouraging him and assuring him it was OK to let go.

The days after that were a blur to her now. She had occupied herself by making the funeral arrangements and by meeting and greeting Gerry's relatives and old school friends that she hadn't seen for years. She remained so solid and calm through it all. She was just thankful that, after months, his suffering was over. It didn't occur to her to feel the anger or bitterness that she felt now for the life that was taken away from her. That feeling didn't arrive until she went to collect her husband's death certificate.

And then that feeling made a grand appearance.

As she sat in the crowded waiting room of her local health clinic, waiting for her number to be called, she wondered why on earth Gerry's number had been called so early in his life. She was sandwiched between a young couple and an elderly one – the picture of what she and Gerry had once been, and a glimpse of the future they could have had. And it all just seemed unfair. While the noise of screaming children was amplified in the room, Holly felt squashed between the shoulders of her past and her lost future, and she felt suffocated. She shouldn't have to be there.

None of her friends had to be there.

None of her family had to be there.

In fact the majority of the population of the world didn't have to be in the position she was in right then.

It didn't seem fair.

Because it just wasn't fair.

After presenting the official proof of her husband's death to bank managers and insurance companies, as if the look on her face wasn't proof enough, Holly returned home to her nest and locked herself away from the rest of the world that contained hundreds of memories of the life she had once had. The life she had been very happy with. So why had she been given another one, and a far worse one at that?

That was two months ago, and she hadn't left the house until today. And what a welcome she had been given, she thought, smiling down at the envelopes. Gerry was back.

Holly could hardly contain her excitement as she furiously dialled Sharon's number with trembling hands. After reaching a few wrong numbers she eventually calmed herself and concentrated on dialling correctly.

'Sharon!' she squealed as soon as the phone was picked up. 'You'll never guess what. Oh my God, I can't believe it!'

'Eh, no . . . it's John, but I'll get her for you now.' A worried John rushed off to get Sharon.

'What, what, what?' panted a very out-of-breath Sharon. 'What's wrong? Are you OK?'

'Yes, I'm fine!' Holly started giggling hysterically, not knowing whether to laugh or cry and suddenly forgetting how to structure a sentence.

John watched as Sharon sat down at her kitchen table, looking very confused while she tried with all her strength to make sense of the rambling Holly. It was something about Mrs Kennedy giving Holly a brown envelope with a bedside lamp in it. It was all very worrying.

'STOP!' shouted Sharon, much to Holly and John's surprise. 'I cannot understand a word you are saying, so please,' Sharon spoke very slowly, 'slow down, take a deep breath and start from the very beginning, preferably using words from the English language.'

Suddenly she heard quiet sobs from the other end.

'Oh, Sharon,' Holly's words were quiet and broken, 'he wrote me a list. Gerry wrote me a list.'

Sharon froze in her chair while she digested this information.

John watched his wife's eyes widen and he quickly pulled out a chair and sat next to her, shoving his head towards the telephone so he could hear what was going on.

'OK, Holly, I want you to get over here as quickly but as *safely* as you can.' Sharon paused again and swatted John's head away as if he was a fly so she could concentrate on what she had just heard. 'This is . . . great news?'

John stood up from the table, insulted, and began to pace the kitchen floor, trying to guess what the news could be.

'Oh, it is, Sharon,' sobbed Holly, 'it really is.'

'OK, make your way over here now and we can talk about it.'

'OK.'

Sharon hung up the phone and sat in silence.

'What? What is it?' demanded John.

'Oh, sorry, love. Holly's on the way over. She . . . em . . . she said that eh . . .'

'WHAT, for Christsake?'

'She said that Gerry wrote her a list.'

John studied her face and tried to decide if she was serious. Sharon's worried blue eyes stared back at him and he realised she was. He joined her at the table and they both sat in silence and stared at the wall, lost in thought.

CHAPTER SIX

'Wow,' was all Sharon and John could say as the three of them sat around the kitchen table in silence, staring at the contents of the package that Holly had emptied as evidence. Conversation between them had been minimal for the last few minutes as they all tried to decide how they felt. It had gone something like this:

'But how did he manage to . . . ?'

'But how didn't we notice him . . . well . . . ? God.'

'When do you think he . . . ? Well, I suppose he was on his own sometimes . . .'

Holly and Sharon just sat looking at each other while John stuttered and stammered his way through trying to figure out just when, where and how his terminally ill friend had managed to carry out this idea all alone without anyone finding out.

'Wow,' he eventually repeated after coming to the conclusion that Gerry had done just that. He had carried it out alone.

38

'I know,' Holly agreed. 'So the two of you had absolutely no idea then?'

'Well, I don't know about you, Holly, but it's pretty clear to me that John was the mastermind behind all of this,' Sharon said sarcastically.

'Ha-ha,' John replied drily. 'He kept his word, anyway, didn't he?' John looked to both of the girls with a smile on his face.

'He sure did,' Holly said quietly.

'Are you OK, Holly? I mean, how do you feel about all this? It must be . . . weird,' asked Sharon again, clearly concerned.

'I feel fine.' Holly was thoughtful. 'Actually, I think it's the best thing that could have happened right now! It's funny, though, how amazed we all are, considering how much we went on about this list. I mean, I should have been expecting it.'

'Yeah, but we never expected any of us to ever do it!' said John.

'But why not?' questioned Holly. 'This was the whole reason for it in the first place! To be able to help your loved ones after you go.'

'I think Gerry was the only one who took it really seriously.'

'Sharon, Gerry is the only one of us who is gone. Who knows how seriously anyone else would have taken it?'

There was a silence.

'Well, let's study this more closely then,' perked up John, suddenly starting to enjoy himself. 'There's how many envelopes?'

'Em . . . there's ten,' counted Sharon, joining in with the spirit of their new task.

'OK, so what months are there?' John asked. Holly sorted through the pile.

'There's March, which is the lamp one I've already opened, April, May, June, July, August, September, October, November and December.'

'So there's a message for every month left in the year,' Sharon said slowly, lost in thought. They sat in silence, thinking the same thing: Gerry had known he wouldn't live past February.

Holly looked happily at her friends. Whatever Gerry had in store for her was going to be interesting, but he had already succeeded in making her feel almost normal again, laughing with John and Sharon while they guessed what the envelopes contained. It was as though he was still with them.

'Hold on!' John exclaimed very seriously.

'What?'

His blue eyes twinkled. 'It's April now and you haven't opened this month's envelope yet.'

'Oh, of course! Should I do it now?'

'Go on,' encouraged Sharon.

Holly picked up the envelope and slowly opened it. There were only eight more to open after this and she wanted to treasure every second before it became another memory. She pulled out the little card.

A disco diva must always look her best. Go shopping for an outfit as you'll need it for next month!
   PS. I love you . . .

'Ooooh,' John and Sharon squealed with excitement, 'he's getting cryptic!'

40

CHAPTER SEVEN

Holly lay on her bed, switching the lamp on and off, with a smile on her face like a demented woman. She and Sharon had gone shopping in Bed Knobs and Broomsticks in Malahide, and both girls had eventually agreed on the beautifully carved wooden stand and the cream shade that matched the cream and wooden furnishings of the master bedroom (of course they had chosen the most ridiculously expensive one, it would have been wrong to spoil tradition). And although Gerry hadn't physically been there with her as she bought it, she felt as though they had made the purchase together.

She had drawn the curtains of her bedroom in order to test her new merchandise. The bedside lamp had a softening effect on the room, making it appear warmer. How easily this could have ended their nightly arguments, but perhaps neither of them wanted to end them. It had become a routine, something familiar that made them feel closer. How she would give anything to have one of those little arguments now. And she would gladly get out of her cosy bed for him, she would gladly walk on the cold floor for him, and she would gladly bruise herself on the bedpost whilst fumbling in the dark for the bed. But that time was gone.

The sound of Gloria Gaynor's 'I Will Survive' snapped her back to the present as she realised her mobile phone was ringing.

'Hello?'

'G'day, mate, I'm hooooome!' shrieked a familiar voice.

'Oh my God, Ciara! *I didn't know you were coming home!*'

'Well, neither did I, actually, but I ran out of money and decided to surprise you all!'

'Wow, I bet Mum and Dad were surprised all right.'

'Well, Dad did drop the towel with fright when he stepped out of the shower.'

Holly covered her face with her hands, 'Oh, Ciara, he didn't!'

'No hugs for Daddy when I saw him!' Ciara laughed.

'Oh, yuck, yuck, yuck. Change the subject, I'm having horrible visions,' Holly laughed.

'OK, well, I was calling to tell you that I was home, obviously, and that Mum's organising dinner tonight to celebrate.'

'Celebrate what?'

'Me being alive.'

'Oh, OK. I thought you might have an announcement or something.'

'That I'm alive.'

'O . . . K. So who'll be there?'

'The whole family.'

42

'Did I mention that I'm going to the dentist to have all my teeth pulled out? Sorry I can't make it.'

'I know, I know, I said the same thing to Mum, but we haven't all been together for ages. Sure, when's the last time you've even seen Richard and Meredith?'

'Oh, good ol' Dick – he was in flying form at the funeral. Had lots of wise and comforting things to say to me like, "Did you not consider donating his brain to medical science?" Yes, he's a fantastic brother all right.'

'Oh gosh, Holly, I'm sorry, I forgot about the funeral.' Her sister's voice changed. 'I'm sorry I couldn't make it.'

'Ciara, don't be silly. We both decided it was best you stay,' Holly said briskly. 'It's far too expensive to be flying back and forth from Australia so let's not bring it back up, OK?'

'OK.'

Holly quickly changed the subject. 'So when you say the whole family, do you mean . . . ?'

'Yes, Richard and Meredith are bringing our adorable little niece and nephew. And Jack and Abbey are coming, you'll be pleased to know. Declan will be there in body but probably not in mind, Mum, Dad and me, of course, and you WILL be there.'

Holly groaned. As much as Holly moaned about her family she had a great relationship with her brother Jack. He was only two years older than she, so they had been close when growing up, and he had always been very protective of her. Their mother had called them her 'two little elves', because they were always getting up to mischief around the house, usually aimed at their eldest brother, Richard. Jack was similar to Holly in both looks and personality, and she considered him to be the most normal of her siblings. It also helped that she got along with his partner of seven years, Abbey, and when Gerry was alive the four of them often met up for dinner and drinks. When Gerry was alive . . . God, that didn't sound right.

Ciara was a different kettle of fish altogether. Jack and Holly were convinced she was from the planet Ciara, population: one. Ciara had the look of their father – long legs and dark hair. She also had various tattoos and piercings on her body as a result of her travels around the world. A tattoo for every country, her dad used to joke. A tattoo for every man, Holly and Jack were convinced.

Of course, this carry-on was all frowned upon by the eldest sibling, Richard (or Dick, as he was known to Jack and Holly). Richard was born with the serious affliction of being an eternal old man. His life revolved around rules and regulations and obedience. When he was younger he had one friend and they had a fight when they were ten, and after that Holly could never remember him bringing anyone home, having any girlfriends or ever going out to socialise. She and Jack thought it was a wonder he even met his equally joyless wife, Meredith – probably at an anti-happiness convention.

It wasn't as though Holly had the *worst* family in the world, it was just that they were such a strange mix of people. The huge clashes of personalities usually led to arguments at the most inappropriate times or, as Holly's parents preferred to call them, 'heavy discussions'. They *could* get along, but that was with everyone really trying and being on their best behaviour.

Holly and Jack often met up for lunch or for drinks,

44

just to catch up on each other's lives. She enjoyed his company and considered him to be not only a brother but a real friend. Lately they hadn't seen much of each other. Jack understood Holly well and knew when she needed her space.

The only time Holly caught up on her younger brother, Declan's, life was when she called at the house looking for her parents and he would answer. Declan wasn't a great conversationalist. He was an overgrown 'boy' who didn't yet quite feel comfortable in the company of adults so Holly never really knew that much about him. Although she was aware of his unbreakable loyalty to his band, The Orgasmic Fish (whom she had yet to see perform), and if it wasn't a guitar that he had in his hand, it was a video camera. A nice guy, he just had his head up in the clouds a bit.

Ciara, her twenty-four-year-old little sister, had been away for the entire year and Holly had missed her. They were never the kind of sisters to swap clothes and giggle about boys – their tastes differed so much – though as the only two girls in a family of brothers, they formed a bond. But Ciara was closer to Declan; both of them were dreamers. With Jack and Holly inseparable as children and friends as adults, that left Richard. He was out on his own in the family but Holly suspected he liked that feeling of being separated from those he couldn't quite understand. Holly was dreading his lectures on all-things-boring, his insensitive questioning of her life and just the whole feeling of being frustrated by comment after comment at the dinner table. But it was a welcome-home dinner for Ciara, and Jack would be there; Holly could count on him.

But was Holly looking forward to tonight? Absolutely not.

Holly reluctantly knocked on the door and immediately heard the pounding of tiny feet flying towards the door, followed by a voice so loud that should not have belonged to a child.

'Mummy! Daddy! It's Aunty Holly, it's Aunty Holly!'

It was nephew Timothy, nephew Timothy.

His happiness was suddenly crushed by a stern voice (although it was unusual for her nephew to be happy about Holly's arrival. Things must be even more boring in there than usual). 'Timothy! What did I tell you about running in the house? You could fall and hurt yourself. Now go stand in the corner and think about what I said. Do I make myself clear?'

'Yes, Mummy.'

'Ah, come on, Meredith, will he hurt himself on the carpet or on the comfy padded couch?'

Holly laughed to herself; Ciara was definitely home. Just as Holly was contemplating escape, the door swung open and there stood Meredith. She looked even more sour-faced and unwelcoming than usual.

'Holly.' She nodded her head in acknowledgement.

'Meredith,' Holly imitated.

Once in the living room Holly looked around for Jack, but to her disappointment he was nowhere to be seen. Richard stood in front of the fireplace, dressed in a surprisingly colourful sweater; perhaps he was letting his hair down tonight. He had his hands in his pockets and was rocking back and forth from his heels to the balls of his toes like a man mid-lecture. His lecture was aimed at their father, Frank, who sat uncomfortably in his favourite armchair, looking like a chastised schoolboy. Richard was so lost in his story he didn't see Holly. She blew her poor father a kiss from across the room, not wanting to be brought into their conversation. He smiled at her and pretended to catch her kiss.

Declan was slumped on the couch wearing his ripped jeans and South Park T-shirt, puffing furiously on a cigarette while Meredith warned him of the dangers of smoking. 'Really? I didn't know that,' he said, sounding worryingly interested while stabbing out his cigarette. Meredith's face looked satisfied until Declan winked at Holly, reached for the box and immediately lit up another one. 'Tell me some more, please, I'm just dying to know.' Meredith stared back at him in disgust.

Ciara was hiding behind the couch, throwing pieces of popcorn at the back of Timothy's head. He stood facing the wall in the corner of the room, too afraid to turn round. Abbey was pinned to the floor and being bossed around by little five-year-old Emily and an evil-looking doll. She caught Holly's eye and mouthed 'Help' to her.

'Hi, Ciara.' Holly approached her sister, who jumped up and gave her a big hug, squeezing Holly a bit tighter than usual. 'Nice hair.'

'You like it?'

'Yeah, pink is really your colour.'

Ciara looked satisfied. 'That's what I tried to tell them,' she said, squinting at Richard and Meredith. 'So how's my big sis?' Ciara asked softly, rubbing Holly's arm affectionately.

'Oh, you know,' Holly smiled weakly. 'I'm hanging in there.'

47

'Jack is in the kitchen helping your mum with the dinner, if you're looking for him, Holly,' Abbey announced, then widening her eyes and mouthing 'Help me' again.

Holly raised her eyebrows at Abbey. 'Really? Well, isn't he great, helping out Mum?'

'Oh, Holly, you know how much Jack just *loves* cooking. Can't get enough of it,' she said sarcastically.

Holly's dad chuckled to himself, which stopped Richard in his tracks.

'What's so funny, Father?'

Frank shifted in his seat nervously. 'I just find it remarkable that all this happens in one tiny little test tube.'

Richard let out a disapproving sigh at his father's stupidity. 'Yes, but you have to understand these are so minuscule, Father, it's rather fascinating. The organisms combine with the . . .' And away he went again while his father settled back down in his chair and tried to avoid eye contact with Holly.

Holly tiptoed quietly into the kitchen where she found her brother at the table with his feet up on a chair, munching on some food. 'Ah, here he is, the Naked Chef himself.'

Jack smiled and stood up. 'There's my favourite sister.' He scrunched up his nose. 'I see you got roped into coming to this thing as well.' He walked towards her and held out his arms to offer her one of his big bear hugs. 'How are you?' he said quietly into her ear.

'I'm OK, thanks.' Holly smiled sadly and kissed him on the cheek before turning to her mother. 'Darling Mother, I am here to offer my services at this extremely stressful and busy time of your life,' Holly said, planting a kiss on her mother's flushed cheek.

'Oh, aren't I just the luckiest woman in the world, having such caring children like you?' Elizabeth said sarcastically. 'Tell you what, you can just drain the water from the potatoes there.'

'Mum, tell us about the time when you were a little girl during the famine and the spuds were gone,' Jack said, putting on an exaggerated Irish accent.

Elizabeth hit him across the head playfully with the tea towel. 'Ah sure, 'tis years before my time, son.'

'Sure, 'tis true,' said Jack.

'No, you t'aren't at all,' joined in Holly.

They both stopped and stared at her. 'Since when is there such a word as "t'aren't"?' laughed her mum.

'Ah, shut up, the both of you.' Holly joined her brother at the table.

'I hope you two won't be getting up to any mischief tonight. I would like this to be an argument-free zone for a change.'

'Mother, I am shocked the thought even crossed your mind.' Jack winked across to Holly.

'All right,' she said, not believing a word of it. 'Well, sorry, my babies, but there's nothing else to be done here. Dinner will be ready in a few minutes.'

'Oh.' Holly was disappointed.

Elizabeth joined her children at the table and the three of them stared at the kitchen door, all thinking the same thing.

'No, Abbey,' squealed Emily loudly, 'you're not doing what I tell you,' and she burst into tears. This was shortly followed by a loud guffaw from Richard; he must have cracked a joke because he was the only one laughing.

'But I suppose it's important that we all stay here and keep an eye on the dinner,' Elizabeth added.

'OK, everyone, dinner is served,' announced Elizabeth, and the family made their way to the dining room. There was an awkward moment like at a children's birthday party while everyone scuffled to sit beside their best friend. Eventually Holly was satisfied with her position at the table and settled down with her mother on her left at the end of the table and Jack to her right. Abbey sat with a scowl on her face as she had been placed between Jack and Richard. Jack would have some making up to do when he got home. Declan sat opposite Holly and wedged in between him was an empty seat where Timothy should be sitting, then Emily and Meredith, then Ciara. Holly's father got a raw deal, sitting at the head of the table between Richard and Ciara, but he was such a calm man he was the best one for the job.

Everyone oohed and aahed as Elizabeth brought out the food and its aroma filled the room. Holly had always loved her mother's cooking; she was never afraid to experiment with new flavours and recipes, a trait that had not been passed down to her daughter.

'Hey, poor little Timmy must be starving out there,' Ciara exclaimed to Richard. 'He must have done his time by now.'

She knew she was skating on thin ice but she loved the danger of it and, more importantly, she loved to wind up Richard. After all, she had to make up for lost time – she had been away for a year.

'Ciara, it's important that Timothy knows when he has done something wrong,' explained Richard.

'Yeah, but couldn't you just tell him?'

The rest of the family tried hard not to laugh.

'He needs to know that his actions will lead to serious consequences so he will not repeat it.'

'Ah well,' she said, raising her voice a few decibels, 'he's missing all this yummy food. Mmm mmm mmm,' she said, licking her lips.

'Stop it, Ciara,' Elizabeth snapped.

'Or you'll have to stand in the corner,' Jack added sternly.

The table erupted with laughter – bar Meredith and Richard, of course.

'So, Ciara, tell us about your adventures in Australia,' Frank moved swiftly on.

Her eyes lit up. 'Oh, I had the most amazing time, Dad. I would definitely recommend going there to anyone.'

'Awful long flight, though,' Richard said.

'Yeah, it is but it's so worth it.'

'Did you get any more tattoos?' Holly asked.

'Yeah, look.' With that, Ciara stood up at the table and pulled down her trousers, revealing a butterfly on her behind.

Mum, Dad, Richard and Meredith protested in outrage while the others sat in convulsions of laughter. Finally, when Ciara had apologised and Meredith had removed her hands from Emily's eyes, the table settled down.

'They are revolting things,' Richard said in disgust.

'I think butterflies are pretty, Daddy,' said Emily with big innocent eyes.

'Yes, some butterflies are pretty, Emily, but I'm talking

about tattoos. They can give you all sorts of diseases and problems.' Emily's smile faded.

'Hey, I didn't exactly get this done in a dodgy place sharing needles with drug users, you know. The place was perfectly clean.'

'Well, that's an oxymoron if ever I heard one,' sniffed Meredith.

'Been in one recently, Meredith?' Ciara asked a bit too forcefully.

'Well, em . . . n-n-n-no,' she stuttered, 'I have never been in one, thank you very much, but I am sure they are.' Then she turned to Emily. 'They are dirty, horrible places, Emily, where only dangerous people go.'

'Is Aunt Ciara dangerous, Mummy?'

'Only to five-year-old little girls with red hair,' Ciara said, stuffing her face with potatoes.

Emily froze.

'Richard dear, do you think that Timmy might want to come in now for some food?' Elizabeth asked politely.

'It's Timothy,' Meredith interrupted.

'Yes, Mother, I think that would be OK.'

A very sorry little Timothy walked slowly into the room with his head down, and took his place silently beside Declan. Holly's heart leaped out to him. How cruel to treat a child like that, how cruel to stop him from being a child . . . Her sympathy diminished immediately as she felt his foot kick her shin underneath the table. They should have left him out there.

'So, Ciara, come on, give us the gossip. Do anything wild and wonderful out there?' Holly pushed for more information.

'Oh yeah, I did a bungee jump, actually – well, I did

a few. I have the photo here.' She reached into her back pocket and everyone looked away just in case she was planning on revealing any more bits of her anatomy. Thankfully she took out only her wallet and passed the photo from it around the table.

'The first one I did was off a bridge and my head hit the water when I fell . . .'

'Oh, Ciara, that sounds dangerous,' her mother said with her hands across her face.

'Oh no, it wasn't dangerous at all,' she reassured her.

The photograph was passed to Holly, and she and Jack burst out laughing. Ciara dangled upside down from a rope with her face contorted in the middle of a scream of pure terror. Her hair (it was blue at that time) was shooting out in all directions as though she had been electrocuted.

'Attractive photo, Ciara. Mum, you must get that framed for over the fireplace,' Holly joked.

'Yeah!' Ciara's eyes lit up. 'That would be a cool idea.'

'Sure, darling, I'll just take down the one of you making your Holy Communion and replace it with that,' Elizabeth said sarcastically.

'Well, I don't know which one would be scarier,' said Declan.

'Holly, what are you doing for your birthday?' asked Abbey, leaning across towards her. She was clearly dying to get out of the conversation she was having with Richard.

'Oh, that's right!' shouted Ciara. 'You're gonna be thirty next week!'

'I'm not doing anything big at all,' she warned everyone. 'I don't want any surprise party or anything, PLEASE.'

'Oh, you have to—' said Ciara.

'No, she doesn't have to if she doesn't want to,' her father interrupted, and winked supportively at Holly.

'Thank you, Dad. I'm just going to have a girly night out clubbing or something. Nothing mad, nothing wild.'

Richard tutted as the photograph reached him and passed it on to his father, who chuckled to himself over the sight of Ciara.

'Yes, I agree with you, Holly,' said Richard, 'those birthday celebrations are always a bit embarrassing. Grown adults acting like children, doing "Rock the boat" on the floor and drinking far too much. You're quite right.'

'Well, I actually quite enjoy those parties, Richard,' Holly shot back, 'but I just don't feel in the celebratory mood this year, that's all.'

There was a silence for a moment before Ciara piped up, 'A girly night it is then.'

'Can I tag along with the camera?' asked Declan.

'For what?'

'Just for some footage of clubs and stuff for college.'

'Well, if it'll help . . . but as long as you know I won't be going to all the trendy places that you like.'

'No, I don't mind where you g— OW!' he shouted, and stared menacingly at Timothy.

Timmy stuck his tongue out at him and the conversation continued. After the main course was finished Ciara disappeared out of the room, returned with a bulging bag in her hand and announced, 'Presents!'

Timmy and Emily cheered. Holly hoped that Ciara had remembered to get them something.

Her father received a colourfully painted boomerang

that he pretended to throw down to his wife; Richard was given a T-shirt with the map of Australia on it, which he immediately began to teach to Timmy and Emily at the table; Meredith quite comically wasn't given anything; Jack and Declan were given T-shirts with perverted pictures and a caption saying, 'I've been to the bush', and Elizabeth received a collection of old aboriginal recipes. Holly was touched by her dream catcher made from brightly coloured feathers and sticks.

'So all your dreams come true,' Ciara whispered in her ear before kissing her on the cheek.

Thankfully Ciara had bought sweets for Timmy and Emily, which looked strangely like the sweets they could buy from the local shop. These were briskly taken away by Richard and Meredith, who claimed they would rot their teeth.

'Well, give them back then so I can rot my own,' Ciara demanded.

Timmy and Emily looked around sadly at everyone's presents and were immediately chastised by Richard for not concentrating on the map of Australia. Timmy made a face at Holly and a warm feeling returned to her heart. As long as the kids kept acting as if they deserved their treatment, that was OK with her.

'Right, we better hit the road, Richard, or the children will fall asleep where they sit,' announced Meredith. The children were wide awake and were kicking Holly and Declan repeatedly under the table.

'Well, before everybody goes disappearing –' Holly's father announced loudly over the chatter. The table grew silent – 'I would like to propose a toast to our beautiful daughter Ciara.' He smiled at her and Ciara lapped up all the attention. 'We missed you, love, and we're glad you're home safely,' Frank finished. He lifted his glass into the air. 'To Ciara!'

'To Ciara!' everyone repeated.

As soon as the door closed behind Richard and Meredith everyone else began to leave one by one. Holly stepped into the chilly air and walked to her car alone. Her mum and dad stood at the door waving her off but she still felt so lonely. Usually she left dinner parties with Gerry, or if not *with* him then she was returning home *to* him. But not tonight or the next night or the night after that.

CHAPTER EIGHT

On her birthday, Holly stood in front of the full-length mirror and inspected herself. She had carried out Gerry's orders and had purchased a new outfit. What for, she didn't know but several times a day she had to drag herself away from the temptation of opening the envelope for May. There were only two days left until she could and the anticipation left her no room to think of anything else.

She had settled on wearing an all-black outfit to suit her current mood. Black fitted trousers slimmed her legs and were tailored perfectly to sit over her black boots. A black corset that made her look like she had a bigger chest finished the outfit off perfectly. Leo had done a wonderful job on her hair, tying it up and allowing strands to fall in loose waves around her shoulders. Holly ran her fingers through her hair and smiled at the memory of her time at the hairdressers . . .

She had arrived at the salon with her face flushed, and out of breath. 'Oh, I'm so sorry, Leo. I got caught on the phone and didn't realise the time.'

'Don't worry, love. Whenever you make an appointment I have the staff trained to pencil it in for half an hour later. COLIN!' he yelled, clicking his fingers in the air.

Colin dropped everything and ran.

'God, are you taking horse tranquillisers or something? The length of your hair already, and I just cut it a few weeks ago.'

He pumped vigorously on the chair, raising Holly higher. 'Anything special tonight?' he asked.

'The big three-0,' she said, biting her lip.

'What's that, your local bus route?'

'No! I'm the big three-0!'

'Of course I knew that, love. COLIN!' he yelled again, snapping his fingers in the air once more.

Colin appeared from the staff room behind Holly with a cake in his hand, followed by a row of hairdressers joining Leo in a chorus of 'Happy Birthday'. Holly was dumbfounded. She battled the tears that were welling in her eyes and failed miserably. By this stage the entire salon had joined in and Holly was so overwhelmed by their show of love. When it was over everyone applauded and normal business resumed.

Holly couldn't speak.

'Christ Almighty, Holly, one week you're in here laughing so hard you practically fall off your chair and the next visit you're crying!'

'Oh, but that was just so special, Leo, thank you,' she said, drying her eyes and giving him a huge hug and a kiss.

'Well, I had to get you back after you mortified me,' he said, shrugging her off, uncomfortable with the sentimentality.

Holly laughed, remembering Leo's surprise fiftieth birthday party. The theme had been 'feathers and lace'. Holly had worn a beautiful tight-fitting lace dress, and Gerry, who was always game for a laugh, had worn a pink feather boa to match his pink shirt and tie. Leo claimed to have been excruciatingly embarrassed but everyone knew he was secretly delighted with all the attention. The next day, Leo had rung every guest who had attended the party and left a threatening message on their machine. Holly had been terrified to make an appointment with him for weeks after that in case he butchered her hair. Word had it that business was very slow for Leo that week.

'Well, you enjoyed the stripper that night, anyway,' Holly teased.

'Enjoyed? I went out with him for a month after that. The bastard.'

A slice of cake arrived in front of each customer and everyone turned to thank her.

'Don't know why they're thanking you,' Leo muttered under his breath. 'I'm the one who bloody bought it.'

'Don't worry, Leo, I'll make sure your tip covers the cost.'

'Are you mad? Your tip wouldn't cover the cost of my bus fare home.'

'Leo, you live next door.'

'Exactly!'

Holly pouted her lip and pretended to sulk.

Leo laughed. 'Thirty years old and you're still acting like a baby. Where are you off to tonight?'

'Oh, nowhere mad. I just want a low-key, nice quiet night out with the girls.'

'That's what I said at my fiftieth. Who's going?'

'Sharon, Ciara, Abbey, and Denise – haven't seen her for ages.'

'Ciara home?'

'Yeah, her and her pink hair.'

'Merciful hour! She'll stay away from me if she knows what's good for her. Right, missus, you look fab, you'll be the belle of the ball – have fun!'

Holly stopped daydreaming and gazed at her reflection in the mirror. She didn't look thirty or feel thirty. But then again what was being thirty supposed to feel like? When she was younger, thirty seemed so far away, she'd thought that a woman of that age would be wise and knowledgeable, settled in her life with a husband and children and a career. She had none of those things. She still felt as clueless as when she was twenty, only with a few grey hairs, and crow's feet around her eyes. She sat down on the edge of the bed and continued to stare at herself. There was nothing about being thirty worth celebrating.

The doorbell rang and Holly could hear the excited chatter of the girls outside. She tried to perk herself up, took a deep breath and plastered a smile on her face.

'Happy birthday!' they all yelled in unison.

She stared back at their smiling faces and was immediately cheered by their enthusiasm. She ushered them into the living room and waved hello to the camera being brandished by Declan.

'No, Holly, you're supposed to ignore him!' hissed Denise, and dragged her by the arm onto the couch where they all surrounded her and immediately started thrusting presents in her face.

'Open mine first!' squealed Ciara, knocking Sharon out of the way so hard that she toppled off the couch. Sharon froze in horror, unsure of how to react, then burst into giggles.

'OK, calm down, everyone,' said the voice of reason (Abbey), struggling to help up a hysterical Sharon. 'I think we should pop open the bubbly first and *then* open the pressies.'

'OK, but as long as she opens mine first,' pouted Ciara.

'Ciara, I promise to open yours first.' Holly spoke as though addressing a child.

Abbey raced into the kitchen and returned with a tray full of champagne flutes.

'Anyone for champers, sweetie darlings?'

The flutes had been a wedding gift and one of the glasses had Gerry and Holly's name inscribed on it, which Abbey had tactfully removed from the set. 'OK, Holly, you can do the honours,' Abbey said, handing her the bottle.

Everyone ran for cover and ducked as Holly began to remove the cork. 'Hey, I'm not that bad, everyone!'

'Yeah, she's an old pro at this by now,' said Sharon, appearing from behind the couch with a cushion on her head.

The girls all cheered as they heard the pop and crawled out from their hiding places.

'The sound of heaven,' Denise said dramatically, holding her hand up to her heart.

'OK, now open my present,' Ciara screamed again.

'Ciara!' they all shouted.

'After the toast,' added Sharon.

Everyone held up her glass.

61

'OK, here's to my bestest friend in the whole world who has had such a difficult year, but throughout all has been the bravest and the strongest person I've ever met. She's an inspiration to us all. Here's to her finding happiness for the next thirty years of her life! To Holly!'

'To Holly,' they all chorused. Everyone's eyes were sparkling with tears as they all took sips of their drinks, except of course for Ciara, who had already knocked back her glass of champagne and was scrambling to give her present to Holly.

'OK, first you have to wear this tiara because you are our princess for the night, and secondly here's my present from me to you!'

The girls helped Holly put on the sparkling tiara that luckily went perfectly with her glittery corset. At that moment, surrounded by her friends, she really did feel like a princess.

Holly carefully removed the sellotape from the neatly wrapped parcel.

'Oh, just rip it open,' said Abbey to everyone's surprise.

Holly looked at the box inside, confused. 'What is it?'

'Read it!' Ciara said excitedly.

Holly began to read aloud from the box, 'It's a battery operated . . . oh my God! Ciara! You naughty girl!' Holly and the girls laughed hysterically.

'Well, I'll definitely need this,' Holly laughed, holding the box up to the camera.

Declan looked as if he was about to throw up.

'Do you like it?' Ciara asked, searching for approval. 'I wanted to give it to you at dinner last week but I didn't think it would be appropriate.'

'Gosh! Well, I'm glad you saved it till now!' Holly laughed, giving her sister a hug.

'OK, me next,' Abbey said, putting her parcel on Holly's lap. 'It's from me and Jack so don't expect anything like Ciara's.'

'Well, I would worry if Jack gave me something like that,' Holly said, opening it. 'Oh, Abbey, it's beautiful!' Holly said, holding up the sterling silver-covered photo album.

'For your new memories,' Abbey said softly.

'Oh, it's perfect,' Holly said, wrapping her arms round her and squeezing her. 'Thank you.'

'OK, well, mine is less sentimental but as a fellow female I'm sure you will appreciate it,' said Denise, handing her an envelope.

'Oh, brilliant! I've always wanted to go here,' Holly exclaimed as she opened it. 'A weekend of pampering at Haven's health and beauty clinic!'

'God, you sound like you're on *Blind Date*,' teased Sharon.

'Let us know when you want to make an appointment, it's valid for a year, and the rest of us can book the same time. Make a holiday out of it!'

'Oh, that's a great idea, Denise. Thank you!'

'OK, last but not least!' Holly winked at Sharon. Sharon fidgeted with her hands nervously while she watched Holly's face.

The present was a large silver photo frame with a photograph of Sharon, Denise and Holly at the Christmas Ball two years ago. 'Oh, I'm wearing my spensive white dress!' sobbed Holly playfully.

'*Before* it was ruined,' pointed out Sharon.

'God, I don't even remember that being taken!'

'I don't even remember being there,' mumbled Denise.

Holly continued to stare at the photo sadly while she walked over to the fireplace. That had been the last ball that she and Gerry had been to, as he had been too ill to attend last year's.

'Well, this will take pride of place,' Holly announced, walking over to the mantelpiece and placing it beside her wedding photo.

'OK, girls, let's get some serious drinking done!' screamed Ciara, and everyone dived to safety as another bottle of champagne was popped open.

Two bottles of champagne and several of red wine later the girls stumbled out of the house and piled into a taxi. Through the hilarity and shouting, someone managed to explain to the taxi driver where they were going. Holly insisted on sitting in the passenger seat and having a heart-to-heart with Nick, the driver, who probably wanted to kill her by the time they reached town.

'Bye, Nick!' they all shouted to their new best friend before falling out onto the kerb, where they watched him drive off at high speed. They had decided (while drinking their third bottle of wine) to chance their luck at Dublin's most stylish club, Boudoir. The club was reserved for the rich and famous only, and it was a well-known fact that if you weren't either, you then had to have a membership card to be granted access. Denise walked up to the door coolly waving her video store membership card in the bouncer's faces. Amazingly, they stopped her.

The only famous faces the girls saw overtaking them to enter the club, as they fought with the bouncers to get in, were some newsreaders from the national TV station, whom Denise smiled at and hilariously kept repeating, 'Good evening,' very seriously to their faces. Unfortunately, after that Holly remembered no more.

Holly awoke with her head pounding. Her mouth was as dry as Gandhi's sandal and her vision was impaired. She leaned up on one elbow and tried to open her eyes, which were somehow glued together. She squinted around. It was bright, very bright, and the room seemed to be spinning. Something very odd was going on. Holly caught sight of herself in the mirror ahead and startled herself. Had she been in an accident last night? She ran out of energy and collapsed flat on her back again. Suddenly the house alarm began wailing and she lifted her head slightly from the pillow and opened one eye. Oh, take whatever you want, she thought, just as long as you bring me a glass of water before you go. After a while she realised it wasn't the alarm but the phone ringing beside her bed.

'Hello?' she croaked.

'Oh good, I'm not the only one,' said a desperately ill-sounding voice on the other end.

'Who are you?' croaked Holly again.

'My name is Sharon, I think,' came the reply, 'although don't ask me who Sharon is because I don't know. The man beside me in bed seems to think I know him.'

Holly heard John laughing loudly in the background.

'Sharon, what happened last night? Please enlighten me.'

'Alcohol happened,' said Sharon drowsily, 'lots and lots of alcohol.'

'Any other information?'

'Nope.'

'Know what time it is?'

'Two o'clock.'

'Why are you ringing me at this hour of the morning?'

'It's the afternoon, Holly.'

'Oh. How did that happen?'

'Gravity or something. I was out that day from school.'

'Oh God, I think I'm dying.'

'Me too.'

'I think I'll just go back to sleep. Maybe when I wake up the ground will have stopped moving.'

'Good idea. Oh, and, Holly, welcome to the thirties club.'

Holly groaned. 'I have not started as I mean to go on. From now on I will be a sensible, mature thirty-year-old woman.'

'Yeah, that's what I said too. Good night.'

'Night.' Seconds later Holly was asleep. She awoke at various stages during the day to answer the phone, the conversations all seeming part of her dreams. And she made many trips to the kitchen for water to rehydrate herself.

Eventually, at nine o'clock that night, Holly succumbed to her stomach's screaming demands for food. As usual there was nothing in the fridge so she decided to treat herself to a Chinese takeaway. She sat snuggled up on the couch in her pyjamas watching the very best of Saturday night TV while stuffing her face. After the trauma of being without Gerry for her birthday the previous day, Holly was surprised to notice that she felt very content with herself. It was the first time since

Gerry died that she was comfortable with her own company. There was a slight chance she could make it without him.

Later that night Jack called her on her mobile. 'Hey, sis, what are you doing?'

'Watching TV, having Chinese,' she said.

'Well, you sound in good form. Unlike my poor girlfriend, who's suffering here beside me.'

'I'm never going out with you again, Holly,' she heard Abbey scream weakly in the background.

'You and your friends perverted her mind,' he joked.

'Don't blame me. She was doing just fine all by herself as far as I remember.'

'She says she can't remember anything.'

'Neither can I. Maybe it's something that happens as soon as you hit thirty. I was never like this before.'

'Or maybe it's just an evil plan you all hatched so you wouldn't have to tell us what you got up to.'

'I wish it was . . . Oh, thanks for the pressie by the way, it's beautiful.'

'Glad you like it. It took me ages to find the right one.'

'Liar.'

He laughed. 'Anyway, I was ringing to ask you if you're going to Declan's gig tomorrow night.'

'Where is it?'

'Hogan's pub.'

'No way. There is no way I'm ever setting foot in a pub again, especially to listen to some loud rock band with screeching guitars and noisy drums,' Holly told him.

'Oh, it's the old, "I'm never drinking again" excuse, is it? Well, don't drink then. Please come, Holly. Declan's really excited about it and no one else will come.'

'Ha! So I'm the last resort, am I? Nice to know you think so highly of me.'

'No, you're not. Declan would love to see you there and we hardly got a chance to talk at dinner. We haven't gone out for ages,' he pleaded.

'Well, we're hardly going to have a heart-to-heart with the Orgasmic Fish banging out their tunes,' she said sarcastically.

'They're actually called Black Strawberries now, which has a much sweeter ring to it, I think,' he laughed.

Holly held her head in her hands and groaned, 'Oh, please don't make me go, Jack.'

'You're going.'

'OK, but I'm not staying for the whole thing.'

'We can discuss that when we get there. Declan will be chuffed when I tell him; the family never usually goes to these things.'

'OK then, about eight-ish?'

'Perfect.'

Holly hung up and sat stuck to the couch for another few hours. She felt so full, she couldn't move. Maybe that Chinese hadn't been such a good idea after all.

CHAPTER NINE

Holly arrived in Hogan's pub feeling a lot fresher than the day before, but her reactions were still a little slower than usual. Her hangovers seemed to be getting worse as she got older, and yesterday took the gold medal for the hangover of all hangovers. She had gone for a long walk along the coast from Malahide to Portmarnock earlier that day, and the crisp fresh breeze had helped to clear her fuzzy head. She had called in to her parents for Sunday dinner, when they presented her with a beautiful Waterford Crystal vase for her birthday. It had been a wonderful relaxing day and she almost had to drag herself off the comfortable couch to go to Hogan's.

Hogan's was a popular three-storey building situated in the centre of town, and even on a Sunday the place was jammed. The first floor was a trendy nightclub that played all the latest music from the charts. It was where the young beautiful people went to show off their latest fashions. The ground floor was a traditional Irish pub for the older crowd (usually containing old men perched up on their bar stools, bent over their pints, contemplating life). A few nights a week there was a traditional Irish music band that played all the old favourites, which was popular with the young and old. The basement, where bands usually played, was dark and dingy, and the clientele was purely students. Holly seemed to be the oldest person in there. The bar consisted of a tiny counter in the corner of the long hall and was surrounded by a huge crowd of young students dressed in scruffy jeans and ripped T-shirts, pushing each other violently in order to be served. The bar staff also looked as if they should be in school, and were rushing around at a hundred miles per hour with sweat dripping from their faces.

The basement was stuffy, with no ventilation or air conditioning at all, and Holly was finding it difficult to breathe in the smoky air. Practically everyone around her seemed to be smoking and her eyes were already stinging. She dreaded to think what it might be like in an hour's time.

She waved at Declan to let him know she was there but decided not to make her way over as he was surrounded by a crowd of girls. She didn't want to cramp his style. Holly had missed out on the whole student scene when she was younger. She had decided not to go to college after school and instead begun working as a secretary, moving from job to job every few months, ending with the awful job she had left so she could spend time with Gerry while he was sick. She doubted she would have stayed in it that much longer anyway. Gerry had studied Marketing at Dublin City University but he never socialised much with his college friends. Instead he chose to go out with Holly, Sharon and John, Denise and whoever she was with at the time. Looking around at everyone, Holly didn't feel that she had missed anything special.

Finally Declan managed to tear himself away from his female fans and made his way over to Holly.

'Well, hello, Mr Popular. I feel privileged you chose me to speak to next.' All the girls stared Holly up and down and wondered what the hell Declan saw in this older woman.

Declan laughed and rubbed his hands together cheekily. 'I know! This band business is great. Looks like I'll be getting a bit of action tonight,' he said cockily.

'As your sister it's always a pleasure to be informed of that,' Holly replied sarcastically. She was finding it impossible to maintain a conversation with Declan as he refused eye contact with her and instead was scouring the crowds.

'OK, Declan, just go, why don't you, and flirt with these beauties instead of being stuck here with your old sister?'

'Oh no, it's not that,' he said defensively. 'It's just that we were told there might be a record company guy coming to see us play tonight.'

'Oh, cool!' Holly's eyes widened with excitement. This obviously meant a lot to her brother and she felt guilty for never taking an interest in it before. She glanced around and tried to spot someone who might be a record company person. What would they look like? It's not as if they would be sitting in the corner with a notebook scribbling furiously. Finally her eyes fell upon a man who seemed much older than the rest of the crowd, more her own age. He was dressed in a black leather jacket, black slacks and a black T-shirt, and stood with his hands on his hips staring at the stage. Yes, he was definitely a record company guy. He had stubble all around his jaw and looked like he hadn't been to bed for days. He probably smelled bad as well. Or else he was just a weirdo who liked to go to student nights and ogle all the young girls. Also a possibility.

'Over there, Deco!' Holly raised her voice over the noise and pointed at the man.

Declan looked excited and his eyes followed to where her finger pointed. His smile faded as he obviously recognised the man. 'No, it's just DANNY!' he yelled, and wolf-whistled to grab the guy's attention.

Danny twirled round, trying to find his caller, nodded his head in recognition and made his way over.

'Hey, man,' Declan said, shaking his hand.

'Hi, Declan, how are you set?' The man looked stressed.

'Yeah, OK,' Declan nodded unenthusiastically. Somebody must have told Declan that acting like you didn't care was cool.

'Sound check go OK?'

'There were a few problems but we sorted them out.'

'So everything's OK?'

'Sure.'

'Good.' His face relaxed and he turned to face Holly. 'Sorry for ignoring you there. I'm Daniel.'

'Nice to meet you. I'm Holly.'

'Oh, sorry,' Declan interrupted. 'Holly, this is the owner; Daniel, this is my sister.'

'Sister? Wow you look nothing alike.'

'Thank God,' Holly mouthed to Daniel so Declan couldn't see, and he laughed.

'Hey, Deco, we're on!' yelled a blue-haired boy at him.

'See you two later,' and Declan ran off.

'Good luck!' yelled Holly after him. 'So you're a Hogan,' she said, turning to face Daniel.

'Well, no, actually I'm a Connolly,' he smiled. 'I just took over the place a few weeks ago.'

'Oh.' Holly was surprised. 'I didn't know they'd sold it. So are you going to change it to Connolly's then?'

'Can't afford all the lettering on the front. It's a bit long.'

Holly laughed. 'Well, everyone knows the name Hogan's at this stage; it would probably be stupid to change it.'

Daniel nodded in agreement. 'That was the main reason, actually.'

Suddenly Jack appeared at the main entrance and Holly waved him over. 'I'm so sorry I'm late. Did I miss anything?' he said, giving her a hug and a kiss.

'Nope, he's just about to go on now. Jack, this is Daniel, the owner.'

'Nice to meet you,' Daniel said, shaking his hand.

'Are they any good?' Jack asked him, nodding his head in the direction of the stage.

'To tell you the truth, I've never even heard them play,' Daniel said worriedly.

'That was brave of you!' laughed Jack.

'I hope not too brave,' he said, turning to face the front as the boys took to the stage.

'I recognise a few faces here,' Jack said, scanning the crowd. 'Most of them are under eighteen as well.'

A young girl dressed in ripped jeans and a belly top walked slowly by Jack with an unsure smile on her face.

73

She placed her finger over her lip. Jack smiled and nodded back.

Holly looked at Jack questioningly. 'What was that about?'

'Oh, I teach her English. She's only sixteen or seventeen. She's a good girl, though.' Jack stared after her as she walked by, then added, 'But she'd better not be late for class tomorrow.'

Holly watched the girl down a pint with her friends, wishing she had had a teacher at school like Jack; all the students seemed to love him. And it was easy to see why: he was a lovable kind of person. 'Well, don't tell *him* they're under eighteen,' Holly said under her breath, nodding in the direction of Daniel.

The crowd cheered and Declan took on his moody persona as he lifted his guitar strap over his shoulder. The music started and after that there was no chance of carrying on any kind of conversation. The crowd began to jump up and down, and once too often Holly's foot was stomped on. Jack just looked at her and laughed, amused at her obvious discomfort.

'CAN I GET YOU TWO A DRINK?' Daniel yelled, making a drinking motion with his hand. Jack asked for a pint of Budweiser while Holly settled for a 7-Up. They watched Daniel battle through the moshing crowd and climb behind the bar to fix the drinks. He returned minutes later with their glasses and a stool for Holly. She and Jack turned their attention back to the stage and watched their brother perform. The music really wasn't Holly's type of thing, and it was so loud and noisy it was difficult for her to tell if they were actually any good. It was a far cry from the soothing sounds of her favourite Westlife CD.

After four songs Holly had had enough, and gave Jack a hug and a kiss goodbye. 'TELL DECLAN I STAYED TILL THE END!' she yelled. 'NICE MEETING YOU, DANIEL! THANKS FOR THE DRINK!' she screamed, and made her way back to civilisation and cool fresh air.

Her ears continued to ring all the way home in the car. It was ten o'clock by the time she got there. Only two more hours till May. And that meant she could open another envelope.

Holly sat at her kitchen table nervously drumming her fingers on the wood. She gulped back her third cup of coffee and uncrossed her legs. Staying awake for just two more hours had proved more difficult than she'd anticipated; she was obviously still tired from overindulging at her party the night before last. She tapped her feet under the table with no particular rhythm, and then crossed her legs again. It was eleven thirty. She had the envelope on the table in front of her and she could almost see it sticking its tongue out and singing 'Nah nah na-nah nah.'

She picked it up and ran her hands over it. Who would know if she opened it early? Sharon and John had probably forgotten there was even an envelope for May, and Denise was no doubt conked out after the stress of her two-day hangover. Holly could just as easily lie if they ever asked her, but then again they probably wouldn't even care. No one would know and no one would care.

But that wasn't true.

Gerry would know.

Each time Holly held the envelopes in her hand she felt a connection with Gerry. The last two times she'd

75

opened them she'd felt as though Gerry were sitting right beside her and laughing at her reactions. She felt as if they were playing a game together, even though they were in two different worlds. But she could *feel* him, and he would know if she cheated, he would know if she disobeyed the rules of their game.

After another cup of coffee Holly was bouncing off the walls. The small hand of the clock seemed to be auditioning for a part in *Baywatch* with its slow-motion run around the dial, but eventually it struck midnight. Once again she slowly turned the envelope over and treasured every moment of the process. Gerry sat opposite her at the table. 'Go on: open it!'

She carefully tore open the seal and ran her fingers along it, knowing the last thing that touched this was Gerry's tongue. She slid the card out of its pouch and opened it.

Go on, disco diva! Face your fear of karaoke at Club Diva this month, and you never know, you might be rewarded . . .
PS. I love you . . .

She felt Gerry watching her and the corners of her lips lifted into a smile. She began to laugh, repeating, 'NO WAY!' whenever she caught her breath. Finally she calmed down and announced to the room, 'Gerry! You bastard! There is absolutely no way I am going through with this!'

Gerry laughed louder.

'This is *not* funny. You know how I feel about karaoke, and I refuse to do it. Nope. No way. Not doing it.'

'You have to do it, you know,' laughed Gerry.

'I do not have to do this!'

'Do it for me.'

'I am not doing it for you, for me or for world peace. I hate karaoke!'

'Do it for me,' he repeated.

The sound of the phone caused Holly to jump in her seat.

It was Sharon. 'OK, it's five past twelve, what did it say? John and I are dying to know!'

'What makes you think I opened it?'

'Ha!' Sharon snorted. 'Twenty years of friendship qualifies me as an expert; now come on, tell us what it says.'

'I'm not doing it,' Holly stated bluntly.

'What? You're not telling us?'

'No, I'm not doing what he wants me to do.'

'Why, what is it?'

'Oh, just Gerry's *pathetic* attempt at being *humorous*,' she snapped at the ceiling.

'I'm intrigued now,' Sharon said. 'Tell us.'

'Holly, spill the beans, what is it?' John was on the downstairs phone.

'OK . . . Gerry wants me . . . to . . . singatakaraoke,' she rushed out.

'Huh? Holly, we didn't understand a word you said,' Sharon gave out.

'No, I did,' interrupted John. 'I think I heard something about karaoke. Am I right?'

'Yes,' Holly replied.

'And do you have to sing?' enquired Sharon.

'Ye-eess,' she replied slowly. Maybe if she didn't say it, it wouldn't have to happen.

The others burst out laughing so loud, Holly had to remove the phone from her ear. 'Phone me back when the two of you shut up,' she said angrily, hanging up.

A few minutes later they called back.

'Yes?'

She heard Sharon snort down the phone, relapse into a fit of the giggles and then the line went dead.

Ten minutes later she phoned back.

'Yes?'

'OK.' Sharon had an overly serious 'let's get down to business' tone in her voice. 'I'm sorry about that, I'm fine now. Don't look at me, John,' she said away from the phone. 'I'm sorry, Holly, but I just kept thinking about the last time you—'

'Yeah, yeah, yeah,' Holly interrupted, 'you don't need to bring it back up. It was *the most embarrassing day of my life* so I just happen to remember it. That's why I'm not doing it.'

'Oh, Holly, you can't let a stupid thing like that put you off!'

'Well, if that wouldn't put a person off, then they're clinically insane!'

'Holly, it was only a little fall . . .'

'Yes, thank you! I remember it just fine! Anyway, I can't even sing, Sharon; I think I established that fact marvellously the last time!'

Sharon was very quiet.

'Sharon?'

More silence.

'Sharon, you still there?'

There was no answer.

'Sharon, are you laughing?' Holly gave out.

Holly heard a little squeak and the line went dead.

'What wonderfully supportive friends I have,' she muttered under her breath.

'Oh, Gerry!' she yelled. 'I thought you were supposed to be helping me, not turning me into a nervous wreck!'

She got very little sleep that night.

CHAPTER TEN

'Happy birthday, Holly! Or should I say Happy belated birthday?' Richard laughed nervously. Holly's mouth dropped open in shock at the sight of her older brother standing on her doorstep. This was a rare occurrence; in fact it may even have been a first. She opened and closed her mouth like a goldfish, completely unsure what to say.

'I brought you a potted mini phalaenopsis orchid,' he said, handing her a plant. 'They have been shipped fresh, budding and are ready to bloom.' He sounded like an advertisement.

Holly was even more stunned. She fingered the tiny pink buds. 'Gosh, Richard, orchids are my favourite!'

'Well, you have a nice big garden here anyway, nice and . . .' he cleared his throat, 'green. Bit overgrown, though . . .' he trailed off and began that annoying rocking thing he did with his feet.

'Would you like to come in or are you just passing through?' Please say no, please say no. Despite the thoughtful gift, Holly was in no mood for Richard's company.

'Well, yes, I'll come in for a little while so.' He wiped his feet for a good two minutes at the door before stepping into the house. He reminded Holly of her old maths teacher at school, dressed in a brown knitted cardigan with brown trousers that stopped just at the top of his neat little brown loafers. He hadn't a hair on his head out of place and his fingernails were clean and perfectly manicured. Holly could imagine him measuring them with a little ruler every night to see that they didn't outgrow the required European standard length for fingernails, if such a thing existed.

Richard never seemed comfortable in his own skin. He looked as if he was being choked to death by his tightly knotted (brown) tie, and he always walked as if he had a barge pole shoved up his backside. On the rare occasions that he smiled, the smile never quite managed to reach his eyes. He was the drill sergeant of his own body, screaming at it and punishing himself every time he lapsed into human mode. The sad thing was that he thought he was better off than everyone else for it. Holly led him into the living room and placed the ceramic pot on top of the TV for the time being.

'No, no, Holly,' Richard said, wagging a finger at her as though she was a naughty child, 'you shouldn't put it there. It needs to be in a cool, draught-free location away from harsh sunlight and heat vents.'

'Oh, of course.' Holly picked the pot back up and searched around the room in panic for a suitable place. What had he said? A draught-free, warm location? How did he always manage to make her feel like an incompetent little girl?

'How about that little table in the centre? It should be safe there.'

Holly did as she was told and placed the pot on the table, half expecting him to say 'good girl'. Thankfully he didn't.

Richard took his favourite position at the fireplace and surveyed the room. 'Your house is very clean,' he commented.

'Thank you. I just, eh . . . cleaned it.'

He nodded as if he already knew.

'Can I get you a tea or a coffee?' she asked, expecting him to say no.

'Yes, great,' he said, clapping his hands together. 'Tea would be splendid. Just milk no sugar.'

Holly returned from the kitchen with two mugs of tea and placed them down on the coffee table. She hoped the steam rising from the mugs wouldn't murder the poor plant. It being a heat vent and all.

'You just need to water it regularly and feed it during the spring months.' He was still talking about the plant. Holly nodded, knowing full well she would not do either of those things.

'I didn't know you had green fingers, Richard,' she said, trying to lighten the atmosphere.

'Only when I'm painting with the children,' he laughed, cracking a rare joke.

'Do you do much work in your garden?' Holly was anxious to keep the conversation flowing; as the house was so quiet every silence was amplified.

'Oh, yes, I love to work in the garden.' His eyes lit

up. 'Saturdays are my garden days,' he said, smiling into his mug of tea.

Holly felt as though a complete stranger was sitting beside her. She realised she knew very little about her brother and he equally knew very little about her. But that was the way Richard had always liked to keep things. He had distanced himself from the family even when they were younger. He never shared exciting news with them or even told them how his day went. He was just full of facts, facts and more facts. The first time the family had even heard of Meredith was the day they both came over for dinner to announce their engagement. Unfortunately, by that stage it was too late to convince him not to marry the flame-haired, green-eyed dragon. Not that he would have listened, anyway.

'So,' she announced far too loudly for the echoing room, 'anything strange or startling?' Like why are you here?

'No, no, nothing strange. Everything is ticking over as normal.' He took a sip of tea, then a while later added, 'Nothing startling either, for that matter. I just thought I would pop in and say hello while I was in the area.'

'Ah, right. It's unusual for you to be over this side of the city,' Holly laughed. 'What brings you to the dark and dangerous world of the north side?'

'Oh, you know, just a little business,' he mumbled to himself. 'But my car's parked on the other side of the river, of course!'

Holly forced a smile.

'Just joking,' he added. 'It's just outside the house . . . It will be safe won't it?' he asked seriously.

'I think it should be OK,' Holly said. 'There doesn't

83

seem to be anyone suspicious hanging around the cul-de-sac in broad daylight today.' Her humour was lost on him. 'How's Emily and Timmy – sorry, I mean Timothy?' An honest mistake for once.

Richard's eyes lit up, 'Oh, they're good, Holly, very good. Worrying, though.' He looked away and surveyed her living room.

'What do you mean?' Holly asked, thinking that perhaps Richard may open up to her.

'Oh, there isn't one thing in particular, Holly. Children are a worry in general.' He pushed the rim of his glasses up his nose and looked her in the eye. 'But I suppose you're glad you will never have to worry about all this children nonsense,' he said, laughing.

There was a silence.

Holly felt as if she had been kicked in the stomach.

'So have you found a job yet?' he continued on.

Holly sat frozen on her chair in shock. She couldn't believe he had had the audacity to say that to her. She was insulted and hurt and she wanted him out of her house. She really wasn't in the mood to be polite to him any more, and certainly couldn't be bothered explaining to his narrow little mind that she hadn't even begun looking for a job yet as she was still grieving the death of her spouse – 'nonsense' that he wouldn't have to experience for another fifty years or so.

'No,' she spat out.

'So what are you doing for money? Have you signed on the dole?'

'No, Richard,' she said, trying not to lose her temper. 'I haven't signed on the dole. I get *widow's* allowance.'

'Ah, that's a great, handy thing, isn't it?'

'Handy is not quite the word I would use. Devastatingly depressing is more like it.'

The atmosphere was tense. Suddenly he slapped his leg with his hand, signalling the end of the conversation. 'I better motor on so and get back to work,' he announced, standing up and exaggerating a stretch as though he had been sitting down for hours.

'OK then,' Holly was relieved. 'You better leave while your car is still there.'

Once again her humour was lost on him as he was peering out the window to check.

'You're right; it's still there, thank God. Anyway, nice to see you and thank you for the tea.'

'You're welcome, and thank you for the orchid,' Holly said through gritted teeth.

He marched down the garden path and stopped midway to look at the garden. He nodded his head disapprovingly and shouted to her, 'You really must get someone to sort this mess out,' and drove off in his brown family car.

Holly fumed as she watched him drive away, and banged the door shut. That man made her blood boil so much she felt like knocking him out. He just hadn't a clue . . . about anything.

CHAPTER ELEVEN

'Oh, Sharon, I just *hate* him,' Holly moaned to her friend on the phone later that night.

'Just ignore him, Holly. He can't help himself, he's an idiot,' she replied angrily.

'But that's what annoys me even more. Everyone says he can't help himself or it's not his fault, but he's a grown man, Sharon. He's thirty-six years old. He should bloody well know when to keep his mouth shut. He says those things deliberately,' Holly fumed.

'I really don't think he does, Holly,' Sharon said soothingly. 'I genuinely think he called round to wish you a happy birthday . . .'

'Yeah! And what's that about?' Holly ranted. 'Since *when* has he ever called round to my house to give me a birthday present? NEVER! That's when!'

'Well, thirty is more of a big deal than any other—'

'Not in his eyes it's not! He even said so at dinner the other day. If I recall, his exact words were,' she mimicked his voice, 'I don't agree with silly celebrations blah blah blah I'm a sap blah blah blah. He really is a Dick.'

Sharon laughed at her friend sounding like a ten-year-old. 'OK, so he's an evil monster of a being who deserves to burn in hell!'

Holly paused. 'Well, I wouldn't go that far, Sharon . . .'

Sharon laughed. 'Oh, I just can't please you at all, can I?'

Holly smiled weakly. Gerry would know exactly how she was feeling, he would know exactly what to say and exactly what to do. He would give her one of his famous hugs and all her problems would melt away. She grabbed a pillow from her bed and hugged it tight. She couldn't remember the last time she had hugged someone, *really* hugged someone. And the depressing thing was that she couldn't imagine ever embracing anyone the same way again.

'Helloooo? Earth to Holly? You still there or am I talking to myself again?

'Oh, sorry, Sharon, what did you say?'

'I said have you given any more thought to this karaoke business?'

'Sharon!' Holly yelped. 'No more thought is required on that subject.'

'OK, calm down, woman! I was just thinking that we could hire a karaoke machine and set it up in your living room. That way, you'll be doing what he wants minus the embarrassment! What do you think?'

'No, Sharon, it's a great idea but it won't work; he wants me to do it in Club Diva, wherever that is.'

'Ah! So sweet! Because you're his disco diva?'

'I think that was the general idea,' Holly said miserably.

'Ah! That's a lovely idea, although Club Diva? Never heard of it.'

'Well, that's that settled then. If no one knows where it is, then I just can't do it, can I?' Holly said, satisfied she had found a way out.

They both said their goodbyes but as soon as Holly had hung up, the phone rang again.

'Hi, sweetheart.'

'Mum!' Holly said accusingly.

'Oh God, what have I done now?'

'I received a little visit from your evil son today and I'm not very happy.'

'Oh, I'm sorry, dear, I tried to call you earlier to tell you he was on his way over but I kept getting that bloody answering machine. Do you ever turn your phone on?'

'That is not the point, Mum.'

'I know, I'm sorry. Why, what did he do?'

'He opened his mouth. There lies the problem in itself.'

'Oh no, and he was so excited about giving you that present.'

'Well, I'm not denying the fact that the present was very nice and thoughtful but he said some of the most insulting things without batting an eyelid!'

'Do you want me to talk to him for you?'

'No, it's OK; we're big boys and girls now. But thanks, anyway. So what are you up to?' Holly was anxious to change the subject.

'Ciara and I are watching a Denzel Washington film. Ciara thinks she's going to marry him someday,' Elizabeth laughed.

'I am too!' Ciara shouted in the background.

'Well, sorry to burst her little bubble but tell her he's already married.'

'He's married, honey,' Elizabeth passed on the message.

'Hollywood marriages . . .' Ciara mumbled.

'Are the two of you on your own?' Holly asked.

'Frank is down the pub and Declan is at college.'

'College? But it's ten o'clock at night!' Holly laughed. Declan was probably out somewhere doing something illegal and using college as an excuse. She didn't think her mum would be so gullible to believe that line, especially after having four other children.

'Oh, he's a very hard worker when he puts his mind to it, Holly. He's working on some project. I don't know what it is; I don't listen half the time.'

'Mmm,' Holly replied, not believing a word of it.

'Anyway, my future son-in-law is back on television so I must be off,' Elizabeth laughed. 'Would you like to come round and join us?'

'Thanks but no, I'm OK here.'

'All right, love, but if you change your mind you know where we are. Bye, dear.'

Back to her empty, silent house.

Holly woke up the next morning still fully dressed and lying on her bed. She could feel herself slipping into her old habits again. All her positive thoughts of the past few weeks were melting away bit by bit every day. It was so bloody tiring trying to be happy all the time and she just didn't have the energy any more. Who cared if the house was a mess? Nobody but she was going to see it, and she certainly didn't care one way or the other. Who cared if she didn't wear make-up or wash for a week? She had no intention of impressing anyone. The only guy she was seeing regularly was the pizza delivery boy, and she even had to tip him to make him smile. *Who bloody cared?*

Her phone vibrated beside her, signalling a text message. It was from Sharon.

Club Diva no 36700700
Think bout it. Wud b fun.
Do it 4 Gerry?

Gerry's bloody dead, she felt like texting back. But ever since she had begun opening the envelopes he didn't feel dead to her. It was as though he was just away on holiday and he was writing her letters so he wasn't *really* gone. Well, the very least she could do was ring the club and suss out the situation. That didn't mean she had to go through with it.

She dialled the number and a man answered. She couldn't think of anything to say and quickly hung up again. Oh, come on, Holly, she told herself, it's really not that difficult. Just say a friend is interested in singing.

Holly braced herself and pressed redial.

The same voice answered, 'Club Diva.'

'Hi, I was wondering if you do karaoke nights there?'

'Yes, we do. They are on a . . .' she heard him leafing through some pages, 'yeah, sorry, they're on a Thursday.'

'Thursday?'

'No, sorry, sorry, hold on . . .' He leafed through some pages again. 'No, they're on a Tuesday night.'

'Are you sure?'

'Yes, they are definitely on a Tuesday.'

'OK, em, well, I was wondering if, em . . .' Holly took a deep breath and began the sentence again. 'My friend might be interested in singing and she was wondering what she would have to do?'

There was a long pause on the other end.

'Hello?' Was this person stupid?

'Yeah, sorry, I don't actually organise the karaoke nights so . . .'

'OK.' Holly was losing her temper. It had taken a lot to summon up the courage to actually make the call and some underqualified unhelpful little twit wasn't going to ruin it for her. 'Well, is there anyone there who might have a clue?'

'Eh, no, there isn't. The club isn't actually open yet. It's very early in the morning still,' came the sarcastic response.

'Well, thank you very much. You've been a terrific help,' she matched his sarcasm.

'Excuse me, if you can just bear with me for a moment, I'll try and find out for you.' Holly was put on hold and was forced to listen to 'Greensleeves' for the next five minutes.

'Hello? Are you still there?'

'Barely,' she said angrily.

'OK, I'm very sorry about the delay but I just made a phone call there. What's your friend's name?'

Holly froze; she hadn't planned on this. Well, maybe she could just give her name and then get 'her friend' to call back and cancel if she changed her mind.

'Em, her name is Holly Kennedy.'

'OK, well, it's actually a karaoke competition on Tuesday nights. It goes on for a month and every week two people out of ten are chosen till the last week of the month, where the six people sing again in the final.'

Holly gulped and felt butterflies in her tummy. She didn't want to do this.

'But unfortunately,' he continued, 'the names have all been entered a few months in advance so you can tell your friend that maybe she could try again at Christmas. That's when the next competition is on.'

'Oh, OK.'

'By the way, the name Holly Kennedy rings a bell. Would that be Declan Kennedy's sister?'

'Eh, yeah. Why, do you know her?' asked a shocked Holly.

'I wouldn't say I know her I just met her briefly here the other night with her brother.'

Was Declan going around introducing girls as his sister? The sick and twisted little . . . No, that couldn't be right.

'Declan played a gig in Club Diva?'

'No, no,' the man laughed, 'he played with his band downstairs in the basement.'

Holly quickly digested the information until the facts finally clicked in place.

'Is Club Diva in Hogan's?'

He laughed again. 'Yeah, it's on the top floor. Maybe I should advertise a bit more!'

'Is that Daniel?' Holly blurted out and then kicked herself for being so stupid.

'Eh, yeah, do I know you?'

'Em, no! No, you don't! Holly just mentioned you in conversation, that's all.' Then she realised how that sounded. 'Very briefly in conversation,' she added. 'She said you gave her a stool.' Holly began hitting her head softly against the wall.

Daniel laughed again. 'Oh, OK, well, tell her if she wants to sing in the karaoke at Christmas I can put her name down now for it. You wouldn't believe the amount of people that want to sign up.'

'Really?' Holly said weakly. She felt like a fool.

'Oh, by the way, who am I speaking to?'

Holly paced her bedroom floor. 'Em, Sharon. You're speaking to Sharon.'

'OK, Sharon, well, I have your number on caller ID so I'll call you if anyone backs out.'

'OK, thanks a lot.'

And he hung up.

Holly leaped into bed, throwing the duvet over her head as she felt her face burn with embarrassment. She hid under the covers, cursing herself for being such a bimbo. Ignoring the phone ringing, she tried to convince herself she hadn't been a complete idiot. Eventually, after she had persuaded herself she could show her face in public again (it took a long time) she crawled out of bed and hit the button on her answering machine. The electronic voice announced she had one message.

'Hi, Sharon, I must have just missed you. It's Daniel here from Club Diva,' he paused and then, laughing, added, 'in Hogan's. Em, I was just looking through the list of names in the book and it seems somebody already entered Holly's name a few months back. In fact it's one of the first entries. Unless it's another Holly Kennedy . . .' he trailed off. 'Anyway, call me back when you get a chance so we can sort it out. Thanks.'

Holly sat shocked on the edge of her bed, unable to move.

CHAPTER TWELVE

Sharon, Denise and Holly sat by the window in Bewley's café overlooking Grafton Street. They often met up there to watch the world go by. Sharon always said it was the best window shopping she could ever do as she had a bird's-eye view of all her favourite stores.

'I can't believe Gerry organised all this!' gasped Denise when she heard the news.

'It'll be a bit of fun, won't it?' Sharon said excitedly.

'Oh God.' Holly had butterflies in her stomach just at the thought of it. 'I still really, really, *really* don't want to do it but I feel I have to finish off what Gerry started.'

'That's the spirit, Hol!' cheered Denise. 'And we'll all be there to cheer you on!'

'Now hold on a minute, Denise,' Holly said, dampening the celebratory tone, 'I just want you and Sharon there, no one else. I don't want to make a big deal out of this at all. Let's keep it between us.'

'But, Holly!' Sharon protested. 'It is a big deal! No one ever thought you'd do karaoke again after last time . . .'

'Sharon!' warned Holly. 'One must not speak of such things. One is still scarred from that experience.'

'Well, I think one is a daft cow for not getting over it,' mumbled Sharon.

'So when's the big night?' Denise changed the subject, sensing bad vibes.

'Next Tuesday,' Holly groaned, bending forward and banging her head playfully on the table repeatedly. The surrounding tables of customers stared at her curiously.

'She's just out for the day,' Sharon announced to the room, pointing at Holly.

'Don't worry, Holly; that gives you seven days exactly to transform yourself into Mariah Carey. No problem at all,' Denise said, smiling at Sharon.

'Oh, please, we would have a better chance teaching Lennox Lewis how to do ballet,' said Sharon.

Holly looked up from banging her head, 'Well, thanks for the encouragement, Sharon.'

'Ooh, but imagine Lennox Lewis in a pair of tights, that tight little arse dancing around . . .' Denise said dreamily.

Holly and Sharon stopped growling at each other to stare at their friend.

'You've lost the plot, Denise.'

'What?' Denise said defensively, snapping out of her fantasy. 'Just imagine those big muscular thighs . . .'

'That would snap your neck in two if you went near him,' Sharon finished for her.

'Now *there's* a thought,' Denise said, widening her eyes.

'I can see it all now,' Holly joined in, staring off into

space. 'The deaths column would read: "Denise Hennessey, tragically died after being crushed to death by the most tremendous thunder thighs after briefly catching a glimpse of heaven . . ."'

'I like that,' she agreed. 'Ooh, and what a way to die! Give me a slice of that heaven!'

'OK, you,' Sharon interrupted, pointing her finger at Denise, 'keep your sordid little fantasies to yourself, please. And you,' she pointed at Holly, 'stop trying to change the subject.'

'Oh, you're just jealous, Sharon, because your husband couldn't snap a matchstick between his skinny little thighs,' teased Denise.

'Excuse me, but John's thighs are perfectly fine. I just wish mine could be more like his,' Sharon finished.

'Now you,' Denise pointed at Sharon, 'keep your sordid little fantasies to yourself.'

'Girls, girls!' Holly snapped her fingers in the air. 'Let's focus on me now, focus on me,' she gracefully motioned with her hands, bringing them towards her chest.

'OK, Ms Selfish, what are you planning on singing?'

'I have no idea, that's why I called this emergency meeting.'

'No, it's not, you told me you wanted to go shopping,' Sharon said.

'Oh, really?' Denise looked at Sharon and raised an eyebrow. 'I thought you were both coming to visit me on my lunch break.'

'You are both correct,' Holly asserted. 'I am shopping for ideas and I need you both.'

'OK, OK!' Sharon exclaimed excitedly. 'I think I've got an idea. What was that song we sang for the whole two weeks in Spain and we couldn't get it out of our heads? It used to bug the hell out of us?'

Holly shrugged her shoulders. If it bugged the hell out of them it was hardly a very good choice.

'I don't know, I wasn't invited on that holiday,' muttered Denise.

'Oh, you know the one, Holly!'

'I can't remember.'

'Oh, you have to!'

'Sharon, I don't think she can remember,' Denise said frustratedly to Sharon.

'Oh, what was it?' Sharon put her face in her hands, irritated. Holly shrugged her shoulders at Denise again. 'OK, I've got it!!' she announced happily, and began to sing loudly in the café. '"Sun, sea, sex, sand, come on boy, give me your hand!".'

Holly's eyes widened and her cheeks flushed with embarrassment as the surrounding tables turned to stare. She turned to Denise for support in silencing Sharon.

'"Ooh ooh ooh *so sexy*, *so sexy!*"' Denise joined in with Sharon. Some people stared with amusement but most with loathing while Denise and Sharon warbled their way through the tacky European dance song that was a hit a few summers previously. Just as they were about to sing the chorus for the fourth time (neither of them could remember the verses) Holly silenced them.

'Girls, I can't sing that song! Besides, the verses are rapped by a guy!'

'Well, at least you wouldn't have to sing too much,' chuckled Denise.

'No way! I am not rapping at a karaoke competition!'

'OK, well, what CD are you listening to at the moment?' Denise got serious again.

'Westlife?' She looked at them hopefully.

'Then sing a Westlife song,' Sharon encouraged. 'That way, at least you'll know all the words.'

Sharon and Denise began to laugh uncontrollably. 'You might not get the tune right,' Sharon forced out between hacking laughs.

'But at least you'll know the words!' Denise managed to finish for her before the two of them doubled over at the table.

First Holly was angry but looking at both of them crouched over holding their stomachs in hysterics, she had to chuckle. They were right, Holly was completely tone deaf and hadn't a note in her head. Finding a song she could actually sing was going to prove impossible.

Finally, after the girls had settled down again, Denise looked at her watch and moaned about having to get back to work. They left Bewley's, much to the other customers' delight. 'The miserable sods will probably throw a party now,' Sharon had mumbled, passing their tables.

The three girls linked arms and walked down Grafton Street, heading towards the clothes store where Denise was manager. The day was sunny with just a light chill in the air; Grafton Street was busy as usual with people running around on their lunch breaks while shoppers slowly meandered up the street taking full advantage of the lack of rain. At every stretch of the road there was a busker fighting for attention from the crowds, and Denise and Sharon embarrassingly did a quick Irish dance as they passed a man playing the fiddle. He winked at

98

them and they threw some money into his tweed cap on the ground.

'Right, you ladies of leisure, I'd better head back to work,' Denise said, pushing the door to her shop open. As soon as her staff saw her they scarpered from gossiping at the counter and immediately began to tidy the clothes rails. Holly and Sharon tried not to laugh. They said their goodbyes and both headed up to Stephen's Green to collect their cars.

'"Sun, sea, sex, sand,"' Holly quietly sang to herself. 'Oh shit, Sharon, you've got that stupid song in my head now,' she complained.

'You see, there you go with that "shit Sharon" thing again. So negative, Holly.' Sharon began humming the song.

'Oh, shut up!' Holly laughed, hitting her on the arm.

CHAPTER THIRTEEN

It was four o'clock by the time Holly eventually got out of town and started heading home to Swords. Evil Sharon had convinced Holly to go shopping after all, which resulted in her splashing out on a ridiculous top she was far too old to wear. She really needed to watch her spending from now on. Her funds were running low and without regular income she could sense tense times ahead. She needed to start thinking about getting a job, but she was finding it hard enough to get out of bed in the morning as it was – another depressing nine-to-five job wasn't going to help matters. But it would pay the bills. Holly sighed loudly. All these things she had to handle by herself. She spent too much time on her own thinking about them. She needed people around her, like today with Denise and Sharon, as they always took her mind off things.

She phoned her mum and checked if it was all right for her to call round.

'Of course you can, love, you're always welcome.' Then

Elizabeth lowered her voice to a whisper. 'Just as long as you know that Richard is here.' Christ! What was with all the little visits all of a sudden?

Holly contemplated heading straight home when she heard that, but convinced herself she was being silly. He was her brother and, as annoying as he was, she couldn't go on avoiding him forever.

She arrived to an extremely loud and crowded house, and it felt like old times again, hearing screams and shouts in every room. Her mum was setting an extra place at the table just as Holly walked in.

'Oh, Mum, you should have told me you were having dinner,' Holly said, giving her a hug and a kiss.

'Why, have you eaten already?'

'No, actually I'm starving but I hope you didn't go to too much trouble.'

'No trouble at all, dear. It just means that poor Declan will have to go without food for the day, that's all,' she said, teasing her son, who was taking his seat. He made a face at her.

The atmosphere was so much more relaxed this time around – or maybe it had just been Holly who was uptight last time they met up.

'So, Mr Hard Worker, why aren't you in college today?' she said sarcastically.

'I've been in college all morning,' Declan replied, making a face. 'And I'm going back in at eight o'clock, actually.'

'That's very late,' said his father, pouring gravy all over his plate. Frank always ended up with more gravy than food.

'Yeah, but it was the only time I could get the editing suite.'

'Is there only one editing suite, Declan?' piped up Richard.

'Yeah.' Ever the conversationalist.

'And how many students are there?'

'It's only a small class so there are twelve of us.'

'Don't they have the funds for any more?'

'For what, students?' Declan teased.

'No, for another editing suite.'

'No, it's only a small college, Richard.'

'I suppose the bigger universities would be better equipped for things like that. They're better all round.'

And there was the dig they were all waiting for.

'No, I wouldn't say that. The facilities are top of the range, there's just fewer people so less equipment. And the lecturers aren't inferior to university lecturers. They're a bonus because they work in the industry as well as lecturing. In other words, they practise what they preach. It's not just textbook stuff.'

Good for you, Declan, Holly thought, and winked across the table at him.

'I wouldn't imagine they get paid well doing that, so they probably have no choice but to lecture too.'

'Richard, working in film is a very good job; you're talking about people who have spent years in college studying for degrees and masters . . .'

'Oh, you get a degree for that, do you?' Richard was amazed. 'I thought it was just a little course you were doing.'

Declan stopped eating and looked at Holly in shock. Funny how Richard's ignorance still amazed everyone.

'Who do you think makes all those gardening programmes you watch, Richard?' Holly interfered.

'They're not just a crowd of people who are doing a little course.'

The thought that there was a skill involved had never even crossed his mind. 'Great little programmes they are,' he agreed.

'What's your project on, Declan?' Frank asked.

Declan finished chewing his food before he spoke. 'Oh, it's too messy to go into but basically it's on club life in Dublin.'

'Ooh, will we be in it?' Ciara broke her unusual silence.

'Yeah, I might just show the back of your head or something,' he joked.

'Well, I can't wait to see it,' Holly said encouragingly.

'Thanks.' Declan put his knife and fork down and started laughing, 'Hey, what's this I hear about you singing in a karaoke competition next week?'

'What?' Ciara yelled, her eyes nearly popping out of her head.

Holly pretended not to know what he was talking about.

'Ah, come on, Holly!' he persisted. 'Danny told me!' He turned to the rest of the table and explained, 'Danny is the owner of the place where I did the gig the other night and he told me Holly has entered a karaoke competition in the club upstairs.'

Everyone oohed and aahed and talked about how great it was.

Holly refused to give in. 'Declan, Daniel's just playing games with you. Sure, everyone knows I can't sing! Now, come on,' she addressed the rest of the table. 'Honestly, if I was singing in a karaoke competition I *think* I would

103

tell you all.' She laughed as if the thought was so ridiculous. In fact the thought *was* so ridiculous.

'Holly,' Declan chuckled, 'I saw your name on the list. Don't lie.'

Holly put her knife and fork down. She suddenly wasn't hungry any more.

'Holly, why didn't you tell us you're going to sing in a competition?' her mother asked.

'Because I can't sing!'

'Then why are you doing it?' Ciara burst out laughing.

She may as well tell them, otherwise Declan would beat it out of her and she didn't like lying to her parents.

'OK, it's a really complicated story, but basically Gerry entered my name in months ago because he really wanted me to do it and as much as I *don't* want to do it, I feel I have to go through with it. It's stupid, I know.'

Ciara stopped laughing abruptly.

Holly felt paranoid by her family staring at her, and she nervously tucked her hair behind her ears.

'Well, I think that's a wonderful idea,' her dad suddenly announced.

'Yes,' added her mum, 'and we'll all be there to support you.'

'No, Mum, you really don't have to. It's no big deal.'

'There's no way my sister is singing in a competition without me being there,' declared Ciara.

'Here, here,' said Richard. 'We'll all go so. I've never been to a karaoke before. It should be . . .' he searched his brain for the right word, '. . . fun.'

Holly groaned and closed her eyes, wishing she had gone straight home from town.

Declan was laughing hysterically, 'Yes, Holly, it'll be
. . . hmmm . . .' he said, scratching his chin, '. . . fun!'

'When is it on?' Richard said, taking out his diary.

'Eh . . . Saturday,' Holly lied, and Richard began
writing it down.

'It is not!' Declan burst out. 'It's next Tuesday, you
liar!'

'Shit!' cursed Richard, much to everyone's surprise.
'Has anyone got any Tippex?'

Holly could not stop going to the toilet. She was nervous
and had had practically no sleep the night before. And
she looked how she felt. There were huge bags around
her bloodshot eyes and her lips were bitten.

The big day had arrived, her worst nightmare – singing
in public.

Holly wasn't even the kind of person who sang in the
shower for fear of cracking all the mirrors. But man, was
she spending time in the toilet today. There was no better
laxative than fear, and Holly felt as if she had lost a
stone in just one day. Her friends and family had been
as supportive as ever, sending her good luck cards. Sharon
and John had even sent her a bouquet of flowers, which
she placed on the draught-free, heat-vent-free coffee table
beside her half-dead orchid. Denise had 'hilariously' sent
her a sympathy card.

Holly dressed in the outfit Gerry had told her to buy
last month and cursed him throughout. There were far
more important things to worry about right now than
irrelevant little details like how she looked. She left her
hair down so it covered her face as much as possible and
piled on the waterproof mascara as though it was going

to prevent her from crying. She could foresee the night ending in tears. She tended to have psychic powers when it came to facing the shittiest days of her life.

John and Sharon collected Holly in a taxi and she refused to talk to them, cursing everyone for forcing her to do this. She felt physically sick and she couldn't sit still. Every time the taxi stopped at a red light she contemplated jumping out and running for dear life but by the time she would build up the courage the lights would go green again. Her hands fidgeted nervously and she kept opening and closing her bag, pretending to Sharon she was searching for something just to keep herself occupied.

'Relax, Holly,' Sharon said soothingly, 'everything will be fine.'

'Fuck off,' she snapped.

They continued on in silence for the rest of the journey: even the taxi driver didn't speak. After a tense journey they finally reached Hogan's, and John and Sharon had a hell of a time trying to stop Holly ranting (something about preferring to jump in the Liffey) and persuading her to go inside. Much to Holly's horror, the club was absolutely jammed and she had to squeeze by everyone to make her way to her family, who had saved a table (right beside the toilet as requested).

Richard was sitting awkwardly on a stool, looking out of place in a suit. 'So tell me about these rules, Father. What will Holly have to do?'

Holly's dad explained the 'rules' of karaoke to Richard and her nerves began to build even more.

'Gosh, that's terrific, isn't it?' Richard said, staring around the club in awe. Holly didn't think he had ever been in a nightclub before.

The sight of the stage terrified Holly. It was much bigger than she had expected and there was a huge screen on the wall for the crowd to see the words of the songs. Jack was sitting with his arm draped around Abbey's shoulders; they both gave her supportive smiles. Holly scowled at them and looked away.

'Holly the funniest thing happened earlier on,' Jack said laughing. 'Remember that guy Daniel we met last week?'

Holly just stared at him, watching his lips moving but not giving a damn about what he said. 'Well, me and Abbey got here first to keep the table and we were having a kiss and your man came over and whispered in my ear that you were gonna be here tonight. He thought we were going out and that I was doing the dirt!' Jack and Abbey laughed hysterically.

'Well, I think that's disgusting,' Holly said, and turned away.

'No,' Jack tried to explain, 'he didn't know that we were brother and sister. I had to explain . . .' Jack trailed off as Sharon shot him a warning look and silenced him.

'Hi, Holly,' Daniel said, approaching her with a clipboard in his hand. 'OK, here's the order of tonight: first up is a girl called Margaret, then a guy called Keith and then you're up after him. Is that OK?'

'So I'm third.'

'Yeah, after—'

'That's all I need to know,' Holly snapped rudely. She just wanted to get out of this stupid club and wished that everyone would stop annoying her and leave her alone to wish evil thoughts on them all. She wished the ground would swallow her up, that a natural disaster would occur and everyone would have to evacuate the building. In fact, that was a good idea. She searched around frantically for a button to raise the fire alarm, but Daniel was still talking away to her.

'Look, Holly, I'm really sorry to disturb you again, but could you tell me which of your friends is Sharon?' He looked as if he was afraid she was going to bite his head off. So he should be, she thought, narrowing her eyes.

'Her over there.' Holly pointed to Sharon. 'Hold on, why?'

'Oh, I just wanted to apologise for the last time we spoke.' He started to walk towards Sharon.

'Why?' Holly said, the panic in her voice making him turn around again.

'We just had a minor disagreement on the phone last week.' He looked at her confused.

'You know you really don't need to do that. She's probably forgotten about it completely by now,' she stammered. This was the last thing she needed.

'Yeah, but I would still like to apologise,' and he headed over to Sharon. Holly leaped from her stool.

'Sharon, hi, I'm Daniel. I just wanted to apologise about the confusion on the phone last week.'

Sharon looked at him as though he had ten heads. 'Confusion?'

'You know, on the phone?'

John placed his arm protectively around Sharon's waist. 'On the phone?'

'Eh . . . yes, on the phone,' he nodded.

'What's your name again?'

'Em, it's Daniel.'

108

'And we spoke on the phone?' Sharon said with a smile appearing on her face.

Holly gestured wildly to her behind Daniel's back.

Daniel cleared his throat nervously. 'Yes, you called the club last week and I answered – does that ring a bell?'

'No, sweetie, you've got the wrong girl,' Sharon said politely.

John threw Sharon a dirty look for calling him sweetie; if it was up to him he would have told him where to go.

Daniel brushed his hand through his hair and appeared to be more confused than everyone else. He began to turn round to face Holly.

Holly nodded her head frantically to Sharon.

'Oh . . .' Sharon said, looking as though she finally remembered. 'Oh – Daniel!' she yelled a bit over enthusiastically. 'God, I am so sorry, my brain cells seem to be going a bit dead.' She laughed like a mad woman. 'Must be too much of this,' she chortled, picking up her drink.

Relief washed over Daniel's face. 'Good, I thought it was me going mad there for a minute! OK, so you remember us having that conversation on the phone?'

'Oh, *that* conversation we had on the phone. Listen, don't worry about it,' she said, waving her hand dismissively.

'It's just that I only took over the place a few weeks ago and I wasn't too sure of the exact arrangements for tonight.'

'Don't worry . . . we all need our time . . . to adjust . . . to things . . . you know?' Sharon looked at Holly to see if she had said the right thing or not.

'OK then. Well, it's nice to finally meet you in person,'

Daniel laughed. 'Can I get you a stool or anything?' he joked.

Sharon and John sat on their stools and stared back at him in silence, not knowing what to say to this strange man.

John watched with suspicion as Daniel walked away.

'What was that all about?' Sharon screamed at Holly as soon as he was out of earshot.

'Oh, I'll explain it to you later,' said Holly. She turned to face the stage as their karaoke host stepped on stage.

'Good evening, ladies and gentlemen!' he announced.

'Good evening!' shouted Richard, looking excited. Holly rolled her eyes to heaven.

'We have an exciting night ahead of us . . .' he went on and on and on in his DJ voice while Holly danced nervously from foot to foot. She desperately needed the toilet again.

'So first up tonight we have Margaret from Tallaght who is going to sing the theme to *Titanic*, "My Heart Will Go On" by Celine Dion. Please put your hands together for the wonderful Margaret!' The crowd went wild. Holly's heart raced. The hardest song in the world to sing – typical.

When Margaret started to sing, the room became so quiet you could almost hear a pin drop. Holly watched everyone's faces. They were all staring at Margaret in amazement, including Holly's family, the traitors. Margaret's eyes were closed and she sang with such passion, as though she had lived every line of the song. Holly hated her and contemplated tripping her up on her way back to her seat.

'Wasn't that incredible?' the DJ announced. The crowd

110

cheered again; Holly prepared herself not to hear that sound after she sang. 'Next up we have Keith. You may remember him as last year's winner and he's singing "America" by Neil Diamond. Give it up for Keith!' Holly didn't need to hear any more and rushed to the toilet.

She paced up and down and tried to calm herself, but her knees were knocking, her stomach was twisted in knots and she felt the beginnings of vomit rising to her mouth. She looked at herself in the mirror and tried to take big deep breaths. It didn't work, as it only made her feel dizzy. The crowd applauded outside and Holly froze. She was next.

'Wasn't Keith terrific, ladies and gentlemen?'

Lots of cheers again.

'Perhaps Keith is going for the record of winning two years in a row. Well, it doesn't get any better than that!'

It was about to get a lot worse.

'Next we have a newcomer to the competition and her name is Holly and she's singing . . .'

Holly ran to the toilet and locked herself in. There was no way in this world they were getting her out of there.

'So, ladies and gentlemen, please put your hands together for Holly!'

There was a huge applause.

CHAPTER FOURTEEN

It was three years ago that Holly had taken to the stage for her debut karaoke performance.

Not coincidentally, it was three years *since* Holly had taken to the stage to do karaoke.

A huge crowd of her friends had gone to their local pub in Swords to celebrate one of the lad's thirtieth birthdays. Holly had been extremely tired as she had been working overtime for the past two weeks and she really wasn't in the mood to go out partying. All she wanted was to go home, have a nice long bath, put on the most unsexy pair of pyjamas she owned, eats lots of chocolate and snuggle up on the couch in front of the TV with Gerry.

After standing on an overcrowded Dart all the way from Blackrock to Sutton Station, Holly was definitely not in the mood to stand all night in a packed stuffy pub. On the train, half her face had been squashed up against the window and the other half lodged underneath the sweaty armpit of a very unhygienic man.

Right behind her a man was breathing alcoholic fumes rather loudly down her neck. It didn't help matters that every time the train swayed he 'accidentally' pressed his big beer belly up against her back. She had suffered through this ordeal everyday going to work and coming home for two weeks and she could take it no longer. She wanted her pyjamas.

Finally she arrived at Sutton Station and the very clever people there thought it was a great idea to all get *on* the train while passengers tried to get off. It took her so long to fight her way through the crowd to get *off* the train that by the time she reached the platform she saw her feeder bus drive off, packed with happy little people smiling out the window at her. And because it was after six o'clock, the coffee shop had closed and she was left standing in the freezing cold waiting for another half-hour till the next bus arrived. On top of everything else, this strengthened her desire to cuddle up in front of the fire.

But a good evening at home was not to be. Her beloved husband had other plans. She arrived home tired and extremely pissed off to a crowded house and thumping music. People she didn't even know were wandering around her living room with cans of beer in their hands and slumping themselves on the couch she had intended to inhabit for the next few hours. Gerry stood at the CD player acting DJ and trying to look cool. At that moment in time she had never seen him look so uncool in her life.

'What is wrong with you?' Gerry asked her after seeing her storming upstairs to the bedroom.

'Gerry, I am tired, I am pissed off, I am not in the

mood to go out tonight and you didn't even ask me if it was all right to invite all these people over. And, by the way, WHO ARE THEY?' she yelled.

'They're friends of Conor's and, by the way, THIS IS MY HOUSE TOO!' he yelled back.

Holly placed her fingers on her temples and began to gently massage her head, she had such a headache and the music was driving her crazy.

'Gerry,' she said quietly, trying to stay calm, 'I'm not saying that you can't invite people over. It would be fine if you had planned it in advance and told me. *Then* I wouldn't care, but today of all days when I am so so tired . . .' her voice became weaker and weaker with every word, 'I just wanted to relax in my own house.'

'Oh, everyday's the same with you,' he snapped. 'You never want to do anything any more anyway. Every single night, you come home in your cranky moods and bitch at me about everything!'

Holly's jaw dropped. 'Excuse me! I have been working hard!'

'And so have I, but you don't see me biting your head off every time I don't get my own way.'

'Gerry this isn't about me getting my own way, this is about you inviting the whole street into our h—'

'IT'S FRIDAY,' he yelled, silencing her, 'IT'S THE WEEKEND! When is the last time you went out? Leave your work behind and let your hair down, for a change. Stop acting like such a GRANNY!' And he stormed out of the bedroom and slammed the door.

After spending a long time in the bedroom hating Gerry and dreaming of a divorce she managed to calm

114

down and think rationally about what he had said. And he was right. OK, he wasn't right in the way he had phrased it but she *had* been cranky and bitchy all month and she knew it.

Holly was the type of person who finished work at 5 p.m. and had her computer switched off, lights off, desk tidied and was running for her train by 5.01 p.m. whether her employers liked it or not. She never took her work home, never stressed about the future of the business because, quite frankly, she didn't care, and phoned in sick as many Monday mornings as possible without running the risk of being fired. But due to a momentary lapse of concentration when looking for new employment, she had found herself accepting an office job that forced her to take paperwork home, agree to work late and worry about the business, which she was not happy with *at all*. How she even managed to stay there for an entire month was anybody's guess but, nevertheless, Gerry had been right. Ouch, it even hurt to think it. She hadn't gone out with him or her friends for weeks and fell asleep the minute her head hit the pillow every night. Come to think of it, that was probably Gerry's main problem, never mind the bitchiness.

But tonight would be different. She intended showing her neglected friends and husband that she was still the fun and frivolous Holly who could drink them all under the table and still manage to walk the white line all the way home. This show of antics began by preparing home-made cocktails. God only knows what was in them, but they worked their magic, and at eleven o'clock they were all dancing down the road to the pub where karaoke was taking place. Holly demanded to be first up and heckled the karaoke host until she got her way. The pub was jammed and that night there was a very rowdy crowd who were out on a stag night. It was as though a film crew had arrived in the pub hours earlier and worked away, setting the scene for disaster. They couldn't have done a better job.

The DJ gave Holly a huge build-up after believing her lies of being a professional singer. Gerry lost all power of speech and sight from laughing so hard but she was determined to show him that she could still let her hair down. He needn't plan that divorce just yet. Holly decided to sing 'Like a Virgin' and dedicated it to the man who was getting married the next day. As soon as she started singing, Holly had never heard so many boos in her whole life and at such a loud volume. But she was so drunk she didn't care and continued on singing to her husband, who seemed to be the only one without a moody face.

Eventually, when people began to throw things at the stage, and when the karaoke host himself encouraged them to boo even louder, Holly felt that her work there had been done. When she handed him back the microphone there was a cheer so loud that people from the pub next door came running in. There were all the more people to see Holly trip down the steps in her stilettos and fall flat on her face. They all watched as her skirt went flying over her head to reveal the old underwear, which had once been white and which she hadn't bothered to change when she got home from work.

Holly was taken to hospital to see to her broken nose.

Gerry lost his voice from laughing so loudly and Denise and Sharon helped matters by taking photographs of the scene of the crime, which Denise then chose as the cover for the invitations to her Christmas party with the heading, 'Let's get legless!'

Holly vowed *never* to do karaoke again.

CHAPTER FIFTEEN

'Holly Kennedy? Are you here?' the karaoke host's voice boomed. The crowd's applause died down into a loud chatter as everyone looked around in search of Holly. Well, they would be a long time looking, she thought as she lowered the toilet seat lid and sat down to wait for the excitement to settle so they could move on to their next victim. She closed her eyes, rested her head on her hands, and prayed for this moment to pass. She wanted to open her eyes and be at home safely, a week from now. She counted to ten, praying for a miracle and then slowly opened them again.

She was still in the toilet.

Why couldn't she, at least just this once, suddenly find magical powers?

Holly knew this would happen. From the moment she opened that envelope and read Gerry's third letter, she foresaw tears and humiliation. Her nightmare had come true.

Outside, the club sounded very quiet and a sense of

calm engulfed her as she realised they were moving on to the next singer. Her shoulders relaxed and she unclenched her fists, her jaw relaxed and air flowed more easily into her lungs. The panic was over but she decided to wait until the next singer began before she made a run for it. She couldn't even climb out the window – well, not unless she wanted to plummet to her death.

Outside the cubicle Holly heard the toilet door open and slam. Uh-oh, they were coming to get her, whoever *they* were.

'Holly?'

It was Sharon.

'Holly, I know you're in there so just listen to me, OK?'

Holly sniffed back the tears that were beginning to well.

'OK, I know that this is an absolute nightmare for you and I know you have a major phobia about this kind of thing but you need to relax, OK?'

Sharon's voice was so soothing, Holly's shoulders once again relaxed.

'Holly, I hate mice, you know that.'

Holly frowned, wondering where this little pep talk was going.

'And my worst nightmare would be to walk out of here to a room full of mice. Now could you imagine me?'

Holly smiled at the thought and remembered the time when Sharon moved in with Gerry and Holly for two weeks after she had caught a mouse in her house. John, of course, had been granted conjugal visits.

'Yeah, well, I would be right here where you are now and nothing in the whole world would bring me out.' She paused.

'What?' the DJ's voice said into the microphone, and then started laughing, 'Ladies and gentlemen, it appears that our singer is currently in the toilets.' The entire room erupted in laughter.

'Sharon!' Holly's voice trembled in fear. She felt as though the angry mob were about to break down the door; strip her of her clothes and carry her over their heads to the stage for her execution. Panic took over for the third time.

Sharon rushed her next sentence. 'Anyway, Holly, all I'm saying is that you don't have to do this if you don't want to. Nobody here is forcing you . . .'

'Ladies and gentlemen, let's let Holly know that she's up next!' yelled the DJ. 'Come on!'

Everybody began to stamp their feet and chant her name.

'OK, well, at least nobody who cares about you is forcing you to do this,' stammered Sharon, now under pressure from the approaching mob. 'But if you don't do this, I know you will never be able to forgive yourself. Gerry wanted you to do this for a reason.'

'HOLLY! HOLLY! HOLLY!'

'Oh, Sharon!' Holly repeated, panicking. Suddenly the walls of the cubicle felt like they were closing in on her, beads of sweat formed on her forehead. She had to get out of there. She burst through the door. Sharon's eyes widened at the sight of her distraught friend, who looked like she had just seen a ghost. Her eyes were red and puffy with black lines of mascara streaming down her

120

face (that waterproof stuff never works) and her tears had washed the rest of her make-up away.

'Don't mind them, Holly,' Sharon said coolly. 'They can't make you do anything you don't want to do.'

Holly's lower lip began to tremble.

'Don't!' Sharon said, gripping her by the shoulders and looking her in the eye. 'Don't even think about it!'

Her lip stopped trembling but the rest of her didn't. Finally, Holly broke her silence. 'I can't sing, Sharon,' she whispered, her eyes wide with terror.

'I know that,' Sharon said, laughing, 'and your family knows that! Screw the rest of them! You are never gonna see any of their ugly mugs EVER AGAIN! Who cares what they think? I don't, do you?'

Holly thought about it for a minute. 'No,' she whispered.

'I didn't hear you – what did you say? Do you care what they think?'

'No,' Holly said, a little stronger.

'Louder!' Sharon shook her by the shoulders.

'No!' Holly yelled.

'Louder!'

'NOOOOOOOOO! I DON'T CARE WHAT THEY THINK!' Holly screamed so loud the crowd began to quieten down outside. The two of them smiled at each other and then began to giggle at their stupidity.

'Just let this be another silly Holly day so we can laugh about it a few months from now,' Sharon pleaded with her.

Holly cast one last look at her reflection in the mirror, took a deep breath and charged towards the door like a woman on a mission. She opened the door to her adoring fans, who were all still chanting her name. They all began to cheer when they saw her and she took an extremely theatrical bow and headed towards the stage to the sound of claps and laughter, and a yell from Sharon saying, 'Screw them!'

Holly had everybody's attention now, whether she liked it or not. If she hadn't run into the toilet the people who were chatting down the back of the club probably wouldn't even have noticed her singing, but now she had attracted even more interest.

She stood with her arms folded and stared at the audience in shock. The music had started without her even noticing, and she missed the first few lines of the song. The DJ stopped the track and put it back to the start.

There was complete silence. Holly cleared her throat and the sound echoed around the room. Holly stared down at Denise and Sharon for help and her whole table gave her the thumbs-up. Ordinarily Holly would have laughed at how corny they all looked but right then it was strangely comforting. Finally the music began again and Holly held the microphone tightly in her two hands and prepared to sing. With an extremely shaky and timid voice she sang: '"What would you do if I sang out of tune? Would you stand up and walk out on me?"'

Denise and Sharon howled with laughter at the wonderful choice of song and gave her a big cheer. Holly struggled on, singing dreadfully and looking as if she was about to burst into tears. Just when she felt she was about to hear boos again, her family and friends joined in with the chorus. '"Ooh, I'll get by with a little help from my friends; yes I'll get by with a little help from my friends."'

The crowd turned to her table of family and friends and laughed, and the atmosphere warmed a little more. Holly prepared herself for the high note coming up and yelled at the top of her lungs, '"Do you *neeeed* anybody?"' She even managed to give herself a fright with the volume and a few people helped her out to sing, '"I need somebody to love."'

'"Do you *neeeed* anybody?"' she repeated, and held the microphone out to the crowd to encourage them to sing and they all sang, '"I need somebody to love,"' and gave themselves a round of applause. Holly felt less nervous now and battled her way through the rest of the song. The people down the back resumed chatting, the bar staff carried on serving drinks and smashing glasses until Holly felt that she was the only one listening to herself.

When she had finally finished singing, a few polite tables up the front and her own table to the right were the only people to acknowledge her. The DJ took the microphone from her hand and managed to say between laughs, 'Please give it up for the incredibly brave Holly Kennedy!'

This time her family and friends were the only people to cheer. Denise and Sharon approached her with cheeks wet from tears of laughter.

'I'm so proud of you!' Sharon said, throwing her arms around Holly's neck. 'It was awful!'

'Thanks for helping me, Sharon.' Holly hugged her friend.

Jack and Abbey cheered, and Jack shouted, 'Terrible! Absolutely terrible!'

Holly's mother smiled encouragingly at her, knowing she had passed her special singing talent down to her daughter, and Holly's father could barely look her in the eye he was laughing so much. All Ciara could manage was to repeat over and over again, 'I never knew anyone could be so bad.'

Declan waved at her across the room with a camera in his hand and gave her the thumbs-down. Holly hid in the corner at the table and sipped on her water while she listened to everyone congratulating her on being so desperately awful. Holly couldn't remember the last time she had felt so proud.

John shuffled over to Holly and leaned against the wall beside her where he watched the next act on stage in silence. Eventually he plucked up the courage to speak and said, 'Gerry's probably here, you know,' and looked at her with watery eyes.

Poor John, he missed his best friend too. She gave him an encouraging smile and looked around the room. He was right. Holly *could* feel Gerry's presence. She could feel him wrapping his arms around her and giving her one of his hugs she missed so much.

After an hour the singers had finally finished and Daniel and the DJ headed off to tot up the votes. Everyone had been handed a voting slip as they paid at the door and Holly couldn't bring herself to write her own name down so she gave her slip to Sharon. It was pretty obvious that Holly wasn't going to win but that had never been her intention. And on the off chance that she did win she shuddered at the thought of having to return in two weeks' time to repeat the whole experience. She hadn't learned a thing from it, only that she hated karaoke even more. Last year's winner, Keith, had brought along at least thirty of his friends, which meant that he was a sure winner, and Holly doubted very much that her 'adoring fans' in the crowd would vote for her.

The DJ played a pathetic CD of a drum roll as the winners were about to be announced. Daniel took to the stage once again in his black leather jacket and black slacks uniform and was greeted by wolf-whistles and screams from the girls. Worryingly, the loudest of these girls was Ciara. Richard looked excited and crossed his fingers at Holly, a very sweet but incredibly naïve gesture, she thought. He obviously didn't understand the 'rules' properly.

There was a bit of embarrassment as the drum-roll began to skip and the DJ rushed over to his equipment to shut it down. The winners were announced undramatically, in dead silence. 'OK, I'd like to thank everyone for taking part in tonight's competition. You provided us all with some terrific entertainment.' That last part was directed at Holly and she slithered down her seat in embarrassment. 'So the two people that will be going through to the final are –' Daniel paused for dramatic effect – 'Keith and Samantha!'

Holly jumped up with excitement and danced around in a huddle with Denise and Sharon. She had never felt such relief in her life. Richard looked on very confused while the rest of Holly's family congratulated her on her victorious losing.

'I voted for the blonde one,' Declan announced with disappointment.

'That's just because she had big tits,' Holly laughed.

'Well, we all have our own individual talents,' Declan agreed.

Holly wondered what hers were as she sat back down. It must be a wonderful feeling to win something, to know that you have a gift. Holly had never won anything in her life. She didn't do any sports, couldn't play an instrument – now that she thought about it she didn't have *any* hobbies or special interests. What would she put down on her CV when she eventually got around to applying for a job? 'I like to drink and shop' wouldn't go down very well. She sipped her drink thoughtfully. Holly had lived her life being interested in Gerry – in fact, everything she did revolved around him. In a way, being his wife was all she was good at; being his partner was all she knew. Now what did she have? No job, no husband and she couldn't even sing in a karaoke competition properly, never mind win it.

Sharon and John seemed engrossed in a heated discussion, Abbey and Jack were gazing into each other's eyes like love-struck teenagers, as usual, Ciara was intent on getting to know Daniel better and Denise was . . . Actually, where was Denise?

Holly looked around the club and spotted her sitting on the stage swinging her legs and striking a very provocative pose for the karaoke host. Holly's parents had left hand in hand just after her name wasn't announced as a winner, which left . . . Richard.

Richard sat squashed beside Ciara and Daniel, looking around the room like a lost puppy and taking a sip from his drink every few seconds out of paranoia. Holly realised she must have looked like him – a complete loser.

But at least this loser had a wife and two children to go home to, unlike Holly, who had a date with a microwave dinner.

Holly moved over and sat on the high stool opposite Richard, and struck up a conversation.

'You enjoying yourself?'

He looked up from his drink, startled that someone had spoken to him. 'Yes, thank you, I'm having fun, Holly.'

If that was him having fun Holly dreaded to think what he looked like when he wasn't.

'I'm surprised you came, actually. I didn't think this would be your scene.'

'Oh, you know . . . you have to support the family.' He stirred his drink.

'So where's Meredith tonight?'

'Emily and Timothy,' he said, as if that explained it all.

'You working tomorrow?'

'Yes,' he said, suddenly knocking back his drink, 'so I best be off. You were a great sport tonight, Holly.' He looked around awkwardly at his family, deciding whether to interrupt them and say goodbye but eventually deciding against it. He nodded to Holly and off he went, manoeuvring his way through the dense crowd.

Holly was once again alone. As much as she wanted to grab her bag and run home she knew she should sit this one out. There would be plenty of times in the future when she would be alone like this, the only singleton in the company of couples, and she needed to adapt. She felt awful though, and also angry with the others who didn't even notice her. Then she cursed herself for being so childish. She couldn't have asked for more supportive friends and family. Holly wondered whether this had been Gerry's intention. Did he think that this situation was what she needed? Did he think that this would help her? Perhaps he was right because she was certainly being tested. It was forcing her to become braver in more ways than one. She had stood on a stage and sang to hundreds of people and now she was stuck in a situation where she was surrounded by couples. Whatever his plan was, she was being forced to become braver without him. Just sit it out, she told herself.

Holly smiled as she watched her sister nattering away to Daniel. Ciara was nothing like her at all; she was so carefree and confident, and didn't seem to worry about anything. For as long as Holly could remember, Ciara had never managed to hold down a job or a boyfriend. Her brain was always somewhere else, lost in the dream of visiting another far-off country. Holly wished she could be more like her. She had been to far-flung places too, but always with Gerry by her side, and never for more than a few weeks. Unlike Ciara, Holly was a home-bird and could never imagine herself moving away from her family and friends and leaving the life she had made for herself here. At least, she could never have left the life she had once had.

She turned her attention to Jack, who was still lost in a world with Abbey. She even wished she could be more like him; he absolutely loved his job as a secondary school teacher. He was the cool English teacher that all the teenagers respected, and whenever Holly and Jack passed one of his students on the street they always greeted him with a big smile and a 'Hiya, sir!' All the girls fancied him and all the boys wanted to be like him when they got older. Holly sighed loudly and drained her drink. Now she was bored.

Daniel looked over. 'Holly, can I get you a drink?'

'Ah no, it's OK, thanks, Daniel. I'm heading home soon anyway.'

'Ah, Hol!' protested Ciara. 'You can't go home so early! It's your night!'

Holly didn't feel as though it was her night. She felt rather as if she had gate-crashed a party and didn't know anyone there.

'No, I'm all right, thanks,' she assured Daniel again.

'No, you're staying,' Ciara insisted. 'Get her a vodka and Coke, and I'll have the same again,' she ordered Daniel.

'Ciara!' Holly exclaimed, embarrassed at her sister's rudeness.

'No, it's OK!' Daniel assured her. 'I asked.' And he headed off to the bar.

'Ciara, that was so rude,' Holly gave out to her sister.

'What? It's not like he has to pay for it; he owns the bloody place,' she said defensively.

'That still doesn't mean you can go around demanding free drinks—'

'Where's Richard?' Ciara interrupted.

'Gone home.'

'Shit! How long ago?' She jumped down from her seat in a panic.

'I dunno, about five or ten minutes. Why?'

'He's supposed to be driving me home!' She threw everyone's coats into a pile on the floor while she rooted around for her bag.

129

'Ciara, you'll never catch him now, he's been gone far too long.'

'No, I will. He's parked ages away and he'll have to drive back down this road to get home. I'll get him while he's passing.' She finally found her bag and legged it out the door yelling, 'Bye, Holly! Well done, you were shite!' before disappearing.

Holly was once again alone. Great, she thought, watching Daniel carrying the drinks back to the table. Now she was stuck talking to him all by herself.

'Where's Ciara gone?' Daniel said, placing the drinks on the table and sitting down opposite Holly.

'Oh, she said to say she's really sorry but she had to chase my brother for a lift.' Holly bit her lip guiltily, knowing full well that Ciara hadn't even given Daniel a second thought as she raced out the door. 'Sorry for being so rude to you earlier as well.' Then she started laughing, 'God, you must think we're the rudest family in the world. Ciara's a bit of a motor mouth; she doesn't mean what she says half the time.'

'And you did?' he smiled.

'At the time, yes.' She laughed again.

'Hey, it's fine, just means there's more drink for you,' he said, sliding a shot glass across the table to her.

'Ugh, what is this?' Holly wrinkled her nose up at the smell.

Daniel looked away awkwardly and cleared his throat. 'I can't remember.'

'Oh, come on!' Holly laughed. 'You just ordered it! It's a woman's right to know what she's drinking, you know!'

Daniel looked at her with a smile on his face. 'It's

called a BJ. You should have seen the barman's face when I asked for one. I don't think he knew it was a shot!'

'Oh God,' Holly laughed, 'what's Ciara doing drinking this? It smells awful!'

'She said she found it easy to swallow.' He started laughing again.

'Oh, I'm sorry, Daniel. She really is ridiculous sometimes.' Holly shook her head over her sister.

Daniel stared past Holly's shoulder with amusement. 'Well, it looks like your friend is having a good night, anyway.'

Holly turned and saw Denise and the DJ wrapped around each other beside the stage. Her provocative poses had obviously worked.

'Oh no, not the horrible DJ who forced me to come out of the toilet,' Holly groaned.

'That's Tom O'Connor from Dublin FM.' Daniel laughed. 'He's a friend of mine.'

Holly covered her face in embarrassment.

'He's working here tonight because the karaoke went out live on the radio,' he said seriously.

'WHAT?' Holly nearly had a heart attack for the twentieth time that night.

Daniel's face broke out into a smile, 'Only joking; just wanted to see the look on your face.'

'Oh my God, don't do that to me,' Holly said, putting her hand on her heart. 'Having the people in here listening to me was bad enough, never mind the entire city as well.' She waited for her heart to stop pounding while Daniel stared at her with an amused look in his eye.

'If you don't mind me asking, if you hate it so much why did you enter?' he asked carefully.

'Oh, my hilarious husband thought it would be funny to enter his tone-deaf wife into a singing competition.'

Daniel laughed. 'You weren't *that* bad! Is your husband here?' he asked. 'I don't want him thinking I'm trying to poison his wife with that awful concoction.' He nodded towards the shot glass.

Holly looked around the club and smiled. 'Yeah, he's definitely here . . . somewhere.'

CHAPTER SIXTEEN

Holly secured her bed sheet onto the washing line with a peg and thought about how she had bumbled around for the remainder of May trying to get her life into some sort of order. Days went by when she felt so happy and content, and *confident* that her life would be OK, and then as quickly as the feeling came it would disappear and she would feel sadness setting in again. She tried to find a routine she could fall into so that she felt as though she belonged in her body and her body belonged in this life, instead of wandering around like a zombie, watching everybody else live theirs while she waited for hers to end.

Unfortunately the routine hadn't turned out exactly as she hoped it would. She found herself immobile for hours in the sitting room, reliving every single memory that she and Gerry had shared. She spent most of that time thinking about every argument they'd had, wishing she could take them back, wishing she could take back every horrible word she had ever said to him. She prayed that

Gerry had known her words had only been spoken in anger and that they had not reflected her true feelings. She tortured herself for the times she had acted selfishly, going out with her friends for the night when she was mad at him instead of staying home with him. She chastised herself for walking away from him when she should have hugged him, when she held grudges for days instead of forgiving him, when she went straight to sleep some nights instead of making love to him. She wanted to take back every moment she knew he had been so angry with her and hated her. She wished all her memories were of the good times but the bad times kept coming back to haunt her. They had all been such a waste.

And nobody had told them that they were short on time.

There were her happy days, when she would walk around in a daydream with nothing but a smile on her face, catching herself giggling as she walked down the street when a joke of theirs would suddenly pop into her head.

Then she would fall into days of deep dark depression; then finally build up the strength to be positive and to snap out of it for another few days. But the tiniest and simplest thing would trigger off her tears again. That was her routine. It was a tiring process and most of the time she couldn't be bothered battling with her mind. It was far stronger than her body.

Friends and family came and went; sometimes helping her with her tears, other times making her laugh. But even in her laughter there was something missing. She never seemed to be truly happy; she just seemed to be passing time till she waited for something else. She was tired of just existing; she wanted to live. But what was the point in living when there was no *life* in it. These questions went through her mind over and over again till she reached the point of not wanting to wake up from her dreams that felt so real.

Deep down, she knew it was normal to feel like this. She didn't particularly think she was losing her mind. She knew that people said that one day she would be happy again and that this feeling would just be a distant memory. It was getting to that feeling that was the hard part.

She read and reread Gerry's letter over and over again, analysing each word and each sentence, and each day coming up with a new meaning. But she could sit there till the cows came home trying to read between the lines and guess the hidden message. The fact was that she would never *really* know *exactly* what he meant because she would never speak to him *ever again*. It was this that she had the most difficulty trying to come to terms with.

Now May had gone and June had arrived, bringing bright long evenings and beautiful mornings. And along with these sunny days June also brought clarity. There was no hiding indoors as soon as it got dark, no lie-ins until the afternoon. It seemed as though the whole of Ireland had come out of hibernation, taken a big stretch and a yawn, and suddenly started living again. It was time to open all the windows and air the house, to free it of the ghosts of the winter and dark days, to get up early with the songbirds and go for a walk and look people in the eye and smile and say hello instead of hiding under layers of clothes with eyes to the ground while running from destination to destination, ignoring the world. It was time to stop hiding in the dark and to hold your head up high and come face to face with the truth.

June also brought another letter from Gerry.

Holly had sat out in the sun, revelling in the new brightness of life and nervously yet excitedly read the fourth letter. She loved the feel of the card and the bumps of Gerry's handwriting under her finger as it ran over the dried ink. Inside, his neat script had listed the items that belonged to him that remained in the house, and beside each of his possessions he explained what he wanted Holly to do with them and where he wished for them to be sent. At the bottom it read:

> *PS. I love you, Holly, and I know you love me.*
> *You don't need my belongings to remember me*
> *by, you don't need to keep them as proof that I*
> *existed or still exist in your mind. You don't need*
> *to wear my sweater to feel me around you; I'm*
> *already here . . . <u>always</u> wrapping my arms*
> *around you.*

That had been difficult for Holly to come to terms with. She almost wished he would ask her to do karaoke again. She would have jumped from an aeroplane for him; run a thousand miles, anything except empty out his wardrobes and rid herself of his presence in the house. But he was right and she knew it. She couldn't hang on to his things for ever. She couldn't pretend to herself that he was coming back to collect them. The physical Gerry was gone; he didn't need his clothes.

136

It was an emotionally draining experience. It took her days to complete. She relived a million memories with every garment and piece of paper she bagged. She held each item near to her before saying goodbye. Every time it left her fingers it was like saying goodbye to a part of Gerry all over again. It was difficult; so difficult – and at times too difficult.

She informed her family and friends of what she was about to do and although they all offered their assistance and support time and again, Holly knew she had to do this alone. She needed to take her time; say a proper goodbye because she wouldn't be getting anything back. Just like Gerry, his things couldn't return.

Despite Holly's wishes of wanting to be alone, Jack had called round a few times to offer some brotherly support and Holly had appreciated it. Every item had a history and they would talk and laugh about the memories surrounding it. He was there for her when she cried and he was there when she finally clapped her hands together, ridding her skin of the dust that remained. It was a difficult job, but one that needed to be done. And one, that was made easier by Gerry's help. Holly didn't need to worry about making all the big decisions, Gerry had already made them for her. Gerry was helping her and, for once, Holly felt as though she was helping him too.

She laughed as she bagged the old, dusty cassettes of his favourite rock band from his schooldays. At least once a year Gerry came across the old shoebox during his efforts to control the mess that grew inside his closet. He would blast the heavy metal music from every loudspeaker in the house just to torment Holly with its

137

screeching guitars and badly produced sound quality. She always told him she couldn't wait to see the end of the tapes, but now the relief didn't wash over her as she once hoped it would.

Lying in a crumpled ball in the back corner of the wardrobe her eyes rested upon Gerry's lucky football jersey. It was still covered in grass and mud stains, fresh from its last victorious day on the pitch. She held it close to her and inhaled deeply, the smell of beer and sweat faint, but still there. She put it aside to be washed and passed on to John.

So many objects, so many memories. Each were being labelled and packed away in bags just as they were in her mind. To be stored in an area that would sometimes be called upon to teach and help in the future. Objects that were once so full of life and importance but that now lay limp on the floor. Without him they were just *things*.

Gerry's wedding tuxedo, his suits, shirts and ties that he would moan about having to wear every morning before going to work. The fashions of the years gone by, the eighties shiny suits and shell tracksuits bundled away. A snorkel from their first time scuba-diving, a shell that he had picked up off the ocean floor ten years ago, his collection of beer mats from every country they had visited. Letters and birthday cards from friends and family sent over the years. Valentine's Day cards from Holly. Childhood teddies and dolls put aside to be sent back to his parents. Records of bills, his golf clubs for John, books for Sharon, memories, tears and laughter for Holly.

His entire life bundled into twenty refuse sacks.

His and her memories bundled away into Holly's mind.

Each item unearthed dust, tears, laughter and memories. She bagged the items, cleared the dust, wiped her eyes and filed away the memories for safe-keeping.

Holly's mobile began to ring, disrupting her thoughts, and she dropped the laundry basket onto the grass under the washing line and ran through the patio doors into the kitchen to answer the phone.

'Hello?'

'I'm gonna make you a star!' Declan's voice screeched hysterically on the other end, and he broke into uncontrollable laughter.

Holly waited for him to calm down while she tried to figure out what he could be talking about. 'Declan, are you drunk?'

'Maybe jus a lil bit, but that's completely irrevelant,' he hiccuped.

'Declan, it's ten o'clock in the morning!' Holly laughed. 'Have you been to bed yet?'

'Nope,' he hiccuped again. 'I'm on the train home now and will be in bed in proximately three hours.'

'Three hours! Where are you?' Holly laughed. She was enjoying this as it reminded her of when she used to call Jack at all hours of the morning from all sorts of locations after misbehaving on a night out.

'I'm in Galway. The wards were on last night,' he said, as if she should know.

'Oh, sorry for my ignorance but what awards were you at?'

'I told you!'

'No, you didn't.'

'I told Jack to tell you, the bastard . . .' he stumbled over his words.

139

'Well, he didn't,' she interrupted, 'so now you can tell me.'

'The student media wards were on last night and I won!' he yelled, and Holly heard what sounded like the entire carriage celebrating with him. She was delighted.

'And the prize is that my film is gonna be aired on Channel Four next week! Can you blieve it!' There were more cheers this time, and Holly could barely hear what he was saying. 'You're gonna be famous, sis!' was the last thing she heard before the line went dead.

She rang round her family to share the good news but learned that they had all received similar phone calls. Ciara had stayed on the phone for ages chattering like an excited schoolgirl about how they were going to be on TV, and eventually her story ended with her marrying Denzel Washington.

It was decided that the family would gather in Hogan's pub next Wednesday to watch the documentary being aired. Daniel had kindly offered Club Diva to Declan as the venue so they could watch it on the big wall screen. Holly was so excited for her brother, and rang Sharon and Denise to let them know the good news.

'Oh, this is brill, Holly!' Sharon whispered excitedly.

'Why are you whispering?' Holly whispered back.

'Oh, old wrinkly face here decided it would be a great idea to ban us from accepting personal calls,' moaned Sharon referring to her boss. 'She says we spend more time chatting on the phone to friends than doing business so she's been patrolling our desks all morning. I swear I feel like I'm back at school again with the old hag keeping her eye on us.' Suddenly she spoke up and became businesslike. 'May I take your details, please?'

Holly laughed. 'Is she there?'

'Yes, absolutely,' Sharon continued.

'OK, well, I won't keep you very long then. The details are that we're all meeting up in Hogan's on Wednesday night to watch it so you're welcome to come.'

'That's great . . . OK.' Sharon pretended to take her details.

'Brilliant, we'll have fun. Sharon what will I wear?'

'Hmm . . . brand new or second-hand?'

'No, I really can't afford anything new. Even though you forced me to buy that top a few weeks ago I'm refusing to wear it on the grounds that I am no longer eighteen. So probably something old.'

'OK . . . red.'

'The red top I wore to your birthday?'

'Yes, exactly.'

'Yeah, maybe.'

'What's your current state of employment?'

'To be honest I haven't even started looking yet.' Holly chewed the inside of her mouth and frowned.

'And date of birth?'

'Ha-ha, shut up, you bitch,' Holly laughed.

'I'm sorry, we only give motor insurance to ages twenty-four and older. You're too young, I'm afraid.'

'I wish. OK I'll speak to you later.'

'Thank you for calling.'

Holly sat at the kitchen table wondering what she should wear next week; she wanted something new. She wanted to look sexy and gorgeous, for a change, and she was sick of all her old clothes. Maybe Denise had something in her shop. She was about to call when she received a text message from Sharon.

141

Hag rite bhind me
Tlk 2 u l8r xxx

Holly picked up the phone and called Denise at work.

'Hello, Casuals,' answered a very polite Denise.

'Hello, Casuals, Holly here. I know I'm not supposed to call you at work but I just wanted to tell you that Declan's documentary won some student award thingy and it's gonna be aired on Wednesday night.'

'Oh, that's so cool, Holly! Are we gonna be in it?' she asked excitedly.

'Yeah, I think so. So we're all meeting up in Hogan's to watch it that night. You up for that?'

'Of course! I can bring my new boyfriend too,' she giggled.

'What new boyfriend?'

'Tom!'

'The karaoke guy?' Holly asked in shock.

'Yeah, of course! Oh, Holly, I'm so in love!' she giggled childishly again.

'In love? But you only met him a few weeks ago!'

'I don't care; it only takes a minute . . . as the saying goes.'

'Wow, Denise . . . I don't know what to say!'

'Tell me how great it is!'

'Yeah . . . wow . . . I mean . . . of course . . . It's really great news.'

'Oh, try not to sound too enthusiastic, Holly,' she said sarcastically. 'Anyway I can't wait for you to meet him. You'll absolutely love him. Well, not as much as I do but you'll certainly really *really* like him . . .' she rambled on about how great he was.

'Denise, aren't you forgetting that I've met him already?' Holly interrupted her in the middle of a story about how Tom had saved a child from drowning.

'Yeah, I know you have, but I would rather you meet him when you're not acting like a demented woman hiding in toilets and shouting into microphones.'

'Look forward to it then . . .'

'Yeah, cool, it's gonna be great! I've never been to my own premiere before!' she said excitedly.

Holly rolled her eyes at her dramatics and they said their goodbyes.

Holly barely got any housework done that morning as she spent most of the time talking on the phone. Her mobile was burning and it was giving her a headache. She shuddered at the thought. Every time she had a headache it reminded her of Gerry. She hated to hear her loved ones complaining of headaches and migraines, and would immediately launch herself at them, telling them how they should take it more seriously and go see their doctors. She ended up petrifying everyone with her stories and they eventually stopped telling her whenever they felt ill.

She sighed loudly. She was turning into such a hypochondriac even her doctor was sick of the sight of her. She went running to her in a panic over the tiniest little things: if she had a pain in her leg or a cramp in her stomach. Last week she was convinced there was something wrong with her feet; her toes just didn't look quite right. Her doctor had examined them seriously and then had immediately started to scribble her prescription down on a slip of paper while Holly watched in terror.

Eventually she handed her the piece of paper, and scrawled messily in that handwriting only doctors can perfect was: 'Buy bigger shoes.'

It may have been funny but it cost her forty euro.

Holly had spent the last few minutes on the phone listening to Jack ranting and raving about Richard. Richard had paid him a little visit too. Holly wondered whether he was just trying to bond with his siblings after years of hiding from them. Well, it was too little too late for most of them, it seemed. It was certainly very difficult trying to hold a conversation with someone who hadn't yet mastered the art of politeness.

Oh, stop, stop, stop! she silently screamed to herself. She needed to stop worrying, stop thinking, stop making her brain go into overdrive, and she certainly needed to stop talking to herself. She was driving herself crazy.

She finally finished hanging out the washing more than two hours later and piled another load into the machine. She switched the radio on in the kitchen, had the television blaring from the living room and went about her housework. Perhaps that would drown out the whinging little voice from her head.

CHAPTER SEVENTEEN

Holly arrived at Hogan's and pushed her way through the old men in the pub to the stairs to Club Diva. The traditional band was in full swing and the crowd was joining in with all their favourite Irish songs. It was only seven thirty so Club Diva wasn't officially open yet, and the empty space looked like a completely different venue from the one where she had been so terrified in a few weeks ago. She was the first to arrive and settled herself at a table right in front of the big screen so she would have a perfect view of her brother's documentary.

A glass smashing over by the bar made her jump, and she looked up to see who had joined her in the room. Daniel's head emerged from behind the bar with a dustpan and brush in his hand.

'Oh, hiya, Holly. I didn't realise anyone had come in.'

'I came early, for a change.' She walked over to the bar to greet him. He looked different tonight, she thought, inspecting him.

'God, you're really early,' he said. 'The others probably won't be here for another hour or so.'

Holly looked confused and glanced at her watch. 'But it's seven thirty – the show starts at eight, doesn't it?'

Now Daniel looked confused. 'No, I was told nine o'clock but I could be wrong . . .' he reached for that day's paper and looked at the TV page. 'Yep, nine o'clock, Channel Four.'

Holly rolled her eyes. 'Oh, no, I'm sorry, I'll wander around town for a bit and come back later so,' she said hopping off her stool.

'Hey, don't be silly.' Daniel flashed his pearly whites. 'The shops are all closed by now and you can keep me company – that's if you don't mind . . .'

'Well, I don't mind if you don't mind.'

'I don't mind,' he said firmly.

'Then I'll stay so,' she said happily, hopping back on to her stool.

Daniel leaned his hands against the taps in a typical barman pose. 'So now that that's settled, what can I get you?' he said smiling.

'Well, this is great, no queuing or shouting my order across the bar or anything,' she joked. 'I'll have a sparkling water, please.'

'Nothing stronger?' He raised his eyebrows. His smile was infectious; it seemed to reach from ear to ear.

'No, I'd better not or I'll be drunk by the time everyone gets here.'

'Good thinking,' he agreed, and reached behind him to the fridge to retrieve the bottled water.

Holly realised what it was that made him look so different: he wasn't in his trademark black. He was wearing faded blue jeans and an open light blue shirt, with a white T-shirt underneath, that complemented his blue eyes so that they seemed to twinkle even more than usual. The sleeves of his shirt were rolled up to just below his elbows, and Holly could see his muscles through the light fabric. She quickly averted her eyes as he slid the glass towards her.

'Can I get you anything?' she asked him.

'No, thanks, I'll take care of this one.'

'No, please,' Holly insisted. 'You've bought me plenty of drinks. It's my turn.'

'OK, I'll have a Budweiser then, thanks.' He leaned against the bar and continued to stare at her.

'What? Do you want me to get it?' Holly laughed, jumping off her stool and walking round the bar. Daniel stood back and watched her with amusement.

'I always wanted to work behind a bar when I was a kid,' she said, grabbing a pint glass and pulling down on the tap. She was enjoying herself.

'There's a spare job if you're looking for one,' Daniel said, closely watching her work.

'No, thanks, I think I do a better job on the other side of the bar,' she laughed, filling the pint glass.

'Mmm . . . well, if you're ever looking for work you know where to come,' Daniel said, after taking a gulp of his pint. 'You did a good job.'

'It's not exactly brain surgery,' she smiled, bouncing across to the other side of the bar. She took out her purse and handed him money. 'Keep the change.'

'Thanks,' he smiled, turning to open the cash register and she scorned herself for checking out his bum. It was nice, though – firm, but not as nice as Gerry's, she decided.

'Has your husband deserted you again tonight?' he teased, walking round the bar to join her.

Holly bit her lip and wondered how to answer him. Now wasn't really the time to talk about something so depressing to someone who was only making chitchat, but she didn't want the poor man to keep asking her every time he saw her. He would soon realise the truth, which would cause him even more embarrassment.

'Daniel,' she said softly, 'I don't mean to make you uncomfortable but my husband passed away.'

Daniel stopped in his tracks and his cheeks blushed slightly, 'Oh, Holly, I'm sorry, I didn't know,' he said sincerely.

'It's OK, I know you didn't.' She smiled to show him she wasn't upset by his mistake.

'Well, I didn't meet him the other night but if someone had told me, I would have gone to the funeral to pay my respects.' He sat beside her at the bar.

'Oh no, Gerry died in February, Daniel. He wasn't here the other night.'

Daniel looked confused. 'But I thought you told me he was here . . .' he trailed off, thinking he had misheard.

'Oh, yeah,' Holly looked down at her feet with embarrassment. 'He wasn't here,' she said, looking around the club, 'but he was here.' She put her hand on her heart.

'Ah, I see.' He finally understood, 'Then you were even braver the other night than I thought, considering the circumstances,' he said gently.

Holly was surprised at how at ease he seemed. Usually people stuttered and stammered their way through a sentence and either wandered off or changed the subject. She felt relaxed in his presence, though, as if she could

148

talk openly without fear of crying. Holly smiled and briefly explained the story of the list.

'So that's why I ran off after Declan's gig that time,' Holly laughed.

'It wasn't because they were so terrible, by any chance?' Daniel joked, then he looked lost in thought. 'Ah yes, that's right, that was the thirtieth of April.'

'Yeah, I couldn't wait any longer to open the note,' Holly explained.

'Hmm . . . when's the next one?'

'July,' she said excitedly.

'So I won't be seeing you on the thirtieth of June then,' he said drily.

'Now you're getting the gist,' she laughed.

'I have arrived!' announced Denise to the empty room as she swanned in, dolled up to the nines in the dress she had worn to the ball last year. Tom strolled in behind her, laughing and refusing to take his eyes off her.

'God, *you're* dressed up,' Holly remarked, staring her friend up and down. In the end Holly had decided to wear a pair of jeans, black boots and a very simple black top. She hadn't been in the mood to get all dressed up after all, especially as they were only sitting in an empty club, but Denise hadn't quite grasped that concept.

Tom and Daniel greeted each other with hugs. 'Baby, this is Daniel, my best friend,' Tom said, introducing Daniel to Denise. Daniel and Holly raised their eyebrows at each other and smiled, both registering the use of the word 'baby'.

'Hi, Tom.' Holly shook his hand after Denise had introduced her and he kissed her on the cheek. 'I'm sorry about the last time I met you. I wasn't feeling very sane that night.' Holly blushed at the memory of the karaoke.

'That's no problem,' Tom smiled kindly. 'If you hadn't entered then I wouldn't have met Denise, so I'm glad you did.'

After a while Holly discovered she was enjoying herself; she wasn't just pretending to laugh or finding things mildly amusing, she was genuinely happy. The thought of that made her even happier, as did the knowledge that Denise had finally found someone she really loved.

Minutes later the rest of the Kennedy family arrived, along with Sharon and John. Holly ran down to greet her friends.

'Hiya, hon,' Sharon said, giving her a hug. 'You here long?'

Holly started laughing. 'I thought it was on at eight o'clock so I came at half seven.'

'Oh no.' Sharon looked anxious.

'Don't worry, it was fine. Daniel kept me company,' Holly said, pointing him out.

'Him?' John said angrily. 'Watch yourself with him, Holly. He's a bit of an oddball. You should have heard the stuff he was saying to Sharon the other night.'

Holly guessed she'd caused this confusion, and quickly excused herself from their company to join her family.

'Meredith not with you tonight?' she asked Richard.

'No she's not,' he snapped back rudely, and headed over to the bar.

'Why does he bother coming to these things at all?' she moaned to Jack as he held her head to his chest and rubbed her hair, playfully consoling her.

'OK everyone!' Declan was standing on a stool to

150

address the gathering. 'Because Ciara couldn't decide what to wear tonight, we're all late and *my* documentary is about to start any minute,' he said proudly, 'so if you can just all shut up and sit down, that would be great.'

'Oh, Declan . . .' His mother admonished him for his rudeness.

Holly searched the room for Ciara and spotted her glued to Daniel's side at the bar. She laughed to herself and settled down to watch the documentary. As soon as the announcer introduced it everybody cheered but were quickly hushed by an angry Declan, who didn't want them to miss a thing.

The title *Girls and the City* appeared over a beautiful night-time shot of Dublin, and Holly became nervous. The words 'The Girls' appeared over a black screen, followed by footage of Sharon, Denise, Abbey and Ciara all squashed up beside each other in the back of a taxi.

Sharon was speaking: 'Hello! I'm Sharon and this is Abbey, Denise and Ciara.'

Each of the girls posed for her close-up as she was introduced.

'And we're heading to our best friend Holly's house because it's her birthday . . .'

The scene changed to the girls surprising Holly with shouts of 'Happy Birthday' at her front door. Then the camera returned to Sharon in the taxi. 'Tonight it's gonna be just us girls and NO men . . .'

The scene switched to Holly opening the presents and holding the vibrator up to the camera and saying, 'Well, I'll definitely need this,' before returning to Sharon in the taxi saying: 'We are gonna do lots and *lots* of drinking . . .'

Now Holly was popping open the champagne, then the girls were knocking back shots in Boudoir, and eventually there was Holly with her crooked tiara on her head and drinking out of a champagne bottle with a straw.

'We are gonna go clubbing . . .'

There was a shot of the girls in Boudoir, doing some very embarrassing moves on the dance floor.

'But nothing too mad! We're gonna be good girls tonight!' said Sharon sincerely.

The next scene showed the girls, protesting wildly, being escorted out of the club by three bouncers.

Holly's jaw dropped and she stared in shock at Sharon, who was equally surprised. The men laughed their hearts out and slapped Declan on the back, congratulating him for exposing their partners. Holly, Sharon, Denise, Abbey and even Ciara slithered down in their seats with humiliation.

What on earth had Declan done?

CHAPTER EIGHTEEN

There was complete silence in the club as everyone stared at the screen in anticipation. Holly held her breath; she was nervous now about what was going to appear. Perhaps the girls would be reminded of what exactly they had all conveniently succeeded in forgetting about that night. The truth terrified her. After all, how drunk must they all have been to forget completely the events of that night? Unless, somebody was lying, in which case, they should be even more nervous right now. Holly looked around at the girls. They were all chewing on their finger-nails. Holly crossed her fingers.

A new title appeared on the screen: 'The Gifts'.

'Open mine first,' shrieked Ciara from the television, thrusting her present towards Holly and shoving Sharon off the couch and on to the floor. Everyone in the club laughed while they watched Abbey dragging a horrified Sharon to her feet. Ciara left Daniel's side and tiptoed over to the rest of the girls for security. Everyone oohed and aahed, as one by one Holly's birthday presents were unveiled. A lump formed in Holly's throat as Declan zoomed in on the two photographs on the mantelpiece while Sharon's toast was made.

Once again a new title took over the screen, 'Journey to the City', and showed the girls scrambling over one another to get into the taxi. It was obvious they were pretty pissed by now. Holly was shocked; she had actually thought she was quite sober at that stage.

'Oh, Nick,' Holly moaned drunkenly to the taxi driver from the passenger seat, 'I'm thirty today, can you believe it?'

Nick the taxi driver, who couldn't give a flying flute what age she was, glanced over at her and laughed, 'Sure, you're only a young one still, Holly,' his voice low and gravelly. The camera zoomed in on Holly's face and she cringed at the sight of herself. She looked so drunk, so *sad*.

'But what am I gonna do, Nick?' she whinged. 'I'm thirty! I have no job, no husband, no children and I'm thirty! Did I tell you that?' she asked him, leaning towards him.

Beside her in the club, Sharon giggled. Holly thumped her.

In the background the girls were all chattering excitedly to one another. It sounded as if they were talking over one another; it was hard to see how any type of conversation was going on.

'Ah, enjoy yourself tonight, Holly. Don't get caught up in silly emotions on your birthday. Worry about all that shite tomorrow, love.' Nick sounded so caring, and Holly made a mental note to call him and thank him.

The camera stayed with Holly as she leaned her head

154

against the window and remained silent, lost in thought for the rest of the journey. Holly couldn't get over how lonely she looked. She didn't like it. She looked around the room in embarrassment and caught Daniel's eye. He winked at her in encouragement. She smiled weakly and turned back to face the screen in time to see herself screaming to the girls on O'Connell Street.

'OK, girls. We are going to Boudoir tonight and *no one* is going to stop us from getting in, *especially* not any *silly bouncers* who *think* they own the place.' And she marched off in what she'd thought at the time was a straight line. All the girls cheered and followed after her.

The scene immediately jumped to the two bouncers outside Boudoir shaking their heads. 'Not tonight, girls, sorry.'

Holly's family howled with laughter.

'But you don't understand,' Denise said calmly to the bouncers. 'Do you not know who we are?'

'No,' they both said, and stared over their heads, ignoring them.

'Huh!' Denise put her hands on her hips and pointed to Holly. 'But this is the very, very extremely famous . . . em . . . Princess Holly from the royal family of . . . Finland.'

On camera Holly frowned at Denise.

Her family once again howled with laughter. 'You couldn't write a script better than this,' Declan laughed.

'Oh, she's royalty, is she?' the bouncer with a moustache smirked.

'Indeed she is,' Denise said seriously.

'Finland got a royal family, Paul?' moustache man turned to his colleague.

'Don't think so, boss.'

Holly fixed the crooked tiara on her head and gave them both a royal wave.

'You see?' Denise said, satisfied. 'You men will be very embarrassed if you don't let her in.'

'Supposing we let her in, then you'll have to stay outside,' moustache man said, and motioned for the people behind them in the queue to pass them and enter the club. Holly gave them a royal wave as they passed.

'Oh, no, no, no, no,' Denise protested. 'You don't understand. I am her . . . lady-in-waiting so I need to be with her at all times.'

'Well then, you won't mind waiting till she comes out at closing time,' Paul smirked.

Tom, Jack and John all started laughing, and Denise slithered down even further in her seat.

Finally Holly spoke, 'Oh, one *must* have a drink. One is *dreadfully* thirsty.'

Paul and moustache man snorted and tried to keep straight faces while still staring over the girl's heads.

'No, honestly, girls, not tonight. You need to be a member.'

'But I am a member, of the royal family!' Holly said sternly. 'Off with your heads!' she commanded, pointing at the both of them.

Denise quickly forced Holly's arm down. 'Honestly, the princess and I will be no trouble at all. Just let us in for a few drinks,' she pleaded.

Moustache man stared down at the two of them, then raised his eyes to the sky. 'All right then, go on in,' he said, stepping aside.

'God bless you,' Holly said, making the sign of the cross at them as she passed.

'What is she, a princess or a priest?' laughed Paul as she entered the club.

'She's out of her mind,' laughed moustache man, 'but it's the best excuse I've heard while I've been on the job,' and the two of them sniggered. They regained their composure as Ciara and her entourage approached the door.

'Is it OK if my film crew follow me in?' Ciara said confidently in a brilliant Australian accent.

'Hold on while I check with the manager.' Paul turned his back and spoke into a walkie-talkie. 'Yeah, that's no problem, go ahead,' he said, holding the door open for her.

'That's that Australian singer, isn't it?' moustache man said to Paul.

'Yeah. Good song, that.'

'Tell the boys inside to keep an eye on the princess and her lady,' said moustache man. 'We don't want them bothering that singer with the pink hair.'

Holly's father choked on his drink from laughing, and Elizabeth rubbed his back for him while chortling herself.

As Holly watched the image of the inside of Boudoir on the screen she remembered being disappointed by the club. There had always been a mystery as to what Boudoir looked like. The girls had read in a magazine that there was a water feature into which Madonna had apparently jumped one night. Holly had imagined a huge waterfall cascading down the wall of the club that continued to flow in little bubbling streams while all the glamorous people sat around it and occasionally dipped their glasses

157

into it to fill them with more champagne. Holly had imagined a champagne waterfall. What she got was an oversized fish bowl in the centre of the circular bar. What that had to do with anything she didn't know. Her dreams were shattered. The room wasn't as big as she thought it would be, and was decorated in rich reds and gold. On the far side of the room there was a huge gold curtain acting as a partition, which was blocked by another menacing-looking bouncer.

At the top of the room the main attraction was the massive king-size bed, which was tilted on a platform towards the rest of the club. On top of the gold silk sheets were two skinny models dressed in no more than gold body paint and tiny gold thongs. It was all a bit too tacky.

'Look at the size of those thongs!' gasped Denise in disgust. 'I have a plaster on my baby finger bigger than those.'

Beside her in Club Diva, Tom chuckled and began to nibble on Denise's baby finger. Holly looked away and returned her gaze to the screen.

'Good evening and welcome to the twelve o'clock news. I'm Sharon McCarthy.' Sharon stood in front of the camera with a bottle in her hand serving as a microphone. Declan had angled the camera so that she could get Ireland's famous newsreaders in the shot.

'Today is the thirtieth birthday of Princess Holly of Finland. Her royal self and her lady-in-waiting finally succeeded in being granted access to the famous celebrity hang-out Boudoir. Also present is Australian rock chick Ciara and her film crew and . . .' She held her finger to her ear as though she were receiving more information.

'News just in. It appears that Ireland's favourite newsreader, Tony Walsh, was seen smiling just moments ago. Here beside me I have a witness to the fact. Welcome, Denise.' Denise posed seductively at the camera. 'Denise, tell me, where were you when this event was taking place?'

'Well, I was just over there beside his table when I saw it happening.' Denise sucked in her cheekbones and smiled at the camera.

'Can you explain to us what happened?'

'I was just standing there minding my own business when Mr Walsh took a sip of his drink and then shortly afterwards he smiled.'

'Gosh, Denise, this is fascinating news. And are you sure it was a smile?'

'Well, it could have been trapped wind causing him to make a face but others around me also thought it was a smile.'

'So there were others who witnessed this?'

'Yes, Princess Holly beside me here, saw the whole thing.'

The camera panned across to Holly where she stood drinking from a champagne bottle with a straw. 'So, Holly, can you tell us, was it wind or a smile?'

Holly looked confused, then rolled her eyes, 'Oh, wind. Sorry, I think it's this champagne that's doing it to me.'

Club Diva erupted in laughter. Jack as usual laughed the loudest. Holly hid her face in shame.

'OK then . . .' Sharon said, trying not to laugh, 'so you heard it here first. The night when Ireland's grimmest presenter was seen smiling. Back to you at the studio.' Sharon's smile faded as she looked up and saw Tony

159

Walsh standing beside her, not surprisingly without a smile on his face.

Sharon gulped and said, 'Good evening,' and the camera was switched off. Everyone in the club was laughing at this stage, including the girls. Holly was finding the whole thing just so ridiculous that she had to laugh.

The camera was switched back on and this time it was focused on the mirror in the ladies' toilet. Declan was filming from outside through a slit in the doorway and Denise and Sharon's reflections were clearly visible.

'I was only having a laugh,' Sharon huffed, fixing her lipstick.

'Don't mind the miserable sod, Sharon. He just doesn't want the camera in his face all night, especially on his night off. I can understand that.'

'Oh, you're on his side, I suppose,' Sharon said grumpily.

'Ah, shut up, you moany old whore,' Denise snapped.

'Where's Holly?' Sharon asked, changing the subject.

'Don't know. Last time I saw her she was doing a few funky moves on the dance floor,' said Denise. The two of them looked at each other and laughed.

'Ah . . . our poor little disco diva,' said Sharon sadly. 'I hope she finds someone gorgeous out there tonight and snogs the face off him.'

'Yeah,' agreed Denise. 'Come on then, let's go find her a man,' she added, putting her make-up back in her bag.

Just after the girls left, a toilet flushed, the cubicle door opened and out stepped Holly.

In Club Diva, Holly's big smile faded quickly when she saw her face on the screen.

Through the crack in the door Holly's reflection was

visible in the mirror; her eyes were red from crying. She blew her nose and stared miserably at herself for a while. She took a deep breath, opened the door and carried on downstairs to her friends.

Holly hadn't remembered crying that night – in fact, she thought she had got through it very well. She rubbed her face while she worried about what else was coming up that she couldn't remember.

Finally the scene changed and the words 'Operation Gold Curtain' came up.

Denise screamed, 'Oh my God, Declan, you bastard!' very loudly, and rushed to hide in the toilet.

She had obviously remembered something.

Declan chuckled and lit himself another cigarette.

'OK, girls,' Denise was announcing, 'it is now time for Operation Gold Curtain.'

'Huh?' Sharon and Holly announced groggily from the couch where they had collapsed in a drunken stupor.

'Operation Gold Curtain!' Denise exclaimed excitedly, trying to drag them to their feet. 'It's time to infiltrate the VIP bar!'

'You mean this isn't it?' Sharon said sarcastically, looking around the club.

'No! That's where the real celebs go!' Denise pointed at the gold curtain, which was blocked by possibly the biggest and tallest man on the planet.

'I don't really care where the celebs are, to be honest, Denise,' piped up Holly. 'I'm fine here where I am,' and she snuggled into the cosy couch.

Denise groaned and rolled her eyes, 'Girls! Abbey and Ciara are in there, why aren't we?'

Jack looked curiously across at his girlfriend. Abbey

161

shrugged her shoulders weakly and held her face in her hand. None of this was jogging anybody's memory except Denise's, and she had fled the room. Jack's smile suddenly faded and he slid down in his chair and crossed his arms. It was obviously all right for his sisters to act the fool but his girlfriend was a different matter. Jack placed his feet up on the chair in front of him and quietened down for the rest of the documentary.

Once Sharon and Holly had heard that Abbey and Ciara were in the room they sat up attentively and listened to Denise's plan.

'OK, girlies, here's what we're gonna do . . .'

Holly turned away from the screen and nudged Sharon. Holly couldn't remember doing or saying any of these things at all; she was beginning to think Declan had hired lookalike actors as a horrible practical joke. Sharon turned to face her with wide worried eyes and shrugged. Nope, she wasn't there that night either.

The camera followed the three girls as they very suspiciously approached the gold curtain and loitered around like idiots. Sharon finally built up the courage to tap the giant on the shoulder, causing him to turn round and provide Denise with enough time to escape under the curtain. She got down on her hands and knees and stuck her head through to the VIP bar while her bum and legs stuck out from the other side of the curtain.

Holly kicked her in the bum to hurry her along.

'I can see them!' Denise hissed loudly. 'Oh my God! They're speaking to that Hollywood actor guy!' She took her head back out from under the curtain and looked at Holly with excitement. Unfortunately Sharon was running out of things to say to the giant bouncer and he turned his head just in time to catch Denise.

'No, no, no, no, no!' Denise said calmly again. 'You don't understand! This is Princess Holly of Sweden!'

'Finland,' Sharon corrected her.

'Sorry, Finland,' Denise said, remaining on her knees. 'I am bowing to her. Join me!'

Sharon quickly got on her knees and the two of them began to worship her feet. Holly looked around awkwardly as everyone in the club began to stare and she once again gave them the royal wave. Nobody seemed very impressed.

'Oh, Holly!' her mother said, trying to catch her breath after laughing so hard.

Big burly bouncer turned his back and spoke into his walkie-talkie. 'Boys, got a situation with the princess and the lady.'

Denise looked at both the girls in panic and mouthed, 'Hide!' The girls jumped to their feet and fled. The camera searched through the crowds for them but couldn't find them.

From her seat in Club Diva, Holly groaned loudly and held her head in her hands as it clicked with her what was about to happen.

CHAPTER NINETEEN

Paul and moustache man rushed upstairs to the club and met the very big man at the gold curtain.

'What's going on?' moustache man asked him.

'Those girls you told me to keep my eye on tried to crawl through to the other side,' big man said seriously. You could tell by looking at him that his previous job involved killing people. He was taking this breach of security very seriously.

'Where are they?' moustache man asked.

Big man cleared his throat and looked away, 'They're hiding, boss.'

Moustache man rolled his eyes. 'They're hiding?'

'Yes, boss.'

'Where? In the club?'

'I think so, boss.'

'You think so?'

'Well, they didn't pass us on our way in so they must still be here,' Paul piped up.

'OK,' moustache man sighed. 'Well, let's start

looking, then. Get someone to keep an eye on the curtain.'

The camera followed the three bouncers as they patrolled the club, looking behind couches, under tables, behind curtains and they even got someone to check the toilets. Holly's family laughed hysterically at the scene unfolding before their eyes.

There was a bit of commotion at the top of the club and the bouncers headed towards the noise to sort it out. A crowd was beginning to gather, and the two skinny dancers dressed in gold body paint had stopped dancing and were staring with horrified expressions at the bed. The camera panned across. Underneath the gold silk sheets there appeared to be three pigs fighting under a blanket. Sharon, Denise and Holly rolled around screaming at each other, trying to make themselves as flat as possible so they wouldn't be noticed. The crowd thickened and soon enough the music was shut down. The three big lumps under the bed stopped squirming and suddenly froze, not knowing what was going on outside.

The bouncers counted to three and pulled the covers off the bed. Three very startled-looking girls, like deer caught in headlights, stared back at them, lying there as flat as they could with their arms stiffly by their sides.

'*One* just had to get forty winks before *one* left,' Holly said in her royal accent, and the other girls burst out laughing.

'Come on, princess, the fun's over,' said Paul. The three men accompanied the girls outside, assuring them that they would never be allowed back into the club ever again.

'Can I just tell my friends that we're gone?' Sharon asked.

The men tutted and looked away.

'Excuse me? Am I talking to myself? I asked you if it was OK if I go in and tell my friends that we had to leave?'

'Look, stop playing around, girls,' moustache man said angrily. 'Your friends aren't in there. Now off you go, back to your beds.'

'Excuse me,' Sharon repeated angrily, 'I have two friends in the VIP bar; one of them has pink hair and the other one—'

'Girls!' the bouncer raised his voice. 'She does not want anyone bothering her. She is no more your friend than the man on the moon. Now clear off before you get yourselves into more trouble.'

Everyone in the club howled with laughter.

The scene changed to 'The Long Journey Home', and all the girls were in the taxi. Abbey sat like a dog, with her head hanging out of the open window by order of the taxi driver. 'You're not throwing up in my cab. You either stick your head out the window or you walk home.' Abbey's face was almost purple and her teeth were chattering but she wasn't going to trek all the way home. Ciara sat with her arms crossed, in a huff, angry with the girls for forcing her to leave the club so early but, more embarrassingly, for blowing her cover as a famous rock singer. Sharon and Denise had fallen asleep with their heads resting on one another.

The camera turned round to focus on Holly, who was sitting in the passenger seat once again. But this time she wasn't talking the ear off the taxi driver; she rested her head on the back of the seat and stared straight ahead out into the dark night. Holly knew what she was thinking as she watched herself. Time to go home to that big empty house all alone again.

'Happy birthday, Holly,' a very cold Abbey's tiny little voice trembled.

Holly turned round to smile at her and came face to face with the camera. 'Are you *still* filming with that thing? Turn it off!' and she knocked the camera out of Declan's hand.

The End.

As Daniel went to turn the lights up in the club, Holly slipped quickly away from the gang and escaped through the nearest door. She needed to collect her thoughts before everyone started talking. She found herself in a tiny storeroom surrounded by mops and buckets and empty kegs. What a stupid place to hide, she thought. She sat down on a barrel and thought about what she had just seen. She was in shock. She felt confused and angry at Declan; he had told her that he was making a documentary about club life. She distinctly remembered him not mentioning anything about making a show of her and her friends. And he had literally made a show of them. If he had asked her politely whether he could do it that would have been a different matter. Although she still wouldn't have agreed to it.

But the last thing she wanted to do right now was to scream at Declan in front of everyone. Apart from the fact that it had completely humiliated her, Declan had actually filmed it and edited it very well. If it was anyone else but her on the TV, Holly would have thought it most deserving of the award. But it *was* her so therefore it *didn't* deserve to win . . . Parts of it had been funny, she agreed, and she didn't mind so much the bits of her and her friends being so silly; it was more the sneaky shots of her unhappiness that bothered her.

Thick salty tears trickled down her face and she wrapped her arms around her body to comfort herself. She had seen on television how she truly felt. Lost and alone. She cried for Gerry, she cried for herself with big heaving sobs that hurt her ribs whenever she tried to catch her breath. She didn't want to be alone any more and she didn't want her family seeing the loneliness she tried so hard to hide from them. She just wanted Gerry back and didn't care about anything else. She didn't care if he came back and they fought every day, she didn't care if they were broke and had no house and no money. She just wanted him. She heard the door open behind her and felt big strong arms wrapping themselves round her frail body. She cried as though months of built-up anguish were all tumbling out at once.

'What's wrong with her? Didn't she like it?' she heard Declan ask worriedly.

'Just leave her be, son,' her mum said softly, and the door was closed behind them again as Daniel stroked Holly's hair and rocked her softly.

Finally, after crying what felt like all the tears in the world, Holly stopped and let go of Daniel. 'Sorry,' she sniffed, drying her face with the sleeves of her top.

'There's no need to be sorry,' he said, gently removing her hand from her face and handing her a tissue.

She sat in silence while trying to compose herself.

'If you're upset about the documentary, then there's

no need,' he said, sitting down on a crate of glasses opposite her.

'Yeah, right,' she said sarcastically, wiping her tears again.

'No, really,' he insisted. 'I thought it was really funny. You all looked like you were having a great time.'

'Pity that's not how I felt,' she said sadly.

'Maybe that's not how you felt but the camera doesn't pick up on feelings, Holly.'

'You don't have to try to make me feel better.' Holly was embarrassed at being consoled by a stranger.

'I'm not *trying* to make you feel better, I'm just saying it like it is. Nobody but you noticed whatever it is that's upsetting you. I didn't see anything so why should anyone else?'

Holly felt mildly better. 'Are you sure?'

'I'm sure I'm sure,' Daniel said, smiling. 'Now you really have to stop hiding in all the rooms in my club. I might take it personally,' he laughed.

'Are the girls OK?' Holly asked, hoping it was just her being stupid after all.

There was loud laughter from outside.

'They're fine, as you can hear.' He nodded towards the door. 'Ciara's delighted everyone will think she's a star, Denise has finally come out of the toilet and Sharon just can't stop laughing. Although Jack's giving Abbey a hard time about throwing up on the way home.'

Holly chuckled.

'So you see, nobody even noticed what you saw.'

'Thanks, Daniel.' She took a deep breath and smiled at him.

'You ready to go face your public?'

'Think so.' Holly stepped outside to the sounds of laughter. The lights were up and everyone was sitting around the table and happily sharing jokes and stories. Holly sat beside her mum. Elizabeth wrapped her arm round her daughter and gave her a kiss on the cheek.

'Well, I thought it was great,' announced Jack enthusiastically. 'If only we could get Declan to go out with the girls all the time, then we'd know what they get up to, eh, John?' he winked at Sharon's husband.

'Well, I can assure you,' Abbey spoke up, 'that what you saw is not a regular girls' night out.'

The boys weren't having any of it.

'So is it OK?' Declan asked Holly, afraid he had upset her.

Holly threw him a look.

'I thought you would like it, Hol,' he said worriedly.

'I might have liked it if I had *known* what you were doing,' she snapped back.

'But I wanted it to be a surprise,' he said genuinely.

'I hate surprises.' She rubbed her stinging eyes.

'Let that be a lesson to you, son,' Frank warned Declan. 'You shouldn't go around filming people without them knowing what you're doing. It's illegal.'

'I bet they didn't know that when they chose him for the award,' Elizabeth agreed.

'You're not gonna tell them, are you, Holly?' Declan asked worriedly.

'Not if you're nice to me for the next few months,' Holly said slyly, twisting her hair around her finger.

Declan made a face. He was stuck and he knew it. 'Yeah, whatever,' he said, waving her away.

'To tell you the truth, Holly, I have to admit I thought

170

it was quite funny,' giggled Sharon. 'You and your Operation Gold Curtain.' She thumped Denise playfully on the leg.

Denise rolled her eyes. 'I can tell you all something – I am *never* drinking again.'

Everyone laughed and Tom put his arm round her shoulders.

'What?' she said innocently. 'I really mean it.'

'Speaking of drink, would anyone like one?' Daniel stood up from his chair. 'Jack?'

'Yeah, a Budweiser, thanks.'

'Abbey?'

'Em . . . a white wine, please,' she said politely.

'Frank?'

'A Guinness, thanks, Daniel.'

'I'll have the same,' said John.

'Sharon?'

'Vodka and Coke, please. Holly you want the same?'

Holly nodded.

'Tom?'

'JD and Coke, please, Dan.'

'Me too,' said Declan.

'Denise?' Daniel tried to hide his smile.

'Em . . . I'll have a . . . gin and tonic please.'

'Ha!' everyone jeered her.

'What?' She shrugged her shoulders as though she didn't care. 'One drink is hardly going to kill me . . .'

Holly was standing over the sink with her sleeves rolled up to her elbows, scrubbing the pots, when she heard the familiar voice.

'Hi, honey.'

171

She looked up and saw him standing at the open patio doors. 'Hello, you,' she smiled.

'Miss me?'

'Of course.'

'Have you found that new husband yet?'

'Of course I have. He's upstairs in bed asleep,' she laughed, drying her hands.

Gerry shook his head and tutted. 'Shall I go up and suffocate him for sleeping in our bed?'

'Ah, give him another hour or so,' she joked, looking at her watch. 'He needs his rest.'

He looked happy, she thought, fresh-faced and still as beautiful as she remembered. He was wearing her favourite blue top she had bought him one Christmas. He stared at her from under his long eyelashes with his big brown puppy eyes.

'Are you coming in?' she asked, smiling.

'No, I just popped by to see how you are. Everything going OK?' he leaned against the door jamb with his hands in his pockets.

'So, so,' she said, weighing her hands in the air. 'Could be better.'

'I hear you're a TV star now,' he grinned.

'A very reluctant one,' she laughed.

'You'll have men falling all around you,' he assured her.

'Falling all around me is right,' she joked. 'The problem is they keep missing the target.' She pointed to herself. He laughed. 'I miss you, Gerry.'

'I haven't gone far,' he said softly.

'You leaving me again?'

'For the time being.'

172

'See you soon,' she smiled.

He winked at her and disappeared.

Holly woke up with a smile on her face and felt as if she had slept for days. 'Good morning, Gerry,' she said happily, staring up at the ceiling.

The phone rang beside her. 'Hello?'

'Oh my God, Holly, just take a look at the weekend papers,' Sharon said in a panic.

CHAPTER TWENTY

Holly immediately leaped out of bed, threw on a tracksuit and drove to her nearest newsagent. She reached the newspaper stand and began to leaf through the pages in search of what Sharon had been raving about. The man behind the counter coughed loudly and Holly looked up at him.

'This is not a library, young lady. You'll have to buy that,' he said, nodding at the newspaper in her hand.

'I know that,' she said, irritated by his rudeness. Honestly, how on earth was anyone supposed to know which paper they wanted to buy if they didn't even know which paper had what they were looking for? She ended up picking up every single newspaper from the stand and slammed them down on the counter, smiling sweetly at him.

The man looked startled and started to scan them into the register one by one. A queue began to form behind her.

Holly stared longingly at the selection of chocolate

bars displayed in front of her and looked around to see if anyone was looking at her. *Everyone* was staring. She quickly turned back to face the counter. Finally her arm jumped up and grabbed the two king-size chocolate bars nearest to her on the shelf from the bottom of the pile. One by one the rest of the chocolate began to slide on to the floor. The teenager behind her snorted and looked away, laughing, as Holly bent down with a red face and began to pick them up. So many had fallen she had to make several trips up and down. The shop was silent apart from a few coughs from the impatient queue behind her. She sneakily added another few packets of sweets to her pile, 'For the kids,' she said loudly to the news-agent, hoping everyone behind her would also hear.

He just grunted at her and continued scanning the items. Then she remembered she needed to get milk so she rushed from the queue to the end of the shop to retrieve a pint of milk from the fridge. A few women tutted loudly as she made her way back to the top of the queue where she added the milk to her pile. The newsagent stopped scanning to stare at her, she stared back blankly at him.

'Mark,' he yelled.

A spotty young teenager appeared from one of the shopping aisles with a pricing gun in his hand. 'Yeah?' he said grumpily.

'Open the other till, will ya, son? We might be here for a while.' The newsagent glared at Holly.

She made a face at him.

Mark dragged his body over to the second till, all the time staring at Holly. What? she thought defensively. Don't blame me for you having to do your job. He took over the till and the entire queue behind her rushed over to the other side.

Satisfied that no one was staring at her any more she grabbed a few packets of crisps from below the counter and added them to her purchases. 'Birthday party,' she mumbled.

In the queue beside her, the teenager quietly asked for a packet of cigarettes.

'Got any ID?' Mark asked loudly.

The teenager looked around in embarrassment with a red face. Holly snorted at him and looked away.

'Anything else?' the newsagent asked sarcastically.

'No, thank you, that will be all,' she said through gritted teeth. She paid her money and fumbled with her purse, trying to put all the change back in.

'Next,' the newsagent nodded to the customer behind her.

'Hiya, can I have twenty Benson and—'

'Excuse me,' Holly interrupted the man, 'could I have a bag please?' She stared at the huge pile of groceries in front of her.

'Just a moment,' he said rudely, 'I'll deal with this gentleman first. Yes, sir, cigarettes, is it?'

'Please,' the customer said, looking at Holly apologetically.

'Now,' the newsagent said, returning to Holly, 'what can I get you?'

'A bag.' She clenched her jaw.

'That'll be twenty cents please.'

Holly sighed loudly and reached into her handbag, searching through the mess to find her purse again. Another queue formed behind her.

'Mark, take over the till again, will you?' the man said arrogantly.

Holly took the coin out of her purse, slammed it down on the counter and began to fill the bag with her items.

'Next,' the newsagent said again, looking over her shoulder to the next customer. Holly felt under pressure to get out of the way and began stuffing the bag full in panic.

'I'll wait till the lady here is ready,' the customer said politely.

Holly smiled at him appreciatively and turned to leave the shop. She was walking away grumbling to herself when Mark, the boy behind the counter, startled her by yelling, 'Hey, I know you! You're the girl from the telly!'

Holly swirled round in surprise and the plastic handle broke from the weight of all the newspapers. Everything fell onto the floor and her chocolate, sweets and crisps went rolling in all directions.

The friendly customer got down on his knees to help her gather her belongings while the rest of the shop watched in amusement, wondering who the girl from the telly was.

'It is you, isn't it?' the boy laughed.

Holly smiled up weakly at him from the floor.

'I knew it!' He clapped his hands together with excitement. 'You're cool!'

Yeah, she really felt cool, on her knees on the floor of a shop, searching for bars of chocolate. Holly's face went red and she nervously cleared her throat, 'Em . . . excuse me, could I have another bag, please?'

'Yeah, that'll be—'

'There you go,' the friendly customer interrupted him,

placing a twenty-cent coin down on the counter. The newsagent looked perplexed and continued serving the customers.

'I'm Rob,' the man said, helping Holly put all her chocolate back into the bag, then holding his hand out.

'I'm Holly,' she said, a little embarrassed by his over-friendliness, and took his hand. 'And I'm a chocoholic.'

He laughed.

'Thanks for the help,' she said gratefully, getting to her feet.

'No problem.' He held the door open for her. He was good-looking, she thought, a few years older than she, and he had the oddest coloured eyes, a kind of a grey-green colour. She squinted at him and took a closer look.

He cleared his throat.

She blushed, suddenly realising she had been staring at him like a fool. She walked out to her car and placed the bulging bag on the back seat. Rob followed her over. Her heart did a little flip.

'Hi again,' he laughed. 'Em . . . I was wondering if you would like to go for a drink?' Then he laughed, glancing at his watch. 'Actually, it's a bit too early for that. How about a coffee?'

He was a very confident man and he rested himself coolly against the car opposite Holly, his hands in the pockets of his jeans with his thumbs resting outside and those weird eyes just staring back at her. However, he didn't make her feel uncomfortable, he was just very relaxed, as though asking a stranger out for coffee was the most natural thing in the world. Was this what people did these days?

'Em . . .' Holly thought about it. What harm could it

do to go for a coffee with a man who had been so polite to her? The fact that he was absolutely gorgeous also helped. But regardless of his looks, Holly really craved company, and he seemed like a nice decent man to talk to. Sharon was out and Denise was at work and Holly couldn't keep calling over to her mother's house; Elizabeth had work to do too. Holly really needed to start meeting new people. Many of Gerry and Holly's other friends had been people with whom Gerry worked, but once he had died all those 'friends' of theirs hadn't been too much of a familiar feature around her house. At least she knew who her true friends were.

She was just about to say yes to Rob when he glanced down at her hand and his smile faded. 'Oh, sorry, I didn't realise . . .' He backed away from her awkwardly as though she had some kind of disease. 'I have to rush off anyway.' He smiled quickly at her and scarpered off down the road.

Holly stared after him, confused. Had she said something wrong? Had she taken too long to decide? Had she broken one of the silent rules of this new meeting-people game? She looked down at the hand that had caused him to run away from her and saw her wedding ring sparkle back at her. She sighed loudly and rubbed her face tiredly.

Just then the teenager from the shop walked by with a gang of friends and a cigarette in his mouth and snorted at her.

She just couldn't win.

Holly slammed the door of her car and looked around. She wasn't in the mood to go home, she was sick of staring at the walls all day every day and talking to herself. It was still only ten o'clock in the morning and beautifully sunny and warm outside. Across the road her local café, The Greasy Spoon, was setting up tables and chairs outside. Her stomach grumbled. A nice big Irish breakfast was exactly what she needed. She took her sunglasses from the glove compartment of her car, carried her newspapers with both hands and wandered across the road.

A plump lady was cleaning the tables. Her hair was tied back tightly in a large bun, and a bright red and white checked apron covered her flowery dress. Holly felt like she had walked straight into a country kitchen.

'Been a while since these tables have seen sunlight,' the woman said happily to Holly as she approached the café.

'Yeah, it's a beautiful day, isn't it?' Holly said, and the two of them stared up at the clear blue sky. It was funny how good weather in Ireland always seemed to be the conversation of the day with everyone. It was such a rare sight that everyone felt blessed when it finally arrived.

'You want to sit out here, love?'

'Yes, I will. Might as well make the most out of it. It'll probably be gone in an hour,' Holly laughed, taking a seat.

'You need to think positively, love.' The waitress busied herself around Holly. 'Right, I'll get you the menu,' she said, turning to leave.

'No, it's OK,' Holly called after her, 'I know what I want. I'll have the Irish breakfast.'

'No problem, love,' the woman smiled, and her eyes widened when she saw the pile of newspapers on the table, 'You thinking of starting your own newsagents?' she chuckled.

Holly looked down at the pile and laughed at the sight

of the *Arab Leader* lying on the top. She had grabbed every single paper and hadn't even thought to check what they were. She doubted very much the *Arab Leader* contained any articles about the documentary.

'Well, to tell you the truth, love,' the woman said, cleaning the table beside her, 'you'd be doing us all a favour if you put that miserable ol' bastard out of business.' She glared across the road to the newsagent. Holly laughed as the woman waddled back into the café.

Holly just sat there for a while, watching the world go by. She loved catching snippets of people's conversations as they walked past; it gave her a sneaky peak into the lives of others. She loved to guess what people did for a living, where they were heading as they rushed by, where they lived, if they were married or single . . . Sharon and Holly always used to sit in Bewley's overlooking Grafton Street and they would do their people spotting. They would create little scenarios in their heads to pass the time, although Holly seemed to be doing this very regularly these days – just another demonstration of how her mind was caught up in other people's lives instead of focusing on her own.

For example, the new little scenario she was creating involved the man walking down the path holding hands with his wife. Holly decided that he was secretly gay and the man headed toward them was his lover. Holly watched their faces as they approached each other, wondering if they would make eye contact. They went one better than that, and Holly tried not to giggle as the three of them stopped just in front of her table.

'Excuse me? Have you got the time?' lover asked secretly gay man and wife.

181

'Yes, it's a quarter past ten,' secretly gay man answered him, looking at his watch.

'Thanks a lot,' lover said, touching his arm, and walked on.

Now it was as clear as day to Holly that that had been secret code for a rendezvous later. She continued her people spotting for a little while longer until she eventually got bored and decided to live her own life for a change.

Holly flicked through the pages of the tabloids and came to a small article in the review section that caught her eye.

Girls and the City a Hit in the Ratings
by Tricia Coleman

For any of you unfortunate people who missed out on the outrageously funny TV documentary *Girls and the City* last Wednesday, do not despair because it will be back on our screens soon.

The hilarious fly-on-the-wall documentary, directed by Irishman Declan Kennedy, follows five Dublin girls out for a night on the town. They lift the lid on the mysterious world of celebrity life in trendy club Boudoir and provide us with thirty minutes of stomach-aching laughter.

The show proved to be a success when first aired on Channel 4, the latest TAM ratings revealing 4 million people tuned in in the UK. The show is to be repeated again Sunday night at 11p.m. on Channel 4. This is must-see TV, so don't miss it!

Holly tried to keep her cool as she read through the article. It was obviously great news for Declan but disastrous for her. Having that documentary aired once was bad enough, never mind a second time. She really needed to have a serious talk with him about this. She had let him off lightly the other night because he had been so excited and she didn't want to make a scene, but at this stage she had enough problems on her plate without having to worry about this too.

She flicked through the rest of the papers and saw what it was Sharon was ranting about. Every single tabloid had an article about the documentary and one had even printed a photograph of Denise, Sharon and Holly from a few years ago. How they got their hands on it she did not know. Thank God the broadsheets contained some real news or Holly would have really worried about the world. She wasn't too happy with the use of the words, 'mad girls', 'drunken girls', and the description from one of the papers that they were 'well up for it'. What did that even mean?

Holly's food finally arrived and she stared at it in shock, wondering how on earth she was going to get through it all.

'That'll fatten you up, love,' the plump lady said, placing it on the table. 'You need a bit of meat on your bones; you're far too skinny,' she warned her, waddling off again. Holly felt pleased at the compliment.

The plate was piled high with sausages, bacon, eggs, hash browns, black and white pudding, baked beans, fried potatoes, mushrooms, tomatoes and five slices of toast. Holly looked around her with embarrassment, hoping no one would think she was a complete pig. She saw that annoying teenager heading towards her with his gang of friends again and she picked up her plate and ran inside. She hadn't much of an appetite lately; but she finally felt ready to eat and she wasn't going to let some stupid spotty teenager ruin her breakfast for her.

Holly must have stayed in The Greasy Spoon much longer than she thought, because by the time she reached her parents' house in Portmarnock it was almost two o'clock. Against her prediction, the sun was still sitting high in the cloudless blue sky. She looked across at the crowded beach in front of the house and found it difficult to tell where the sky ended and the sea began. Busfuls of people where continuously being unloaded across the road, and there was a lovely smell of sun-tan lotion in the air. There were gangs of teenagers hanging around the grassy area with CD players blaring out the latest tunes. The sound and the smell brought back every happy childhood memory for Holly.

Holly rang the doorbell for the fourth time and still no one answered. She knew somebody had to be home because the bedroom windows were wide open upstairs. Her mum and dad would never leave them open if they weren't home, especially with throngs of strangers wandering around the area. Holly walked across the grass and pressed her face against the living-room window to see if there was any sign of life. She was just about to give up and wander over to the beach when she heard the screaming match between Declan and Ciara.

'CIARA, GET THE DAMN DOOR!'

'NO, I SAID! I . . . AM . . . BUSY!'

'WELL, SO AM I!'

Holly rang the doorbell again, just to add fuel to the fire.

'DECLAN!' Ouch, that was a bloodcurdling scream.

'GET IT YOURSELF, YOU LAZY COW!'

'HA! *I'M* LAZY?'

Holly took out her mobile phone and rang the house.

'CIARA, ANSWER THE PHONE!'

'NO!'

'Oh, for Christsake,' Holly snapped loudly, and hung up the phone. She dialled Declan's mobile number.

'Yeah?'

'Declan, open the goddamn fucking door now or I'll kick it in,' Holly growled.

'Oh sorry, Holly, I thought Ciara had answered it,' he lied.

He opened the door in his boxer shorts and Holly stormed in. 'Jesus Christ! I hope you two don't carry on like that *every* time the doorbell rings.'

He shrugged his shoulders noncommittally, 'Mum and Dad are out,' he said lazily, and headed up the stairs.

'Hey, where are you going?'

'Back to bed.'

'No you are not,' Holly said calmly, 'you are going to sit down here with me,' she patted the couch, 'and we're gonna have a nice long chat about *Girls and the City*.'

'No,' Declan moaned. 'Do we have to do this now? I'm really, really tired.' He rubbed his eyes with his fists.

Holly had no sympathy for him, 'Declan, it's two o'clock in the afternoon, how can you still be tired?'

'Because I only got home a few hours ago,' he said,

185

cheekily winking at her. Now she definitely had no sympathy for him; she was just plain jealous.

'Sit!' she ordered him.

He moaned again and dragged his weary body over to the couch where he collapsed and stretched out along the entire thing, leaving no room for Holly. She rolled her eyes and dragged her dad's armchair closer to Declan.

'I feel like I'm with a shrink,' he laughed, crossing his arms behind his head and staring up at her.

'Good, because I'm really going to pick your brains.'

Declan whinged again, 'Oh, Holly, do we have to? We just talked about this the other night.'

'Did you honestly think that was all I was going to say? "Oh, I'm sorry, Declan, but I didn't like the way you publicly humiliated me and my friends. See you next week"?'

'Obviously not.'

'Come on, Declan,' she said, softening her tone, 'I just want to understand why you thought it would be such a great idea not to tell me you were filming me and my friends?'

'You *knew* I was filming,' he said defensively.

'For a documentary about *club life*!' Holly raised her voice in frustration at her younger brother.

'And it *was* about club life,' Declan laughed.

'Oh, you think you're so bloody clever,' she snapped at him, and he stopped laughing. She counted to ten and breathed slowly to prevent herself from attacking him.

'Come on, Declan,' she said quietly. 'Do you not think that I am going through enough right now without having to worry about this as well? And without even asking me? I cannot for the life of me understand why you would do it!'

Declan sat up on the couch and became serious for a change, 'I know, Holly, I know you've been through hell but I thought this would cheer you up. I wasn't lying when I said I was going to film the club because that's what I had planned on doing. But when I brought it back to college to begin the edit everyone thought that it was just so funny that I couldn't *not* show it to people.'

'Yeah, but you put it on TV, Declan.'

'I didn't know that was the prize, honestly,' he said, wide-eyed. 'Nobody knew, not even my lecturers! How could I say no to it when I won?'

Holly gave up and ran her fingers through her hair.

'I honestly thought you would like it,' he smiled. 'I checked with Ciara and *even she* said you'd like it. I'm sorry if I upset you,' he mumbled.

Holly continued nodding her head through his explanation, realising he genuinely had good intentions, however misguided. Suddenly she stopped. What had he just said? She sat up, alert in her seat. 'Declan, did you just say that Ciara knew about the tape?'

Declan froze in his seat and tried to think of a way to back himself out of the corner he found himself in. Coming up with nothing, he threw himself back onto the couch and covered his head with a cushion, knowing he had just started World War Three.

'Oh, Holly, don't say anything to her. She'll kill me!' came his muffled reply.

Holly bounded out of her seat and stormed upstairs, thumping her feet on every stair to show Ciara she was *really* mad. She yelled threats at Ciara all the way up and pounded on her bedroom door.

'Don't come in!' yelled Ciara from inside.

'You are in so much trouble, Ciara!' Holly screamed. She burst her way inside, putting on her most terrifying face.

'I told you not to come in!' wailed Ciara.

Holly was about to start screaming all sorts of insulting things at her sister but stopped herself when she saw Ciara sitting on the floor with what looked like a photo album on her lap and tears streaming down her face.

CHAPTER TWENTY-ONE

'Oh, Ciara, what's wrong?' Holly said soothingly. She was worried; she couldn't remember the last time she had seen Ciara cry. In fact, she didn't even know Ciara knew *how* to cry. Whatever had reduced her to tears must be something serious.

'Nothing's wrong,' Ciara said, snapping the photo album shut and sliding it under her bed. She seemed embarrassed to be caught crying and she wiped her face roughly, trying to look as if she didn't care.

Downstairs on the couch, Declan peeped his head out from under the cushion. It was eerily quiet up there; he hoped they hadn't done anything stupid to one another. He tiptoed upstairs and listened outside the door.

'Something *is* wrong,' Holly said, crossing the room to join her sister on the floor. She wasn't sure how to deal with Ciara like this. This was a complete role reversal; ever since they were kids it had always been Holly who had done all the crying. Ciara was supposed to be the strong one.

'I'm fine,' Ciara snapped.

'OK,' Holly said looking around, 'but if there's something on your mind that's upsetting you, you know you can talk to me about it, don't you?'

Ciara refused to look at her and just nodded her head. Holly began to stand up to leave her sister in peace when all of a sudden Ciara burst into tears again. Holly quickly sat back down and wrapped her arms protectively round her younger sister. Holly stroked Ciara's silky pink hair while she cried quietly.

'Do you want to tell me what's wrong?' she asked softly.

Ciara gurgled some sort of reply and sat up to slide the photo album back out from under the bed. She opened it with trembling hands and flicked a few pages.

'Him,' she said, sadly pointing to a photograph of her and some guy Holly didn't recognise. In fact, Holly barely recognised her sister. She looked so different and so much younger. The photograph was taken on a beautiful sunny day on a boat overlooking the Sydney Opera House. Ciara was sitting happily on his knee with her arms wrapped round his neck and he was staring at her with a huge smile on his face. Holly couldn't get over how pretty Ciara looked. She had blonde hair, which Holly had never seen on her sister before, and a great big smile on her face. Her features looked much softer – she didn't look as if she was going to bite someone's head off for a change.

'Is that your boyfriend?' Holly asked gently.

'Was,' Ciara sniffed, and a tear landed on the page.

'Is that why you came home?' she asked softly, wiping a tear from her sister's face.

Ciara nodded.

'Do you want to tell me what happened?'

Ciara gasped for breath. 'We had a fight.'

'Did he . . .' Holly chose her words carefully, 'he didn't hurt you or anything did he?'

Ciara shook her head. 'No,' she spluttered, 'it was just over something really stupid and I said I was leaving and he said he was glad . . .' She trailed off as she started sobbing again.

Holly held her in her arms and waited till Ciara was ready to talk again.

'He didn't even come to the airport to say goodbye to me.'

Holly rubbed Ciara's back soothingly as though she was a baby who had just drunk her bottle. She hoped Ciara wouldn't throw up on her. 'Has he called you since?'

'No, and I've been home for two months, Holly,' she wailed. She looked up at her older sister with such sad eyes Holly felt like crying too. She didn't like the sound of this guy at all for hurting her sister. Holly smiled at her encouragingly. 'Then do you think that maybe he's not the right kind of person for you?'

Ciara started crying again. 'But I love Mathew, Holly, and it was just a stupid fight. I only booked the flight because I was angry. I didn't think he would let me go . . .' She stared for a long time at the photograph.

Ciara's bedroom windows were wide open and Holly listened to the familiar sound of the waves and the laughter coming from the beach. Holly and Ciara had shared this room together as they grew up, and a weird sense of comfort now embraced her as she smelled the same smells and listened to the familiar noises.

Ciara began to calm down. 'Sorry, Hol.'

'Hey, you don't need to be sorry at all,' she said, squeezing her hand. 'You should have told me all this when you came home instead of keeping it all inside.'

'But this is only minor compared to what's happened to you. I feel stupid even crying about it.' She wiped her tears, angry with herself.

Holly was shocked, 'Ciara, this *is* a big deal. Losing someone you love is always hard, no matter if they're alive or . . .' She couldn't finish the sentence. 'Of course you can tell me anything.'

'It's just that you've been so brave, Holly. I don't know how you do it. And here I am crying over a stupid boyfriend I went out with for only a few months.'

'Me? Brave?' Holly laughed. 'I wish.'

'Yes, you are,' Ciara insisted. 'Everyone says so. You've been so strong through everything. If I were you I'd be lying in a ditch somewhere.'

'Don't go giving me ideas, Ciara,' Holly smiled at her, wondering who on earth had called her brave.

'You're OK, though, aren't you?' Ciara said, worriedly studying her face.

Holly looked down at her hands and slid her wedding ring up and down her finger. She thought about that question for a while and the two girls became lost in their own thoughts. Ciara, suddenly calmer than Holly had ever seen her, sat by her side patiently awaiting Holly's reply.

'Am I OK?' Holly repeated the question to herself. She looked ahead at their collection of teddy bears and dolls that their parents had refused to throw out. 'I'm lots of things Ciara,' Holly explained, continuing to roll her ring around on her fingers. 'I'm lonely, I'm tired, I'm sad, I'm happy, I'm lucky, I'm unlucky; I'm a million different things everyday of the week. But I suppose OK is one of them.' She looked to her sister and smiled sadly.

'And you're brave,' Ciara assured her. 'And calm and in control. And organised.'

Holly shook her head slowly, 'No, Ciara, I'm not brave. You're the brave one. You were always the brave one. As for being in control, I don't know what I'm doing from one day to the next.'

Ciara's forehead creased and she shook her head wildly. 'No, I am far from being brave, Holly.'

'Yes you are,' Holly insisted. 'All those things that you do like jumping out of aeroplanes and snow boarding off cliffs . . .' Holly trailed off as she tried to think of more crazy things her little sister did.

Ciara shook her head in protest. 'Oh no, my dear sister. That's not brave, that's *foolish*. Anybody can bungee jump off a bridge. You could do it,' Ciara nudged her.

Holly's eyes widened, terrified at the thought and she shook her head.

Ciara's voice softened. 'Oh, you would *if you had to,* Holly. Trust me, there's nothing brave about it.'

Holly looked at her sister and matched her tone, 'Yes, and if your husband died you would cope *if you had to*. There's nothing brave about it. There's no choice involved.'

Ciara and Holly stared at each other, aware of the other's battle.

Ciara was the first to speak. 'Well, I guess you and I are more alike than we thought.' She smiled at her big sister and Holly wrapped her arms round her small frame and hugged her tightly, 'Who would have thought?'

Holly thought her sister looked like such a child, with her big innocent blue eyes. She felt as though they were both children again, sitting on the floor where they used to play together during their childhood, and where they would gossip when they were teenagers.

They sat in silence, listening to the sounds outside.

'Was there something you were going to scream at me about earlier on?' Ciara asked quietly in a childish voice. Holly had to laugh at her sister for trying to take advantage.

'No, forget about it, it was nothing,' Holly replied, staring out at the blue sky.

From outside the door, Declan wiped his brow and breathed a sigh of relief; he was in the clear. He tiptoed silently back into his bedroom and hopped back into bed. Whoever this Mathew was he owed him big time. His phone beeped, signalling a message, and he frowned as he read the text. Who the hell was Suzanne? Then a grin crept across his face as he remembered last night.

CHAPTER TWENTY-TWO

It was eight o'clock when Holly finally drove up her driveway, and it was still bright. She smiled; the world never felt quite so depressing when it was bright. She had spent the day with Ciara, chatting about her adventures in Australia. Ciara had changed her mind at least twenty times in the space of a few hours about whether or not she should call Mathew in Australia. By the time Holly left, Ciara was adamant she would never speak to him again, which probably meant she had already called him by now.

She walked up the path to the front door and stared at the garden curiously. Was it her imagination or did it look a little tidier? It was still a complete mess, with weeds and overgrown shrubs sprouting up everywhere, but something about it looked different.

The sound of a lawnmower started and Holly spun round to face her neighbour, who was out working in his garden. She waved over to thank him, presuming it was he who had helped her, and he held his hand up in response.

It had always been Gerry's job to do the garden. He wasn't necessarily a keen gardener, it was just that Holly was an incredibly unkeen one and somebody had to do the dirty work. It had been agreed between them that there was no way in the world Holly was going to waste her day off toiling in the soil. As a result, their garden was simple; just a small patch of grass surrounded by a few shrubs and flowers. As Gerry knew very little about gardening he often planted flowers in the wrong season, or put them in the wrong place so they ended up dying. Now the garden just looked like an overgrown field. When Gerry died, the garden had died along with him.

Which reminded her of the orchid in her house. She rushed inside, filled a jug with water and poured it over the extremely thirsty-looking plant. It didn't look very healthy at all and she promised herself she wouldn't let it die under her care. She threw a chicken curry into the microwave and sat down to wait at the kitchen table. Outside on the road she could still hear the kids playing happily. She always used to love when the bright evenings came; it meant Mum and Dad would let them all play outside longer, which meant she wouldn't have to go to bed till later than usual and that had always been a treat. Holly thought back over her day and decided it had been a good one, apart from one incident . . .

She looked down at the rings on her wedding finger and she immediately felt guilty. When that man Rob had walked away from her Holly had felt so awful. He had given her that look as if she was about to initiate an affair when that was the last thing in the world she would ever do. She had felt guilty for even *considering* accepting his invitation to go for a coffee.

If Holly had left her husband because she absolutely couldn't stand him any more she could understand being able eventually to be attracted to someone else. But her husband had died when they were both still very much in love and she couldn't just fall out of love all of a sudden just because he wasn't around any more. She still *felt* married, and going for coffee today would have seemed as if she was betraying Gerry. The very thought disgusted her. Her heart, soul and mind still belonged with him.

Holly twisted her ring around on her finger, lost in thought. At what point should she take her wedding ring off? Gerry was gone almost six months now. Where was the rulebook for widows that explained when exactly the ring should be taken off? And when it finally did come off, where would she put it, where *should* she put it? In the bin? Beside her bed so she could be reminded of him every single day? She continued to twist the ring around her finger and plagued herself with question after question. No, she wasn't quite ready to give up her Gerry yet. As far as she was concerned he was still living.

The microwave beeped. She took the dish out and threw it straight into the bin. She had suddenly lost her appetite.

Later that night Denise rang her in a tizzy. 'Switch Dublin FM on, quick!'

Holly raced to the radio and flicked the switch, 'I'm Tom O'Connor and you're listening to Dublin FM. If you've just joined us we are talking about bouncers. In light of the amount of persuasion it took the *Girls and the City* girls to blag their way into Boudoir, we wanna know what your thoughts on bouncers are. Do you like

197

them? Do you not? Do you agree or understand why they are the way they are? Or are they too strict? The number to call is . . .'

Holly picked the phone back up, having forgotten for a moment that Denise was still on the other end.

'Well?' Denise said, giggling.

'What the hell have we started, Denise?'

'I know,' she chuckled. It was obvious she was loving every minute of it. 'Did you see the papers today?'

'Yeah, it's all a bit silly really. I agree it was a good documentary but the stuff they were writing was just stupid.'

'Oh, honey, I love it! And I love it even more because I'm in it!'

'I bet you do,' Holly laughed.

They both remained quiet while they listened to the radio. Some guy was giving out about bouncers and Tom was trying to calm him down.

'Oh, listen to my baby,' Denise said. 'Doesn't he sound so sexy?'

'Em . . . yeah,' Holly mumbled. 'I take it you two are still together?'

'Of course.' Denise sounded insulted by the question. 'Why wouldn't we be?'

'Well, it's been quite a while now, Denise, that's all,' Holly quickly tried to explain so she wouldn't hurt her friend's feelings. 'And you always said you couldn't be with a man for over a month, that you hate being tied down to one person.'

'Yes, well, I said I *couldn't* be with a man for over a period of a month but I never said I *wouldn't*. Tom is different, Holly,' Denise added breathily.

Holly was surprised to hear this from Denise, the girl who wanted to remain single for the rest of her life. 'Oh, so what's so different with Tom then?' Holly rested the phone between her ear and her shoulder and she settled down in the chair to examine her nails.

'Oh, there's just this *connection* between us. It's like he's my soul mate. He's so thoughtful, always surprising me with little gifts and taking me out for dinner and spoiling me. He makes me laugh *all the time* and I just love being with him. I haven't got sick of him like all the other guys. *Plus* he's good-looking.'

Holly stifled a yawn. Denise tended to say this after the first week of going out with all her new boyfriends and then she would quickly change her mind. But then again, perhaps Denise meant what she said this time; after all they had been together for several weeks now.

'I'm very happy for you,' Holly replied genuinely.

The two girls began listening to a bouncer speaking on the radio.

'Well, first of all I just want to tell you that for the past few nights we have had I don't know how many princesses and ladies queuing up at our door. Since that bloody programme was aired people seem to think we're going to let them in if they're royalty! And I just want to say, girls, it's not going to work again so don't bother!'

Tom kept laughing and tried to hold himself together. Holly flicked the switch off on the radio.

'Denise,' Holly said seriously, 'the world is going mad.'

The next day Holly dragged herself out of bed to go for a stroll in the park. She needed to start doing some exercise before she turned into a complete slob and she also needed to start thinking seriously about job-hunting. Everywhere she went she tried to picture herself working in that environment. She had definitely ruled out clothes stores (the possibility of having a boss like Denise had talked her out of that one), restaurants, hotels, pubs and she certainly didn't want another nine-to-five office job, which left . . . nothing. Holly decided she wanted to be like the woman in the film she had seen last night; she wanted to work in the FBI so she could run around solving crimes and interrogating people and then eventually fall in love with her partner, whom she hated when they first met. However, seeing as she neither lived in America nor had any police training, the chances of that happening didn't seem too hopeful. Maybe there was a circus she could join somewhere . . .

She sat down on a park bench opposite the playground and listened to the children's screams of delight. She wished she could go in and play on the slide and be pushed on the swings instead of sitting here and watching. Why did people have to grow up? Holly realised she had been dreaming of going back to her youth all weekend.

She wanted to be irresponsible, she wanted to be looked after, to be told that she didn't have to worry about a thing and that someone else would take care of everything. How easy life would be without having grown-up problems to worry about. And then she could grow up all over again and meet Gerry all over again and force him to go to the doctor months earlier and then she would be sitting beside Gerry here on the bench watching their children playing. What if, what if, what if . . .

She thought about the stinging remark Richard had made about never having to bother with all that children nonsense. It angered her just thinking about it. She wished so much that she could be worrying about all that children nonsense right now. She wished she could have a little Gerry running around the playground while she shouted at him to be careful and did other mummy things, like spit on a tissue and wipe his pudgy little dirty face.

Holly and Gerry had only started talking about having children a few months before he was diagnosed. They had been so excited about it and used to lie in bed for hours trying to decide names, creating scenarios in their heads of what it would be like to be parents. Holly smiled at the thought of Gerry being a father; he would have been terrific. She could imagine him being so patient while he sat helping the kids with their homework at the kitchen table. She could imagine him being so overprotective if his daughter ever brought a boy home. Imagine if, imagine if, imagine if . . .

But Holly needed to stop living her life in her head, remembering old memories and dreaming of impossible dreams. It would never get her anywhere.

Well, talk of the devil, Holly thought to herself, seeing Richard leaving the playground with Emily and Timmy. He looked so relaxed, she thought, watching him in surprise as he chased the children around the park. They looked as though they were having fun, not a very familiar sight. She sat up on the bench and zipped up her extra layer of thick skin in preparation for their conversation.

'Hello, Holly!' Richard said happily, spotting her and walking across the grass to her.

'Hello!' Holly said, greeting the kids as they ran over

to her and gave her a big hug. That made a nice change. 'You're far from home,' she said to Richard. 'What brings you all the way over here?'

'I brought the children to see Grandma and Granddad, didn't I?' he said, ruffling Timmy's head.

'*And* we had McDonald's,' Timmy said excitedly, and Emily cheered.

'Oh, yummy!' Holly said, licking her lips. 'You lucky things. Isn't your daddy the best?'

Richard looked pleased.

'Junk food?' Holly questioned her brother.

'Ah,' he waved his hand dismissively and sat down beside her, 'everything in moderation, isn't that right, Emily?'

Five-year-old Emily nodded her head as though she had completely understood her father. Her big green eyes were wide and innocent and her nodding head was sending her red ringlets bouncing. She was eerily like her mother and Holly had to look away. Then she felt guilty and looked back and smiled . . . then had to look away again. There was something about those eyes and that hair that scared her.

'Well, one McDonald's meal isn't going to kill them,' Holly agreed with her brother.

Timmy grabbed at his throat and pretended to choke. His face went red as he made gagging noises and he collapsed on the grass and lay very still. Richard and Holly laughed. Emily looked as if she was going to cry.

'Oh dear,' Richard joked, 'looks like we were wrong, Holly. The McDonald's did kill Timmy.'

Holly looked at her brother in shock for calling his

son Timmy, but she decided not to mention it. It was obviously just a slip of the tongue.

Richard got up and threw Timmy over his shoulder. 'Well, we better go bury him now and have a funeral.' Timmy giggled as he dangled upside down on his father's shoulder.

'Oh, he's alive!' Richard laughed.

'No, I'm not,' giggled Timmy.

Holly watched in amusement at the family scene before her. It had been a while since she had witnessed anything like this. None of her friends had children and Holly was very rarely around any. There was obviously something seriously wrong with her if she was doting on Richard's children. And it wasn't the wisest decision to become broody when there was no man in your life.

'OK, we best be off,' laughed Richard. 'Bye, Holly.'

'Bye, Holly,' the children cheered, and Holly watched Richard walk off with Timmy slung over his right shoulder, as little Emily hopped, skipped and danced along beside him while gripping his hand.

Holly stared in amusement at the stranger walking off with two children. Who was this man who claimed to be her brother? Holly certainly had never met *that* man before.

CHAPTER TWENTY-THREE

Barbara finished serving her customers and as soon as they left the building she ran into the staffroom and lit up a cigarette. The travel agent's had been so busy all day and she had to work all through her lunch break. Melissa, her colleague, had called in sick that morning although Barbara knew very well she had partied too hard the night before and any sickness she might have was self-inflicted. So she was stuck in this boring job all by herself today. And, of course, it was the busiest day they'd had in ages. As soon as November came, with those horrible depressing dark nights and dark mornings and piercing wind and sheets of rain . . . everyone came running in the door, booking holidays to beautiful hot sunny countries. Barbara shuddered as she heard the wind rattle the windows and made a note to herself to check for any special holiday deals.

Her boss had finally gone out to run some errands and she had flown into the staffroom as quickly as she could to light up a cigarette. The bell over the door sounded and Barbara cursed the customer entering the shop for disturbing her precious break. She puffed on the cigarette furiously, almost making herself dizzy, reapplied her glossy red lipstick, made sure her name badge was still pinned on and sprayed her perfume all around the room, so her boss wouldn't notice the smoke. She left the staff room expecting to see a customer sitting behind the counter but instead the old man was still slowly making his way over. Barbara tried not to stare and began pressing random buttons on her keypad.

'Excuse me?' the man's weak voice called to her.

'Hello, sir, how can I help you?' she said for the hundredth time that day. She didn't mean to be rude by staring at him but she was surprised at how young the man actually was. From far away his slumped figure looked like that of a pensioner. His body was hunched and the walking stick in his hand seemed to be the only thing preventing him from collapsing to the floor in front of her. His skin was very white and pasty, as though he hadn't seen the sun for years, but he had big brown puppy eyes that seemed to smile at her from under his long lashes. She couldn't help but smile back at him.

'I was hoping to book a holiday,' he said quietly, 'but I was wondering if you could help me choose a place.'

Usually Barbara would have silently screamed at the customer for making her do this unbelievably impossible task. Most of her customers were so fussy that she could be sitting there for hours with them flicking through brochures and trying to persuade them where to go when the truth is she really couldn't give a toss where they went. But this man seemed pleasant so she was glad to help. She surprised herself.

'No problem, sir. Why don't you take a seat there and we'll search through the brochures.' She pointed to the chair in front of her and looked away again so she didn't have to watch his struggle to sit down.

'Now,' she said, full of smiles, 'is there any country in particular that you would like to go to?'

'Em . . . Spain . . . Lanzarote, I think.'

Barbara was glad; this was going to be a lot easier than she'd thought.

'And is it a summer holiday you're looking for?'

He nodded slowly.

They worked their way through the brochure and finally the man found a place that he liked. Barbara was happy that he took her advice into account, unlike some of her other customers, who just ignored every single bit of her knowledge.

'OK, any month in particular?' she said, looking at the prices.

'August?' he asked, and those big brown eyes looked so deep into Barbara's soul she just wanted to jump over the counter and give him a big hug.

'August is a good month,' she agreed with him. 'Would you like a sea view or a pool view? The sea view is an extra thirty euro,' she added quickly.

He stared into space with a smile on his face as though he was already there. 'A sea view, please.'

'Good choice. Can I take your name and address, please?'

'Oh . . . this isn't actually for me . . . it's a surprise for my wife and her friends.'

Those brown eyes looked sad. Barbara cleared her throat nervously, 'Well, that's very thoughtful of you, sir,' she felt she had to add. 'Could I have their names then, please?'

She finished taking his details and he settled the bill. She began to print the arrangements from the computer to give to him.

'Oh, do you mind if I leave the details here with you? I want to surprise my wife and I would be afraid of leaving papers around the house in case she finds them.'

Barbara smiled; what a lucky wife he had.

'I won't be telling her till July so do you think it could be kept quiet till then?'

'That's no problem at all, sir. Usually the flight times aren't confirmed till a few weeks before anyway, so we would have no reason to call her. I'll give the other staff strict instructions not to call the house.'

'Thank you for your help, Barbara,' he said, smiling sadly with those puppy eyes.

'It's been a pleasure Mr—?'

'It's Gerry,' he smiled again.

'Well, it's been a pleasure, Gerry. I'm sure your wife will have a wonderful time. My friend went there last year and she loved it.' Barbara felt the need to reassure him his wife would be fine.

'Well, I'd better head back home before they think I've been kidnapped. I'm not even supposed to be out of bed, you know.' He smiled again and a lump formed in Barbara's throat.

She jumped to her feet and ran round the other side of the counter to hold the door open for him. He smiled appreciatively as he walked past her and she watched as he slowly climbed into the taxi that had been waiting outside for him. Just as Barbara was about to close the door her boss walked in and it banged against his head. She looked over at Gerry, who was still waiting in the taxi to move out onto the road and he laughed and gave her the thumbs-up.

Her boss threw her a look for leaving the counter unattended and marched into the staffroom. 'Barbara,' he yelled, 'have you been smoking in here again?'

She rolled her eyes and turned to face him.

'God, what's wrong with you? You look like you're about to burst into tears!'

It was the first of July and Barbara sat grumpily behind the counter of Swords travel agents. Everyday she had worked this summer had been beautiful and sunny, but the last two days she'd had off it had pissed down with rain. Today was typically the complete opposite. It was the hottest day of the year, all her customers kept on bragging as they strolled in in their little shorts and skimpy tops, filling the room with the smell of coconut sun cream. Barbara squirmed in her chair in her uncomfortable and incredibly itchy uniform. She felt as if she was back at school again. She banged on the fan once again as it stalled.

'Oh, leave it, Barbara,' Melissa moaned. 'That'll only make it worse.'

'As if that could be possible,' Barbara grumbled, and spun round in her chair to face the computer where she pounded on the keypad.

'What is it with you today?' Melissa asked.

'Oh, nothing much,' Barbara said through gritted teeth. 'It's just the hottest day of the year and we're stuck in this *crappy* job in this *stuffy* room with *no air conditioning* in these horrible *itchy uniforms*.' She shouted each word towards her boss's office, hoping he would hear. 'That's all.'

Melissa sniggered. 'Look, why don't you go outside for a few minutes to get some air and I'll deal with this next customer,' she said, nodding to the woman making her way in.

'Thanks, Mel,' Barbara said, relieved at finally being able to escape. She grabbed her cigarettes. 'Right, I'm going to get some fresh air.'

Melissa looked down at her hand and rolled her eyes. 'Hello, can I help you?' she smiled at the woman.

'Yes, I was wondering if Barbara still works here?'

Barbara froze just as she was reaching the door and contemplated whether to run outside or to go back to work. She groaned and headed back to her seat. She looked at the woman behind the counter. She was pretty, she decided, but her eyes looked tired and drawn as she stared frantically from one girl to the other.

'Yes, I'm Barbara.'

'Oh, good!' The lady looked relieved and she dived on to the stool in front of her. 'I was afraid you might not work here any more.'

'She wishes,' Melissa muttered under her breath.

'Can I help you?'

'Oh God, I really hope you can,' the lady said a bit hysterically, and rooted through her bag. Barbara raised her eyebrows over at Melissa and the two of them tried to hold in their laughs.

'OK,' she said eventually, pulling a crumpled envelope out of her bag. 'I received this today from my husband and I was wondering if you could explain it to me.'

Barbara frowned as she stared at the dog-eared piece of paper on the counter. A page had been torn out of a holiday brochure and written on it were the words: 'Swords Travel Agent. Attn: Barbara.'

Barbara frowned again and looked at the page more closely. 'My friend went there two years ago on holiday but other than that it means nothing to me. Did you not get any more information?'

The lady shook her head vigorously.

'Well, can't you ask your husband for more information?' Barbara was confused.

'No, he's not here any more,' she said sadly, and tears welled in her eyes. Barbara panicked. If her boss saw her making someone cry she really would be given her marching orders. She was on her last warning as it was.

'OK then, can I take your name, and maybe it will come up on the computer?'

'It's Holly Kennedy.' Her voice shook.

'Holly Kennedy, Holly Kennedy . . .' Melissa was listening in on their conversation. 'That name rings a bell. Oh, hold on, I was about to call you this week! That's weird! I was under strict instructions by Barbara not to ring you until July for some reason—'

'Oh!' Barbara interrupted her friend, finally realising what was going on. 'You're Gerry's wife?' she asked hopefully.

'Yes!' Holly threw her hands to her face in shock. 'He was in here?'

'Yes, he was,' Barbara smiled encouragingly. 'He was a lovely man,' she said, reaching out to Holly's hand on the counter.

Melissa stared at the two of them, not knowing what was going on.

Barbara's heart went out to the lady across the counter: she was so young and it must be so hard for her right now. But Barbara was delighted to be the bearer of good news.

'Melissa, can you get Holly some tissues, please, while I explain to her exactly why her husband was here.' She beamed across the counter at Holly, then let go of Holly's hand to tap away at the computer while Melissa returned with a box of tissues.

'OK, Holly,' Barbara said softly, 'Gerry has arranged a holiday for you and a Sharon McCarthy and a Denise Hennessey to go to Lanzarote for one week, arriving on the thirtieth of July to return home on the fifth of August.'

Holly's hands flew to her face again in shock, and tears poured from her eyes.

'He was adamant that he found the perfect place for you,' Barbara continued, delighted at her new role. She felt like one of those television hosts who sprang surprises on their guests. 'That's the place you're going to,' she said, tapping the crumpled page in front of her. 'You'll have a fab time, believe me. When my friend was there she just loved it. There are loads of restaurants and bars around and . . .' She trailed off, realising Holly probably didn't give a damn about whether she had a good time or not.

'When did he come in?' Holly asked, still in shock.

Barbara tapped away on the computer. 'The booking was made on the twenty-eighth of November.'

'November?' Holly gasped. 'He shouldn't even have been out of bed then! Was he on his own?'

'Yes, but there was a taxi waiting outside for him the whole time.'

'What time was this at?' Holly asked quickly.

'I'm sorry but I really can't remember. It was quite a long time ago—'

'Yes, of course, I'm sorry,' Holly interrupted.

Barbara completely understood. If that was her husband – well, if she ever met someone worthy of ever becoming her husband – she would also want to know every single detail. Barbara told her as much as she could remember until Holly could think of no more questions to ask.

'Oh, thank you, Barbara, thank you so much.' Holly reached over the counter and gave her a big hug.

'No problem at all,' Barbara hugged her back, feeling satisfied with her good deed for the day. 'Come back and let us know how you get on,' she smiled. 'Here's your details.' She handed Holly a thick envelope and watched her walk away. She sighed, thinking her crappy job might not be so crappy after all.

'What on earth was that all about?' Melissa was dying to find out. Barbara began to explain the story.

'OK, girls, I'm taking my break now. Barbara, no smoking in the staffroom.' Their boss closed and locked his door and then turned to face them. 'Christ Almighty, what *are* you two crying about now?'

CHAPTER TWENTY-FOUR

Holly eventually arrived at her house and waved to Sharon and Denise, who were sitting on her garden wall sunbathing. They jumped up as soon as they saw her and rushed over to greet her.

'God, you both got here quick,' she said, trying to inject energy into her voice. She felt completely and utterly drained, and she really wasn't in the mood to have to explain everything to the girls right now. But she would have to.

'Sharon left work as soon as you called and she collected me from town,' Denise explained, studying Holly's face and trying to assess how bad the situation was.

'Oh, you didn't have to do that,' Holly said lifelessly, as she tried to put the key in the door.

'Hey, have you been working in your garden?' Sharon asked, looking around and trying to lighten the atmosphere.

'No, my neighbour's been doing it, I think.' Holly

pulled the key from the door and searched through the bunch for the correct one.

'You think?' Denise tried to keep the conversation going while Holly battled with yet another key in the lock.

'Well, it's either my neighbour or a little leprechaun lives down the end of my garden,' she snapped, getting frustrated with the keys. Denise and Sharon looked at each other and tried to figure out what to do. They motioned to one another to stay quiet as Holly was obviously stressed.

'Oh, fuck it!' Holly yelled, and threw her keys on the ground. Denise jumped back, just managing to avoid the heavy bunch from slamming into her ankles.

Sharon picked them up. 'Hey, hon, don't worry about it,' she said light-heartedly. 'This happens to me all the time. I swear the bloody things jump around on the keyring deliberately just to piss us off.'

Holly smiled wearily, thankful that somebody else could take control for a while. Sharon slowly worked her way through the keys, talking calmly to her in a singsong voice as though Holly was a child. The door finally opened and Holly rushed in to turn the alarm off. Thankfully she remembered the number: the year Gerry and she had met and the year they got married. As if she could ever forget those numbers.

'OK, why don't you two make yourselves comfortable in the living room and I'll follow you in a minute?' Sharon and Denise did as they were told while Holly headed into the toilet to splash cold water on her face. She needed to snap out of this daze, take control and be as excited about this holiday as Gerry had intended.

When she felt a little more alive she joined the girls in the living room.

She pulled the footrest over to the couch and sat opposite the girls.

'OK, I'm not going to drag this one out. I opened the envelope for July today and this is what it said.' She rooted in her bag for the small card, which had been attached to the brochure that she'd shown to the girl at the travel agent and handed it to them. It read:

Have a good Holly day!
PS. I love you . . .

'Is that it?' Denise wrinkled up her nose, unimpressed. Sharon nudged her in the ribs. 'Ow!'

'Well, Holly, I think it's a lovely note,' Sharon lied. 'It's so thoughtful and it's . . . a lovely play on words.'

Holly had to giggle. She knew Sharon was lying because she always flared her nostrils when she wasn't telling the truth. 'No, you fool!' she said, hitting Sharon over the head with a cushion.

Sharon began to laugh. 'Oh good, because I was beginning to worry there for a second.'

'Sharon, you are always so supportive you make me sick sometimes!' Holly grinned. 'Now this is what else was inside.' She handed them the crumpled page that was torn from the brochure.

She watched with amusement as the girls tried to figure out Gerry's writing and Denise finally held her hand up to her mouth. 'Oh my God!' she gasped, sitting forward on her seat.

'What what what?' Sharon demanded, and leaned

forward with excitement. 'Did Gerry buy you a holiday?'

'No.' Holly shook her head seriously.

'Oh.' Sharon and Denise both sat back in their seats with disappointment.

Holly allowed an uncomfortable silence to lapse between them until she spoke again.

'Girls,' she said with a smile beginning to spread across her face, 'he bought *us* a holiday!'

The girls opened a bottle of wine and squealed with excitement.

'Oh, this is incredible,' Denise said after the news had sunk in. 'Gerry's such a sweetie.'

Holly nodded, feeling proud of her husband, who had once again managed to surprise them all.

'So you went down to see this Barbara person?' Sharon asked.

'Yes, and she was the sweetest girl,' Holly smiled. 'She sat with me for ages telling me about the conversation they had that day. He went in at the end of November.'

'November?' Sharon looked thoughtful. 'That was after the second operation.'

Holly nodded. 'The girl said he was pretty weak when he went in.'

'Isn't it funny that none of us had any idea at all?' Sharon said.

They all nodded silently.

'Well, it looks like we're all off to Lanzarote!' Denise cheered, and she held her glass up. 'To Gerry!'

'To Gerry!' Holly and Sharon joined in.

'Are you sure Tom and John won't mind?' Holly asked, suddenly aware that the girls had partners to think of.

'Of course John won't mind!' Sharon laughed. 'He'll probably be delighted to be rid of me for a week!'

'Yeah, and me and Tom can go away for a week another time, which actually suits me fine,' agreed Denise, 'because that way we're not stuck together for two weeks on our first holiday together!' she laughed.

'Sure, you two practically live together anyway!' Sharon laughed, nudging her.

Denise gave a quick smile but didn't answer and the two of them dropped the subject. That annoyed Holly because they were always doing that. She wanted to hear how her friends were getting on in their relationships but nobody seemed to tell her any of the juicy gossip any more out of fear of hurting her. People seemed to be afraid to tell her about how happy they were or about the good news in their lives. Then again they also refused to moan about the bad things. So instead of being informed of what was really going on in her friends' lives she was stuck with this mediocre chitchat about . . . nothing really, and it was starting to bother her. She couldn't be shielded from other people's happiness for ever – what good would that do her?

'I have to say that leprechaun really is doing a great job on your garden, Holly,' Denise cut into her thoughts as she looked out the window.

Holly blushed. 'Oh, I know. I'm sorry for being a bitch earlier, Denise,' she apologised. 'I suppose I should really go next door and thank him properly.'

After Denise and Sharon had headed off home Holly grabbed a bottle of wine from the stash under the stairs and carried it next door to her neighbour. She rang the bell and waited.

'Hi, Holly,' Derek said, opening the door, 'come in, come in.'

Holly looked past him and into the kitchen, and saw the family sitting around the table eating dinner. She backed away from the door slightly.

'No, I won't disturb you. I just came by to give you this,' she handed him the bottle of wine, 'as a token of my thanks.'

'Well, Holly, this is really thoughtful of you,' he said, reading the label. Then he looked up with a confused expression on his face. 'But thanks for what, if you don't mind me asking?'

'For tidying up my garden,' she said, blushing. 'I'm sure the entire estate was cursing me for ruining the appearance of the street,' she laughed.

'Holly, your garden certainly isn't a worry to anyone – we all understand – but I haven't been tidying it for you, I'm sorry to say.'

'Oh.' Holly cleared her throat, feeling very embarrassed. 'I thought you had been.'

'No, no . . .'

'Well, you wouldn't by any chance know who has been?'

'I have no idea,' he said, puzzled. 'I thought it was you, to be honest,' he laughed. 'How odd.'

Holly wasn't quite sure what to say next.

'So perhaps you would like to take this back,' he said awkwardly, thrusting the wine bottle towards her.

'Oh no, that's OK,' she laughed again, 'you can keep that as thanks for . . . not being neighbours from hell. Anyway, I'll let you get back to dinner.' She ran off down the driveway with her face burning with embarrassment.

What kind of fool wouldn't know who was tidying her own garden?

She knocked on a few more doors around the estate and to her embarrassment nobody seemed to know what she was talking about. Everyone seemed to have jobs and lives and, remarkably enough, they didn't spend their days monitoring her garden. She returned to her house even more confused. As she walked in the door the phone was ringing and she ran to answer it.

'Hello?' she panted.

'What were you doing, running a marathon?'

'No I was chasing leprechauns,' Holly explained.

'Oh, cool.'

The oddest thing was that Ciara didn't even question her.

'It's my birthday in two weeks.'

Holly had completely forgotten. 'Yeah, I know,' she said matter-of-factly.

'Well, Mum and Dad want us all to go out for a family dinner . . .'

Holly groaned loudly.

'Exactly.' And she screamed away from the phone, 'Dad, Holly said the same thing as me.'

Holly giggled as she heard her father cursing and grumbling in the background.

Ciara returned to the phone and spoke loudly so her father could hear. 'OK, so my idea is to go ahead with the family dinner but to invite friends as well so that it can actually be an enjoyable night. What do you think?'

'Sounds good,' Holly agreed.

Ciara screamed away from the phone, 'Dad, Holly agrees with my idea.'

'That's all very well,' Holly heard her dad yelling, 'but I'm not paying for all those people to eat.'

'He has a point,' Holly added. 'Tell you what, why don't we have a barbecue? That way Dad can be in his element and it won't be so expensive.'

'Hey, that's a cool idea!' Ciara screamed away from the phone once again, 'Dad, what about having a barbecue?'

There was a silence.

'He's loving that idea,' Ciara came back. 'Mr Super Chef will once again cook for the masses.'

Holly smirked at the thought. Her dad got so excited when they had barbecues; he took the whole thing incredibly seriously and stood by the grill constantly, watching over his wonderful creations. Gerry had been like that too. What was it with men and barbecues? Probably because it was the only way that the two of them could actually cook. Either that or they were closet pyromaniacs.

'So will you tell Sharon and John, Denise and her DJ bloke, and will you ask that Daniel guy to come too? He's yummy!' Ciara demanded.

'Ciara, I hardly know the guy. Ask Declan to ask him; he sees him all the time.'

'No, because I want you to subtly tell him that I love him and want to have his babies. Somehow I don't think Declan would feel very comfortable doing that.'

Holly groaned.

'Stop it!' Ciara gave out. 'He's *my* birthday treat!'

'OK,' Holly gave in, 'but why do you want all my friends there? What about your friends?'

'Holly, I've lost contact with all my friends, I've been

away for so long. And all my other friends are in Australia and the stupid bastards haven't bothered to call me,' Ciara huffed.

Holly knew to whom she was specifically referring. 'But don't you think this would be a great opportunity to catch up with your old friends – you know, invite them to a barbecue? It's a nice relaxed atmosphere.'

'Yeah, right. What would I have to tell them when they start asking questions? Have you a job? Eh . . . no. Have you a boyfriend? Eh . . . no. Where do you live? Eh . . . actually I still live with my parents. How pathetic would I sound?'

Holly gave up. 'OK, whatever . . . Anyway I'll call the others and . . .'

Ciara had already hung up.

Holly decided to get the most awkward phone call out of the way first and she dialled the number to Hogan's.

'Hello, Hogan's.'

'Hi, can I speak to Daniel Connolly, please?'

'Yeah, hold on.' She was put on hold and 'Greensleeves' belted out into her ear.

'Hello?'

'Hi, Daniel?'

'Yeah, who's this?'

'It's Holly Kennedy.' She paced nervously around her bedroom, hoping he would recognise the name.

'Who?' he yelled as the noise in the background became louder.

Holly dived on to her bed in embarrassment. 'Holly Kennedy? Declan's sister?'

'Oh, Holly, hiya. Hold on a second while I go somewhere quieter.'

Holly was stuck listening to 'Greensleeves' again, and she danced around her bedroom and started singing along.

'Sorry, Holly,' Daniel said, picking up the phone again. He started laughing. 'You like "Greensleeves"?'

Holly's face went scarlet. 'Em, no, not really.' She couldn't think of what else to say, then she remembered why she was ringing.

'I was just ringing to invite you to a barbecue.'

'Oh great, yeah, I would love to go.'

'It's Ciara's birthday on Friday week – you know my sister, Ciara?'

'Eh . . . yes, the one with the pink hair.'

Holly laughed. 'Yeah, stupid question, everyone knows Ciara. Well, she wanted me to invite you to the barbecue and to subtly tell you that she wants to marry you and have your babies.'

Daniel started laughing. 'Yes . . . that was very subtle all right.'

Holly wondered whether he was interested in her sister, if she was his type.

'She'll be twenty-five,' Holly added for some unknown reason.

'Oh . . . right.'

'Em, well, Denise and your friend Tom are coming as well, and Declan will be there with his band, of course, so you'll know plenty of people.'

'Are you going?'

'Of course!'

'Good. I'll know even more people then, won't I?' he laughed.

'Oh great, she'll be delighted you're coming.'

'Well, I would feel rude for not accepting an invitation from a princess.'

At first Holly thought he was flirting and then she realised he was referring to the documentary so she mumbled some sort of incoherent answer.

He was just about to hang up the phone when a thought suddenly popped into her head. 'Oh, there's just one more thing.'

'Go for it,' he laughed.

'Is that position behind the bar still available?'

CHAPTER TWENTY-FIVE

Thank God it was a beautiful day, Holly thought as she locked her car and walked round to the back of her parents' house. The weather had drastically changed this week and it had rained and rained continuously. Ciara was in hysterics about what would become of her barbecue, and she had been hell to be with all week. Luckily for everyone's sake the weather had returned to its former splendour. Holly already had a good tan from lying out in the sun all month, one of the perks of not having a job, and she felt like showing it off today by wearing a cute little denim skirt she had bought in the summer sales and a simple tight white T-shirt that made her look even browner.

Holly was proud of the present she had bought Ciara and she knew she would love it – a butterfly belly-button ring, which had a little pink crystal in each wing. She had chosen it to co-ordinate with Ciara's new butterfly tattoo, and her pink hair, of course. She followed the sounds of laughter and was glad to see that the garden was already full with family and friends. Denise had arrived with Tom and Daniel, and they had all flaked out on the grass. Sharon had turned up without John and she was sitting chatting to Holly's mum, no doubt discussing Holly's progress in life. Well, she was out of the house, wasn't she? Holly frowned as she noted Jack was once again not present. Ever since he had helped her carry out the task of cleaning Gerry's wardrobe, he had been unusually distant. Even as children Jack had always been great at understanding Holly's needs and feelings without her having to point it out to him, but when she had told him that she needed space after Gerry's death, she didn't mean she wanted to be *completely* ignored and isolated. It was so out of character for him not to be in contact for so long. Nerves fluttered through Holly's stomach and she prayed that he was all right.

Ciara was standing in the centre of the garden, screaming at everyone and loving being the centre of attention. She was dressed in a pink bikini top, to match her pink hair, and blue denim cut-offs.

Holly approached her with her present, which was immediately grabbed from her hand and ripped open. She needn't have bothered wrapping it so neatly.

'Oh, Holly, I love it!' Ciara exclaimed and threw her arms round her sister.

'I thought you would,' Holly said, glad she had chosen the right thing because no doubt her beloved sister would have let her know about it if she hadn't.

'I'm gonna wear it now, actually,' Ciara said, ripping out her current belly-button ring and piercing the butterfly through her skin.

'Ugh,' Holly shuddered, 'I could have lived without seeing that, thank you very much.'

There was a gorgeous smell of barbecued food in the air and Holly's mouth began to water. She wasn't surprised to see all the men huddled around the barbecue, with her dad taking pride of place. Hunter men must provide food for women.

Holly spotted Richard and marched over. Ignoring the small talk she just charged right in. 'Richard, did you tidy my garden?'

Richard looked up from the barbecue with a confused expression on his face. 'Excuse me, did I what?' The rest of the men stopped their conversation and stared.

'Did you tidy my garden?' she repeated with her hands on her hips. She didn't know why she was acting so angry with him, just a force of habit probably, because if he had tidied it he had done her a huge favour. It was just annoying to keep returning home to see another section of her garden cleared and not to know who was doing it.

'When?' Richard looked around at the others frantically, as though he had been accused of murder.

'Oh, I don't know when,' she snapped. 'During the days for the past few weeks.'

'No, Holly,' he snapped back. 'Some of us have to work, you know.'

Holly glared at him and her father interjected, 'What's this, love? Is someone working on your garden?'

'Yes, but I don't know who,' she mumbled, rubbing her forehead and trying to think again. 'Is it you, Dad?'

Frank shook his head wildly, hoping his daughter hadn't finally lost the plot.

'Is it you, Declan?'

'Eh . . . think about it, Holly,' he said sarcastically.

She turned to the stranger standing next to her father. 'Is it you?'

'Um . . . no, I just flew into Dublin . . . um . . . for the . . . um weekend,' he replied nervously with an English accent.

Ciara started laughing. 'Let me help you, Holly. IS ANYBODY HERE WORKING ON HOLLY'S GARDEN?' she yelled.

The whole party stopped what they were doing and shook their heads, blank expressions on their faces.

'Now wasn't that much easier?' Ciara cackled.

Holly looked with disbelief at her sister and joined Denise, Tom and Daniel on the far side of the garden.

'Hello, Daniel,' Holly leaned over to greet Daniel with a kiss on the cheek.

'Hi, Holly. Long time no see.' He handed her a can from beside him.

'You still haven't found that leprechaun yet?' Denise laughed.

'No,' Holly said, stretching her legs out in front of her and resting back on her elbows, 'but it is just *so* odd!' She explained the story to Tom and Daniel.

'Do you think maybe your husband organised it?' Tom blurted out, and Daniel threw his friend a look.

'No,' Holly said, looking away, angry that a stranger knew her private business. 'It's not part of that.' She scowled at Denise for telling Tom her business.

Denise just held her hands up helplessly and shrugged.

Holly turned to Daniel, ignoring the other two. 'Thanks for coming, Daniel.'

227

'No problem at all. I was glad to come.'

It was weird, seeing him out of his usual wintery clothes; he was dressed in a navy vest and navy combat shorts that went just below his knees, with a pair of navy trainers. She watched his biceps as he took a slug of his beer. She had no idea he was that fit.

'You're very brown,' she commented, trying to think of an excuse for being caught staring at his biceps.

'And so are you,' he said, purposely staring at her legs.

Holly laughed and tucked them up underneath her. 'A result of unemployment. What's your excuse?'

'I was in Miami for a while last month.'

'Ooh, lucky you. Did you enjoy it?'

'Had a great time,' he nodded, smiling. 'Have you ever been?'

She shook her head, 'But at least us girls are heading off to Spain shortly. Can't wait.' She rubbed her hands together excitedly.

'Yes, I heard that. I'd say that was a nice surprise for you.' He gave her a smile, his eyes crinkling at the corners.

'You're telling me.' Holly shook her head, still not quite believing it.

They chatted together for a while about his holiday and their lives in general and Holly gave up eating her burger in front of him, as she could find no easy way of consuming it without tomato ketchup and mayonnaise dribbling down her mouth.

'I hope you didn't go to Miami with another woman or poor Ciara will be devastated,' she joked, and then kicked herself for being so nosy.

'No, I didn't,' Daniel said seriously. 'We broke up a few months ago.'

228

'Oh, I'm sorry to hear that,' she said genuinely. 'Were you together long?'

'Seven years.'

'Wow, that is a long time.'

'Yeah.' He looked away and Holly could tell he didn't feel comfortable talking about it so she quickly changed the subject.

'By the way, Daniel,' she lowered her voice to a hushed tone and he moved his head closer, 'I just wanted to thank you so much for looking out for me the way you did after the documentary. Most men run a mile when they see a girl cry; you didn't, so thank you.' Holly smiled gratefully.

'No problem at all, Holly. I don't like to see you upset.' Daniel returned the smile.

'You're a good friend,' Holly said, thinking aloud.

Daniel looked pleased. 'Why don't we go out for drinks or something before you go away?'

'Maybe I can get to know as much about you as you know about me.' Holly laughed. 'I think you know my whole life story by this stage.'

'Yeah, I'd like that,' Daniel agreed, and they arranged a time to meet.

'Oh, by the way, did you give Ciara that birthday present?' Holly asked excitedly.

'No,' he laughed. 'She's been kind of . . . busy.'

Holly turned round to look at her sister and spotted her flirting with one of Declan's friends, much to Declan's disgust. Holly laughed at her sister. So much for wanting Daniel's babies.

'I'll call her over, will I?'

'Go on,' Daniel laughed.

'Ciara!' Holly called. 'Got another pressie for you!'

'Ooh!' Ciara screamed with delight and abandoned a very disappointed-looking young man.

'What is it?' She collapsed on the grass beside them.

Holly nodded over at Daniel. 'It's from him.'

Ciara excitedly turned to face him.

'I was wondering if you would like a job working behind the bar in Club Diva?'

Ciara's hands flew to her mouth. 'Oh, Daniel, that would be brill!'

'Have you ever worked behind a bar?'

'Yeah, loads of times.' She waved her hand dismissively.

Daniel raised his eyebrows.

'Oh, I've done bar work in practically every country I've been to, honestly!' she said excitedly.

Daniel smiled. 'So do you think you'll be able for it?'

'Ooh, would I ever?' she squealed, and threw her arms around him.

Any excuse, Holly thought as she watched her sister practically strangling Daniel. His face started to turn red and he made 'rescue me' faces towards Holly.

'OK, OK, that's enough, Ciara,' she laughed, dragging her off Daniel. 'You don't want to kill your new boss.'

'Oh, sorry,' Ciara said backing off. 'This is *so* cool! I have a *job*, Holly!' she squealed again.

'Yes, I heard,' Holly laughed.

Suddenly the garden became very quiet and Holly looked round to see what was happening. Everyone was facing the conservatory as Holly's parents appeared at the door with a large birthday cake in their hands singing 'Happy Birthday'. Every one else joined in and Ciara lapped up all the attention. As her parents stepped outside Holly spotted someone following behind them carrying a huge bouquet of flowers. Her parents walked towards Ciara and placed the birthday cake on the table before her and the stranger behind slowly removed the bouquet from in front of his face.

'Mathew!' Ciara gasped.

Holly grabbed Ciara's hand as her face went white.

'I'm sorry for being such a fool, Ciara,' Mathew's Australian accent echoed around the garden. Some of Declan's friends smirked loudly, obviously feeling uncomfortable at this open show of emotion. He actually looked as if he was acting out a scene from an Australian soap, but then again drama always seemed to work for Ciara. 'I love you! Please take me back!' he announced, and everyone turned to stare at Ciara to see what she would say.

Her lower lip started to tremble and she leaped up from the grass, ran over to Mathew and jumped on him, wrapping her legs round his waist and her arms round his neck.

Holly was overcome with emotion, and tears welled in her eyes at the sight of her sister being reunited with the man she loved. Declan grabbed his camera and began filming.

Daniel put his arm round Holly's shoulders and gave her an encouraging squeeze.

'I'm sorry, Daniel,' Holly said, wiping her eyes, 'but I think you've just been dumped.'

'Not to worry,' he laughed. 'I shouldn't mix business with pleasure anyway.' He seemed relieved.

Holly continued to watch as Mathew spun Ciara round in his arms.

231

'Oh, get a room!' Declan yelled with disgust, and everyone laughed.

Holly smiled at the jazz band as she passed and looked around the bar for Denise. They had arranged to meet up in the girls' favourite bar, Juicy, favoured for its extensive cocktail menu and relaxing music. Holly had no intention of getting drunk tonight as she wanted to be able to enjoy her holiday as much as she could, starting the next day. She intended to be bright-eyed and bushy-tailed for her week of relaxation from Gerry. She spotted Denise snuggling up to Tom on a comfortable large black leather couch in a conservatory area that overlooked the River Liffey. Dublin was lit up for the night and all its colours were reflected in the water. Daniel sat opposite Denise and Tom, sucking fiercely on a strawberry daiquiri, eyes surveying the room. Nice to see Tom and Denise were ostracising everyone again.

'Sorry I'm late,' Holly apologised, approaching her friends. 'I just wanted to finish packing before I came out.'

'You're not forgiven,' Daniel said quietly into her ear as he gave her a welcoming hug and kiss.

Denise looked up at Holly and smiled, Tom waved slightly and they returned their attention to each other.

'I don't know why they even bother inviting other people out. They just sit there staring into each other's eyes, ignoring everyone else. They don't even talk to each other! And then they make you feel like you've inter-rupted them if you strike up a conversation. I think they've got some weird telepathic conversation going on there,' Daniel said, sitting down again and taking

232

another sip from his glass. He made a face at the sweet taste. 'And I really need a beer.'

Holly laughed. 'Oh, so all round it sounds like you've been having a fantastic night.'

'Sorry,' Daniel apologised. 'It's just been so long since I've spoken to another human being, I've forgotten my manners.'

Holly grinned. 'Well, I've come to rescue you.' She picked up the menu and surveyed the choice of drinks before her. She chose a drink with the lowest alcohol content and settled down in the cosy chair. 'I could fall asleep here,' she remarked, snuggling further down.

Daniel raised his eyebrows. 'Then I would *really* take it personally.'

'Don't worry, I won't,' she assured him. 'So, Mr Connolly, you know absolutely *everything* about me. Tonight I am on a mission to find out about you, so be prepared for my interrogation.'

Daniel smiled. 'OK, I'm ready.'

Holly thought about her first question. 'Where are you from?'

'Born and reared in Dublin.' He took a sip of the red cocktail and winced again. 'And if any of the people I grew up with saw me drinking this stuff and listening to jazz, I'd be in trouble.'

Holly giggled.

'After I finished school I joined the army,' he continued.

Holly raised her eyes, impressed. 'Why did you decide to do that?'

He didn't even think about it. 'Because I hadn't a clue what I wanted to do with my life, and the money was good.'

'So much for saving innocent lives.'

'I only stayed with the army for a few years.'

'Why did you leave?' Holly sipped on her lime-flavoured drink.

'Because I realised I had urges to drink cocktails and listen to jazz music and they wouldn't permit it in the army barracks,' he explained.

'Really, Daniel,' Holly laughed.

He smiled. 'Sorry, it just wasn't for me. My parents had gone down to Galway to run a pub and the idea of that appealed to me. So I moved to Galway to work there and eventually my parents retired, I took over the pub, decided a few years ago that I wanted to own one of my own, worked really hard, saved my money, took out the biggest mortgage ever and moved back to Dublin and bought Hogan's. And here I am, talking to you.'

'Well, that's a wonderful life story, Daniel.'

'Nothing special, but a life all the same.' He returned her smile.

'So where does the ex come into all this?' Holly asked.

'Laura's right in between running the pub in Galway and leaving to come to Dublin.'

'Ah . . . I see.' Holly nodded, understanding. She drained her glass and picked up the menu again. 'I think I'll have Sex on the Beach.'

'When? On your holidays?' Daniel teased.

Holly thumped him playfully on the arm. Not in a million years.

CHAPTER TWENTY-SIX

'We're all going on our summer Holly days!' the girls sang in the car all the way to the airport. John had offered to drive them there but he was fast regretting it. They were acting as though they had never left the country before. Holly couldn't remember the last time she had felt so truly excited. She felt as if she was back at school and was off on a trip. Her bag was packed with sweets, chocolate and magazines, and the girls couldn't stop singing cheesy songs in the back of the car. Their flight wasn't until 9 p.m. so they wouldn't arrive at their accommodation until the early hours of the morning.

They arrived at the airport and piled out of the car while John lifted their suitcases from the boot. Denise ran across the road and into the departure lounge as if doing so would get her to Lanzarote any faster but Holly stood back from the car and waited for Sharon, who was saying her goodbyes to her husband.

'You'll be careful now, won't you?' he asked her worriedly. 'Don't be doing anything stupid over there.'

'John, of course I'll be careful.'

John wasn't listening to a word she said. 'Because it's one thing messing around over here but you can't act like that in another country, you know.'

'John,' Sharon said, wrapping her arms around his neck, 'I'm just going for a nice relaxing holiday; you don't need to worry about me.'

He whispered something in her ear and she nodded. 'I know, I know.'

They gave each other a long goodbye kiss and Holly watched her life-long friends embrace. She felt around in the front pocket of her bag for the August letter from Gerry. She would be able to open it in a few days, lying on the beach. What luxury. The sun, sand, sea *and* Gerry all in one day.

'Holly, take care of my wonderful wife for me, will you?' John asked, breaking into Holly's thoughts.

'I will, John. We're only going for a week, you know,' Holly laughed, and gave him a hug.

'I know but after seeing what you girls get up to on your nights out, I'm just a little worried,' he smiled. 'You enjoy yourself, Holly. You deserve the rest.'

John watched them as they dragged their luggage across the road and into the airport.

Holly paused as she entered and took in a deep breath. She loved airports. She loved the smell, the noise, the whole atmosphere as people walked around happily tugging their luggage, looking forward to going on their holidays or heading back home. She loved to see people arriving and being greeted with a big cheer by their families, and she loved to watch them all giving each other emotional hugs. It was a perfect place for people spotting. The airport always gave her a feeling of anticipation in the pit of her stomach as though she was about to do something amazing. Queuing at the boarding gate felt like waiting to go on a roller coaster ride at a theme park, like an excited little child.

Holly followed Sharon and they joined Denise halfway down the extremely long check-in queue.

'I told you we should have come earlier,' Denise moaned.

'Well, then we would be waiting at the boarding gate for just the same amount of time,' reasoned Holly.

'Yeah, but at least there's a bar there,' explained Denise, 'and it's the only place in this entire stupid building that us smoker freaks can smoke in,' she mumbled.

'Good point,' Holly said.

'Now can I just point out something to you two before we even leave – I'm not going to be doing any crazy drinking or having any wild nights. I just want to be able to relax by the pool or on the beach with my book, enjoy a few meals out and go to bed early,' Sharon said seriously.

Denise looked at Holly in shock. 'Is it too late to invite someone else, Hol? What do you reckon? Sharon's bags are still packed and John can't be too far down the road.'

Holly laughed. 'No, I have to agree with Sharon on this one. I just want to go and relax and not do anything too stressful.'

Denise pouted like a child.

'Oh, don't worry, pet,' Sharon said softly, 'I'm sure there will be other kids your age who you can play with.'

Denise threw her the finger. 'Well, if they ask me if I have anything to declare when we get there I'm telling everyone my two friends are dry shites.'

Sharon and Holly sniggered.

After thirty minutes of queuing they finally checked in and Denise ran around the shop like a mad woman, buying a lifetime's supply of cigarettes.

'Why is that girl staring at me?' Denise said through gritted teeth, eyeing up the woman at the end of the bar.

'Probably because you're staring at her,' Sharon responded, checking her watch. 'Only fifteen more minutes.'

'No, honestly, girls,' Denise turned back round to face them, 'I'm not being paranoid here. She is definitely staring at us.'

'Well then, why don't you go over to her and ask her if she wants to take it outside,' Holly joked, and Sharon smirked.

'Oh, here she comes,' Denise said, and turned her back to her.

Holly looked up and saw a skinny blonde-haired girl with big fake tits heading towards them. 'You better get those knuckle-dusters out, Denise. She looks like a dangerous one,' Holly teased, and Sharon almost choked on her drink.

'Hi, there!' the girl squeaked.

'Hello,' Sharon said, trying not to laugh.

'I didn't mean to be rude by staring but I just had to come over and see if it was really you!'

'It's me all right,' Sharon said, 'in the flesh.'

'Oh, I just *knew* it!' the girl squealed, and jumped up and down with excitement. Unsurprisingly her chest stayed still. 'My friends kept telling me I was wrong but I *knew* it was you! That's them over there.' She turned round and pointed to the end of the bar, and the other

238

four spice girls twinkled their fingers back. 'My name's Cindy . . .'

Sharon nearly choked on her water again.

'. . . and I'm just the biggest fan of all of you,' she squealed excitedly. 'I just love that show that you're all in. I've watched it dozens and dozens of times! You play Princess Holly, don't you?' she said, pointing a manicured nail in Holly's face.

Holly opened her mouth to speak but Cindy kept on talking.

'And you play her lady!' she pointed at Denise. 'And *you*,' she squealed even louder, pointing at Sharon, 'you were friends with that Australian rock star!'

The girls looked at each other worriedly as she pulled out a chair and sat down at their table.

'You see, I'm an actress myself . . .'

Denise rolled her eyes.

'. . . and I would just love to work on a show like yours. When are you making the next one?'

Holly opened her mouth to explain that they weren't actually actresses but Denise beat her to it.

'Oh, we're in discussions right now about our next project,' she lied.

'How fantastic!' Cindy clapped her hands. 'What's it about?'

'Well, we can't really say right now but we have to go to Hollywood for filming.'

Cindy looked as if she was going to have a heart attack. 'Oh my God! Who's your agent?'

'Frankie,' Sharon interrupted Denise, 'so Frankie and us are all going to Hollywood.'

Holly couldn't hold her laugh in.

239

'Oh, don't mind her, Cindy, she's just excited,' explained Denise.

'Wow, and so you should be!' Cindy looked down at Denise's boarding pass on the table and nearly had heart failure. 'Wow, you girls are going to Lanzarote too!'

Denise grabbed her boarding pass and shoved it in her bag, as if that would make a difference.

'I'm going there with my friends. They're just over there.' She turned round *again* and waved at them *again* and they waved back *again*. 'We're staying in a place called Costa Palma Palace. Where are you guys staying?'

Holly's heart sunk. 'Oh I can't quite remember the name, girls, can you?' She looked to Sharon and Denise with wide eyes.

They shook their heads vigorously.

'Oh well, not to worry.' Cindy shrugged her shoulders happily. 'I'll see you when we land anyway! I better go now and board. I wouldn't want the plane to fly off without me!' she squeaked so loudly that the surrounding tables turned to stare. She gave each of the girls a big hug and tottered off back to her friends.

'Looks like we needed those knuckle-dusters after all,' Holly said miserably.

'Oh, it doesn't matter,' perked up Sharon, always the optimist. 'We can just ignore her.'

They all stood up and headed over to the boarding gate. As they made their way to their seats on the plane Holly's heart sunk once again and she immediately dived onto the seat on the far side of the aisle. Sharon sat down beside her and Denise's face was a picture when she realised who she had to sit next to.

'Oh, fab! You get to sit beside me!' Cindy squeaked at Denise.

Denise threw Sharon and Holly the nastiest look and plonked herself beside Cindy.

'See? I told you that you'd find yourself a little friend to play with,' Sharon whispered to Denise.

Sharon and Holly broke into fits of laughter.

CHAPTER TWENTY-SEVEN

Four hours later the plane glided over the sea and landed at Lanzarote airport. Everyone cheered and applauded and no one on the plane was more relieved than Denise.

'Oh, I have the biggest headache,' she complained to the girls as they made their way to the luggage reclaim. 'That bloody girl just talks and talks and talks.' She massaged her temples and closed her eyes, relieved at the peace.

Sharon and Holly spotted Cindy and her crew making their way over to them and dashed off into the crowd, leaving Denise standing alone with her eyes closed.

They beat their way through the rabble so they had a good view of the luggage. Everybody thought it would be a great idea to stand right next to the conveyer belt and to lean forward so that nobody beside could see what was coming. They stood there for almost a half an hour before the conveyer belt even started moving and a further half an hour later they were still standing there waiting for their bags while the majority of the crowd had headed outside to their coaches.

'You bitches,' Denise said, angrily approaching them, dragging her suitcase behind her. 'You still waiting for your bags?'

'No I just find it strangely comforting standing here and watching the same leftover bags going around and around and around. Why don't you go on ahead to the coach and I'll just stay here and continue enjoying myself?' Sharon said.

'Well, I hope they lost your case,' Denise snapped, 'or even better, I hope your bag bursts open and all your big knickers and bras are spread all over the conveyer belt for everyone to see.'

Holly looked at Denise with amusement. 'You feel better now?'

'Not until I have a cigarette,' she replied, but she still managed to smile.

'Ooh, there's my bag!' Sharon said happily, and swung it off the conveyer belt, managing to whack Holly in the shins.

'OW!'

'Sorry, but must save clothes.'

'If they lost my clothes I'm going to sue them,' Holly said angrily. By now everyone had left and they were the only people still inside. 'Why am I always the last person waiting for my bags?' she asked her friends.

'Murphy's law,' Sharon explained. 'Ah, here it is.' She grabbed the suitcase and once again whacked it against Holly's already sore shins.

'OW! OW! OW!' Holly yelled, rubbing her legs, 'Could you at least swing the bloody thing the other way?'

'Sorry,' Sharon looked apologetic, 'I only swing one way, darling.'

The three of them headed off to meet their holiday rep.

'Stop, Gary! Get off me!' they heard a voice screeching as they rounded a corner. They followed the sound and spotted a young woman dressed in a red holiday rep uniform being attacked by a young man also dressed in a holiday rep uniform. The girls approached her and she straightened herself up.

'Kennedy, McCarthy and Hennessey?' she said in a thick London accent.

The girls nodded.

'Hi, I'm Victoria and I'm your holiday rep for the next week.' She plastered a smile on her face. 'So follow me and I'll show you to the coach.' She winked cheekily at Gary and led the girls outside.

It was two o'clock in the morning, and yet a warm breeze greeted them as they stepped outside. Holly smiled at the girls; now they were really on holiday.

When they stepped on the coach everybody cheered and Holly silently cursed them all, hoping this wasn't going to be a cheesy 'let's all make friends' holiday.

'Woo-hoo,' Cindy sang over to them. She was standing up and waving over at them. 'I kept you all a seat back here!'

Denise sighed loudly over Holly's shoulder and the girls trudged down to the back seat of the bus. Holly was fortunate enough to sit next to the window where she could ignore the rest of them. With luck Cindy would understand that she wanted to be left alone, the major hint being the fact that Holly had ignored her since the moment she had tottered over to their table.

Forty-five minutes later they reached Costa Palma

Palace and the excitement once again returned to Holly's stomach. There was a long driveway in and tall palm trees lined the centre of the drive. A large fountain was lit up with blue lights outside the main entrance and, to her annoyance, everybody on the bus cheered once again when they pulled up outside. The girls were booked into a studio apartment that was a nice neat size, containing one bedroom with twin beds, a small kitchen and living area with a sofa bed, a bathroom and a balcony. Holly stepped on to the balcony and looked out to the sea. Although it was too dark to see anything Holly could hear the water gently lapping up against the sand. She closed her eyes and listened.

'Cigarette, cigarette, must have cigarette,' Denise joined her, ripping the cigarette packet open and inhaling deeply. 'Ah! That's much better; I no longer have the desire to kill people.'

Holly laughed; she was looking forward to spending time with her friends.

'Hol, do you mind if I sleep on the sofa bed? That way I can keep the door open and smoke . . .'

'Only if you do keep the door open, Denise,' Sharon yelled from inside. 'I'm not waking up in the morning to the stink of smoke.'

'Thanks,' Denise said happily.

At nine o'clock that morning Holly was woken up to the sound of Sharon stirring. Sharon whispered to her she was going down to the pool to save them some sun beds.

Fifteen minutes later she returned to the apartment. 'The Germans have nicked all the sun beds,' she said grumpily. 'I'll be down on the beach if you want me.'

Holly sleepily mumbled a response and fell back asleep again.

At ten o'clock Denise jumped on her in bed and they decided to get up and join Sharon at the beach.

The sand was hot, and they had to keep moving so as not to burn the soles of their feet. As proud as Holly had been about her tan back in Ireland, it was obvious they had just arrived on the island. They were the whitest people there. They spotted Sharon sitting under the shade of an umbrella, reading her book.

'Oh, this is so beautiful, isn't it?' Denise smiled, looking around.

'Heaven,' Sharon agreed.

Holly gazed about, hoping Gerry had come to the same heaven. Nope, no sign of him. All around her there were couples: couples massaging sun cream onto each other's bodies, couples walking hand in hand along the beach, couples playing beach tennis and, directly in front of her sun bed, a couple snuggled up together sunbathing. But Holly didn't have time to be depressed as Denise had stepped out of her sundress and was hopping around on the hot sand in nothing but a skimpy leopardskin thong, demanding attention.

'Will one of you put sun cream on me?'

Sharon put her book down and stared at her over the rim of her reading glasses. 'I'll do it but you can put the cream on your tits and bum yourself.'

'Damn,' Denise joked. 'Don't worry about it, I'll go ask someone else then.' She sat at the end of Sharon's sun bed while she applied the cream. 'You know what, Sharon?'

'What?'

'You'll get an awful tan line if you keep that sarong on.'

Sharon looked down at herself and pulled the little skirt further down her legs. 'What tan? I never get a tan. Denise, didn't you know that the colour blue was the new brown.'

Holly and Denise laughed. As much as Sharon tried to tan over the years she just ended up getting sunburned and then it would peel. She had finally given up trying for a tan and accepted the fact that her skin was meant to be pale.

'Besides, I look like such a blob these days I wouldn't want to scare everyone off.'

Holly looked at her friend, annoyed at her for calling herself a blob. She had put a little bit of weight on but was by no means fat.

'Why don't you go up to the swimming pool then, and scare all those Germans away?' Denise joked.

'Yeah, girls, we really need to get up earlier tomorrow to get a place by the pool. The beach gets boring after a while,' Holly suggested.

'Don't vorry. Ve vill get ze Germans,' joked Sharon.

The girls relaxed by the beach for the rest of the day, occasionally dipping themselves into the sea to cool down. They ate lunch at the beach bar and generally had a lazy day just as they had planned. Holly gradually felt all the stress and tension working its way out of her muscles, and for a few hours she felt free.

That night they successfully managed to avoid the Barbie brigade and they enjoyed dinner in one of the many restaurants that lined the busy street not far from the apartment complex.

'I can't believe it's ten o'clock and we're heading back to the apartment already,' Denise said, staring longingly at the huge choice of bars around them.

People overflowed from the bars onto the streets, music, vibrating from every building, mixing together to form an unusual eclectic sound. Holly could almost feel the ground pulsing beneath her. Conversation between them stopped as they took in the sights, sounds and smells around them. There was loud laughter, clinking glasses and singing coming from every direction. Neon lights flashed and buzzed, each bar battling for custom. On the street, bar owners fought hard against each other to convince passers-by to enter, handing out leaflets, free drinks and concessions.

Tanned young bodies hung out in big groups around the outdoor tables and strolled confidently by them on the street, the smell of coconut sun cream rich in the air. Looking at the average age of the clientele, Holly felt old.

'Well, we can go to a bar for a few drinks if you want,' she said uncertainly, watching the younger ones dancing around on the street.

Denise stopped walking and assessed the bars.

'All right, beautiful.' A very attractive man stopped and flashed his pearly whites at Denise. He had an English accent. 'Are you coming in here with me?'

Denise stared at the young man for a while, lost in thought. Sharon and Holly smirked at each other, knowing that Denise wouldn't be going to bed early after all. In fact, Denise may not get to bed at all tonight, knowing her.

Finally Denise snapped out of her trance and

straightened herself up. 'No, thank you. I have a boyfriend and I love him!' she announced proudly. 'Come on girls!' she said to Holly and Sharon, and walked off in the direction of the apartment.

The two girls remained on the street, mouths open in shock. They couldn't quite believe it. They had to run to catch up with her.

'What are you two gawking at?' Denise smiled.

'You,' Sharon said, still shocked. 'Who are you and what have you done with my man-eating friend?'

'OK,' Denise held her hands up in the air and grinned, 'maybe being single isn't all it's cracked up to be.'

Holly lowered her eyes and kicked a stone along the path as they made their way back to their resort. It sure wasn't.

'Well, good for you, Denise,' Sharon said happily, wrapping her arm round Denise's waist and giving her a little squeeze.

A silence fell between them and Holly listened as the music faded away slowly, leaving only a beat of the bass in the distance.

'That street made me feel so old,' Sharon said suddenly.

'Me too!' Denise's eyes widened. 'Since when did people start going out so young?'

Sharon began to laugh. 'Denise, the people aren't getting younger; *we* are getting older, I'm afraid.'

Denise thought about that for a while. 'Well, it's not like we're *old*, old for God's sake. I mean it's not exactly time for us to hang up our dancing shoes and grab our walking sticks. We could stay out all night if we wanted to, we just . . . are tired. We've had a long day . . . oh God, I do sound old.' Denise rambled on to herself as

249

Sharon was too busy watching Holly, head down, still kicking a stone along the path.

'Holly, are you OK? You haven't said a word in a while.'

'Yeah, I was just thinking,' Holly said quietly, keeping her head down.

'Thinking about what?' Sharon asked softly.

Holly's head shot up. 'Gerry.' She looked at the girls. 'I was thinking about Gerry.'

'Let's go down to the beach,' Denise suggested and they slipped out of their shoes and allowed their feet to sink into the cooling sand.

The sky was clear black and a million little stars twinkled down on them, as if someone had thrown glitter up into a massive black net. The full moon rested itself low over the horizon, reflecting its beam and showing where the sea met the sky. The girls sat in its path along the shore. The musical water gently lapped before them, calming them, relaxing them. The air was warm but a slight breeze brushed past Holly, causing her hair to tickle her skin. She closed her eyes, took a deep breath and filled her lungs with fresh air.

'That's why he brought you here, you know,' Sharon said, watching her friend relaxing.

Holly's eyes remained closed and she smiled.

'You don't talk about him enough, Holly,' Denise said, casually making designs with her finger in the sand.

Holly slowly opened her eyes. Her voice was quiet but warm and silky. 'I know.'

Denise looked up from drawing circles in the sand. 'Why not?'

Holly paused for a while and looked out to the black

sea. 'I don't know how to talk about him.' She paused again. 'I don't know whether to say "Gerry was" or "Gerry is". I don't know whether to be sad or happy when I talk about him to other people. It's like if I'm happy when I talk about him, certain people judge and expect me to be crying my eyes out. When I'm upset when talking about him it makes people feel uncomfortable.' She stared out to the sparkling black sea and her voice was quieter when she spoke again. 'I can't tease about him in conversation like I used to because it feels *wrong*. I can't talk about things he told me in confidence because I don't want to give his secrets away, because they're *his* secrets. I just don't quite know *how* to remember him in conversation. It doesn't mean I don't remember him up here,' she tapped her temples.

The three girls continued to sit cross-legged on the soft sand.

'Me and John talk about Gerry all the time.' Sharon looked at Holly with glittering eyes. 'We talk about the times he made us laugh, which was *a lot*. We even talk about the times we fought. Things we loved about him, things he did that *really* annoyed us.'

Holly raised her eyebrows.

Sharon continued, 'Because to us, that's just how Gerry was. He wasn't all nice. We remember *all* of him and there's absolutely *nothing* wrong with that.'

There was a long silence.

Denise was the first to speak. 'I wish my Tom had known Gerry.' Her voice trembled a little.

Holly looked at her in surprise.

'Gerry was my friend too,' Denise said, tears pricking in her eyes. 'And Tom doesn't even know him at all. So

251

I try to tell him things about Gerry all the time, just so he knows that not long ago one of the nicest men on this earth was *my* friend and I think *everyone* should have known him.' Her lip wobbled and she bit down on it hard. 'But I can't believe that someone I now love so much, who knows everything else about me, doesn't know a friend who I loved for ten years.'

A tear ran down Holly's cheek and she reached out to hug her friend. 'Well then, Denise, we'll just have to keep telling Tom about him, won't we?'

They didn't bother meeting up with their holiday rep the next morning, as they had no intention of going on any tours or taking part in any silly sports tournaments. Instead, they got up early and took part in the sun bed dance, running around trying to throw their towels on the sun beds to reserve their positions for the day. Unfortunately, they still didn't manage to get up early enough. ('Don't those bloody Germans ever sleep?' Sharon gave out.) Finally, after Sharon had sneakily thrown a few towels away from some unattended beds, the girls managed to get three beds together.

Just as Holly found herself nodding off she heard piercing screams and a crowd ran by her. For some reason, Gary, the holiday rep the girls had seen at the airport, thought it would be a really funny idea to dress in drag and be chased around the swimming pool by Victoria. Everyone around the pool cheered them on as the girls rolled their eyes. Eventually Victoria caught Gary and they both managed to fall on top of each other into the swimming pool.

Everyone applauded.

Minutes later, as Holly was taking a quiet swim, a woman announced into a microphone attached to her head that she was going to begin aqua aerobics in the pool in five minutes. Victoria and Gary, helped by the Barbie brigade, ran round all the sun beds, dragging everyone up and forcing them to take part.

'Ah, would you ever fuck off!' Holly heard Sharon screaming as someone tried to drag her into the pool. Holly was soon forced out of the pool by what looked like an approaching herd of hippopotami, who were about to dive in for their much-needed aqua aerobics session. They sat through an incredibly annoying half-hour session of aerobics with the instructor yelling out the movements into the headpiece. When it was finally over they announced a water polo tournament was about to take place, so the girls immediately jumped up and headed over to the beach for some peace and quiet.

'You ever hear from Gerry's parents, Holly?' Sharon asked as they lounged on their Lilos in the sea.

'Yeah, they send me postcards every few weeks, telling me where they are and how they're getting on.'

'So they're still on that cruise?'

'Yeah.'

'Do you miss them?'

'To be honest, their son's gone and they have no grand-children so I don't really think they feel we have any connection any more.'

'That's bullshit, Holly. You were married to their son and that makes you their daughter-in-law. That's a very strong connection.'

'Oh, I don't know,' she sighed. 'I just don't think that's enough for them.'

'They're a bit backward, aren't they?'

'Yeah, *very*. They hated me and Gerry "living in sin", as they said. Couldn't wait for us to get married. And *then* they were even worse when we did! They couldn't understand why I wouldn't change my name.'

'Yeah, I remember that,' Sharon laughed. 'His mum gave me an earful at the wedding. She said it was the woman's duty to change her name as a sign of respect to her husband. Imagine that? The cheek of her!'

Holly laughed.

'Ah well, you're better off without them being around anyway,' Sharon assured her.

'Hello, girls.' Denise floated out to meet them.

'Hey, where have you been?' Holly asked.

'Oh, I was just chatting to some bloke from Miami. Really nice guy.'

'Miami? That's where Daniel went on holiday,' Holly replied, lightly running her fingers through the clear blue water.

'Hmm,' Sharon mused, 'nice guy, Daniel, isn't he?'

'Yeah, he's a really nice guy,' Holly agreed. 'Very easy to talk to.'

'Tom was telling me he's really been through the wars recently,' Denise said, turning to lie on her back.

Sharon's ears pricked up at the sound of gossip, 'Why's that?'

'Oh, he was engaged to be married to some chick and it turns out she was sleeping with someone else. That's why he moved to Dublin and bought the pub, to get away from her.'

'I know. It's awful, isn't it?' Holly said sadly.

'Where did he live before?' Sharon asked.

'Galway. He used to run a pub there,' Holly explained.

'Oh,' Sharon said, surprised, 'he doesn't have a Galway accent.'

'Well, he grew up in Dublin and joined the army, then he left and moved to Galway where his family own a pub, then he met Laura, they were together for seven years, were engaged to be married but she cheated on him so they broke up and he moved back to Dublin and bought Hogan's.' Holly caught her breath.

'Don't know much about him, do you?' Denise teased.

'Well, if you and Tom had paid the slightest bit of attention to us the other night in the pub, then maybe I wouldn't know so much about him.' Holly rolled her eyes at Sharon. 'Honestly, Sharon, they invite me and Daniel out and then they ignore us both.' She pretended to be insulted.

Denise sighed loudly. 'God, I really miss Tom.'

'Did you tell the guy from Miami that?' Sharon laughed.

'No I was just chatting to him,' Denise said defensively. 'To be honest, nobody else interests me. It's really weird – it's like I can't even *see* any other men, I don't even *notice* them. And as we are currently surrounded by hundreds of half-naked men I think that's saying a lot.'

'I think they call it love, Denise,' Sharon smiled.

'Well, whatever it is I've never felt like this before.'

'It's a nice feeling,' Holly said, more to herself.

They lay in silence for a while, lost in their own thoughts, allowing the gentle motion of the waves to soothe them.

'Holy shit!' Denise suddenly yelled, causing the other two to jump. 'Look how far out we are!'

Holly sat up immediately and looked around. They were out so far from the shore everybody on the beach looked like little ants.

'Oh, shit!' panicked Sharon, and as soon as Sharon panicked Holly knew they were in trouble.

'Start swimming quick!' Denise yelled, and they lay on their stomachs and started splashing around with all their might. After a few minutes of tirelessly going at it they gave up, out of breath. To their horror they were even further out than they had been when they started.

It was no use, the tide was moving out too quickly and the waves were just too strong.

CHAPTER TWENTY-EIGHT

'Help!' Denise screamed at the top of her lungs and waved her arms wildly.

'I don't think they can hear us,' Holly said, tears welling in her eyes.

'Oh, could we be any more stupid?' Sharon gave out, and continued to rant on about the dangers of Lilos in the sea.

'Oh, forget about that, Sharon,' Denise snapped. 'We're here now so let's all scream together and maybe they'll hear us.'

They all cleared their throats and sat up on their Lilos as much as they possibly could without causing them to sink under their weight.

'OK one, two, three . . . HELP!' they all yelled, and waved their arms frantically.

Eventually they stopped screaming and stared in silence at the dots on the beach to see if it had made any impact. Everything remained as it was.

'Please tell me there aren't any sharks out here,' Denise whimpered.

'Oh, please, Denise,' Sharon snapped viciously, 'that is the last thing we need to be reminded of right now.'

Holly gulped and stared down into the water. The once-clear blue water had darkened. Holly hopped off her Lilo to see how deep it was and as her legs dangled her heart began to pound. This was bad.

Sharon and Holly tried to swim for it while dragging their Lilos behind them, while Denise continued her bloodcurdling screams.

'Jesus, Denise,' Sharon panted, 'the only thing that's gonna respond to that is a dolphin.'

'Look, why don't you two just stop swimming because you've been at it now for a few minutes and you're still right beside me?'

Holly stopped swimming and looked up, Denise stared back at her.

'Oh.' Holly tried to hold back her tears. 'Sharon, we might as well stop and save our energy.'

Sharon stopped swimming and the three of them huddled together on their Lilos and cried. There was really nothing more they could do, Holly thought, her panic increasing. They had tried shouting for help but the wind was carrying their voices in the other direction; they had tried swimming, which had been completely pointless, as the tide was too strong. It was beginning to get chilly and the sea was looking dark and ugly. What a stupid situation to get themselves into. Through all her fear and worry, Holly managed to surprise herself by feeling completely humiliated.

She wasn't sure whether to laugh or cry, but the unusual

258

sound of both began to tumble out of her mouth, causing Sharon and Denise to stop crying and stare at her as though she had ten heads.

'At least one good thing came out of this,' Holly half-laughed and half-cried.

'There's a good thing?' Sharon said, wiping her eyes.

'Well, the three of us always talked about going to Africa,' she sniggered like a mad woman, 'and by the looks of things I would say we're probably halfway there.'

The girls looked out to sea, to their future destination.

'It's a cheaper mode of transport too,' Sharon joined in.

Denise stared at them as if they were mad, and just one look at her lying in the middle of the ocean, naked except for a leopardskin thong, and with blue lips, was enough to set the girls off laughing.

'What?' Denise looked at them wide-eyed.

'I'd say we're in deep, deep trouble here,' Sharon giggled.

'Yeah,' Holly agreed. 'We're in way over our heads.'

They lay there laughing and crying for a few minutes more till the sound of a speed boat approaching caused Denise to sit up and start waving frantically again. Holly and Sharon laughed even harder at the sight of Denise's chest bouncing up and down as she waved at the approaching lifeguards.

'It's just like a regular night out with the girls,' Sharon laughed, watching Denise being dragged half-naked into the boat by a muscular lifeguard.

'I think they're in shock,' one lifeguard said to the other as they dragged the remaining hysterical girls onto the boat.

'Quick, save the Lilos!' Holly just about managed to blurt out through her laughter.

'Lilo overboard!' Sharon screamed.

The lifeguards looked at each other worriedly, as they wrapped warm blankets around the girls and sped off back to the shore.

As they approached the beach there appeared to be a large crowd gathering. The girls looked at each other and laughed even harder. As they were lifted off the boat there was a huge applause; Denise turned and curtsied to them all.

'They clap now, but where were they when we needed them?' Sharon grumbled.

'Traitors,' Holly agreed.

'There they are!' They heard a familiar squeal and saw Cindy and the Barbie brigade pushing their way through the crowd. 'Oh my God!' she squeaked. 'I saw the whole thing through my binoculars and called the lifeguards. Are you OK?' She looked to each of them frantically.

'Oh, we're fine,' Sharon said rather seriously. 'We were the lucky ones. The poor Lilos never even had a chance.' With that Sharon and Holly cracked up laughing and they were ushered away to be looked at by a doctor.

That night the girls realised the seriousness of what had happened to them and their moods drastically changed. They sat almost in silence throughout dinner, all thinking about how lucky they were to be rescued and kicking themselves for being so careless. Denise squirmed uncomfortably in her chair and Holly noticed she had barely touched her food.

'What's wrong with you?' Sharon said, sucking in a

piece of spaghetti and causing the sauce to splash all over her face.

'Nothing,' Denise said quietly, refilling her glass with water.

They sat in silence for a while longer.

'Excuse me, I'm going to the toilet.' Denise stood up and walked awkwardly to the ladies.

Sharon and Holly frowned at each other.

'What do you think is wrong with her?' Holly asked.

Sharon shrugged. 'Well, she's drunk about ten litres of water through dinner so no wonder she keeps going to the toilet,' she exaggerated.

'I wonder if she's mad at us for going a bit funny out there today.'

Sharon shrugged again and they continued to eat in silence. Holly had reacted unusually out there in the water and it bothered her to think about why she had. After the initial panic of thinking she was going to die, she'd become feverishly giddy as she'd realised that if she did she would be with Gerry, that she didn't care whether she lived or died. Those were selfish thoughts. She needed to change her perspective on her life.

Denise winced as she sat down.

'Denise, what is wrong with you?' Holly asked.

'I'm not telling either of you or you'll laugh,' she said childishly.

'Oh, come on, we're your friends. We won't laugh,' Holly said, trying to keep the smile off her face.

'I said no.' She filled her glass with more water.

'Ah, come on, Denise, you know you can tell us anything. We promise not to laugh.' Sharon said it so seriously that Holly felt bad for smiling.

Denise studied both their faces trying to decide whether they could be trusted.

'Oh, OK,' she sighed loudly, and mumbled something very quietly.

'What?' Holly said, moving in closer.

'Honey, we didn't hear you, you were too quiet,' Sharon said, pulling her chair in as well.

Denise looked around the restaurant to make sure nobody was listening and she moved her head into the centre of the table. 'I said, from lying out in the sea for so long, my bum is sunburned.'

'Oh,' Sharon said, sitting back in her chair abruptly.

Holly looked away to avoid eye contact with Sharon and she counted the bread rolls in the basket to take her mind off what Denise had just said.

There was a long silence.

'See, I told you you would both laugh,' Denise huffed.

'Hey, we're not laughing,' Sharon said shakily.

There was another silence.

Holly couldn't help herself. 'Just make sure you put plenty of sun cream on it so that it doesn't peel.' The two of them broke down.

Denise just nodded her head and waited for them to stop laughing. She had to wait a long time. In fact, hours later, as she lay on the sofa bed trying to sleep, she was still waiting.

The last thing she heard before she went to sleep was a smart remark from Holly. 'Make sure you lie on your front, Denise.'

'Hey, Holly,' Sharon whispered after they had finally calmed down, 'are you excited about tomorrow?'

'What do you mean?' Holly asked yawning.

'The letter!' Sharon replied, surprised that Holly didn't remember immediately. 'Don't tell me that you forgot.'

Holly reached her hand under her pillow and felt around for the letter. In one hour she would be able to open Gerry's sixth letter. Of course she hadn't forgotten.

The next morning Holly awoke to the sound of Sharon throwing up in the toilet. She followed her in and gently rubbed her back and held her hair back.

'You OK?' she asked worriedly after Sharon had eventually stopped.

'Yeah, it's just those bloody dreams I had all night. I dreamed I was on a boat and on a Lilo, I think it made me seasick.'

'I had those dreams too. It was scary yesterday, wasn't it?'

Sharon nodded. 'I'm never going on a Lilo again,' she smiled weakly.

Denise arrived at the bathroom door, already dressed in her bikini. She had borrowed one of Sharon's sarongs to cover up her burned behind and Holly had to bite her tongue to stop herself from teasing her, as she was clearly in a great deal of pain.

When they arrived at the swimming pool, Denise and Sharon joined the Barbie brigade. Well, it was the least they could do, seeing as they were the ones who had called for help. Holly couldn't believe that she had fallen asleep before midnight the previous night. She had planned to get up quietly without waking the girls, sneak out to the balcony and read the letter. How she fell asleep in all her excitement was beyond her, but she couldn't listen to the Barbie brigade any longer. Before Holly was dragged into any conversation she signalled to Sharon that she was leaving and Sharon gave her an encouraging wink, knowing why she was disappearing. Holly wrapped her sarong around her hips and carried her small beach bag containing the all-important letter.

She positioned herself away from all the excited shouts of children and adults playing and ghetto blasters blaring out the latest chart songs. She found a quiet corner and made herself comfortable on her beach towel to avoid more contact with the burning sand. The waves crashed and fell. The seagulls called out to one another in the clear blue sky, flew down, dipped themselves into the cool, crystal water to catch their breakfasts. It was morning and already the sun was hot.

Holly carefully pulled the letter out of her bag as though it was the most delicate thing in the world and she ran her fingers along the neatly written word 'August'. Taking in all the sounds and smells of the world around her she gently tore open the seal and read Gerry's sixth message.

Hi, Holly,

I hope you're having a wonderful holiday. You're looking beautiful in that bikini, by the way! I hope I picked the right place for you. It's where you and I almost went for our honeymoon, remember? Well, I'm glad you got to see it in the end . . .

Apparently if you stand at the very end of the beach near the rocks across from your apartment, and look round the corner to the left, you'll see a lighthouse. I'm told that's where the dolphins

gather . . . not many people know that. I know
you love dolphins . . . tell them I said hi . . .
     PS. I love you, Holly . . .

With shaking hands Holly put the card back into the envelope and secured it safely in a pocket of her bag. She would guard it with her life until she returned home to Dublin where it would take pride of place with the other envelopes in the top drawer of her bedside cabinet. She felt Gerry's eyes on her as she stood up and quickly rolled up the beach towel. She felt as though he was here with her. She quickly ran to the end of the beach that suddenly stopped at a cliff. She put her trainers on and began to climb the rocks so she could see around the corner.

And there it was.

Exactly where Gerry had described it, the lighthouse sat high on the cliff, bright white, as though it was some sort of torch to heaven. Holly carefully climbed over the rocks and made her way round the little cove. She was on her own now. It was completely private. And then she heard the noises: the playful squeaks of dolphins playing near to the shore, away from the view of all the tourists on the beach beside it. Holly collapsed on the sand to watch them play and listen to them talk to one another.

Gerry sat beside her.

He may have even held her hand.

Holly felt happy enough to head back to Dublin, relaxed, destressed and brown. Just what the doctor ordered. That didn't stop her from groaning when the plane landed in

Dublin airport to heavy rain. This time the passengers didn't applaud and cheer, and the airport seemed a very different place from the one she had left last week. Once again Holly was the last person to receive her luggage and an hour later they trudged gloomily out to John, who was waiting in the car.

'Well, it looks like the leprechaun didn't do any more work in your garden while you were away,' Denise said, looking at the garden as they arrived at Holly's home.

Holly gave her friends a big hug and a kiss and made her way into her quiet empty house. There was a horrible musty smell inside, and she made her way to the kitchen patio doors to let the fresh air circulate.

She froze just as she was turning the key in the door and stared outside.

Her entire back garden had been transformed.

The grass was cut. The weeds were gone. The garden furniture had been polished and varnished. A fresh coat of paint gleamed from her garden walls. New flowers had been planted and in the corner, underneath the shade of the great oak tree, sat a wooden bench. Holly was in shock. Who on earth was doing all this?

CHAPTER TWENTY-NINE

In the days following her return from Lanzarote, Holly kept a low profile. Holly, Denise and Sharon were all keen to spend the next few days apart from each other. It wasn't something that they had talked about, but after living in each other's ears all day, every day for a whole week, Holly was sure they all agreed this would be healthy.

Ciara was impossible to get hold of, as she was either working hard at Daniel's club or spending time with Mathew. Jack was spending his last few precious weeks of freedom that the summer holidays brought down in Cork at Abbey's parents' house and Declan was . . . well, who knew where Declan was.

Now she was back, Holly wasn't exactly bored with her life, but she wasn't exactly overjoyed either. It just seemed so . . . nothing and so pointless. She'd had the holiday to look forward to, but now felt as though she had no real reason to get out of bed in the morning. And as she was taking time out from her friends, she really had nobody else to talk to. There was only so much conversation she could have with her parents. Compared to last week's sweltering heat in Lanzarote, Dublin was wet and ugly, which meant she couldn't even work at maintaining her beautiful tan or appreciate her new back garden.

Some days she never even got out of bed – she just watched television and waited . . . waited for next month's envelope from Gerry, wondering what journey he would take her on next. She knew her friends would disapprove after she'd been so positive on holiday, but when he was alive she had lived for him and now he was gone she lived for his messages. Everything was about him. She had truly believed that her purpose in life had been to meet Gerry and enjoy all their days together for the rest of their lives. What was her purpose now? Surely she had one, or perhaps there had been an error in the administration way up above.

Something that she did feel she should do was catch the leprechaun. After further interrogation of her neighbours she still knew nothing more of her mystery gardener. Eventually she had convinced herself that a gardener had made a mistake and that he was working on the wrong garden, so she checked the post every day for a bill that she was going to refuse to pay. But no bill arrived, of that variety anyway. Plenty of others did and she was running out of money fast. She had loans up to her eyeballs, electricity bills, phone bills, insurance bills. Everything that came through her door was a bloody bill and she hadn't a clue how she was going to continue paying them all. But she didn't even care; she had become numb to all those irrelevant problems in life. She just dreamed impossible dreams.

One day Holly realised why the leprechaun hadn't returned. Her garden was only tidied when she wasn't home. So she got out of bed early one morning and drove her car round the corner from her house. She then walked back home and settled down on her bed and waited for her mystery gardener to appear.

After three days, the rain finally stopped and the sun began to shine again. Holly was about to give up hope of ever solving the mystery when she heard a van pull up outside and then someone approach her garden. She jumped out of bed in a panic, unprepared for what she should do, even though she had spent days planning. She peeped over her windowsill and spotted a young boy, about twelve years old, walking down her drive, tugging a lawnmower along behind him. She threw on Gerry's oversized dressing gown and raced down the stairs, not caring what she looked like.

She pulled open the front door, causing the young boy to jump. His arm froze mid-air and his finger hovered just over the doorbell. His mouth dropped open at the sight of the woman in front of him.

'A-HA!' Holly yelled happily. 'I think I've caught my little leprechaun!'

He opened and closed his mouth like a goldfish, unsure of what to say. After a few moments he scrunched up his face as though he was about to cry and screamed, 'Da!'

Holly looked up and down the road in search of his father and decided to squeeze as much information out of the boy before the adult reached them.

'So you're the one who's been working on my garden?' She folded her arms across her chest.

He shook his head wildly and gulped.

'You don't have to deny it,' she said gently. 'You've been caught now.' She nodded over at the lawnmower.

He turned round to stare at it and yelled again, 'Da!' His dad slammed the door of the van and made his way over to her house.

'What's wrong, son?' He wrapped his arm round the child's shoulders and looked at Holly for an explanation.

Holly wasn't going to fall for this little charade. 'I was just asking your son here about your little scam.'

'What scam?' The man looked angry.

'The one where you work on my garden without my permission and then you expect me to pay for it. I've heard about this kind of thing before.' She put her hands on her hips and tried to look as though she couldn't be messed with.

The man looked confused. 'Sorry, I don't know what you're talking about, missus. We've never worked on your garden before.' He stared at the state of her front garden, thinking the woman was insane.

'Not *this* garden, you landscaped my *back* garden.' She smiled and raised her eyebrows, thinking she had caught him.

He laughed back at her. 'Landscaped your garden? Lady, are you mad? We cut grass, that's all. See this? This is a lawnmower, nothing else. All it does is cut the bloody grass.'

Holly dropped her hands from her hips and slowly placed them in the pockets of her gown. Maybe they were telling the truth. 'Are you sure you haven't been in my garden?' she squinted her eyes.

270

'Lady, I have never even worked on this street before, never mind your garden, and I can guarantee I won't be working in your garden in the future.'

Holly's face fell. 'But I thought—'

'I don't care what you thought,' he interrupted. 'In future you try to get your facts straight before you start terrorising my kid.'

Holly looked at the young boy and saw his eyes fill with tears. Her hands flew to her mouth with embarrassment. 'Gosh, I'm so sorry. Just hold on there a minute.'

She rushed into the house to get her purse and returned to squeeze her last fiver into his chubby little hand. His face lit up.

'OK, let's go,' his dad said, turning his son round by the shoulders and leading him down the drive.

'Da, I don't wanna do this job any more,' the boy moaned as they carried on to the next house.

'Ah, don't worry, son, they won't all be as mad as her.'

Holly closed the door and studied her reflection in the mirror. He was right; she had turned into a mad woman; now all she needed was a house full of cats.

The phone rang.

'Hello?' Holly said.

'Hiya, how are you?' Denise asked happily.

'Oh, full of the joys of life,' Holly said.

'Me too!' Denise giggled in response.

'Really? What's got you so happy?'

'Nothing much. Just life in general.'

Of course, just life. Wonderful, wonderful, beautiful life. What a silly question.

'So what's happening?'

'I'm calling to invite you out for dinner tomorrow

271

night. I know it's short notice so if you're too busy . . . cancel whatever it is you have planned!'

'Hold on and let me check my diary,' Holly said sarcastically.

'No problem,' Denise said seriously, and was silent while she waited.

Holly rolled her eyes. 'Oh, look at that, whaddaya know? I appear to be free tomorrow night.'

'Goody!' Denise said happily. 'We're all meeting in Chang's at eight.'

'Who's we?'

'Sharon and John are going, and some of Tom's friends too. We haven't been out together for ages so it'll be fun!'

'OK then, see you tomorrow.' Holly hung up, feeling angry. Had it completely slipped Denise's mind that Holly was still a grieving widow and that life just wasn't fun for her any more?

She stormed upstairs and opened her wardrobe. Now what piece of old and disgusting clothing could she wear tomorrow night and how on earth was she going to afford an expensive meal? She could barely even afford to keep her car on the road. She grabbed all her clothes from her wardrobe and flung them across the room, screaming her head off until she finally felt sane again. Perhaps tomorrow she would buy those cats.

CHAPTER THIRTY

Holly arrived at the restaurant at eight twenty as she had spent hours trying on different outfits and ripping them off again. Eventually she settled with the outfit that she had been instructed to wear by Gerry for the karaoke just so she could feel closer to him. She hadn't been coping very well over the past few weeks; she had had more downs than ups and was finding it harder to pick herself back up again.

As she was walking towards the table in the restaurant her heart sank.

Couples-R-Us.

She paused halfway and quickly sidestepped, hiding behind a wall. She wasn't sure she could go through with this. She hadn't the strength to keep battling with her emotions. She looked around to find the easiest escape route; she certainly couldn't leave the way she had come in or they would definitely see her. She spotted the fire escape beside the kitchen door, which had been left open to clear some of the steam. The moment she stepped

273

out into the cool fresh air she felt free again. She walked across the car park, trying to formulate an excuse to tell Denise and Sharon.

'Hi, Holly.'

She froze and slowly turned round, realising she had been caught. She spotted Daniel leaning against his car, smoking a cigarette.

'Hiya, Daniel.' She walked towards him. 'I didn't know you smoked.'

'Only when I'm stressed.'

'You're stressed?' They greeted each other with a hug.

'I was trying to figure out whether to join happy couples united in there.' He nodded towards the restaurant.

Holly smiled. 'You too?'

He laughed. 'Well, I won't tell them I saw you if that's what you want.'

'So you're going in?'

'Have to face the music sometime,' he said grimly, stabbing out his cigarette with his foot.

Holly thought about what he said. 'I suppose you're right.'

'You don't have to go in if you don't want to. I don't want to be the cause of you having a miserable night.'

'On the contrary, it would be nice to have another loner in my company. There are so very few of our kind in existence.'

Daniel laughed and held out his arm. 'Shall we?'

Holly linked his arm and they slowly made their way into the restaurant. It was comforting to know she wasn't alone in feeling alone.

'By the way, I'm getting out of here as soon as we finish the main course,' he smiled.

'Traitor.' She thumped him on the arm. 'Well, I have to leave early anyway to catch the last bus home.' She hadn't had the money to fill the tank in the car for the past few days.

'Then we have the perfect excuse. I'll say we have to leave early because I'm driving you home and you have to be home by . . . what time?'

'Half eleven?' At twelve she planned on opening the September envelope.

'Perfect,' he smiled, and they made their way into the restaurant, feeling slightly reinforced by each other's company.

'Here they are!' Denise announced as they made their way to the table.

Holly sat down beside Daniel, sticking to her alibi like glue. 'Sorry we're late,' she apologised.

'Holly, this is Catherine and Mick, Peter and Sue, Joanne and Conal, Tina and Bryan, John and Sharon you know, Geoffrey and Samantha, and last but not least this is Des and Simon.'

Holly smiled and nodded at all of them.

'Hi, we're Daniel and Holly,' Daniel said smartly, and Holly giggled beside him.

'We had to order already, if you don't mind,' Denise explained, 'but we just chose loads of different dishes so we can all share them. Is that OK?'

Holly and Daniel nodded.

The woman beside Holly, whose name she couldn't remember, turned to her and spoke loudly. 'So, Holly, what do you do?'

Daniel raised his eyebrows at Holly.

'Sorry, what do I do when?' Holly answered seriously. She hated nosy people and conversations that revolved around what people did for a living, especially when she had just met those people less than a minute ago. She felt Daniel shaking with laughter beside her.

'What do you do for a living?' the woman asked again.

Holly had intended on giving her a funny but slightly rude answer but suddenly stopped herself as all the conversations around the table died down and everyone's attention was focused on her. She looked round with embarrassment and cleared her throat nervously. 'Em . . . well . . . I'm currently between jobs right now.' Her voice shook.

The woman's lips began to twitch and she scraped a piece of bread from between her teeth rudely.

'What is it that you do?' Daniel asked her loudly, breaking the silence.

'Oh, Geoffrey runs his own business,' she said proudly, turning to her husband.

'Oh right, but what is it that *you* do?' Daniel repeated to her.

The lady seemed flushed that her answer hadn't been good enough for him. 'Well, I keep myself busy all day every day doing various things. Honey, why don't you tell them about the company?' She turned to her husband again to divert the attention from herself.

Her husband leaned forward in his seat. 'It's just a small business.' He took a bite out of his bread roll, chewed it slowly and everyone waited while he swallowed so he could continue.

'Small but successful,' his wife added for him.

Geoffrey finally finished eating his bread. 'We make car windshields and sell them to the warehouses.'

'Wow, that's very interesting,' Daniel said drily.

'So what is it that you do, Dermot?' the woman said, turning to look at Daniel.

'Sorry, my name is Daniel, actually. I'm a publican.'

'Right,' she nodded and looked away. 'Awful weather we're having these days, isn't it?' she addressed the table.

Everyone fell into conversation and Daniel turned to Holly. 'Did you enjoy your holiday?'

'Oh, I had a fabulous time,' she smiled. 'We took it easy and relaxed, didn't do anything wild and weird.'

'Just what you needed,' he smiled. 'I heard about your near-death experience.'

Holly rolled her eyes. 'I bet Denise told you that.'

He nodded and laughed.

'Well, I'm sure she gave you the exaggerated version.'

'Not really, she just told me about how you were surrounded by sharks and had to be air-lifted from the sea by a helicopter.'

'She didn't!'

'No, not really,' he laughed. 'Still, that must have been some conversation you were having to not notice you were drifting out to sea!'

Holly's face blushed a little as she recalled that they had been talking about him.

'OK, everyone,' Denise called for attention. 'You're probably wondering why me and Tom invited you all here tonight.'

'Understatement of the year,' Daniel mumbled, and Holly giggled.

'Well, we have an announcement to make.' She looked around at everyone and smiled.

Holly's eyes widened.

'Myself and Tom are getting married!' she squealed, and Holly's hands flew up to her mouth in shock. She had *not* seen that one coming.

'Oh, Denise!' she gasped, and walked round the table to hug them. 'That's wonderful news! Congratulations!'

She looked at Daniel's face: it had gone white.

They popped open a bottle of champagne and everyone raised their glasses as Jemima and Jim or Samantha and Sam or whatever their names were made a toast.

'Hold on! Hold on!' Denise stopped them just before they started. 'Sharon, did you not get a glass?'

Everyone looked at Sharon, who was holding a glass of orange juice in her hand.

'Here you go,' Tom said, pouring her a glass.

'No no no! Not for me, thanks,' she said.

'Why not?' Denise huffed, upset that her friend wouldn't celebrate with her.

John and Sharon looked at each other and smiled. 'Well, I didn't want to say anything because it's Denise and Tom's special night . . .'

Everyone urged her to speak.

'Well . . . I'm pregnant! John and I are going to have a baby!'

John's eyes began to water and Holly just froze in shock in her seat. She had *not* seen that one coming either. Tears filled her eyes as she went over to congratulate Sharon and John. Then she sat down and took deep breaths. This was all too much.

'So let's make a toast to Tom and Denise's engagement and Sharon and John's baby!' Jemima and Jim or Sam and Samantha announced.

Everyone clinked glasses and Holly ate dinner in silence, not really tasting anything.

'You want to make that time eleven o'clock?' Daniel asked quietly, and she nodded in agreement.

After dinner Holly and Daniel made their excuses to leave and nobody really tried to persuade them to stay.

'How much should I leave towards the bill?' Holly asked Denise.

'Oh, don't worry about it.' She waved her hand at her dismissively.

'No, don't be silly. I couldn't let you pay for it. How much honestly?'

The woman beside her grabbed the menu and started adding up the price of all the meals they had bought. There had been so many, but Holly had only picked at her own and had even avoided eating a starter so she could afford it.

'Well, it works out at about fifty each, and that's including all the wine and bottles of champagne.'

Holly gulped and stared down at the thirty euro in her hand.

Daniel grabbed her hand and pulled her up. 'Come on, let's go, Holly.'

She opened her mouth to make the excuse of not bringing as much money as she thought but when she opened her palm and looked at the money, there appeared to be an extra twenty.

She smiled at Daniel gratefully and they both headed out to the car.

They sat in the car in silence, both thinking about what had happened that night. She wanted to feel happy for her friends, really she did, but she couldn't shake off the feeling of being left behind. Everyone else's life was moving on except hers.

Daniel pulled up outside her house. 'Do you want to come in for a tea or coffee or anything?' She was sure he would say no and was shocked when he undid his seat belt and accepted her offer. She really liked Daniel, he was very caring and fun to be with, but right now she just wanted to be alone.

'That was some night, wasn't it?' he said, sitting down on the couch and taking a sip of his coffee.

Holly just shook her head with disbelief. 'Daniel, I have known those girls practically all of my life and I did *not* see any of that coming.'

'Well, if it makes you feel any better I've known Tom for years too and he didn't mention a thing.'

'Although Sharon wasn't drinking when we were away,' she hadn't listened to a word Daniel had said, 'and she did throw up a few mornings, but she said it was seasickness . . .' She trailed off and her brain went into overdrive as things started to add up.

'Seasickness?' Daniel asked, confused.

'After our near-death experience.'

'Oh, right.'

This time neither of them laughed.

'It's funny,' he said, settling down into the couch.

Oh no, Holly thought, he's never going to leave now.

'The lads always said that myself and Laura would be the first to get married,' he continued. 'I just didn't think that Laura would be getting married before me.'

'She's getting married?' Holly asked gently.

He nodded and looked away. 'He used to be a friend of mine too.' He laughed bitterly.

'Obviously not any more.'

'Nope,' he shook his head, 'obviously not.'

'Sorry to hear that,' she said genuinely.

'Ah well, we all get our fair share of bad luck. You know that better than anyone.'

'Huh, fair share,' she repeated.

'I know, there's nothing fair about it but don't worry, we'll have our good luck too.'

'You think?'

'I hope.'

They sat in silence for another while and Holly watched the clock. It was five past twelve. She really needed to get Daniel out of the house so she could open the envelope.

He read her mind. 'So how's the messages from above going?'

Holly sat forward and placed her mug down on the table. 'Well, I've another one to open tonight, actually. So . . .' She looked at him.

'Oh right,' he said, jumping to attention. He sat up quickly in his chair and put his mug down on the table. 'I'd better leave you at it so.'

Holly bit her lip, feeling guilty at ushering him out so quickly, but she was also relieved he was finally going.

'Thanks a million for the lift, Daniel,' she said, following him to the door.

'No problem at all.' He grabbed his coat from the banister and headed out the door. They gave each other a quick hug.

'See you soon,' she said, feeling like a right bitch, and watched him walk to his car in the rain. She waved him off and her guilt immediately faded as soon as she closed the door.

'Right, Gerry,' she said as she headed towards the kitchen and picked up the envelope from the table, 'what have you got in store for me this month?'

CHAPTER THIRTY-ONE

Holly held the tiny envelope tightly in her hands and glanced up at the clock on the wall over the kitchen table. It was twelve fifteen. Usually Sharon and Denise would have called her by now, all excited to hear about what was inside the envelope. But so far neither of them had called. It seemed news of an engagement and a pregnancy beat the news of a message from Gerry these days. Holly scorned herself for being so bitter. She wanted to be back in the restaurant right now celebrating their good news with them like the old Holly would have done. But she couldn't bring herself even to smile for them.

She was jealous of them and their good fortune. She was angry with them for moving on without her. Even in the company of friends she felt alone, in a room of a thousand people she would feel alone. But it was when she roamed the rooms of her quiet house that she felt most alone.

She couldn't remember the last time she had felt truly happy, when somebody or something caused her to laugh so hard her stomach pained her and her jaw ached. She missed going to bed at night with absolutely nothing on her mind; she missed enjoying eating food instead of it becoming something she had to endure in order to stay alive, she hated the butterflies she got in her tummy every time she remembered Gerry. She missed *enjoying* watching her favourite television programmes instead of it being something she would stare blankly at to pass the hours. She hated feeling that she had no reason to wake up; she hated the feelings she had when she *did* wake up. She hated the feeling of having no excitement to look forward to. She missed the feeling of being loved, of sensing Gerry's eyes on her as she entered a room; she missed his touches, his hugs, his words of advice; his words of love.

She hated counting down the days till she could read another one of his messages because they were all she had left of him, and after this one there would only be three more. And she hated to think of what her life might be like when there would be no more Gerry. Memories were fine but you couldn't touch them, smell them or hold them. They were never exactly as the moment was, and they faded with time.

So damn Sharon and Denise – they could go on with their happy lives but for the next few months all Holly had was Gerry. She wiped a tear from her face and she slowly opened her seventh envelope.

Shoot for the moon and if you miss you'll still be among the stars. Promise me you will find a job you love this time!
    PS. I love you . . .

Holly read and reread the letter, trying to discover how it made her feel. She had been dreading going back to work for such a long time, had believed that she wasn't ready to move on, that it was too soon. But now she knew she had no choice. It was time. And if Gerry said it was to be, it would be.

Holly's face broke into a smile. 'I promise, Gerry,' she said happily. Well, it was no holiday to Lanzarote but at least it was one step further to getting her life back on track. She studied his writing for a long time after reading it as she always did, and when she was satisfied with the fact she had analysed every word she rushed over to the kitchen drawer, took out a notepad and pen and began to write her own list of possible jobs.

LIST OF POSSIBLE JOBS.

1. FBI agent – Am not American. Do not want to live in America. Have no police experience.
2. Lawyer – Hated school. Hated studying. Do not want go to college for ten million years.
3. Doctor – Uugghh.
4. Nurse – Unflattering uniforms.
5. Waitress – Would eat all the food.
6. Professional people spotter – Nice idea but no one would pay me.
7. Beautician – Bite my nails and wax as rarely as possible. Do not want to see areas of other people's bodies.
8. Hairdresser – Would not like boss like Leo.
9. Retail Assistant – Would not like boss like Denise.

10. Secretary – NEVER AGAIN.
11. Journalist – Cont spill properly enuff. Ha ha, should be comedienne.
12. Comedienne – *Re* read last joke. Wasn't funny.
13. Actress – Could not possibly out-do my wonderful performance in the critically acclaimed *Girls in the City*.
14. Model – Too small, too fat, too old.
15. Singer – *Re* think idea of comedienne (number 12).
16. Hot-shot advertising businesswoman in control of life – Hmm . . . must do research tomorrow . . .

Holly finally collapsed onto her bed at three in the morning and dreamed of being a big hot-shot advertising woman, making a presentation in front of a huge conference table on the top floor of a skyscraper overlooking Grafton Street. Well, Gerry did say shoot for the moon . . .

She woke up early that morning, excited by her dreams of success, had a quick shower, beautified herself and walked down to her local library to look up jobs on the Internet.

Her heels made a loud noise on the wooden floor as she walked across the room to the librarian's desk, which caused several people to look up from their books and stare at her. She continued clattering across the huge room and her face blushed as she realised everyone was watching her. She slowed down immediately and started to tiptoe so as not to attract any more attention. She felt like one of those cartoon characters on TV who hugely exaggerated their tiptoeing, and her face flared up even more when she realised she looked like a complete idiot. A couple of school kids dressed in their uniforms, who were obviously playing truant for the day, sniggered together as she made her way past their table.

'Shush!' The librarian scowled at the school kids.

Holly decided to keep on walking and quickened her pace. Her heels clicked loudly on the floor and echoed around the room and the sound got faster and faster as she raced to the desk in order to end this humiliation.

The librarian looked up and smiled and tried to appear surprised to see someone standing at the counter. As if she hadn't heard Holly thudding across the room.

'Hi,' Holly whispered, 'I was wondering if I could use the Internet.'

'Excuse me?' the librarian spoke normally and moved her head closer to Holly so she could hear.

'Oh.' Holly cleared her throat, wondering what happened to having to whisper in libraries. 'I was wondering if I could use the Internet.'

'No problem, just over there,' she smiled, directing her over to the row of computers on the far side of the room. 'It's five euro for every twenty minutes online.'

Holly handed over her last ten euro. It was all she had managed to take out of her bank account that morning. She had kept a long line of people waiting behind her at the ATM as she worked her way down from one hundred euro to ten, the ATM beeping embarrassingly every time she entered a sum of money to let her know she had 'insufficient funds'. She couldn't believe that was all she had left, but it had given her even more reason to go job-hunting immediately.

'No, no,' the librarian said, handing back her money. 'You can pay when you finish.'

Holly stared across the floor to the computers. She would have to make another big noise just to get there. She took a deep breath and raced over, passing rows and rows of tables. Holly nearly laughed at the sight of everyone: They were almost like dominos as she passed, each head rising from a book to stare at her. Finally she reached the computers and realised that there was none free. She felt like she had just lost a game of musical chairs. This was getting ridiculous. She raised her hands angrily at the spectators as if to say, 'What are you all looking at?' and they quickly buried their heads in their books again.

Holly stood in the centre of the floor between the rows of tables and computers, drummed her fingers on her handbag and looked around. Her eyes nearly popped out of her head as she spotted Richard tapping away on one of the computers. She tiptoed over to him and tapped him on the shoulder. He jumped with fright and swirled round in his chair.

'Hiya,' she whispered.

'Oh, hello, Holly. What are you doing here?' he said uneasily, as though she had caught him doing something naughty.

'I'm just waiting for a computer,' she explained. 'I'm finally looking for a job,' she added proudly. Even saying the words made her feel like less of a vegetable.

'Oh right.' He turned to face his computer and shut down the screen. 'You can use this one so.'

'Oh no, you don't have to rush for me!' she said quickly.

'Not at all. I was just doing some research for work.'

288

He stood up from his chair and made room for her to sit down.

'All the way over here?' she said surprised. 'Don't they have computers in Blackrock?' she joked. She wasn't quite sure what exactly it was that Richard did for a living, and it would seem rude to ask him after ten years of his working there. She knew it involved him wearing a white coat, wandering around a lab and dropping colourful substances into test tubes. Holly and Jack had always said he was making a secret potion to rid the world of happiness. She felt bad now for ever saying that.

'My work brings me everywhere,' he joked awkwardly.

'Shush!' the librarian said loudly in their direction. Holly's audience once again looked up from their books. Oh, so *now* she was supposed to whisper, Holly thought angrily.

Richard said a quick goodbye, made his way over to pay at the desk and slipped quietly out of the room.

Holly sat down at the computer and the man beside her smiled strangely at her. She smiled back and glimpsed nosily at his computer screen. She nearly gagged at the sight of the porn on his screen and looked away quickly. He continued to stare at her with a scary smile on his face while Holly ignored him and became engrossed in her job-hunting.

Forty minutes later she shut down the computer happily, made her way to the librarian and placed her ten euro on the desk. The woman tapped away on the computer and ignored the money on the counter. 'That's fifteen euro, please.'

Holly gulped as she looked down at her note. 'But I thought you said it was five for twenty minutes.'

'Yes, that's right,' the librarian smiled at her.

'But I was online for only forty minutes.'

'Actually, you were on for forty-four minutes, which cuts into the extra twenty minutes,' the woman said, consulting her computer.

Holly giggled. 'But that's only a few minutes more. It's hardly worth five euro.'

The librarian just continued to smile back at her.

'So you expect me to pay?' Holly asked, surprised.

'Yes, that's the rate.'

Holly lowered her voice and moved her head closer to the woman. 'Look, this is really embarrassing but I actually only have the ten on me now. Is there any way I can come back with the rest later on today?'

The librarian shook her head. 'I'm sorry but we can't allow that. You need to pay the entire amount.'

'But *I don't have* the entire amount,' Holly protested.

She stared back blankly.

'Fine,' Holly huffed, taking out her mobile.

'Sorry, but you can't use that in here.' The librarian pointed to the 'no mobile phones' sign on the counter.

Holly looked up slowly at her and counted to five in her head. 'If you *won't* let me use my phone I *can't* phone somebody for help. If I *can't* phone somebody then they *can't* come down here to give me the money. If they *don't* come down here with the money then I *can't pay you*. So we have a little problem here, don't we?' She raised her voice.

The librarian shuffled nervously from foot to foot.

'Can I go outside to use the phone?'

The woman thought about the dilemma. 'Well, usually we don't allow people to leave the premises without paying but I suppose I can make an exception,' she smiled, and then added quickly, 'as long as you stand just in front of the entrance there.'

'Where you can see me?' Holly said sarcastically.

The woman nervously shuffled papers below the counter and pretended to go back to work.

Holly stood outside the door and thought about who to call. She couldn't call Denise and Sharon. Although they would probably rush home from work she didn't want them to know about her failures in life now that they were both so blissfully happy. She couldn't call Ciara because she was on a day shift at Hogan's, Jack was back teaching, Abbey was too, Declan was at college and Richard wasn't even an option.

Tears rolled down her face as she scrolled down through the list of names in her phone book. The majority of those people hadn't even called her since Gerry had died, which meant she had no other friends to call. She turned her back on the librarian so she wouldn't see that she was upset. What should she do? How embarrassing it was to actually have to call somebody to ask for five euro. The fact she had absolutely nobody to call was even more embarrassing. But she had to or the snotty librarian would probably call the police on her. She dialled the first number that came into her head.

'Hi, this is Gerry, please leave a message after the beep and I'll get back to you as soon as I can.'

'Gerry,' Holly said crying, 'I need you . . .'

Holly stood outside the door of the library and waited. The librarian kept a close watch on her just in case she ran off. Holly made a face at her and turned her back to her.

'Stupid bitch,' she growled.

Finally her mum's car pulled up outside and Holly tried to make herself appear as normal as she could. Watching her mother's happy face as she drove in and parked in the car park brought back memories. Her mum used to collect her from school every day when she was younger and she was always so relieved to see that familiar car come to rescue her after her hellish day. Holly felt like a child. She had always hated school – well, she had until she met Gerry. Then she would look forward to going to school each day so they could sit together and flirt at the back of the class.

Holly's eyes filled with tears again and Elizabeth rushed over to her and wrapped her arms around her. 'Oh, my poor poor Holly . . . What happened, love?' she said, stroking her hair and casting evil glances in at the librarian as Holly explained the story.

'OK, love, why don't you wait out in the car and I'll go in and deal with her?'

Holly did as she was told and sat in the car, flicking through the radio stations as her mum confronted the school bully.

'Silly cow,' her mother grumbled as she climbed back into the car. She glanced over at her daughter who looked so lost. 'Why don't we go home and we can relax?'

Holly smiled gratefully and a tear trickled down her face. Home. She liked the sound of that.

Holly snuggled up on the couch with her mum. She felt like a teenager again. She and her mum always used to cuddle up on the couch and fill each other in on all the gossip in their lives. Holly wished she could have the same giggling conversations with her now.

Her mum broke into her thoughts. 'I rang you last night at home, were you out?'

Holly took a sip of her tea. Oh, the wonders of the magical tea, the answer to all of life's little problems. You have a gossip and you make a cup of tea, you get fired from your job and you have a cup of tea, your husband tells you he has a brain tumour and you have a cup of tea . . .

'Yeah, I went out to dinner with the girls and about a hundred other people I didn't know.' Holly rubbed her eyes tiredly.

'How are the girls?' Elizabeth asked fondly. She had always got along well with Holly's friends, unlike Ciara's, who terrified her.

Holly took a sip of her tea. 'Sharon's pregnant and Denise got engaged,' she replied, staring off into space.

'Oh,' Elizabeth squeaked, not sure how to react in front of her obviously distressed daughter. 'How do you feel about that?' she asked softly, brushing a hair away from Holly's face.

Holly stared down at her hands and tried to compose herself. She wasn't successful and her shoulders began to tremble and she tried to hide her face behind her hair.

'Oh, Holly,' Elizabeth said sadly, putting her cup down and moving closer to her daughter. 'It's perfectly normal to feel like this.'

Holly couldn't even manage to get any words out of her mouth.

The front door banged and Ciara announced to the house, 'We're hoooome!'

'Great,' Holly sniffed, resting her head on her mum's chest.

'WHERE IS EVERYONE?' Ciara shouted, banging doors.

'Just a minute, love,' Elizabeth called out, angry that her moment with Holly had been ruined. It had been a long time since Holly had confided in her; she had chosen to bottle everything up since the funeral and it seemed it had all become too much for her. She didn't want an overexcited Ciara to send her back into her shell again.

'I HAVE NEWS!' Ciara's voice got louder as she got nearer to the living room. Mathew burst open the door, carrying Ciara in his arms. 'Me and Mathew are moving back to Australia!' she yelled happily. She froze as she saw her upset sister in her mum's arms. She quietly jumped down from Mathew's arms, led him out of the room and closed the door silently behind them.

'Now Ciara's going too, Mum.' Holly cried even harder, and Elizabeth cried softly for her daughter.

Holly stayed up late that night talking to her mum about everything that had been bubbling up inside her for the past few months. And although her mother offered many words of kind reassurance, Holly still felt as trapped as before. She stayed in the guest bedroom that night and woke up to a mad house the following morning. Holly smiled at the familiarity of the sound of her brother and sister running around the house, screaming about how they were late for band rehearsals and for work, followed by their dad grumbling at them to get a move on, followed by her mum's gentle pleas for everyone to stay silent so as not to disturb Holly. The world went on, simple as that, and there was no bubble big enough to protect her.

At lunchtime Holly's dad dropped her home and squeezed a cheque for five thousand euro into her hand.

'Oh, Dad, I can't accept this,' Holly said, overcome with emotion.

'Take it,' he said gently, pushing her hand away. 'Let us help you, love.'

'I'll pay back every cent,' she said, hugging him tightly.

Holly stood at the door and waved her father off down the road. She looked at the cheque in her hand and immediately a weight was lifted from her shoulders. She could think of twenty things she could do with this cheque and for once buying clothes wasn't one of them. Walking into the kitchen she noticed the red light flashing on the answering machine on the table in the hall. She sat at the bottom of the stairs and hit the button.

She had five new messages.

One was from Sharon, ringing to see if she was OK because she hadn't heard from her all day. The second was from Denise ringing to see if she was OK because she hadn't heard from her all day. The two girls had obviously been talking to each other. The third was from Sharon, the fourth was from Denise and the fifth was just somebody hanging up. Holly pressed delete and ran upstairs to change her clothes. She wasn't quite ready to talk to Sharon and Denise yet; she needed to get her life in order first so she could be more supportive towards them.

She sat in the spare room in front of her computer and began to type up her CV. She had become an old pro at doing this, having changed jobs so often. It had been a while since she had to worry about going to interviews, though. And if she did get an interview, who would want to hire someone who hadn't been working for a whole year?

It took her two hours to print out something that she finally thought was half decent. In fact she was really proud of what she had done: she had somehow managed to make herself look intelligent and experienced. She laughed evilly loudly, hoping she would manage to fool her future employers into thinking she was a capable worker. Reading back over her CV she decided that even she would hire herself.

On Monday she dressed smartly and drove down to the village in the car she had finally managed to fill with petrol. She parked outside the recruitment office and applied lip-gloss in the rear-view mirror. There was to be no more time-wasting. If Gerry said to find a job, she was going to find a job.

CHAPTER THIRTY-TWO

A few days later Holly sat out on her newly renovated garden furniture in her back garden, sipped on a glass of red wine and listened to the sound of wind chimes making music in the breeze. She looked around at the neat lines of her newly landscaped garden and decided that whoever was working on it had to be a professional. She breathed in and allowed the sweet scent of flowers to fill her nostrils. It was eight o'clock and already it was beginning to get dark. The bright evenings were gone, and everybody was once again preparing for hibernation.

She thought about the message she had received on her answering machine that day. It had been from the recruitment agency, and she'd been shocked to receive a reply from them so quickly. The woman on the phone had said that there had been a great response to her résumé, and already Holly had two job interviews lined up.

Butterflies fluttered around her stomach at the thought

of them. She had never been particularly good at interviews, but then again she had never been particularly keen on any of the jobs she was being interviewed for. This time she felt different; she was excited to get back to work and to try something new. Her first interview was for a job selling advertising space for a magazine that circulated throughout Dublin. It was something she had absolutely no experience in, but she was willing to learn because the idea of it sounded far more interesting than any of her former jobs, which had mostly entailed answering the phone, taking messages and filing. Anything that involved not having to do any of those things all day was a step up.

The second interview was with a leading Irish advertising company, and she knew she had absolutely no hope of getting it. But Gerry had told her to shoot for the moon . . .

Holly also thought about the phone call she had just received from Denise. Denise had been so excited on the phone she didn't seem to be at all bothered by the fact that Holly hadn't talked to her since they went out for dinner last week. In fact, Holly didn't think she had even noticed. Denise had been all talk about her wedding arrangements, and rambled on for almost an hour about what kind of dress she should wear, which flowers she should choose, where she should hold the reception. She started sentences and then forgot to finish them as she jumped from topic to topic. All Holly had to do was make a few noises to let her know she was still listening . . . although she wasn't. The only piece of information she had taken in was that Denise was planning to marry on New Year's Eve, and by the sound of it Tom wouldn't be having a say in how Denise's special day should be run. Holly was surprised to hear they had set a date so soon – she had just assumed it would be one of those long-winded, last-a-few-years kind of engagements, especially as Denise and Tom had only been an item for five months. But Holly didn't worry about that as much as she would have done when she was her old self. She was now a regular subscriber to the finding-love-and-holding-on-to-it-forever magazine. Denise and Tom were right not to waste time worrying about what people thought if they knew in their hearts it was the right decision.

Sharon hadn't called Holly since the day after she had announced her pregnancy, and Holly knew she would have to call her friend soon before the days passed her by and it was too late. This was an important time in Sharon's life and she knew she should be there for her, but she just couldn't bring herself to. She was being jealous, bitter and incredibly selfish, she knew that, but Holly needed to be selfish these days in order to survive. She was still trying to get her head round the fact that Sharon and John were managing to achieve everything that everyone had always assumed Holly and Gerry would do first. Sharon had always said she hated kids, Holly thought angrily.

It began to get chilly and Holly took her glass of wine inside to her warm house where she refilled it. All she could do for the next couple of days was attend her job interviews and pray for success. She went into the sitting room, put her and Gerry's favourite album of love songs on the CD player and snuggled up on the couch with her glass of wine where she closed her eyes and pictured them dancing around the room together.

The following day she was awoken by the sound of a car pulling into her driveway. She got out of bed and threw Gerry's dressing gown on, presuming it was her car being returned from the garage, where she'd left it for its annual service. She peeped out of the curtains and immediately jumped back as she saw Richard stepping out of his car. She hoped he hadn't seen her because she really wasn't in the mood for one of his visits. She paced the bedroom floor, feeling guilty as she ignored the doorbell ringing for the second time. She knew she was being horrible but she just couldn't bear sitting down with him for another awkward conversation. She really hadn't anything to talk about any more; nothing had changed in her life, she had no exciting news, not even any normal news to tell *anybody*, never mind Richard.

She breathed a sigh of relief as she heard him walk away and then his car door bang shut. She stepped into the shower and allowed the warm water to run over her face and she was once again lost in a world of her own. Twenty minutes later she padded downstairs in her disco diva slippers. A scraping noise from outside made her freeze in her step. She pricked her ears up and listened more closely, trying to identify the sound. There it was again: a scraping noise and a rustling, as if somebody were in her garden . . . Holly's eyes widened as she realised that her leprechaun was outside.

She crept into the living room, stupidly thinking the person outside would hear her wandering around her house, and got down on her knees. Peering above the windowsill she gasped as she saw Richard's car still sitting in the driveway. What was even more surprising was the sight of Richard on his hands and knees with a small gardening implement in his hand, digging up the soil and planting new flowers. She crawled away from the window and sat on the carpet in shock, unsure what to do next. The sound of her car being parked outside the house snapped her back to attention and her brain went into overdrive as she tried to figure out whether to answer the door to her mechanic or not. For some reason Richard didn't want Holly to know that he was working on her garden and she decided she was going to respect that wish . . . for now.

She hid behind the couch as she saw the mechanic approach the door and she had to laugh at how ridiculous this all seemed. The doorbell rang and she scurried even further behind the couch as her mechanic walked over to the window and stared in. Her heart beat wildly and she felt as though she were doing something illegal. She covered her mouth and tried to smother her laughs. She felt like a child again. She had always been hopeless at playing hide-and-seek; whenever she felt her seeker coming near her she would always get an attack of the giggles and her hiding place would be found. Then, for the rest of the day, she would have to search for everybody else. She breathed a sigh of relief as she heard the mechanic drop the keys through the letterbox and walk away.

A few minutes later she stuck her head out from behind the couch and checked if it was safe to come out. She stood up and brushed the dust off her clothes, telling herself she was too old to be playing silly games. She peeked out from behind the curtain again and saw Richard packing up his gardening equipment. Holly kicked off her slippers and shoved her feet into her trainers.

On second thought, these silly games were fun and she had nothing else to do. As soon as she saw Richard drive down the road she ran outside and hopped into her car. She was going to follow her leprechaun.

She managed to stay three cars behind him all the way, just like they did in the movies, and she slowed down as she saw him pulling over ahead of her. He parked his car and went into the newsagent and returned with a newspaper in his hand. Holly put her sunglasses on, adjusted her baseball cap and peered over the top of the *Arab Leader* that was covering her face. She laughed at herself as she caught sight of her reflection in the mirror. She looked like the most suspicious person in the world. She watched Richard cross the road and head into The Greasy Spoon. She was slightly disappointed; she was hoping for a far juicier adventure than this.

She sat in her car for a few minutes, trying to formulate a new plan, and jumped with fright when a traffic warden banged on her window.

'You can't park here,' he said, motioning towards the car park. Holly smiled back sweetly and rolled her eyes as she backed into a free space. Surely Cagney and Lacey never had this problem.

Eventually her inner child settled down to have a nap and mature Holly took her cap and glasses off and tossed them onto the passenger seat, feeling foolish. Silly games over. Real life starting now.

She crossed the road and looked around inside the

café for her brother. She spotted him sitting down with his back to her, hunched over his newspaper and drinking a cup of tea. She marched over happily with a smile on her face.

'God, Richard, do you ever go to work?' she joked loudly, causing him to jump. She was about to say more but stopped herself as he looked up at her with tears in his eyes and his shoulders began to shake.

CHAPTER THIRTY-THREE

Holly looked around to see if anyone else in the café had noticed, and she slowly pulled out a chair to sit down beside Richard. Had she said something wrong? She looked at Richard's face in shock, not knowing what to do or say. She could safely admit that she had *never* been in this situation before.

Tears rolled down his face and he tried with all his might to stop them.

'Richard, what's wrong?' she asked, confused, and placed her hand awkwardly on his arm and patted it.

Richard continued to shake with tears.

The plump lady, dressed in a canary-yellow apron this time, made her way round the counter and placed a box of tissues on the table beside Holly.

'Here you go,' she said, handing Richard a tissue. He wiped his eyes and blew his nose loudly, a big old man blow, and Holly tried to hide her smile.

'I'm sorry for crying,' Richard said, embarrassed, avoiding eye contact with her.

'Hey,' she said softly, placing her hand more easily on his arm this time, 'there's nothing wrong with crying. It's my new hobby these days so don't knock it.'

He smiled at her weakly. 'Everything just seems to be falling apart, Holly,' he said sadly, catching a tear with the tissue before it dropped from his chin.

'Like what?' she asked, concerned at her brother's transformation. She had seen so many sides to him over the past few months that he had her slightly baffled.

Richard took a deep breath and gulped back his tea. Holly looked up at the woman behind the counter and ordered another pot.

'Richard, I've recently learned that talking about things helps,' Holly said gently, 'and coming from me that's a huge tip, because I used to keep my mouth shut thinking I was Superwoman.' She smiled at him encouragingly. 'Why don't you tell me about it?'

He looked doubtful.

'I won't laugh, I won't say anything if you don't want me to. I won't tell a soul what you tell me, I'll just listen,' she assured him.

He looked away from her and focused on the salt and pepper shakers at the centre of the table, and then he spoke quietly. 'I lost my job.'

Holly remained silent and waited for him to say more. After a while Richard looked up to face her.

'That's not so bad, Richard,' she said softly then, giving him a smile. 'I know you loved your job but you can find another one. Hey, if it makes you feel any better I used to lose my jobs all the time—'

'I lost my job in April, Holly,' he interrupted her angrily.

'It is now September. There's nothing for me . . . not in my line of work . . .' He looked away.

'Oh . . .' Holly didn't know quite what to say. After a long silence she spoke again. 'But at least Meredith is still working, so you still have a regular income. Just take the time you need to find the right job . . . I know it doesn't feel like it right now but—'

'Meredith left me last month,' he interrupted her again, and this time his voice was weaker.

Holly's hands flew to her mouth. Oh, poor Richard. She had never liked the bitch, but Richard had adored her.

'The kids?' she asked carefully.

'They're living with her,' he said, and his voice cracked.

'Oh, Richard, I'm so sorry.' Holly fidgeted with her hands, not knowing where to put them. Should she hug him?

'I'm sorry too,' he said miserably, and continued to stare at the salt and pepper shakers.

'It wasn't your fault, Richard, so don't go telling yourself it was,' she protested strongly.

'Wasn't it?' he said, his voice beginning to shake. 'She told me I was a pathetic man who couldn't even look after his own family . . .' He broke down again.

'Oh, never mind that silly bitch,' Holly said angrily. 'You are an excellent father and a loyal husband,' she told him strongly, and realised she meant every word of it. 'Timmy and Emily love you because you're fantastic with them so don't mind what that demented woman says to you.' She wrapped her arms around him and hugged her brother while he cried. She felt so angry she wanted to go over to Meredith and punch her in the face – although she had always wanted to do that, but now she even had an excuse.

Richard's tears finally subsided and he pulled away from her and grabbed another tissue. Holly's heart went out to him; he had always tried so hard to do the right thing and to create a perfect life and family for himself, and it hadn't worked out as he had planned. He seemed to be in a great deal of shock.

'Where are you staying?' she asked, suddenly realising that he had had no home to go to for the past few weeks.

'In a B&B down the road. Nice place. Friendly people,' he said, pouring another cup of tea. Your wife leaves you and you have a cup of tea . . .

'Richard, you can't stay there,' Holly protested. 'Why didn't you tell any of us?'

'Because I thought we could work it out, but we can't . . . She's made up her mind.'

As much as Holly wanted to invite him to stay with her she just couldn't. She had far too much to deal with on her own and she was sure Richard would appreciate that.

'What about Mum and Dad?' she asked. 'They would love to be able to help you out.'

Richard shook his head, 'No, Ciara's home now and so is Declan. I wouldn't want to dump myself on them as well. I'm a grown man now.'

'Oh, Richard, don't be silly.' Holly rolled her eyes. 'There's your old room. I'm positive you would be welcome back there,' she tried to persuade him. 'Sure, I even slept there a few nights ago.'

He looked up from staring at the table.

'There is absolutely nothing wrong with returning to the house you grew up in every now and again. It's good for the soul,' she smiled at him.

He looked uncertain. 'Em . . . I don't think that's such a good idea, Holly.'

'If it's Ciara you're worried about then don't. She's heading back to Australia in a few weeks with her boyfriend so the house will be . . . less hectic.'

His face relaxed a little.

Holly smiled. 'So what do you think? Come on, it's a great idea and this way you won't be throwing your money away on some smelly ol' dump. I don't care how nice you say the owners are.'

Richard smiled but it quickly faded. 'I couldn't ask Mother and Father, Holly. I . . . wouldn't know what to say.'

'I'll go with you,' she promised, 'and I'll talk to them for you. Honestly, Richard, they'll be delighted to help out. You're their son and they love you. We all do,' she added, placing her hand over his.

'OK,' he finally agreed, and she linked arms with him, as they headed out to their cars.

'Oh, by the way, Richard, thank you for my garden,' Holly smiled, then leaned over and kissed him on the cheek.

'You know?'

She nodded. 'You have such a huge talent and I'm going to pay you every single penny you deserve as soon as I find a job.'

Her brother's face relaxed into a shy smile.

They got into their cars and drove back to the house they grew up in.

Holly looked at herself in the toilet mirror of the office building where her first job interview was taking place. She had lost so much weight since she had worn all her old suits that she had had to go out and purchase a new one. It was flattering to her new slim figure. The jacket was long and went to just above her knees and it was fastened tightly by one button at the waist. The trousers were just the right fit and fell perfectly over her boots. The outfit was black with light blue lines going through it and she matched it with a light blue top underneath. She felt like a hot-shot advertising business-woman in control of her life, and all she needed to do now was to sound like one. She applied another layer of pink lip-gloss and ran her fingers through her loose curls, which she had decided to allow to tumble onto her shoulders. She took a deep breath and headed back out to the waiting area.

She took her seat again and glanced around at all the other applicants. They looked far younger than Holly and they all seemed to have a thick folder of some kind sitting on their laps. She looked around and started to panic. Sure enough, everybody had one of these folders. She stood up from her seat again and headed over to the secretary.

'Excuse me,' Holly said, trying to get her attention.

The woman looked up and smiled. 'Can I help you?'

'Yes, I was just in the toilet there and I think I must have missed being given a folder.' Holly smiled politely at her.

The woman frowned and looked confused. 'I'm sorry, what folders were handed out?'

Holly turned and pointed to the folders perched on everyone's laps.

The woman smiled and motioned her to come closer with her finger.

Holly tucked her hair behind her ears and moved closer. 'Yes?'

'Sorry, honey, but they're actually portfolios that they brought themselves,' she whispered so that Holly wouldn't be embarrassed.

Holly's face froze. 'Oh. Should I have brought one with me?'

'Well, do you have one?' the woman asked with a friendly smile.

Holly shook her head.

'Well then, don't worry about it. It's not a requirement. People just bring these things to show off,' she said, and Holly giggled.

Holly returned to her seat but continued to worry about this portfolio business. Nobody had said anything to her about any stupid portfolios. Why was she the last to know everything? She tapped her foot and looked around the office while she waited. She got a good feeling from the place; the colours were warm and cosy, and the light poured in from the large Georgian windows. The ceilings were high and there was a lovely feeling of space. Holly could sit there all day thinking. She suddenly felt so relaxed that her heart didn't even jump as her name was called. She walked confidently towards the interview office and the secretary winked at her to wish her good luck. Holly smiled back at her; for some reason she already felt part of the team. She paused just outside the door and took a deep breath.

Shoot for the moon, she whispered to herself, shoot for the moon.

CHAPTER THIRTY-FOUR

Holly knocked lightly on the door and a gruff voice told her to enter. Her heart did a little flip at the sound of it, feeling as if she had been summoned to the principal's office at school. She wiped her clammy hands on her suit and entered the room.

'Hello,' she said more confidently than she felt. She walked across the small room and held out her hand to the man who had stood up from his chair. He greeted her with a big smile and a warm handshake. The face didn't match the grumpy voice at all, thankfully. Holly relaxed a little at the sight of him: he reminded her of her father. He looked to be in his late fifties, with a big cuddly-bear physique, and she had to stop herself from leaping over the desk to hug him. His hair was neat, almost a sparkling silver colour, and she imagined he had been an extremely handsome man in his youth.

'Holly Kennedy, isn't it?' he said, taking his seat and glancing down at her CV in front of him. She sat in the seat opposite him and forced herself to stay calm. She had read every interview technique manual she could get her hands on since drawing up her CV and had tried to put it all into practice, from walking into the room, to the proper handshake to the way she positioned herself in her chair. She wanted to look as if she was experienced, intelligent and highly confident. But she would need more than a firm handshake to succeed in proving that.

'That's right,' she said, placing her handbag on the ground beside her and resting her shaking hands on her lap.

He put his glasses on the end of his nose and flicked through her CV in silence. Holly stared at him intently and tried to read his facial expressions. It wasn't an easy task as he was one of those people who had a constant frown on his face while he read. Well, it was either that or he wasn't at all impressed by what he was seeing. She glanced at his desk while she waited for him to start speaking again. Her eyes fell upon a silver-framed photo, featuring three pretty girls close to her own age, all smiling happily at the camera. She continued to stare at it with a smile on her face and when she looked up she realised he had put the CV down and was watching her. She smiled and tried to appear more businesslike.

'Before we start talking about you I'll explain exactly who I am and what the job entails,' he explained.

Holly nodded, trying to look very interested.

'My name is Chris Feeney and I'm the founder and editor of the magazine, or "the boss man", as everyone likes to call me around here,' he chuckled, and Holly was charmed by his twinkling blue eyes.

'Basically we are looking for someone to deal with the advertising aspect of the magazine. As you know, the running of a magazine or any media organisation is hugely reliant on the advertising we receive. We need the money for our magazine to be published so this job is very important. Unfortunately, our last man had to leave us in a hurry, so I would be looking for somebody who could begin work almost immediately. How would you feel about that?'

Holly nodded. 'That would be no problem at all. In fact, I'm eager to begin work as soon as possible.'

Chris nodded and looked down at her CV again. 'I see you've been out of the workforce for over a year now, am I correct in saying that?' He lowered his head and stared at her over the rim of his glasses.

'Yes, that's right,' Holly nodded, 'and I can assure you that was purely out of choice. Unfortunately my husband was ill and I had to take time off work to be with him.'

She swallowed hard; she knew that this would be an issue for every employer. Nobody wanted to employ someone who had been idle for the past year.

'I see,' he said, looking up at her. 'Well, I hope that he's fully recovered now.' He smiled warmly.

Holly wasn't sure whether that was a question or not and didn't know what to say. Did he want to hear about her personal life? He continued to look at her and she realised he was waiting for an answer.

She cleared her throat. 'Well, no actually, Mr Feeney, unfortunately he passed away in February . . . he had a brain tumour. That's why I felt it was important to leave my job.'

'Gosh.' Chris put down the CV and took his glasses off. 'Of course I can understand that. I'm very sorry to hear it,' he said sincerely. 'It must be hard for you being

313

so young and all . . .' He looked down at his desk for a while, then met her eyes again. 'My wife lost her life to breast cancer just last year so I understand how you may be feeling,' he said generously.

'I'm sorry to hear that,' Holly said sadly, her eyes meeting those of the kind man across the table.

'They say it gets easier,' he smiled.

'So they say,' Holly said grimly. 'Apparently gallons of tea do the trick.'

He started to laugh, a big guffaw of a laugh. 'Yes! I've been told that one too, and my daughters inform me that fresh air is also a healer.'

'Ah yes, the magic fresh air; it does wonders for the heart. Are they your daughters?' she smiled, indicating the photograph.

'Indeed they are,' he said proudly. 'My three little doctors who try to keep me alive,' he laughed. 'Unfortunately, the garden no longer looks like that, though.'

'Wow, is that your garden?' Holly asked wide-eyed. 'It's beautiful; I presumed it was the Botanical Gardens or somewhere like that.'

'That was Maureen's specialty. You can't get me out of the office long enough to sort through that mess.'

'Oh, don't talk to me about gardens,' Holly said, rolling her eyes. 'I'm not exactly Ms Green-fingers myself and the place is beginning to look like a jungle.' Well, it had looked like a jungle, she thought to herself.

They continued to look at each other and smile, and Holly was comforted to hear a story similar to her own. Whether she got the job or not, at least it would be confirmed that she wasn't entirely alone and other people had to cope with what she did.

'Anyway, getting back to the interview,' Chris laughed, 'have you any experience in working with the media at all?'

Holly didn't like the way he said 'at all'. It meant that he had read through her CV and couldn't see any sign of experience for the job.

'Yes, I have, actually.' She returned to business mode and tried so hard to impress him. 'I once worked in an estate agents and I was responsible for dealing with the media regarding the new properties for sale. So I was on the other end of what this job requires and so I know how to deal with companies who are wishing to sell space.'

Chris nodded along. 'But you have never actually worked on a magazine or newspaper or anything like that?'

Holly nodded her head slowly and racked her brains for something to say. 'But I was responsible for printing up a weekly newsletter for a company I worked for . . .' She rambled on and on, grasping at every little straw she could and realising she was sounding rather pathetic.

Chris was too polite to interrupt her as she went through every job she'd ever worked at and exaggerated anything that was in any way advertising- or media-related. Eventually she stopped talking, having grown bored at the sound of her own voice, and she twisted her fingers around each other nervously on her lap. She was underqualified for this job and she knew it, but she also knew that she could do it if he just gave her the chance.

Chris took off his glasses. 'I see. Well, Holly, I can see that you have a great deal of experience in the workplace in various different areas, but I notice that you haven't stayed in any of your jobs for a period longer than nine months . . .'

'I was searching for the right job for me,' Holly said, her confidence now totally shattered.

'So how do I know you won't desert me after a few months?' he smiled, but she knew he was serious.

'Because this *is* the right job for me,' she said seriously. Holly took a deep breath as she felt her chances slipping away from her but she wasn't prepared to give up that easily. 'Mr Feeney,' she said, moving forward to sit on the edge of her chair, 'I'm a very hard worker. When I love something I give it one hundred per cent. I'm a very capable person and what I don't know now I am more than willing to learn so that I can do my best for myself, for you and for the company. If you put your trust in me I promise I won't let you down.' She stopped herself just short of getting down on her knees and begging for the damn job.

She blushed as she realised what she had just done.

'Well then, I think that's a good note to finish on,' Chris said, smiling at her. He stood up from his chair and held his hand out. 'Thank you very much for taking the time to come down here. I'm sure we'll be in touch.'

Holly shook his hand and thanked him quietly, picked her bag up from the ground and felt his eyes burning into her back as she headed towards the door. Just before she stepped outside she turned back to face him. 'Mr Feeney, I'll make sure your secretary brings you in a nice hot pot of tea. It'll do you the world of good.'

She smiled and closed the door to the sound of his loud laughter. The friendly secretary raised her eyebrows at Holly as she passed her desk and the rest of the applicants held onto their portfolios tightly, wondering what the lady had said to make the interviewer laugh so loudly. Holly smiled to herself as she heard Mr Feeney continue to laugh as she made her way out into the fresh air.

Holly decided to drop in on Ciara at work so she could have a bite to eat. She rounded the corner, entered Hogan's pub and searched for a table inside. The pub was packed with people dressed smartly on their lunch breaks from work, and some were even having a few sneaky pints before heading back to the office. Holly found a small table in the corner and settled down.

'Excuse me,' she called out loudly, and clicked her fingers in the air. 'Can I get some service here, please?'

The people at the tables around her threw her the looks for being so rude to the staff, and Holly continued to click her fingers in the air.

'Oi!' she yelled.

Ciara swirled around with a scowl on her face but it broke into a smile when she spotted her sister grinning at her. 'Jesus, I was about to smack the head off you,' she laughed, approaching the table.

'I hope you don't speak to all your customers like that,' Holly teased.

'Not *all* of them,' Ciara replied seriously. 'You having lunch here today?'

Holly nodded. 'Mum told me you were working lunches; I thought you were supposed to be serving in the club upstairs?'

Ciara rolled her eyes. 'That man has got me working

all the hours under the sun. He's treating me like a slave,' Ciara moaned.

'Did I hear someone mention my name?' Daniel laughed, walking up behind her.

Ciara's face froze as she realised he had overheard her. 'No, no . . . I was just talking about Mathew,' she stammered. 'He has me up all hours of the night, I'm like his sex slave . . .' she trailed off and wandered over to the bar to get a notepad and pen.

'Sorry I asked,' Daniel said, staring at Ciara, bewildered. 'Mind if I join you?' he asked Holly.

'Yes,' Holly teased, but pulled out a stool for him. 'OK, what's good to eat here?' She was looking through the menu as Ciara returned with pen in hand.

Ciara mouthed, 'Nothing' behind Daniel's back and Holly giggled.

'The toasted special is my favourite,' Daniel suggested, and Ciara shook her head wildly at Holly.

'What are you shaking your head at?' Daniel said, catching her in the act again.

'Oh, it's just that . . . Holly is allergic to onions,' Ciara stammered again. This was news to Holly.

Holly nodded her head. 'Yes . . . they, eh . . . make my head . . . eh . . . bloat.' She blew her cheeks out. 'Terrible things, those onions are. Fatal, in fact. Could kill me someday.'

Ciara rolled her eyes at her sister who once again had managed to take things way over the top.

'OK, well then, leave the onions out,' Daniel suggested, and Holly agreed.

Ciara stuck her fingers in her mouth and pretended to gag as she walked away.

'You're looking very smart today,' Daniel said, studying her outfit.

'Yes, that was the impression I was trying to give. I was just at a job interview,' Holly said, and winced at the thought of it.

'Oh yeah, that's right,' Daniel smiled. 'Didn't it go well?'

Holly shook her head. 'Well, let's just say I need to buy a smarter-looking suit. I won't be expecting a call from them anytime soon.'

'Not to worry,' Daniel said, smiling. 'There will be plenty of other opportunities. Still have that job upstairs, if you're interested.'

'I thought you gave that job to Ciara. Why is she working downstairs now?' Holly said, looking confused.

Daniel rolled his eyes. 'Holly, you know your sister; we had a bit of a *situation*.'

'Oh no!' Holly laughed. 'What did she do this time?'

'Some guy at the bar said something to her she didn't quite like so she poured him his pint, then served it to him over his head.'

'Oh no!' Holly gasped. 'I'm surprised you didn't fire her!'

'Couldn't do that to a member of the Kennedy family, could I?' he smiled. 'And besides, how would I ever be able to face you again?'

'Exactly,' Holly confirmed. 'You may be my friend but you "gotta respect the family".' Ciara frowned at her sister as she arrived with her plate of food. 'Well, that has to be the worst Godfather impression I've ever heard. Bon appetite,' she said sarcastically, slamming the plate down on the table and turning on her heel.

'Hey!' Daniel frowned, taking Holly's plate away from her, examining her sandwich.

'What are you doing?' she demanded.

'There are onions in it,' he said angrily. 'Ciara must have given the wrong order again.'

'No, no, she didn't.' Holly jumped to her sister's rescue and grabbed the plate back. 'I'm only allergic to red onions,' she blurted out.

Daniel frowned. 'How odd. I didn't think there was a huge difference.'

'Oh, there is.' Holly nodded her head and tried to sound wise. 'They may be part of the same family but the red onion . . . contains deadly toxins . . .' she trailed off.

'Toxins?' Daniel said disbelievingly.

'Well, they're toxic to me, aren't they?' she mumbled, and bit into the sandwich to shut herself up. She found if difficult to eat her sandwich under Daniel's glare without feeling like a pig so she finally gave up and left the remains on her plate.

'Not like it?' he asked worriedly.

'No, I love it, I just had a big breakfast,' she lied, patting her empty stomach.

'So have you had any luck with that leprechaun yet?' he teased.

'Well, actually I found him!' Holly laughed, wiping her greasy hands on her napkin.

'Really? Who was it?'

'Would you believe it was my brother Richard?' she laughed.

'Go away! So why didn't he tell you? Did he want it to be a surprise or something?'

'Something like that, I suppose.'

'He's a nice guy, Richard,' Daniel said, looking thoughtful.

'You think?'

'Yeah, he's a harmless kind of a guy. He has a nice nature.'

Holly nodded her head.

He cut in on her thoughts. 'Have you spoken to Denise or Sharon lately?'

'Just Denise,' she said, looking away guiltily, 'You?'

'Tom has my head done in with all this talk of weddings. Wants me to be his best man. To be honest, I didn't think they would plan it all so soon.'

'Me neither,' Holly agreed. 'How do you feel about it now?'

'Ah,' Daniel sighed, 'happy for him, in a selfish and bitter kind of way.'

'Know how you feel. You haven't spoken to your ex lately or anything?'

'Who, Laura?' he asked, surprised. 'Never want to see the woman again.'

'Is she a friend of Tom's?'

'Not as friendly as they used to be, thank God.'

'So she won't be invited to the wedding then?'

Daniel's eyes widened. 'You know I never even thought of that. God, I hope not. Tom knows what I would do to him if he did invite her.' There was a silence as Daniel contemplated that thought.

'I think I'm meeting up with Tom and Denise tomorrow night to discuss the wedding plans, if you feel like coming out,' he said then.

Holly rolled her eyes. 'Gee, thanks. Well, that just sounds like the best fun ever.'

Daniel started laughing. 'I know, that's why I don't want to go on my own. Call me later if you want to go, anyway.'

Holly nodded.

'Right, here's the bill,' Ciara said, dropping a piece of paper on the table and sauntered off. Daniel watched after her and shook his head.

'Don't worry, Daniel,' Holly laughed. 'You won't have to put up with her for much longer.'

'Why not?' He looked confused.

Uh-oh, Holly thought, Ciara hadn't told him she was moving away. 'Oh, nothing,' she mumbled, rooting through her bag for her purse.

'No, really, what do you mean?' he continued.

'Oh, I mean her shift must be nearly over now,' she said, pulling her purse out of her bag and looking at her watch.

'Oh . . . listen, don't worry about the bill, I'll take care of that.'

'No, I'm not letting you do that,' she said, continuing to search through all the receipts and rubbish in her purse for some money. 'Which reminds me, I owe you twenty.' She placed the money on the table.

'Forget about that.' He waved his hand dismissively.

'Hey, are you going to let me pay for anything?' Holly joked. 'I'm leaving it here on the table anyway, so you'll have to take it.'

Ciara returned to the table and held out her hand for the money.

'It's OK, Ciara, put it on my tab,' Daniel said.

Ciara raised her eyebrows at Holly and winked at her. Then she glanced down at the table and spotted the

322

twenty-euro note. 'Ooh, thanks, sis. I didn't know you were such a good tipper.' She pocketed the money and headed over to serve another table.

'Don't worry,' Daniel laughed, 'I'll take it out of her wages.'

Holly felt relieved finally to be home as she drove down her housing estate. She had got very little sleep the night before, due to pre-interview nerves, and the pressure of the day had worn her out. She was looking forward to opening a bottle of wine and settling down for the night to ponder her next career move.

Her heart began to pound as she spotted Sharon's car outside her house. It had been so long since Holly had spoken to her that she was embarrassed. She contemplated turning the car round and heading off in the other direction but she stopped herself. She needed to face the music sometime before she lost another best friend. If it wasn't too late already.

CHAPTER THIRTY-FIVE

Holly pulled up to her driveway and took a deep breath before getting out of her car. She should have been to visit Sharon first and she knew it, now things just seemed far worse. She walked towards Sharon's car and was surprised to see John stepping out. There was no Sharon to be seen. Her throat became dry; she hoped Sharon was OK.

'Hi, Holly,' John said grimly, banging the car door behind him.

'John! Where's Sharon?'

'I just came from the hospital.' He walked towards her slowly.

Holly's hands flew to her face and tears filled her eyes. 'Oh my God! Is she OK?'

John looked confused. 'Yeah, she's just having a check-up. I'm going back to collect her after I leave here.'

Holly's hands dropped down by her side. 'Oh,' she said, feeling stupid.

'You know, if you're that concerned about her you

should call her.' John held his head high and his icy blue eyes stared straight into hers. Holly could see his jaw clenching and unclenching. She held his stare until the force of his gaze caused her to look away.

'Yeah, I know,' she mumbled. 'Why don't you come inside and I'll make us a cup of tea?' At any other time she would have laughed at herself for saying that; she was turning into one of *them*.

She flicked the switch on the kettle and busied herself while John sat at the table.

'Sharon doesn't know that I'm here so I would appreciate it if you didn't say anything.'

'Oh . . . OK.' Holly felt even more disappointed. Sharon hadn't sent him. She didn't even want to see her; she must have given up on Holly altogether.

'She misses you, you know.' John continued to stare straight at her, not blinking for one moment.

Holly carried the mugs over to the table and sat down. 'I miss her too.'

'It's been two weeks, Holly.'

'It has not been two weeks!' Holly protested weakly, feeling uncomfortable under his stony stare.

'Well, almost two . . . Anyway, it doesn't matter how long it's been exactly, the two of you used to speak to each other every day.' John took the mug from her hand and placed it in front of him.

'Things used to be very different, John,' Holly said angrily. Didn't anybody understand what she was going through? Was she the only sane person in the whole world these days?

'Look, we all know what you've been through—' John started.

325

'I know you all *know* what I've been through, John – that's blatantly obvious – but you all don't seem to understand that I'm *still* going through it!'

There was a silence.

'That's not true at all.' John's voice was quieter and he fixed his gaze on the mug he was rotating on the table before him.

'Yes it is. I can't just move on with my life like you're all doing and pretend that nothing has happened.'

'Do you think that that's what we're doing?'

'Well, let's look at the evidence shall we?' Holly said sarcastically. 'Sharon is having a baby and Denise is getting married—'

'Holly, that's called living,' John interrupted, looking up. 'You seem to have forgotten how to do that. And I'm not saying that I think it's easy for you because I know myself that it's not. I miss Gerry too. He was my best mate. I lived right next door to him all my life. I went to playschool with the guy, for Christsake. We went to primary school together, we went to secondary school together and we played on the same football team. I was his best man at his wedding and he was at mine! Whenever I had a problem I went to Gerry, whenever I wanted to have a bit of fun I went to Gerry. I told him some things that I would never have told Sharon and he told me things he wouldn't have told you. Just because I wasn't married to him doesn't mean that I don't feel like you do. And just because he's dead doesn't mean I have to stop living too.'

Holly sat stunned. John twisted his chair round in order to face her properly. The legs of the chair squeaked loudly in the silence. He took a deep breath before he spoke again.

'Yes it's difficult. Yes it's horrible. Yes it's the worst thing that has ever happened to me in my whole life. But I can't just give up. I can't just stop going to the pub because there's two blokes laughing and joking on the stools Gerry and me used to sit on, and I can't stop going to football matches just because it's somewhere we used to go together all the time. I can remember it all right, and smile about it, but I can't just stop going there.'

Tears welled in Holly's eyes as John continued.

'Sharon knows you're hurting and she understands, but you have to understand that this is a hugely important time in her life too and she needs her best friend to help her through it. She needs your help just like you need hers.'

'I'm trying, John,' Holly sobbed, as hot tears rolled down her cheeks.

'I know you are.' He leaned forward and grabbed her hands. 'But Sharon needs you too. Avoiding the situation isn't going to help anyone or anything.'

'But I went for a job interview today,' she sobbed childishly.

John tried to hide his smile. 'That's great news, Holly. How did it go?'

'Shite,' she sniffed, and John started laughing. He allowed a silence to fall between them before he spoke again.

'She's almost five months pregnant, you know.'

'What? She didn't tell me!'

'She was afraid to,' he said gently. 'She thought you might get mad at her and never want to speak to her again.'

327

'Well, it was stupid of her to think that,' Holly said angrily, and wiped her eyes aggressively.

'Oh really?' he raised his eyebrows. 'So what do you call all this, then?'

Holly looked away. 'I meant to call her, I really did. I picked up the phone every day but I just couldn't do it. Then I would say to myself that I'd call the next day and the next day I would be busy . . . Oh, I'm sorry, John. I'm truly happy for the both of you.'

'Thank you, but it's not me that needs to hear any of this, you know.'

'I know, but I've been so awful! She'll never forgive me now!'

'Don't be stupid, Holly. It's Sharon we're talking about here. It will all be forgotten about by tomorrow.'

Holly raised her eyebrows at him hopefully.

'Well, maybe not *tomorrow*. Next year, perhaps . . . and you'll owe her big time, but she'll eventually forgive you . . .' His icy eyes warmed and twinkled back at her.

'Stop it!' Holly giggled, hitting him on the arm. 'Can I go with you to see her?'

Butterflies fluttered in Holly's stomach as they pulled up outside the hospital. She spotted Sharon looking around as she stood alone outside, waiting to be collected. She looked so cute Holly had to smile. Sharon was going to be a mummy. Holly couldn't believe she was nearly five months pregnant. That meant Sharon had been three months pregnant when they went away on holiday and she hadn't said a word! But, more importantly, Holly couldn't believe that she stupidly hadn't noticed the changes in her friend. Of

328

course she wouldn't have had a bump at only three months but now, as she looked at her dressed in a polo neck and jeans, she could see the swelling of a tiny bump. And it suited her. Holly stepped out of the car and Sharon's face froze.

Oh no, Sharon was going to scream at her. She was going to tell her she hated her and that she never wanted to see her again and that she was a crappy friend and that . . .

Sharon's face broke into a smile and she held her arms out to her. 'Come here to me, you fool,' she said softly.

Holly ran into her arms. There, with her best friend hugging her tight, she felt the tears begin again. 'Oh, Sharon, I'm so sorry. I'm a horrible person. I'm so so so so sorry, please forgive me. I never meant to—'

'Oh, shut up, you whiner and hug me.' Sharon cried too, her voice cracking, and they squeezed each other for a long time.

'Ahem,' John cleared his throat loudly.

'Oh, come here you,' Holly smiled, and dragged him into their huddle.

'I presume this was your idea.' Sharon looked at her husband.

'No, not at all,' he said, winking at Holly. 'I just passed Holly on the street and told her I'd give her a lift . . .'

'Yeah right,' Sharon said, linking arms with Holly as they walked towards the car. 'Well, you certainly gave me a lift, anyway.' She smiled at her friend.

'So what did they say?' Holly asked, squeezing herself forward between the two front seats from the back of the car like an excited little child. 'What is it?'

'Well, you'll never believe this, Holly.' Sharon twisted round in her chair and matched her excitement. 'The doctor told me that . . . and I believe him because apparently he's one of the best . . . anyway, he told me—'

'Come on!' Holly urged her, dying to hear.

'He says it's a baby!'

Holly rolled her eyes. 'Ha-ha. What I mean is, is it a boy or a girl?'

'It's an it for now. They're not too sure yet.'

'Would you want to know what "it" is if they could tell you?'

Sharon scrunched her nose up. 'I don't know, actually. I haven't figured that out yet.' She looked across at John and they smiled excitedly at each other. They shared a secret smile.

A familiar pang of jealousy hit Holly and she sat quietly while she let it pass and the excitement returned.

The three of them headed back to Holly's house. She and Sharon weren't quite ready to leave each other again after just making up. They had so much to talk about. Sitting around Holly's kitchen table, they made up for lost time.

'Sharon, Holly went for a job interview today,' John said when he finally managed to get a word in edgeways.

'Ooh, really? I didn't know you were job-hunting already!'

'Gerry's new mission for me,' Holly smiled.

'Oh, was that what it was this month? I was just dying to know! So how did it go?'

Holly grimaced and held her head in her hands. 'Oh, it was awful, Sharon. I made a total fool of myself.'

'Really? What was the job?'

'Selling advertising space for that magazine, X.'

'Ooh, that's cool. I read that at work all the time.'

'Don't think I know that one; what kind of magazine is it?' John asked.

'It kind of has everything in it: fashion, sports, culture, food, reviews . . . everything really.'

'And adverts,' Holly joked.

'Well, it won't have such good adverts if Holly Kennedy isn't working for them,' Sharon said kindly.

'Thanks, but I really don't think I will be.'

'Why, what was so wrong with the interview? You can't have been that bad.' Sharon looked intrigued as she reached for the pot of tea.

'Oh, I think it's bad when the interviewer asks if you have any experience working on a magazine or newspaper and you tell him you once wrote a newsletter for a shitty company.'

Sharon burst out laughing. 'Newsletter? I hope you weren't referring to that crappy little leaflet that you printed up on the computer to advertise that dive of a company?'

John and Sharon howled with laughter.

'Ah well, it was *advertising* the company . . .' Holly trailed off, feeling even more embarrassed.

'Remember you made us all go out and post them around people's houses in the pissing rain and the freezing cold? It took us days to do!'

'Hey, I remember that,' John laughed. 'Remember you sent me and Gerry out to post hundreds of them one night?'

'Yeah?' Holly was almost afraid to hear what came next.

331

'Well, we shoved them in the skip at the back of Bob's pub and went in for a few pints.' He chuckled at the memory of it and Holly's jaw dropped.

'You sly little bastards!' she laughed. 'Because of you two the company went bust and I lost my job!'

'Oh, I'd say it went bust the minute people took a look at those leaflets, Holly,' Sharon teased. 'Anyway, that place was a kip. You used to moan about it every day.'

'Just one of the many jobs Holly moaned about,' John joked. But he was right.

'Yeah, well, I wouldn't have moaned about this one,' she said sadly.

'There's plenty more jobs out there,' Sharon reassured her. 'You just need to brush up your interview skills.'

'Tell me about it.' Holly stabbed away at the sugar bowl with a spoon.

They sat in silence for a while.

'You published a newsletter,' John repeated a few minutes later, still laughing at the thought of it.

'Shut up, you,' Holly cringed. 'Hey, what else did you and Gerry get up to that I don't know about?' Holly suddenly demanded.

'Ah, a true friend never reveals secrets,' John teased, and his eyes danced with the memories.

But something had been unlocked. And after Holly and Sharon threatened to beat some stories out of him Holly learned things about her husband that night that she never knew before. For the first time since Gerry died, the three of them laughed and talked about him all night, and Holly finally learned how to talk about her husband without being sad. It used to be the four of them together: Holly, Gerry, Sharon and John. This time only three of them gathered to remember the one they had lost. With all their talk, he came alive for them all that night. And soon they would be four again, with the arrival of Sharon and John's baby.

Life went on.

CHAPTER THIRTY-SIX

That Sunday Richard called round to visit Holly with the kids. She had told him he was welcome to bring them by whenever it was his day with them so that they could give Holly and Richard's parents some peace and quiet in their own home for the day. They played outside in the garden while Richard and Holly finished off their dinner and watched them through the patio doors.

'They seem really happy, Richard,' Holly said, watching them playing.

'Yes, they do, don't they?' he smiled. 'I want things to be as normal for them as possible. They don't quite understand what's going on and it's quite difficult to explain.'

'What have you told them?'

'Oh, that Mummy and Daddy don't love each other any more and that I moved away so that we can all be happier. Something along those lines.'

'And they're OK with that?'

Her brother nodded slowly. 'Timothy is, but Emily

is worried that we might stop loving her and that she will have to move away.' He glanced at Holly, his eyes sad.

Poor Emily, Holly thought, watching her dancing around with her scary-looking doll. She couldn't believe that she was having this conversation with Richard. He seemed to be a totally different person these days. Or perhaps it was Holly who had changed; she had a higher tolerance for him now, and found it easier to ignore his annoying little comments, though there were still many of them. But then again she and Richard now had something in common. They both understood what it was like to feel lonely and unsure of themselves.

'How's everything going at Mum and Dad's house?'

Richard swallowed a forkful of mashed potato and nodded. 'Good. They're being extremely generous.'

'Ciara bothering you at all?' Holly felt as if she was questioning her child after his first day of school, wanting to know if the other kids had bullied him. But lately she felt so protective of him. It helped her to help him; it gave her strength.

'Ciara is . . . Ciara,' he smiled. 'We don't see eye to eye on a lot of things.'

'Well, I wouldn't worry about that,' Holly said, trying to stab a piece of pork with her fork. 'The majority of the world wouldn't see eye to eye with her either.' Her fork finally made contact with the pork and she sent it flying off her plate and through the air where it landed on the kitchen counter on the far side of the room.

'And they say pigs don't fly,' Richard remarked.

Holly giggled. 'Hey, Richard, you made a funny!'

He looked pleased with himself. 'I have my moments

too, I suppose,' he said, shrugging his shoulders. 'Although I'm sure you think I don't have many of them.'

Holly speared a carrot, put down her knife and fork and chewed slowly, trying to decide how to phrase what she was going to say. 'We're all different, Richard. Ciara is slightly eccentric, Declan is a dreamer, Jack is a joker, I'm . . . well, I don't know what I am. But you were always very controlled. Straight and serious. It's not necessarily a bad thing, we're all just different.'

'You're very thoughtful,' Richard said after a long silence.

'Pardon?' Holly asked, feeling confused. To cover her embarrassment she stuffed her face with another mouthful of food.

'I've always thought you were very thoughtful,' he repeated.

'When?' Holly asked incredulously, through her mouthful.

'Well, I wouldn't be sitting here eating dinner, with the kids running around having fun outside if you weren't thoughtful now, but I was actually referring to when we were children.'

'I don't think so, Richard. Me and Jack were always so awful to you,' she said softly.

'You weren't *always* awful, Holly.' He gave her an amused smile. 'Anyway, that's what brothers and sisters are for – to make each other's lives as difficult as possible as they grow up. It forms a great basis for life, toughens you up. Anyway, I was the bossy older brother.'

'So how does that make me thoughtful?' Holly asked, feeling she had completely missed the point.

'You idolised Jack. You used to follow him around all

the time and you would do exactly what he told you to do.' He started laughing. 'I used to hear him telling you to say things to me and you would run into my room, terrified, and blurt them out and run away again.'

Holly looked at her plate, embarrassed. She and Jack used to play terrible tricks on Richard.

'But you always came back,' Richard continued. 'You would creep back into my room silently and watch me working at my desk and I knew that was your way of saying sorry.' He smiled at her. 'So that makes you thoughtful. None of our siblings had a conscience in that house of ours, not even me. You were the only one, always the sensitive one.'

He continued eating his dinner and Holly sat in silence, trying to absorb all he had said. She didn't remember idolising Jack but when she thought about it she supposed Richard was right. Jack was her funny, cool, good-looking big brother, who had loads of friends, and Holly used to beg him to let her play with them. She supposed she still felt that way about him. If he called her right now and asked her to go out she would drop everything and go and she had never even realised that before. However, she was spending far more time with Richard than with Jack these days. Jack had always been her favourite brother; Gerry had always got along with Jack the best. It was Jack that Gerry would choose to go out for drinks with during the week, not Richard; it was Jack that Gerry would insist on sitting beside at a family dinner. However, Gerry was gone, and although Jack rang her every now and then he wasn't around as much as he used to be. Had Holly put Jack up on too much of a pedestal? She realised then that she had been making excuses for him every time he didn't call round or phone her when he said he would. In fact, she had been making excuses for him ever since Gerry had died. Was it only their friendship with Gerry that they now had in common?

Richard had, lately, managed to give Holly a regular intake of food for thought. She watched him remove his serviette from his collar and was interested as he folded it into a neat little square with perfect right angles. He obsessively straightened everything on the table so that they were all facing the right way in an orderly fashion. For all Richard's good qualities, which she recognised now, Holly could not live with a man like that at all.

They both jumped as they heard a thump from outside and saw little Emily lying on the ground in floods of tears while a shocked-looking Timmy looked on. Richard leaped out of his chair and hurried outside.

'But she just fell, Daddy, I didn't do anything!' Holly heard Timmy plead with his father. Poor Timmy. She rolled her eyes as she watched Richard dragging him by the arm and ordering him to stand in the corner to think about what he had done. Some people would never really change, she thought wryly.

The next day Holly jumped around the house ecstatically as she replayed the message on the answering machine for the third time.

'Hi, Holly,' came the gruff voice. 'This is Chris Feeney here from X. I'm just calling to say that I was very impressed with your interview. Em . . .' he stalled a bit, 'well, I wouldn't normally say this on an answering machine but no doubt you'll be delighted to know that I've decided to welcome you as a new member of the team. I would love you to start as soon as possible so call me on the usual number when you get a chance and we'll discuss it further. Em . . . goodbye.'

Holly rolled around her bed in terrified delight and pressed the play button again. She had shot for the moon . . . and now she had landed!

CHAPTER THIRTY-SEVEN

Holly stared up at the tall Georgian building and her body tingled with excitement. It was her first day at work and she felt good times were ahead of her. The offices of X were situated in the centre of town, on the second floor, above a small café. Holly had got very little sleep last night, due to nerves and excitement. However, she didn't feel the same dread that she usually felt before starting a new job. She had phoned Chris back immediately (after listening to his voice message another three times) and then she had shared the news with her family and friends. They had been ecstatic, and just before she left the house this morning she had received a beautiful bouquet of flowers from her parents, congratulating her and wishing her luck on her first day.

She felt as though she was starting her first day at school and had gone shopping for a briefcase that made her look extra intelligent. But although she had felt excited when she had sat down to eat her breakfast, she had also felt sad. Sad that Gerry wasn't there to share her exciting new start. They had performed a little ritual every time Holly started a new job, which was quite a regular occurrence. Gerry would wake Holly up with breakfast in bed and then he would pack her bag with ham and cheese sandwiches, an apple, a packet of crisps and a bar of chocolate. Then he would drive her into work on her first day, call her on her lunch break to see if the other kids in the office were playing nicely and later return to collect her and bring her home. Then they would sit together over dinner and he would listen and laugh as Holly explained all the different characters in her office and once again grumble about how much she hated going to work. Mind you, they only ever did that on her first day. Every other day they would tumble out of bed late, race each other to the shower and then wander around the kitchen half-asleep, grumbling while they each grabbed a quick cup of coffee to help kick-start their day. They would give each other a kiss goodbye and go their separate ways. And then they would start all over again the next day. If Holly had known their time was to be so short, she wouldn't have bothered carrying out all those tedious routines . . .

This morning, however, had been a very different scenario. She awoke to an empty house in an empty bed to no breakfast in bed. She didn't have to fight for her right to use the shower first and the kitchen was quiet without the sound of Gerry's fits of morning sneezes. She had allowed herself to imagine that when she woke up Gerry would be miraculously there to greet her because it was tradition, and such a special day that it wouldn't feel right without him. But with death there were no exceptions. Gone meant gone.

Now, poised at the entrance, Holly checked herself to see that her fly wasn't undone, her jacket wasn't tucked into her knickers and that her shirt buttons were fastened properly. Satisfied that she looked presentable she made her way up the wooden staircase to her new office. She entered the waiting room area and the secretary she recognised from the interview came from behind the desk to meet her.

'Hi, Holly,' she said, shaking her hand. 'Welcome to our humble abode.' She held her hands up to display the room. Holly had liked this woman from the moment she had met her at the interview. She looked about the same age as Holly and had long blonde hair and a face that seemed to be always smiling.

'I'm Alice, by the way, and I work out here in reception, as you know. Well, I'll bring you to the boss man now. He's waiting for you.'

'God, I'm not late, am I?' Holly asked worriedly, glancing at her watch. She had left the house early to beat the traffic.

'No, not at all,' Alice said, leading her down to Mr Feeney's office. 'Don't mind Chris and all the other lot, they're all workaholics. They need to get themselves a life, bless them. You wouldn't see me hanging around here anytime after six, that's for sure.'

Holly laughed. Alice reminded her of her former self.

'By the way, don't feel that you have to come in early and stay late just because they do. I think Chris actually lives in his office so you'll never compete with that. The man isn't normal,' she said loudly, tapping on his door and leading her in.

'Who's not normal?' Chris asked gruffly, standing up from his chair and stretching.

'You,' Alice smiled, and closed the door behind her.

'See how my staff treat me?' Chris said, holding out his hand to greet Holly. His handshake was once again warm and welcoming, and Holly felt immediately at ease by the atmosphere between the workers.

'Thank you for hiring me, Mr Feeney,' Holly said genuinely.

'You can call me Chris, and there's no need to thank me. Right, why don't you follow me and I'll show you around the place.' He led her down the hall. The walls were covered with the framed front covers of every copy of X that had been published in the last twenty years.

'There's not much to the place. In here is our office of little ants.' He pushed open the door and Holly looked into the huge office. There were about ten desks in all, and the room was packed with people all sitting in front of their computers and talking on the phone. They looked up and waved politely. Holly smiled at them all, remembering how important first impressions were. 'These are the wonderful journalists that help pay my bills,' Chris explained. 'That's John-Paul, the fashion editor, Mary, our food woman, and Brian, Sean, Gordon, Aishling and Tracey. You don't need to know what they do, they're just wasters.' He laughed and one of the men stuck his fingers up at Chris and continued talking on the phone.

'The rest of the journalists are freelancers so you won't see them hanging around these offices much,' Chris explained, leading her to the room next door. 'This is where all our computer nerds hide. That's Dermot and Wayne and they're in charge of layout and design so

343

you'll be working closely with them and keeping them informed about what advertisements are going where. Lads, this is Holly.'

'Hi, Holly.' They both stood up and shook her hand, and then continued working on their computers again.

'I have them well trained,' Chris remarked, and headed back out to the hall again. 'Down here is the boardroom. We have meetings every morning at eight forty-five.'

Holly nodded to everything he was saying, trying to remember all the names.

'Down those steps are the toilets and I'll show you your office now.'

He headed back down the way they had come and Holly glanced at the walls, feeling excited. This was nothing like she had ever experienced before.

'In here is your office,' he said, pushing the door open and allowing her to walk in ahead of him.

Holly couldn't stop herself from smiling as she looked around at the small room. She had never had her own office before. It was just big enough to fit a desk and filing cabinet in but it was hers. There was a computer sitting on the desk with piles and piles of folders. Opposite the desk was a bookcase crammed with books, yet more folders and stacks of old magazines. The huge Georgian window practically covered the entire back wall behind her desk, and although it was cold and windy outside, the room had a bright and airy feel to it. She could definitely see herself working here.

'It's perfect,' she told Chris, placing her briefcase on the desk and looking around.

'Good,' Chris said. 'The last guy who was here was extremely organised, and all those folders there will explain very clearly what exactly it is you need to do. If you have any problems or any questions about anything at all just come ask me. I'm right next door.' He knocked on the wall that separated their offices.

'Now I'm not expecting miracles from you because I know you're new to this, which is why I expect you to ask lots of questions. Our next edition is due out on the first day of the month.'

Holly's eyes widened: she had a fortnight to fill an entire magazine.

'Don't worry,' he smiled again. 'I want you to concentrate on November's edition. Familiarise yourself with the layout of the magazine. We stick to the same style every month so you will know what kind of pages will need what type of advertisements. This is a lot of work for one person but if you keep yourself organised everything will run smoothly. Speak to Dermot and Wayne and they'll fill you in on the standard layout and if you need anything done just ask Alice. She's there to help everyone.' He stopped talking and looked around. 'So that's about it. Any questions?'

Holly shook her head, 'No, I think you covered just about everything.'

'Right, I'll leave you to it so.' He backed out of the room slowly but paused before closing the door. He watched her surveying the room with satisfaction. 'Holly, I hired you because you seem like a very determined young woman.'

Holly nodded confidently, assuring him he was right.

'I know a hard worker when I see one, haven't been wrong yet.' He gave a small encouraging smile and closed the door softly behind him. Holly immediately sat down at her new desk in her new office, anxious to settle in as quickly as possible. She was slightly scared of her new life. This was the most impressive job she had ever had, and by the sounds of things she was going to be extremely busy, but she was glad. She needed to keep her mind occupied. However, there was no way on earth she had remembered everyone's names so she took out her notepad and pen and wrote down the ones she knew. She opened the folders and got to work.

She was so engrossed in her reading that she realised after a while that she had worked through her lunch break. By the sounds of things, no one else from the office had budged an inch. In her other jobs, Holly would stop working at least half an hour before lunchtime just to think about what she was going to eat. Then she would leave fifteen minutes early and return fifteen minutes late due to 'traffic', even though she would walk to the shop. Holly would daydream the majority of the day, make personal phone calls, especially abroad, because she didn't have to pay the bill, and would be first in queue to collect her monthly pay cheque, which was usually spent within two weeks.

Yes, this was very different from her previous jobs, but she was looking forward to every minute of it.

'Right, Ciara, are you sure you've got your passport?' Elizabeth asked her daughter for the third time since leaving the house.

'Yes, Mum,' Ciara groaned. 'I told you a million billion times, it's right here.'

'Show me,' Elizabeth said, twisting round in the passenger seat.

'No! I'm not showing it to you. You should just take my word for it. I'm not a baby any more, you know.'

Declan snorted and Ciara elbowed him in the ribs. 'Shut up, you.'

'Ciara, just show Mum the passport so you can put her mind at rest,' Holly said tiredly.

'Fine,' she huffed, lifting her bag onto her lap. 'It's in here, look, Mum . . . no, hold on, actually it's in here . . . no, actually maybe I put it in here . . . oh fuck!'

'Jesus Christ, Ciara,' Holly's dad grumbled, slamming on the brakes and turning the car round.

'What?' she said defensively. 'I put it in here, Dad. Someone must have taken it out,' she grumbled, emptying the contents of her bag in the car.

'Bloody hell, Ciara,' Holly moaned as a pair of knickers went flying over her face.

'Ah, shut up,' Ciara grumbled again. 'You won't have to put up with me for much longer.'

Everyone in the car went silent as they realised that was true. Ciara would be in Australia for God only knew how long, and they would all miss her, loud and irritating though she was.

Holly sat squashed beside the window in the back seat of the car with Declan and Ciara as their dad drove them all to the airport to say their goodbyes. Again. Richard was driving Mathew and Jack (ignoring his protestations), and they were probably already at the airport by now. This was their second time returning to the house as Ciara had forgotten her lucky nose ring and had demanded that the car be turned round.

An hour after setting off they reached the airport in what should have only been a twenty-minute drive.

'Jesus, what took you so long?' Jack moaned to Holly when they all finally trudged into the airport with long faces on them. 'I was stuck talking to Dick all on my own.'

'Oh, give it a rest, Jack,' Holly said defensively. 'He's not that bad.'

'Ooh, you've changed your tune,' he teased, his face all mock-surprise.

'No I haven't, you're just singing the wrong song,' she snapped, and walked over to Richard, who was standing alone, watching the world go by. She smiled at her elder brother.

'Pet, keep in touch with us a lot more this time, won't you?' Elizabeth pleaded with her daughter as she hugged her.

'Of course I will, Mum. Oh, please don't cry or you'll get me started too.'

A lump formed in Holly's throat and she fought back the tears. Ciara had been good company over the last few months and had always succeeded in cheering Holly up when she felt that life just couldn't be worse. She would miss her sister, but she understood that she needed to be with Mathew. He was a nice guy and she was happy that they had found each other.

'Take care of my sister.' Holly stood on the tips of her toes to hug the enormous Mathew.

'Don't worry, she's in good hands,' he smiled.

'Look after her now, won't you?' Frank smacked him on the back and smiled.

Mathew was intelligent enough to know it was more of a warning than a question and gave him a very persuasive answer.

'Bye, Richard,' Ciara said, giving him a big hug. 'Stay away from that Meredith bitch now. You're far too good for her.' Ciara turned to Declan. 'You can come over anytime you like, Dec, maybe make a movie or something about me,' she said seriously, giving him a big hug.

'Jack, look after my big sis,' she said, smiling at Holly. 'Ooh, I'm gonna miss you,' she added sadly, squeezing Holly tightly.

'Me too.' Holly's voice shook. She knew it was best for her sister to go, but they had become so close in recent months that a part of Holly wished she would stay.

'OK I'm going now before all you depressing people make me cry,' she said, trying to sound happy.

'Don't go using those rope jumps again, Ciara. They're far too dangerous,' Frank said, looking worried.

'Bungee jumps, Dad!' Ciara laughed, kissing him and her mother on the cheeks again. 'Don't worry, I'm sure I'll find something new to try,' she teased.

Holly stood in silence with her family and watched as Ciara and Mathew walked hand in hand through the boarding gate. Even Declan had a tear in his eye, but pretended his eyes were watering because he was about to sneeze.

'Just look at the lights, Declan.' Jack threw his arm around his baby brother. 'They say that helps you sneeze.'

Declan stared up at the lights and avoided watching his favourite sister walking away. Frank held his wife close to him as she waved, while tears rolled down her cheeks.

They all laughed as the alarm went off as Ciara walked through the security scanner and was ordered to empty her pockets, followed by a frisk.

'Every bloody time,' Jack laughed. 'It's a wonder they agreed to let her into the country at all.'

They all waved goodbye as Ciara and Mathew walked on and her pink hair was eventually lost among the crowd.

'OK,' Elizabeth said, wiping the tears from her face, 'why don't the rest of my babies come back to the house and we can all have lunch?'

They all agreed, seeing how upset their mother was.

'I'll let you go with Richard this time,' Jack said smartly to Holly, and wandered off with the rest of the family, leaving Richard and Holly standing there slightly taken aback.

'So how was your first week at work, darling?' Elizabeth asked Holly as they all sat around the table eating lunch.

'Oh, I love it, Mum,' Holly said, and her eyes lit up. 'It's so much more interesting and challenging than any other job I've done, and all the staff are just so friendly. There's a great atmosphere in the place.'

'Well, that's the most important thing, isn't it?' Frank said, pleased. 'What's your boss like?'

'He's such a doll. He reminds me so much of you, Dad, I just feel like giving him a big hug and a kiss every time I see him.'

'Sounds like sexual harassment in the workplace to me,' Declan joked, and Jack sniggered.

Holly rolled her eyes at her brothers.

'Are you doing any new documentaries this year, Declan?' Jack asked.

'Yeah, on homelessness,' he said with his mouth full of food.

'Declan,' Elizabeth scrunched up her nose at him, 'don't talk with your mouth full.'

'Sorry,' Declan said, and spat the food out on the table.

Jack burst out laughing, while the rest of the family looked away in disgust.

'What did you say you were doing, son?' Frank asked, trying to avoid a family fight.

'I'm doing a documentary on homelessness this year for college.'

'Oh, very good,' he replied, retreating back to a world of his own.

'What member of the family are you using as your subject this time? Richard?' Jack said slyly.

Holly slammed down her knife and fork.

'That's not funny, man,' Declan said seriously, surprising Holly.

'God, why is everyone so touchy these days?' Jack asked, looking around. 'It was just a joke.'

'It wasn't funny, Jack,' Elizabeth said sternly.

'What did he say?' Frank asked his wife after snapping out of his trance.

Elizabeth just shook her head dismissively and he knew not to ask again.

Holly watched Richard, who sat at the end of the table eating quietly. Her heart leaped out to him. He didn't deserve this, and either Jack was being more cruel than usual, or else this was the norm and Holly must have been a fool to have found it funny.

'Sorry, Richard, I was just joking,' Jack said.

'That's OK, Jack.'

'So have you found a job yet?'

'No, not yet.'

'That's a shame,' he said drily, and Holly glared at him. What the hell was his problem?

'Oh, Jack,' Holly sighed, slicing into her chicken breast, 'you really do need to grow up, you know.'

Jack finished his beer and glared at her.

Elizabeth calmly picked up her cutlery and plate of food without a word to anyone and made her way into the living room where she turned the television on and ate her dinner in peace.

Her 'funny little elves' weren't making her laugh any more.

CHAPTER THIRTY-EIGHT

Holly drummed her fingers on her desk and stared out the window. She was absolutely flying through her work this week. She didn't know it was possible to actually *enjoy* work so much. She had happily sat through lunch breaks and had even stayed late, and didn't feel like punching any of her fellow employees in the face yet. But it was only her third week, after all; give her time. The office had developed a light-hearted banter and she would often hear people screaming at each other from office to office. It was all in good humour and she loved it.

She loved feeling that she was a part of the team; as though she were actually doing something that made a huge impact on the finished product. She thought of Gerry every single day when she was at work. Every time she made a deal she thanked him, thanked him for pushing her all the way to the top. She still had her miserable days when she didn't feel worthy of getting out of bed, of course. But the excitement of her job spurred her on.

She heard the radio in Chris's office next door and she smiled. On the hour every hour without fail he turned on the news. And all the news seeped into Holly's brain subconsciously. She had never felt so intelligent in her life.

'Hey!' Holly yelled, banging on the wall. 'Turn that thing down! Some of us are trying to work!'

She heard him chuckle and she smiled. She glanced back down at her work again; a freelancer had written an article on how he had travelled around Ireland trying to find the cheapest pint and it was very amusing. There was a huge gap at the bottom of the page and it was up to Holly to fill it. She flicked through her book of contacts and an idea came to her immediately. She picked up the phone and dialled.

'Hogan's.'

'Hi, Daniel Connolly, please.'

'One moment.'

Bloody 'Greensleeves' again. She put it on speaker phone and danced around the room to the music while she waited. Chris walked in, took one look at her and closed the door again. Holly smiled.

'Hello?'

'Daniel?'

'Yes.'

'Hiya, it's Holly.'

'How are you doin', Holly?'

'I'm grand thanks, you?'

'Couldn't be better.'

'That's a nice complaint.'

He laughed. 'How's that snazzy job of yours?'

'Well, actually that's why I'm calling.' Holly sounded guilty.

'Oh no!' he laughed. 'I have made it company policy not to employ any more Kennedys here.'

Holly giggled. 'Oh damn and I was so looking forward to throwing drinks over the customers.'

He laughed. 'So what's up?'

'Do I remember hearing you say you needed to advertise Club Diva more?' Well, he had actually thought that he was saying it to Sharon, but she knew he wouldn't remember that minor detail.

'I do recall saying that, yes.'

'Good, well, how would you like to advertise it in *X*?'

'Is that the name of the magazine you work on?'

'No, I just thought it would be an interesting question, that's all,' she joked. 'Of course it's where I work!'

'Oh, *of course*, I'd forgotten. That's the magazine that has the offices just round the corner from me. The one that causes you to walk by my front door everyday and yet you still don't call in. Why don't I see you at lunchtime?' he teased. 'Isn't my pub good enough for you?'

'Oh, everyone here eats their lunch at their desks,' she explained. 'So what do you think?'

'I think that's very boring of you all.'

'No, I mean what do you think about the ad?'

'Yeah, sure, that's a good idea.'

'OK, well, I'll put it in the November issue. Would you like it placed monthly?'

'Would you like to tell me how much that would set me back?' he laughed.

Holly totted up the figures and told him.

'Hmm . . .' he said, 'I'll have to think about it, but I'll definitely go for the November edition.'

'Oh, that's great! You'll be a millionaire after this goes to print.'

'I'd better be,' he laughed. 'By the way, there's a launch party for some new drink coming up the week after next. Will I put your name down for an invite?'

'Yeah, that would be great. What new drink is it?'

'Blue Rock. It's a new alcopop that's apparently going to be huge. Tastes like shite but it's free all night so I'll buy the rounds.'

'Wow, you're such a good advertisement for it,' she laughed. 'When is it on?' She took out her diary and made a note of it. 'That's perfect. I can come straight after work.'

'Well, make sure you bring your bikini to work in that case.'

'Make sure I bring my *what*?'

'Your bikini,' he laughed. 'The launch has a beach theme.'

'But it's nearly winter, you nutter.'

'Hey, it wasn't my idea. The slogan is, "Blue Rock, the hot new drink for winter".'

'Uugghh, how tacky.'

'And messy. We're getting sand thrown all over the floor, which will be a nightmare to clean up. Anyway, listen, I'd better get back to work. We're mad busy today.'

'OK, thanks, Daniel. Have a think about what you want your ad to say and get back to me.'

'Will do.'

She stood up and went next door to Chris's office, a thought occurring to her.

'You finished dancing in there?' he chuckled.

'Yeah, I just made up a routine. Came in to show you,' she joked.

'What's the problem?' he said.

'No problem; just an idea.'

'Take a seat.' He nodded to the chair in front of him. Just three weeks ago she had sat there for an interview and now here she was putting ideas forward to her new boss. Funny how life changed so quickly – but then again she had learned that already . . .

'What's the idea?'

'Well, you know Hogan's, round the corner?'

Chris nodded.

'I was just on to the owner and he's going to place an ad in the magazine.'

'That's great, but I hope you don't tell me about every time you fill a space, we could be here all year.'

Holly rolled her eyes. 'That's not it, Chris. Anyway, he was telling me that they're having a launch party on Tuesday week for a new drink called Blue Rock. It has a beach theme, all the staff will be in bikinis and that kind of thing.'

'In autumn?' He raised his eyebrows.

'It's apparently the hot new drink for winter.'

He rolled his eyes. 'Tacky.'

Holly smiled. 'That's what I said. Anyway, I just thought it might be worth covering. I know we're supposed to raise ideas in the meetings but this is happening pretty soon.'

'I understand. That's a great idea, Holly. I'll get one of the lads on to it.'

Holly smiled and stood up from her chair. 'By the way, did you get that garden sorted yet?'

Chris frowned. 'I've had about ten different people come down to look at it. They tell me it'll cost six grand to do.'

'That's a lot of money.'

'Well, it's a big garden. A lot of work needs to be done.'

'What was the cheapest quote?'

'Five and a half grand, why?'

'Because my brother will do it for five,' she blurted out.

'Five?' his eyes nearly popped out of his head. 'Is he any good?'

'Remember I told you my garden was a jungle?'

He nodded.

'Well, no longer. He did a great job on it but the only thing is that he works alone so it takes him longer.'

'For that price I don't care how long it takes. Have you got his business card with you?'

'Eh . . . yeah, hold on and I'll get it.' She stole some impressive-looking card-like paper from Alice's desk, typed up Richard's name and mobile number in a fancy typeface and printed it out, cutting the card into a small rectangle shape.

'That's great,' Chris said, reading it. 'I'll give him a call now.'

'No, no,' Holly said quickly, 'you'll get him easier after the weekend. He's up to his eyeballs today.'

'Right so; thanks, Holly.' She started to head towards the door and stopped when he called out to her, 'Oh, by the way, how are you at writing?'

'It was one of the subjects I learned at school.'

Chris laughed. 'Are you still on that level?'

'Well, I'm sure I could purchase a thesaurus.'

'Good, because I need you to cover that launch thing.'

'Oh?'

'I can't get any of the others – they've already got events to cover that evening – and I can't go to it myself so I have to rely on you.' He shuffled some papers on his desk. 'I'll send one of the photographers down with you; get a few shots of the sand and the bikinis.'

'Oh . . . OK.' Holly's heart raced.

'How does eight hundred words sound?'

Impossible, she thought. As far as she knew she only had fifty words in her vocabulary. 'That's no problem,' she said confidently, and backed out the door.

Shit shit shit shit, she thought; how on earth was she going to pull this one off? She couldn't even spell properly.

She picked up the phone and pressed redial.

'Hogan's.'

'Daniel Connolly, please.'

'One moment.'

'Don't put me on . . . !'

'Greensleeves' started.

'. . . Hold,' she finished.

'Hello?'

'Daniel, it's me,' she said quickly.

'Would you ever leave me alone?' he teased.

'No, I need help.'

'I know you do, but I'm not qualified for that,' he laughed.

'No, seriously, I mentioned that launch to my editor and he wants to cover it.'

'Oh, brilliant. You can forget about that ad so!' he laughed.

'No, not brilliant. He wants *me* to write it.'

'That's great news, Holly.'

'No it's not. I can't write,' she panicked.

'Oh really? That was one of the main subjects in my school.'

'Oh, Daniel, please be serious for a minute . . .'

'OK, what do you want me to do?'

'I need you to tell me absolutely everything you know about this drink and the launch so I can start writing it now and have a few days to work on it.'

'Yes, just one minute, sir,' he yelled away from the phone. 'Look, Holly, I really have to get back to work now.'

'Please,' she whimpered.

'OK, listen, what time do you finish work?'

'Six.' She crossed her fingers and prayed for him to help her.

'Why don't you come around here then, and I'll take you somewhere to have a bite?'

'Oh, thank you so much, Daniel,' and she jumped around her office with relief. 'You're a star!'

She hung up the phone and breathed a sigh of relief. Maybe there was a chance she could get the article done after all, and still manage to keep her job. Then she froze as she went back over the conversation in her head.

Had she just agreed to go on a date with Daniel?

CHAPTER THIRTY-NINE

Holly couldn't concentrate during the last hour of work; she kept on watching the clock, willing the time to go more slowly. For once it was doing the exact opposite. Why didn't it go this fast when she was waiting to open her messages from Gerry? She was dreading her dinner with Daniel before then.

At six o'clock on the dot she heard Alice switch off her computer and clatter down the wooden stairs to freedom. Holly smiled, remembering how she had once felt the same. But then again everything was different when you had a beautiful husband to go home to. If she still had Gerry she would be racing Alice out the door.

She listened as a few of the others packed up their things, and prayed Chris would dump another load of work on her desk just so she would have to stay late and cancel dinner with Daniel. She and Daniel had been out together millions of times, so why was she worrying now? They were the 'two single friends', and every time

361

somebody had a dinner party or arranged a night out the two of them had always been invited to keep each other company, as though they were unable to speak to the other couples at the table. It seemed that people felt that if they invited Daniel, they must invite Holly too. And although they had spent most of the evenings monopolising each other, they had always been in others' company. But something was niggling at the back of Holly's mind. There had been something in his voice that worried her, and something had happened to her stomach earlier when they spoke that made her feel uneasy about meeting up with him. She felt so guilty and ashamed for going out with him and tried to convince herself it was just a business dinner. In fact, the more she thought about it she realised that was exactly what it was. She smiled as she thought about how she had become one of those people who discussed business over dinner. Usually the only business she discussed over food was men and life in general with Sharon and Denise – girls' business.

She shut down her computer and packed her briefcase. Everything she did was in slow motion, as though that would prevent her from having to have dinner with Daniel. She hit herself over the head . . . it was a *business* dinner.

'Hey, don't beat yourself up about it.' Alice leaned in through Holly's door.

Holly jumped with fright. 'Jesus, Alice, I didn't see you there.'

'Everything OK?'

'Yeah,' she said unconvincingly, 'I just have to do something that I really don't want to do. But I kind of want to do it, which makes me not want to do it even more because it seems so wrong even though it's right. You know?'

Alice was staring at her with wide eyes. 'I thought *I* overanalysed things.'

'Oh, don't mind me,' Holly perked up. 'I'm just going nuts.'

'It happens to the best of us.'

'What are you doing back here?' Holly asked, realising she had heard her colleague legging it out the door earlier. 'Does freedom not beckon you?'

'I know,' Alice rolled her eyes, 'but I forgot we had a meeting at six.'

'Oh.' Holly was disappointed. Nobody had told her about any meeting today, which wasn't unusual, because she wasn't required to be at all of them. But it was unusual for Alice to attend one without Holly being asked.

'Is it about anything interesting?' Holly poked around for information, trying to sound uninterested while she busied herself at her desk.

'It's the astrology meeting.'

'Astrology?'

'Yeah, we have it monthly.'

'Oh, am I supposed to be there or am I not invited to it?' She tried not to sound bitter but failed miserably, much to her embarrassment.

Alice laughed. 'Of course you're welcome to come, Holly. I was just about to ask you, which is why I'm standing outside your office.'

Holly put her briefcase down, feeling stupid, and followed Alice into the boardroom where everybody was waiting.

'Everyone, this is Holly's first astrology meeting so let's make her feel welcome,' Alice announced.

Holly took her seat while they all applauded their new member at the table.

Chris rolled his eyes at Holly. 'Holly, I just want you to know in advance that I have absolutely nothing to do with this nonsense and also to apologise to you for being dragged into it.'

'Oh, shut up, Chris,' Tracey waved a hand at her boss, taking her seat at the head of the table, clutching a notepad and pen. 'OK, who wants to go first this month?'

'Let Holly go first,' Alice said generously.

Holly looked around completely baffled. 'But I don't have a clue what's going on.'

'Well, what star sign are you?' Tracey asked.

'Taurus.'

Everyone oohed and aahed and Chris held his head in his hands and tried to look like he wasn't enjoying himself.

'Ooh, great,' Tracey said happily. 'We've never had a Taurus before. OK, so are you married or seeing anyone or single or anything?'

Holly blushed as Brian winked over at her and Chris smiled encouragingly. He was the only one at the table who knew about Gerry. Holly realised this was the first time she had had to answer this question since Gerry died, and she was confused as to how to answer. 'Em . . . no, I'm not really seeing anyone but . . .'

'OK then,' Tracey said, starting to write. 'This month Taurus shall look out for someone tall, dark and handsome and . . .' she shrugged and looked up, 'anybody?'

'Because he will have a big impact on her future,' Alice helped out.

Brian winked at Holly again, obviously finding it very amusing that he was also tall and dark, but quite obviously blind if he thought he was handsome. Holly shuddered and he looked away.

'OK, the career stuff is easy,' Tracey continued. 'So Taurus will be occupied and satisfied by a new workload that comes their way. Lucky day will be a . . .' she thought for a while, 'Tuesday, and lucky colour is . . . blue,' she decided, looking at the colour of Holly's top. 'Right, who's next?'

'Hold on a minute, is this my horoscope for next month?' Holly interrupted, shocked.

Everyone around the table laughed.

'Have we shattered your dreams?' Gordon teased.

'Completely,' she said. 'I love reading my horoscopes. Please tell me this isn't what all magazines do?' she pleaded.

Chris shook his head, 'No, not all magazines do it like this, Holly. Some of them just hire people who have the talent to make it up themselves without involving the rest of the office.' He glared at Tracey.

'Ha-ha, Chris,' she said drily.

'So, Tracey, you're not psychic?' Holly asked sadly.

Tracey shook her head. 'No, not psychic, but I'm good as an agony aunt and at making up crossword puzzles, thank you very much.' She glared at Chris, and he mouthed the word 'wow' at her.

'Ah, you've all ruined it for me now,' Holly laughed, and sat back in her chair, feeling deflated.

'OK, Chris, you're next. This month Gemini will over-work themselves, never leave their office and eat junk food all the time. They need to find some sort of balance in their lives.'

Chris rolled his eyes. 'You write that every month, Tracey.'

'Well, until you change your lifestyle, I can't change what Gemini will do, can I?'

They went through everyone's star sign and Tracey finally gave in to Brian's demands that Leo be desired by the opposite sex all month and win the lottery. Hmm . . . wonder what star sign Brian was. Holly looked at her watch and realised she was very late for her business meeting with Daniel.

'Oh sorry, everybody, I have to rush off,' she said, excusing herself from the table.

'Your tall, dark and handsome man awaits you,' Alice giggled. 'Send him on to me if you don't want him.'

Holly headed outside and her heart beat wildly as she spotted Daniel walking down the road to meet her. The cool autumn months had arrived, so Daniel was back wearing his black leather jacket again, teamed with blue jeans. His dark hair was messy and stubble lined his chin. He had that just-out-of-bed look. Holly's stomach lurched again and she looked away.

'Ooh, I told you!' Tracey said excitedly, as she walked out the door behind Holly and hurried off down the road happily.

'I'm so sorry Daniel,' Holly apologised. 'I got tied up in a meeting and I couldn't call.'

'Don't worry about it, I'm sure it was important,' he smiled at her, and she instantly felt guilty. This was Daniel, her friend, not someone she should be avoiding. What on earth was wrong with her?

366

'So where would you like to go?' he asked.

'How about in there?' Holly said, looking at the small café on the ground floor of her office building. She wanted to go to the least intimate and most casual place possible.

Daniel scrunched up his nose. 'I'm a bit hungrier than that, if you don't mind. I haven't eaten all day.'

They walked along together and Holly pointed out every single café along the way, which Daniel shook his head at every time. Eventually he settled on an Italian restaurant that Holly couldn't say no to. Not because she wanted to go in but because he had said no to every other restaurant on the road.

Inside it was quiet with just a few tables occupied by couples staring lovingly into each other's eyes in the candlelight. Daniel stood up to take his jacket off and Holly quickly blew out the candle on their table when he wasn't looking. He was dressed in a deep blue shirt, highlighting the colour of his eyes and making them seem luminous in the dim restaurant.

'They make you sick, don't they?' Daniel laughed, following Holly's gaze to a couple on the far side of the room, who were holding hands across the table.

'Actually no. They make me sad.'

Daniel hadn't heard her, as he was busy reading the menu. 'What are you having?'

'I'm going to have a Caesar salad.'

Daniel rolled his eyes, 'You women and your salads. Aren't you hungry?'

'Not really.' She shook her head, then blushed as her stomach grumbled loudly.

'I think somebody disagrees with you down there,' he laughed. 'I don't think you ever eat, Holly Kennedy.'

Just not when I'm with you, she thought. 'I just don't have a very big appetite, that's all.'

'Yeah, well, I've seen rabbits eat more than you do,' he laughed.

Holly tried to control the conversation, steering it into safe territory, and they spent the evening talking about the launch party. She wasn't in the mood for discussing their private feelings and thoughts tonight; she wasn't even sure what exactly they were right then. Daniel had kindly brought a copy of the press release so that Holly could look through it in advance and get to work on the article as soon as possible. He also gave her a list of phone numbers for the people who worked at Blue Rock so that Holly could get a few quotes. He was extremely helpful, giving her tips on what angle to take and who to talk to for more information. She was now feeling a lot less panicked about having to write an article – however, a little more panicked about why she had been so uncomfortable with a man that she was certain only wanted to be her friend. She was also still starving, having only eaten a few lettuce leaves.

She stepped outside of the restaurant for a breath of fresh air while Daniel paid the bill. He was an extremely generous man, there was no denying that, and she was glad of his friendship. It just didn't feel quite right for her to be eating in an intimate restaurant with anyone other than Gerry.

She froze and tried to hide her face as she spotted a couple walking towards her who she really did not wish to see. She bent over to pretend to tie her shoelace until she realised she had worn her zip-up boots that day and ended up embarrassingly fumbling with the ends of her trousers.

'Holly, is that you?' she heard the familiar voice. She stared at the two pairs of shoes standing in front of her and slowly looked up to meet their eyes.

'Hello, there!' She tried to sound surprised while nervously steadying herself to her feet.

'How are you?' the woman asked, giving her a hug. 'What are you doing standing out here in the cold?'

Holly prayed that Daniel stayed inside for another while longer. 'Oh, you know . . . I was just having a bite to eat,' she smiled shakily, pointing at the restaurant.

'Oh, we're just about to go in there,' the man said smiling. 'It's a shame we just missed you; we could have eaten together.'

'Yes, yes, it's a shame . . .'

'Well, good for you, anyway,' the woman said, patting her on the back. 'It's good to get out and to do things on your own.'

'Well, actually . . .' Holly glanced at the door again, praying that it wouldn't open. 'Yes, it's nice to do that . . .' she trailed off.

'There you are!' Daniel said, stepping outside. 'I thought you had run off on me.' He wrapped his arm loosely round her shoulders.

Holly smiled at him weakly and turned to face the couple.

'Oh, sorry, I didn't see you there,' Daniel smiled, turning to face them.

The couple stared back at him stonily.

'Eh . . . Daniel, this is Judith and Harold. Gerry's parents.'

CHAPTER FORTY

Holly pressed down on her car horn heavily and cursed the driver in front of her. She was fuming. She was mad at herself for being caught in such a situation last night. She was mad at herself for feeling that she *had* been caught in a bad situation when really there was nothing to it. But she was even angrier at herself for feeling like there was more to it because she had really enjoyed Daniel's company all evening. And she shouldn't be enjoying herself because it didn't feel right, but it had felt so right at the time . . .

She held her hand up to her head and massaged her temples. She had a headache and she was overanalysing things again, and the stupid traffic all the way home was driving her insane. Poor Daniel, she thought sadly. Gerry's parents had been so rude to him and had ended the conversation abruptly and charged into the restaurant, refusing to make eye contact with Holly. Oh, why did they have to see her the one time she was happy? They could have come round to the house any day of the week

370

to see her feeling so miserable and living the perfect grieving widow life. But they hadn't and now they probably thought she was having a great life without their son. Well, screw them, she thought angrily, pushing down on the horn again. Why did it always take people five minutes to move from the traffic lights when they went green?

She had to wait at every single set of traffic lights she came across when all she wanted to do was to go home and throw a tantrum. She picked up her mobile while she waited and called Sharon, knowing she would understand.

'Hello?'

'Hi, John, it's Holly. Can I speak to Sharon?'

'Sorry, Holly, she's asleep. I would wake her for you but she's been absolutely exhausted—'

'No, don't worry,' she interrupted. 'I'll call her tomorrow.'

'Is it important?' he asked, worried.

'No,' she said quietly, 'it's not important at all.' She hung up and immediately dialled Denise's number.

'Hello?' Denise giggled.

'Hiya,' Holly said.

'Are you OK?' Denise giggled again. 'Tom, stop!' she whispered, and Holly realised she had called at a bad time.

'Yeah, I'm fine. I just called for a chat but I can hear you're busy there.' She forced a laugh.

'OK then, I'll call tomorrow, Hol,' Denise replied.

'OK, b—' Holly didn't even get to finish her sentence as Denise had hung up.

She sat at the traffic lights, lost in thought until loud beeps behind her caused her to jump.

She decided to go to her parents' house and talk to Ciara. She would cheer her up. Just as she pulled up outside the house, she remembered Ciara was no longer there and her eyes filled with tears. Once again she had nobody.

She rang the doorbell anyway and Declan answered.

'What's wrong with you?'

'Nothing,' she said, feeling sorry for herself. 'Where's Mum?'

'In the kitchen with Dad talking to Richard. I'd leave them alone for a bit.'

'Oh . . . OK . . .' she felt lost. 'What are you up to?'

'I'm just watching what I filmed today.'

'Is this for the documentary on homelessness?'

'Yeah, do you wanna watch it?'

'Yeah.' She smiled gratefully and settled herself down on the couch. A few minutes into the video and Holly was in tears, but for once they weren't for herself. Declan had done the most amazing interview with an incredible guy who was living on the streets of Dublin. She realised there were people far worse off than she, and the fact that Gerry's parents had bumped into her and Daniel walking out of a restaurant suddenly seemed such a stupid thing to worry about.

'Oh, Declan, that was excellent,' she said, drying her eyes when it had finished.

'Thanks,' he said quietly, taking the video out of the player and packing it in his bag.

'Are you not happy with it?'

He shrugged his shoulders. 'When you end up spending the day with people like that it's kind of hard to be happy about the fact that what he has to say is *so* bad that it

372

makes a great documentary. The worse off he is the better off I am.'

Holly listened with interest. 'No, I don't agree with that, Declan. I think that you filming this will make a difference to him. People will see it and want to help.'

Declan just shrugged, 'Maybe. Anyway, I'm going to bed now, I'm absolutely knackered.' He picked up his bag and kissed her on the top of her head as he passed, which really touched Holly. Her baby brother was finally growing up.

Holly glanced at the clock on the mantelpiece and noticed it was almost twelve. She reached for her bag and took out the October envelope from Gerry. She dreaded the days when there would be no more letters. There were only two left after this. She ran her fingers over the writing once again before tearing the seal open. Holly slid the card out of the envelope and a dried flower which had been pressed between two cards, fell on to her lap. Her favourite, a fragile little sunflower. Along with it, a small pouch had landed on her lap. She studied it with curiosity and realised it was a packet of sunflower seeds. Her hands shook as she touched the delicate petals of the flower, not wanting them to snap between her fingers. Gerry's message read:

A sunflower for my sunflower, to brighten the dark October days you hate so much. Plant some more, safe in the knowledge that a warm and bright summer awaits.

PS. I love you . . .

PPS. Could you please pass this card on to John?

Holly lifted the second card that had fallen onto her lap and read the words through her tears and her laughter.

> *To John,*
> *Happy 32nd Birthday,*
> *You're getting old, my friend, but I hope you have many, many more birthdays. Take care, enjoy life, take care of my wife and Sharon. You're the man now! Lots of love,*
> *Your friend,*
> *Gerry*
> *Told you I'd keep my promise . . .*

Holly read and reread every single word Gerry had written. She sat on that couch for what seemed like hours and thought about how happy John would be to hear from his friend. She thought about how much her life had changed over the past few months. Her working life had definitely improved and she was proud of herself for sticking at it. She loved the feeling of satisfaction she got each day when she switched off her computer and left the office. Gerry had pushed her to be brave; he had encouraged her to want a job that meant more to her in life than just a pay cheque. She wouldn't have needed to search for those extra things if Gerry were still with her. Life without him was emptier but left more room for herself. She'd exchange it all to have Gerry back, though.

That wasn't an option. She needed to start thinking about herself and her own future. Because there was no one else to share the responsibilities with her any more.

* * *

She wiped her eyes and stood up from the couch. She felt a new bounce in her step. She tapped lightly on the kitchen door.

'Come in,' Elizabeth called.

Holly stepped in and looked around at her parents and Richard sitting at the table, holding cups of tea.

'Oh, hello, love,' her mum said happily, getting up to give her a hug and a kiss. 'I didn't hear you come in.'

'I've been here about an hour. I was just watching Declan's documentary.' Holly beamed at her family and felt like giving them all a hug.

'It's great, isn't it?' Frank said, standing up to greet his elder daughter.

Holly nodded and joined them at the table. 'Have you found a job yet?' she asked Richard.

He shook his head sadly and looked as though he were going to cry.

'Well, I did.'

He looked at her disgusted that she could say such a thing. 'Well, I know *you* did.'

'No, Richard,' she smiled, 'I mean I got *you* a job.'

'You what?'

'You heard me,' she grinned. 'My boss will be calling you on Monday.'

His face fell. 'Oh, Holly, that's very nice of you indeed but I have no interest in advertising. My interest is in science.'

'And gardening.'

'Yes, I like gardening.' He looked confused.

'So that's why my boss will be calling you. To ask you to work on his garden. I told him you'll do it for five thousand, I hope that's OK.' She smiled as his jaw dropped.

375

He was completely speechless so Holly kept on talking.

'And here are your business cards,' she said, handing him a large pile of cards that she had printed up.

Richard and her parents picked up the cards and read them in silence.

Suddenly Richard started laughing, jumped out of his chair, pulled Holly with him and danced her around the kitchen while her parents looked on and cheered.

'Oh, by the way,' Richard said, calming down and glancing at the card again, 'you spelled gardener wrong.' He spoke slowly. 'It's not gardner, it is gard-en-er. See the difference?'

Holly stopped dancing and sighed with frustration.

CHAPTER FORTY-ONE

'OK, this is the last one, I promise, girls!' Denise called as her bra was sent flying over the changing-room door.

Sharon and Holly groaned and collapsed in their chairs again.

'You said that an hour ago,' Sharon complained, kicking off her shoes and massaging her swollen ankles.

'Yeah, but I mean it this time. I have a really good feeling about this dress,' Denise said, full of excitement.

'You said *that* an hour ago too,' Holly grumbled, resting her head back on the chair and closing her eyes.

'Don't you go falling asleep on me now,' Sharon warned Holly and her eyes immediately shot open.

They had been dragged to every single wedding gown boutique in the city and Sharon and Holly were exhausted, irritated and extremely fed up. Whatever excitement they had felt for Denise and her wedding had been drained from their systems as Denise tried on dress after dress. And if Holly heard Denise's irritating squeals one more time she would . . .

'Oooh, I love it!' Denise shrieked.

'OK, here's the plan,' Sharon whispered to Holly. 'If she walks out of there looking like a meringue that has sat on a bicycle pump we are going to tell her she looks beautiful.'

Holly giggled. 'Oh, Sharon, we can't do that!'

'Oooh, wait till you see!' Denise shrieked again.

'On second thoughts . . .' Holly looked at Sharon miserably.

'OK, are you ready?'

'Yes,' Sharon groaned unenthusiastically.

'Ta-da!' Denise stepped out of the dressing room and Holly's eyes widened.

'That's so beautiful on you,' the sales assistant, who had been hovering, gushed.

'Oh, stop it!' Denise cried. 'You're no help to me at all! You've loved every single one of them.'

Holly gazed at Sharon uncertainly and tried not to laugh at the look on her face; she looked as if there was a bad smell in the air.

Sharon rolled her eyes and whispered, 'Hasn't Denise ever heard of a thing called commission?'

'What are you two whispering about?' Denise asked.

'Oh, just about how pretty you look.'

Holly frowned at Sharon.

'Oh, do you like it?' Denise squealed again, and Holly winced.

'Yes,' Sharon said unenthusiastically.

'Are you sure?'

'Yes.'

'Do you think Tom will be happy when he looks down the aisle and sees me walking towards him?'

Denise even practised her walk just so the girls could imagine it.

'Yes,' Sharon repeated.

'But are you sure?'

'Yes.'

'Do you think it's worth the money?'

'Yes.'

'Really?'

'Yes.'

'It'll be nicer with a tan, won't it?'

'Yes.'

'Oh, but does it make my bum look enormous?'

'Yes.'

Holly looked at Sharon, startled, realising she wasn't even listening to the questions any more.

'Oh, but are you sure?' Denise carried on, obviously not even listening to the answers.

'Yes.'

'So will I get it?'

Holly expected the sales assistant to start jumping up and down with excitement screaming 'Yessss!' but she managed to contain herself.

'No!' Holly interrupted before Sharon said yes again.

'No?' Denise asked.

'No,' Holly confirmed.

'Do you not like it?'

'No.'

'Is it because it makes me look fat?'

'No.'

'Do you not think Tom will like it?'

'No.'

'Do you think it's worth the money, though?'

379

'No.'

'Oh.' She turned to face Sharon. 'Do you agree with Holly?'

'Yes.'

The sales assistant rolled her eyes and approached another customer, hoping for better luck with her.

'OK then, I trust you two,' Denise said sadly, taking one last look at herself in the mirror. 'To be honest, I wasn't really that keen on it myself.'

Sharon rolled her eyes and put her shoes back on. 'Denise, you said that was the last one. Let's go get something to eat before I drop dead.'

'No, I meant it was the last dress I would try on in *this* shop. There's loads more shops to go to yet.'

'No way!' Holly protested. 'Denise, I am starving to death and at this stage all the dresses are beginning to look the same to me. I need a break.'

'Oh, but this is my wedding day, Holly!'

'Yes, and . . .' Holly tried to think of an excuse, 'and Sharon's pregnant.'

'Oh, OK then, we'll get something to eat,' Denise said, disappointed, and headed back to the changing room.

Sharon elbowed Holly in the ribs. 'Hey, I'm not diseased, you know, just pregnant.'

'It's the only thing that I could think of,' Holly said tiredly.

The three of them trudged into Bewley's café and managed to grab their usual spot by the window overlooking Grafton Street.

'Oh, I hate shopping on Saturdays,' Holly moaned, watching as people bumped and crushed each other on the busy street below.

'Gone are the days of shopping mid-week now you're no longer a lady of leisure,' Sharon teased as she picked up a club sandwich and began stuffing her face.

'I know, and I'm *so* tired, but I feel like I've earned the tiredness this time. Unlike before when I just used to stay up late watching insomniac TV,' Holly said happily.

'Tell us about the little episode with Gerry's parents,' Sharon said with a mouthful of food.

Holly rolled her eyes. 'They were just so rude to poor Daniel.'

'I'm sorry I was asleep. I'm sure if John had known that's what it was about he would have woken me,' Sharon apologised.

'Oh, don't be silly, it wasn't a really big deal. It just felt like it at the time.'

'Too right. They can't tell you who to see and who not to see,' Sharon gave out.

'Sharon, I'm not seeing him.' Holly tried to get the record straight. 'I have no intentions of seeing anyone for at least twenty years. We were just having a business dinner.'

'Oooh, a *business* dinner!' Sharon and Denise giggled.

'Well, that's what it was, but it was also nice to have a bit of company,' Holly admitted. 'And I'm not bitching about you two,' she said quickly before they had a chance to defend themselves. 'All I'm saying is that when everyone else is busy it's nice to have someone else to chat to. Especially male company, you know? And he's easy to get along with and he makes me feel very comfortable. That's all.'

'Yeah, I understand,' Sharon nodded. 'It's good for you to get out and meet new people.'

'So did you find out anything else about him?' Denise leaned forward, her eyes sparkling as she dug for gossip. 'He's a bit of a dark horse, that Daniel.'

'I don't find him secretive at all,' Holly said. 'He told me about that girl he was engaged to. Laura was her name. He said he used to be in the army but left after four years . . .'

'Oooh, I love yummy army men,' Denise drooled.

'And DJs,' Sharon added.

'Oh, and DJs, of course,' Denise replied, laughing.

'Well, I told him my view about the army, anyway,' Holly smiled.

'Oh no, you didn't!' Sharon laughed.

'What's this?' Denise asked.

'So what did he say?' Sharon ignored Denise.

'He just laughed.'

'What's this?' Denise asked again.

'Holly's theory about the army,' Sharon explained.

'And what is it?' Denise asked, irritated.

'Oh, that fighting for peace is like screwing for virginity.'

The girls burst out laughing.

'Yeah, but you can have hours of endless fun trying,' Denise quipped.

'So you haven't mastered it yet?' Sharon asked.

'No, but at every available chance, we try, you know?' Denise replied, and the girls all giggled. 'Well, I'm glad you get along with him, Holly, because you're going to have to dance with him at the wedding.'

'Why?'

'Because it's tradition for the best man to dance with the maid of honour at the wedding.' Her eyes sparkled.

Holly gasped. 'You want me to be your maid of honour?'

Denise nodded excitedly. 'Don't worry, I already asked Sharon and she doesn't mind.'

'Oh, I would love to!' Holly said happily. 'But, Sharon, are you sure you don't mind?'

'Oh, don't worry about me, I'm happy just being a blown-up bridesmaid.'

'You won't be blown up!' Holly laughed.

'Yes I will. I'll be eight months pregnant. I'll need to borrow Denise's marquee to wear as a dress!'

'Oh, I hope you don't go into labour at the wedding,' Denise said, horrified.

'Don't worry, Denise, I won't steal the limelight from you on your day,' Sharon smiled. 'I'm not due till the end of January so that'll be weeks later.'

Denise looked relieved.

'Oh, by the way, I forgot to show you the photograph of the baby!' Sharon said, excitedly rooting through her bag. Finally she pulled out a small photograph of the scan.

'Where is it?' Denise asked, frowning.

'There,' Sharon pointed out the area.

'Whoa! That's one big boy,' Denise exclaimed, moving the picture closer to her face.

Sharon rolled her eyes. 'Denise that's a leg, you fool. We still don't know the sex yet.'

'Oh,' Denise blushed, 'well, congratulations, Sharon. It looks like you're having a little alien.'

'Oh, stop it, Denise,' Holly laughed. 'I think it's a beautiful picture.'

'Good,' Sharon smiled, and looked at Denise, and

Denise nodded at her. 'Because I wanted to ask you something.'

'What?' Holly looked worried.

'Well, John and I would love it if you would be our baby's godmother.'

Holly gasped with shock for the second time that day, and tears filled her eyes.

'Hey, you didn't cry when I asked you to be maid of honour,' Denise huffed.

'Oh, Sharon, I would be honoured!' Holly said, giving her friend a big hug. 'Thank you for asking!'

'Thank you for saying yes! John will be so delighted!'

'Oh, don't you two start crying,' Denise moaned, but Sharon and Holly ignored her and continued hugging.

'Hey!' Denise yelled, causing them to jump from their embrace.

'What?'

Denise pointed out the window. 'I can't believe I never noticed that wedding shop over there! Drink up quick and we'll go there next,' she said excitedly as her eyes darted enthusiastically from dress to dress.

Sharon sighed and pretended to pass out. 'I can't, Denise, I'm pregnant . . .'

CHAPTER FORTY-TWO

'Hey, Holly, I was just thinking,' Alice said to Holly as they were reapplying their make-up in the toilets at work before leaving for the day.

'Oh, no, did it hurt?' Holly teased.

'Ha-ha,' she said drily. 'No, honestly, I was thinking about the horoscope in this month's magazine and I think Tracey may have got it eerily right.'

Holly rolled her eyes. 'How?'

Alice put down her lipstick and turned away from the mirror to face Holly. 'Well, first there was the thing about the tall, dark handsome man who you are now seeing . . .'

'I'm not seeing him, we're just friends,' Holly explained for what felt like the millionth time.

'Whatever you say. Anyway, then there was the thing—'

'I'm not,' Holly repeated.

'Yeah, yeah,' Alice said, disbelieving her. 'Well, then there's the—'

Holly slammed down her make-up bag. 'Alice, I am *not* seeing Daniel.'

'OK, OK,' she held up her hands defensively, 'I get it! You're *not* seeing him, but please stop interrupting me and listen!' She waited for Holly to calm down. 'OK, so the other thing she said was that your lucky day is Tuesday, which is today . . .'

'Wow, Alice, I think you're on to something here,' Holly said sarcastically, applying her lip liner.

'Listen!' Alice said impatiently, and Holly shut up. 'So she also said that blue was your lucky colour. So today, being *Tuesday*, you have been invited by a *tall, dark handsome* man to the launch of *Blue* Rock.' Alice looked pleased with herself as she summed it all up.

'So what?' Holly said, unimpressed.

'So it's a sign.'

'A sign that the colour shirt I happened to be wearing that day was blue, which was why Tracey chose that particular colour, which I happened to be wearing because everything else I owned was dirty. And she just picked the day off the top of her head. It means *nothing*, Alice.'

Alice sighed. 'Oh, ye of little faith.'

'Well, if I am to believe your little theory, as screwed up as it is, then that also means that Brian is going to win the lotto and become the object of every woman's affections,' Holly laughed.

Alice bit her lip and looked sheepish.

'What?'

'Well, Brian won four euro on a scratch card today.'

'Whoopdeedoo,' Holly chortled. 'Well, there's still the problem of at least one human being finding him attractive.'

Alice remained silent.

'What now?' Holly demanded.

'Nothing,' Alice shrugged, and smiled.

'You don't!'

'I don't what?' Alice's face lit up.

'You don't fancy him, do you? You couldn't possibly!'
Alice shrugged. 'He's nice, that's all.'

'Oh, no!' Holly covered her face with her hands.
'You're taking this way too far just to try to prove a
point to me.'

'I'm not trying to prove anything to you,' Alice laughed.

'Well, then I can't believe you fancy him!'

'Who fancies who?' Tracey asked, walking into the
toilet.

Alice shook her head wildly at Holly, begging her
not to tell.

'Oh, nobody,' Holly muttered, staring at Alice in
shock. How could Alice fancy the slime ball of all slime
balls?

'Hey, did you hear Brian won money on a lotto scratch
card today?' Tracey asked them from the cubicle.

'We were just talking about that,' Alice laughed.

'I just might have psychic powers after all, Holly,'
Tracey smirked and flushed the toilet.

Alice winked at Holly in the mirror as Holly headed
out of the bathroom, saying, 'Come on, Alice, we'd better
get going or the photographer will go mad.'

'The photographer's already here,' Alice explained,
applying some mascara.

'Where is he?'

'She.'

'Well then, where is she?'

'Ta-da!' Alice took a camera out of her bag.

'You're the photographer?' Holly laughed. 'Well, at

387

least we can both lose our jobs together when this article is published.'

Holly and Alice pushed through the crowds in Hogan's and made their way upstairs to Club Diva. Holly gasped as they approached the door. A group of young muscular males dressed in swimwear were banging out some Hawaiian drum beats to welcome all the guests. Some very skinny female models, dressed in skimpy bikinis, greeted the girls at the door by wrapping beautiful multi-coloured lei around their necks.

'I feel like I'm in Hawaii,' Alice giggled, snapping away with her camera. 'Oh my God!' she exclaimed as they entered the club.

Holly barely recognised the place. It had been completely transformed. A huge water feature dominated the room, aqua-blue water cascading down it from some rocks.

'Oh, look, Blue Rock!' Alice laughed. 'Very clever.'

Holly smiled; so much for her wonderful powers of journalistic observation. She hadn't even copped that the water was actually the drink itself. Daniel hadn't told her anything about this, which meant she would have to adjust the article so she could hand it in to Chris tomorrow. She looked around the club for Denise and Tom, and saw her being photographed holding her hand up to the camera to show off her sparkly engagement ring. Holly was amused at the big celebrity couple.

The bar staff were also dressed in bikinis and swim-wear, and lined the entrance, bearing trays of blue drinks. Holly lifted a drink from the tray and took a sip, trying not to make a face at its overly sweet taste as a photographer snapped her. As Daniel had said, the floors were scattered with sand, making it appear as if they were at a beach party, and each table was sheltered by a huge bamboo umbrella. The bar stools were all big kettle drums and there was a beautiful barbecue smell in the air. Holly's mouth watered as she spotted the waiters carrying trays of barbecued food to the tables. She darted to the nearest table, helped herself to a kebab, and took a big bite.

'Oh, so you do eat.'

Holly found herself facing Daniel. Chewing valiantly, she swallowed her food.

'Em, hello. I haven't had a thing to eat all day so I am absolutely starving. The place looks great,' she said, looking around, keen to distract him from the sight of her with a mouthful of kebab.

'Yeah, it worked well all right.' He looked pleased. Daniel was slightly more dressed than his staff members: he wore faded blue jeans and a blue Hawaiian shirt with big pink and yellow flowers. He still hadn't shaved and Holly wondered how painful it would be to kiss him with that sharp stubble. Not for her to kiss him, of course. Somebody else . . . Why was she even wondering about it?

'Hey, Holly! Let me get a photo of you and the tall, dark handsome man,' Alice yelled, rushing over with her camera.

Holly was mortified.

Daniel laughed. 'You should bring your friends here more often.'

'She's not my friend,' Holly said through gritted teeth, and posed beside Daniel for the photo.

'Hold on a second,' Daniel said, covering the camera lens with his hand. He took a napkin from the table and wiped the grease and barbecue sauce from Holly's face. Holly's skin tingled at his touch and warmth rushed through her body. She convinced herself it was from blushing so much.

'Now it's gone,' he said, smiling at her, wrapping an arm round her and facing the camera.

Alice skipped away again and continued to snap all around her. Holly turned to Daniel. 'I'm really sorry about the other night. Gerry's parents were so rude to you, and I'm sorry if you felt uncomfortable.'

'Oh, there's no need to apologise again, Holly – in fact there's no need to apologise *at all*. I only felt uncomfortable for you. They shouldn't be able to tell you who to see and who not to see. Anyway, if you're worried about me then there's no need,' he smiled, and placed his hands on her shoulders as though he was going to say something more, but then somebody called him from the bar and he rushed over to sort the problem out.

'But I am *not* seeing you,' Holly muttered to herself. If she had to convince even Daniel of that then they certainly had a problem. She hoped he didn't think there was more to the dinner than there really was. He had called her almost every day since that episode. She realised that she looked forward to his calls. There was that niggling thing at the back of her mind again. Holly wandered over to Denise and joined her on the sun bed where she was sipping on the blue concoction.

'Hey, Holly, I saved this for you.' She pointed to the Lilo in the corner of the room and the two girls giggled, remembering their adventure while on holidays.

'So what do you think of the hot new drink for winter?'

Denise rolled her eyes. 'Tacky. I've only had a few and my head is spinning already.'

Alice ran over to Holly, dragging an enormously muscular man dressed in tiny little shorts. One of his biceps was the size of Alice's waist. She handed the camera to Holly. 'Take a picture of the two of us, will you?'

Holly didn't think that these were the kind of photographs Chris was hoping for but she obliged Alice.

'It's for the screen saver on my computer at work,' Alice explained to Denise.

Holly enjoyed herself that evening, laughing and chatting with Denise and Tom while Alice ran around taking photographs of all the half-naked male models. Holly felt guilty for ever being annoyed by Tom all those months ago at the karaoke competition. He was a sweet guy and he and Denise made a lovely couple. Holly barely got to speak to Daniel as he was too busy being the responsible manager. She watched as he gave orders to his staff and they immediately got to work. It was obvious that they had great respect for him. He got things done. Every time she spotted him heading over to her group, somebody stopped him in his tracks for a chat. Most of the time, he was stopped by skinny young girls in bikinis. They annoyed Holly so she looked away.

'I don't know how I'm going to write this article,' Holly moaned to Alice as they made their way outside into the cold air.

'Don't worry, Holly, you'll be fine. It's only eight hundred words, isn't it?'

'Yeah, *only*,' she said sarcastically. 'You see, I already wrote a draft a few days ago because Daniel gave me all the information. But after seeing all that I'll have to change it extensively. It already almost killed me trying to get this version done in the first place.'

'You're really worried about this, aren't you?'

Holly sighed. 'I just can't write, Alice. I was never any good at putting things into words and describing exactly how things are.'

Alice looked thoughtful. 'Have you got the article in the office?'

Holly nodded.

'Why don't we go there now? I'll look over it, and maybe I'll make a few changes if it needs it.'

'Oh, Alice, thank you so much!' Holly said, hugging her with relief.

The following day Holly sat nervously before Chris and watched him read the article. His face remained grumpy as he turned the page. Alice hadn't just made a few changes to the article, she had completely rewritten it, and Holly thought it was incredible. It was funny yet informative, and she explained the night exactly as it had been. Alice was an extremely talented writer and Holly couldn't understand why she was still working on reception instead of writing for the magazine.

Finally, Chris finished reading and he slowly took off his glasses. He looked up at Holly. Holly's hands fidgeted on her lap; she felt as if she had just cheated on a school exam.

'Holly, I don't know what you're doing in advertising,' Chris finally said. 'You are a fantastic writer. I love it! It's cheeky and funny, yet it gets the point across. It's fabulous.'

Holly smiled weakly. 'Eh . . . thanks.'

'You have such a wonderful talent; I can't believe you tried to hide it from me.'

Holly's smile stayed glued on her face.

'How would you feel about writing every now and again?'

Holly's face froze. 'Well, Chris, I'm really much more interested in the advertising side of things.'

'Oh, of course, and I will pay you more for this too. But if we are ever stuck again at least I know I have another talented writer on the team. Well done, Holly.' He grinned at her and held out his hand.

'Eh . . . thanks,' Holly repeated, shaking his hand weakly. 'I better get back to work now.' She stood up from her chair and walked stiffly out of the office.

'Well, did he like it?' Alice asked loudly, walking down the hall.

'Eh . . . yeah, he loved it. He wants me to write more.' Holly felt guilty for taking all the credit.

'Oh.' Alice looked away. 'Well, aren't you the lucky one?' She continued on to her desk.

CHAPTER FORTY-THREE

Denise banged the till closed with her hip and handed the receipt to the customer. 'Thanks,' she smiled, but the smile quickly faded as soon as the customer turned away from the counter. She sighed loudly, staring at the long queue forming in front of the cash register. She would have to stand at the till all day and she was just dying for a cigarette break. But there was no way she could slip away so she grumpily grabbed the item of clothing from the next customer, de-tagged it, scanned it, and wrapped it.

'Excuse me, are you Denise Hennessey?' she heard a deep voice ask, and she looked up to see where the sexy voice came from. She frowned as she saw a garda before her.

She hesitated while trying to think if she had done anything illegal in the past few days. When she was satisfied that she was crime free she smiled and replied, 'Yes I am.'

'I'm Garda Ryan and I was wondering if you would accompany me to the station, please.'

It was more of a statement than a question and Denise's mouth dropped open in shock. He was no longer sexy garda, he was the evil-lock-her-up-forever-in-a-tiny-cell-with-a-luminous-orange-jumpsuit-and-noisy-flipflops-and-no-hot-water-or-make-up-type garda. Denise gulped and had an image of herself being beaten up by a gang of tough angry women who didn't care about mascara, in the exercise yard at the prison, while the guards looked on and made bets over who would win.

She gulped. 'What for?'

'If you just comply with what I've said, everything will be explained to you down at the station.' He walked round the counter and Denise backed away slowly, looking at the long line of customers helplessly. Everybody just stared back at her, amused by the scene that was unfolding before them.

'Check his ID, love,' one of the customers shouted from the end of the queue.

Denise's voice shook as she demanded to see his ID, which was pointless, as she had never seen a garda ID before, nor knew what a real one would look like. Her hand trembled as she held the ID and studied it closely but didn't read a thing. She was too self-conscious of the crowd of customers and staff that had gathered to stare at her with looks of disgust on their faces. They were all thinking the same thing: she was a criminal.

Denise hardened, refusing to go without a fight. 'I won't go with you until you tell me what this is about.'

He continued towards her again. 'Ms Hennessey, if you just work with me here then there will be no need to use these.' He took out a pair of handcuffs from his trousers pocket.

'But I didn't do anything!' she protested, starting to panic.

'Well, we can discuss that down at the station, can't we?' he began to get irate.

Denise crossed her arms across her chest to show how tough she was. 'I said I will *not* go with you until you tell me what this is about.'

'OK then,' he shrugged, 'if you insist.' He opened his mouth to speak and she yelled as she felt the cold hand-cuffs being snapped around her wrists. It wasn't exactly the first time she had ever worn a pair of handcuffs so she wasn't surprised at how they felt, but she was in so much shock she couldn't speak.

'Good luck, love,' the customer shouted again as she was led by the queue. 'If they send you to Mount Joy tell my Orla I said hi and that I'll be there to visit her at Christmas.'

Denise's eyes widened and images of her pacing a cell, shared with a psycho murderer, jumped into her mind. Maybe she would find a little bird with a broken wing and nurse it and teach it to fly to pass the years inside, just like in the movie . . .

Her face reddened as they stepped out onto Grafton Street and the crowds immediately scattered as soon as they saw the garda and a hardened criminal. Denise kept her eyes peeled to the ground, hoping nobody she knew would spot her. Her heart beat wildly and she briefly thought of escape. She looked around quickly and tried to figure out an escape route but she was already being led toward a mini-bus, the well-known colour blue of the gardaí with blackened-out windows. Denise sat in the front, and although she could sense people behind her, she sat rigidly in her seat, too terrified to turn round and meet her future fellow inmates. She leaned her head against the window and said goodbye to freedom.

'Where are we going?' she asked. The female police officer driving the bus and Garda Ryan ignored her and continued to stare ahead of them.

'Hey!' she shouted. 'We're going in the wrong direction! I thought you said you were taking me to the station?'

They continued to stare straight ahead.

'HEY! WHERE ARE WE GOING?'

No answer.

'I HAVEN'T DONE ANYTHING WRONG!'

Still no answer.

'I'M INNOCENT, GODDAMMIT! INNOCENT, I TELL YOU!'

Denise started kicking the chair in front of her, trying to get their attention. Her blood started to boil when the female garda pushed a cassette into the player and turned the music up. Denise's eyes widened at the choice of song.

Garda Ryan turned round in his seat with a big grin on his face. 'Denise, you have been a very naughty girl.' He stood up and made his way in front of her. She gulped as he started to gyrate his hips to the song 'Hot Stuff'.

She was about to give him a great big kick between his legs when she heard whooping and laughing from the back of the bus. She twisted round and spotted her sisters, Holly, Sharon, and about five other friends, picking themselves up from the floor of the mini bus. She finally figured out what was really happening when her sisters placed a veil on her head while screaming, 'Happy hen party!'

'Oh, you bitches!' Denise spat at them, effing and blinding them until she had used every single curse word invented and even made up a few of her own.

The girls continued to hold their stomachs, doubled up with laughter.

'You are so lucky I didn't kick you in the balls!' Denise screamed at the gyrating garda.

'Denise, this is Ken,' her sister Fiona giggled, 'and he's your stripper for the day.'

Denise narrowed her eyes and continued to curse them, 'I almost had a heart attack, I hope you know! I thought I was going to prison! Oh my God, what will my customers think? And my staff!' Denise closed her eyes as though she was in pain.

'We told the staff about it last week,' Sharon giggled. 'They were all just playing along.'

'Oh, the little bitches,' Denise repeated. 'When I go back to work I'm going to fire the lot of them. But what about the customers?' Denise asked, panicking.

'Don't worry,' her sister giggled, 'we told your staff to inform the customers it was your hen party after you left the shop.'

Denise rolled her eyes, 'Well, knowing *them* they deliberately won't, and if they *don't,* then there will be complaints and if there are complaints I will be *so* fired.'

'Denise! Stop *worrying*! You don't think we would have done this without running it by your boss, do you? It's OK!' Fiona explained. 'They thought it was funny. Now *relax* and enjoy the weekend.'

'Weekend? What the hell are you girls going to do to me next? Where are we going?' Denise looked around at her friends, startled.

'We're going to Galway and that's all you need to know,' Sharon said mysteriously.

'If I wasn't bloody handcuffed I'd slap you all in the face,' Denise threatened.

The girls all cheered as Ken stripped out of his uniform and poured baby oil all over his body for Denise to massage into his skin.

'Men in uniform are so much nicer out of them . . .' Denise mumbled as she watched him flex his muscles before her.

'Lucky she's handcuffed, Ken, or you would be in big trouble!' the girls teased.

'*Big* trouble is right,' Denise mumbled again, staring in shock as the rest of the clothes came off. 'Oh, girls! Thank you so much!' she giggled, her voice taking a very different tone than before.

'Are you OK, Holly?' Sharon asked, handing her a glass of champagne and keeping a glass of orange juice for herself. 'You've barely said a word since we got into the van.'

Holly turned to look out of the window and stared at the green fields as they flew by. The hills were dotted with little white specks as the sheep bravely climbed to new heights, oblivious to the wonderful views. Neat stone walls separated each field and you could see the grey lines, jagged like jigsaw puzzles, for miles, connecting each piece of land together. Holly had yet to find a few pieces for her own puzzled mind.

'Yeah,' she sighed, 'I'm OK.'

'Oh, I really have to ring Tom!' Denise groaned, collapsing onto the double bed she and Holly were sharing in the

399

hotel room. Sharon was fast asleep on the single bed beside them. She had gone to bed much earlier than the girls after eventually becoming bored of their drunken behaviour.

'I'm under strict orders not to let you ring Tom,' Holly yawned. 'This is a girls-only weekend.'

'Oh, please,' Denise whimpered.

'No. I am confiscating your phone.' She grabbed the mobile from Denise's hand and hid it in the press beside the bed.

Denise looked as if she was going to cry. She watched as Holly lay back on the bed and closed her eyes, and she began to formulate a plan. She would wait until Holly was asleep and then she would call Tom. Holly had been so quiet all day it was really starting to irritate Denise. Every time Denise had asked her a question she kept on getting yes/no answers back, and every attempt to strike up a conversation had failed. It was obvious that Holly wasn't enjoying herself, but what really annoyed Denise was to see that Holly wasn't even *trying*, or even *pretending* to be. She could understand that Holly was upset and that she had a lot to deal with at the moment but it was her hen party and she couldn't help feeling that Holly was bringing the atmosphere down.

The room was still spinning. Having closed her eyes, Holly was now unable to sleep. It was five o'clock in the morning, which meant that she had been drinking for almost twelve hours and her head was pounding. Her stomach became queasy as the walls around her spun around and around and around . . . She sat up on the

400

bed and tried to keep her eyes open to avoid the feeling of seasickness.

She turned to face Denise on the bed so that they could talk but the sound of her snores ended all thought of communication between them. Holly sighed and looked around the room. She wanted nothing more than to go home and sleep in her own bed. She felt her way across the bedcovers in the dark for the remote control and flicked on the television. Commercial presentations adorned the screen. Holly watched as they demonstrated a new knife to slice oranges without spraying yourself in the face with the juice; the amazing socks that never got lost in the wash.

Denise snored loudly beside her and kicked Holly in the shins as she changed position. Holly winced and rubbed her leg as she watched with sympathy at Sharon's extremely frustrated struggle to lie on her stomach. Eventually she settled on her side.

Holly rushed to the toilet and hung her head over the pan, prepared for what was inevitably to come. She wished she hadn't drunk so much but with all the talk of weddings and husbands and happiness she had needed all the wine in the bar to prevent her from screaming at everyone to shut up. She dreaded to think what the next two days would be like. Denise's friends were twice as bad as Denise. They were loud and hyper – exactly how girls should be on a hen weekend – but Holly just didn't have the energy to keep up with them. At least Sharon had the excuse of being pregnant; she could pretend she wasn't feeling well or that she was tired. Holly had no excuse apart from the fact that she had turned into a complete bore, and she was saving that excuse for a time when she really needed it.

It felt as if it was only yesterday that Holly had had her own hen party, but in fact it was over seven years ago. She had flown to London with a group of girls for the weekend to party hard but she had ended up missing Gerry so much she had to speak to him on the phone every hour. Back then she had been so excited about what was to come. The future had looked so bright.

She was to marry the man of her dreams and live with him for the rest of their lives. For the entire weekend she was away she had counted the hours until she could return home. She was so excited on the flight back to Dublin. Although they had only been apart for a few days, it had felt like an eternity. He had been waiting for her at arrivals with a huge board in his hand saying 'My future wife'. She had dropped her bags when she saw him and had run into his arms and hugged him *so* tight. She had never wanted to let go; what a luxury it was for people to be able to hold their loved ones whenever they wanted, she thought now bitterly. The scene at the airport had been like a part of a movie, but it was real: real feelings, real emotions, and real love because it was real life. Real life which had now become a nightmare for her.

Yes, she had finally managed to drag herself out of bed every morning; yes, she had even managed to get dressed most of the time. Yes, she had succeeded in finding a new job where she met new people and yes, she had finally started buying food again and feeding herself. But no, she didn't feel ecstatic about any of these things. They were just formalities, something else to check off on the 'things that normal people do' list. None of them filled the hole in her heart; it was like her body had become one great jigsaw just like the green fields with their pretty grey-stone walls connecting the whole of Ireland. She had started working on the corners and the edges of her jigsaw because they were the easy bits but now that they were all in place she needed to do all the bits in between, the hard parts. But nothing she had done so far had managed to fill that hole in her heart; that piece of the jigsaw had yet to be found.

Holly cleared her throat loudly and pretended to have a coughing fit just so the girls would wake up and talk to her. She needed to talk, she needed to cry, she needed to vent all her frustrations and disappointments. But what more could she say to Sharon and Denise that she hadn't said already? What more advice could they give her that they hadn't given her before? Ever since the holiday Holly had opened up to Sharon and Denise a lot more, but now she felt that she was repeating the same old worries over and over again. Sometimes they would succeed in getting through to her and she would feel positive and confident, only to be thrown back into despair days later.

After a while Holly, tired of staring at the four walls, threw on a tracksuit and made her way back downstairs to the hotel bar.

Charlie rolled his eyes as the table down the back of the bar began to roar with laughter again. He wiped down the counter and glanced at his watch: five thirty and he couldn't wait to go home. He had thought he was so lucky when the girls from the hen party had gone to bed earlier than expected, and had been about to tidy up and go home when another gang arrived. And they were still here. In fact he would have preferred if the girls had

403

stayed up instead of this arrogant crowd. They weren't even residents of the hotel but he had to serve them because they included the hotel owner's daughter and her friends.

'Don't tell me you're back for more!' the barman laughed as one of the women from the hen party walked into the room. She walked towards the bar, bumping into the wall as she tried to make her way on to the high stool. Charlie tried not to laugh.

'I just came down for a glass of water,' she hiccuped. 'Oh my God,' she wailed, catching sight of herself in the mirror over the bar. Charlie had to admit that she did look shocking: a bit like the scarecrow on his dad's farm. Her hair was like straw, and sticking out in all directions, her eyes had black circles around them from smudging her mascara and her teeth were stained from red wine.

'There you go,' Charlie said, placing a glass of water on a beer mat in front of her.

'Thanks.' She dipped her finger into her glass and wiped the mascara from her eyes and rubbed the wine stains from her lips.

Charlie began to laugh and she squinted at his nametag. 'What are you laughing at, Charlie?'

'I thought you were thirsty but I would have given you a face cloth if you had asked for one,' he chuckled.

The woman smiled and her features softened. 'I find the ice and lemon helps my skin.'

'Well, that's a new one.' Charlie continued to wipe down the counter. 'Did you girls have fun tonight?'

Holly sighed. 'I suppose.' Fun wasn't a word she used often any more. She had laughed along with the jokes all night, had been excited for Denise, but she hadn't felt as if she was *completely* there. She had felt like the shy girl at school who was always *just there,* but who never spoke and was never spoken to. She didn't recognise the person she had become; she wanted to be able to stop staring at the clock whenever she went out, hoping the night would soon be over so she could go home and crawl into bed. She wanted to stop wishing time would pass and enjoy the moment instead.

'Are you OK?' Charlie stopped wiping the counter and watched her. He had a horrible feeling she was going to cry but he was used to it. A lot of people became emotional when they drank.

'I miss my husband,' she whispered, and her shoulders trembled.

The corners of Charlie's lips turned up into a smile.

'What's so funny?' She looked at him angrily.

'How long are you here for?' he asked.

'The weekend,' she told him, twisting a used tissue around her finger.

He laughed. 'Have you never gone the weekend without seeing him?'

She frowned. 'Only once before,' she finally replied, 'and that was at my own hen party.'

'How long ago was that?'

'Seven years ago.' A tear spilled down her face.

Charlie shook his head. 'That's a long time ago. Well, if you did it once you can do it again,' he smiled. 'Seven years lucky, isn't that what they say?'

Holly snorted into her drink. Lucky her arse.

'Don't worry,' Charlie said gently, 'your husband's probably miserable without you too.'

'Oh God, I hope not,' Holly replied.

'Well then, see? I'm sure he hopes you're not miserable without him either. You're supposed to be enjoying your life.'

'You're right,' Holly said, perking up. 'He wouldn't want me to be unhappy.'

'That's the spirit,' Charlie smiled, and jumped as he saw his boss's daughter coming towards the bar with one of those looks on her face.

'Hey, Charlie,' she yelled, 'I've been trying to get your attention for ages. Maybe if you stopped chatting to the customers at the bar and did a bit of work, me and my friends wouldn't be so thirsty.'

Holly's mouth dropped open with shock. That woman had a nerve, speaking to Charlie like that, and her perfume was so strong it made Holly cough.

'I'm sorry, do you have a problem?' the woman demanded, looking Holly up and down.

'Yes, actually,' Holly slurred, taking a sip of her water. 'Your perfume is disgusting and it's making me want to throw up.'

Charlie started laughing and dropped to his knees behind the counter to pretend to look for a lemon. He tried to block out the sounds of the two women snapping at each other so he would stop.

'What's the delay here?' a deep voice enquired. Charlie shot to his feet at the sound of the woman's fiancé's voice. He was even worse. 'Why don't you sit down, honey, and I'll bring the drinks over?' said the man.

'Fine. At least *someone* is polite around here,' she snapped, looking Holly up and down once more before storming off back to her table. Holly watched her hips working furiously – boom, boom, boom – from side to side as she walked. She must be a model or something, Holly decided. That would explain the tantrums.

'So how are you?' the man beside Holly asked, staring at her chest.

Charlie had to bite his tongue to stop himself from saying anything as he poured a pint of Guinness from the tap and then allowed it to sit on the counter for a while. He had a feeling the woman at the bar wouldn't succumb to Stevie's charms anyway, especially as she seemed to be so head over heels about her husband. Charlie was looking forward to seeing Stevie being ceremoniously dumped.

'I'm fine,' Holly replied shortly, staring straight ahead and deliberately avoiding eye contact.

'I'm Steve,' he said, holding out his hand to her.

'I'm Holly,' she mumbled, and took his hand lightly, not wanting to be overly rude.

'Holly, that's a lovely name.' He held her hand for much too long and Holly was forced to look up. He had big blue sparkly eyes.

'Eh . . . thanks,' she said, embarrassed by his compliment, and her face flushed.

Charlie sighed to himself. Even she had fallen for it, his only hope of satisfaction for the night gone.

'Can I buy you a drink, Holly?' Steve asked smoothly.

'No thanks, I have one here.' She sipped on her water again.

'OK, well, I'm just going to bring these drinks down to my table and then I'll be back to buy the lovely Holly a drink.' He smiled at her creepily as he walked away.

Charlie rolled his eyes as soon as he had turned his back.

'Who the hell is that eejit?' Holly asked, looking bewildered, and Charlie laughed, delighted that she hadn't fallen for him. She was a lady with sense, even if she was crying because she missed her husband after only one day of separation.

Charlie lowered his voice. 'That's Stevie, fiancé of Laura, that blonde bitch who was here a minute ago. Her dad owns this hotel, which means I can't exactly tell her where to go although I would love to. Not worth losing my job over.'

'Definitely worth losing your job over, I should think,' Holly said, staring at the beautiful Laura and thinking nasty thoughts. 'Anyway, good night, Charlie.'

'You off to bed?'

She nodded. 'It's about time; it's after six.' She tapped on her watch. 'I hope you get home soon,' she smiled.

'I wouldn't bet on it,' he replied, and watched her leave the bar. Steve followed after her and Charlie made his way closer to the door just to make sure she was OK. Laura, noticing her fiancé's sudden departure, left the table and arrived at the door at the same time as Charlie. They both stared down the corridor in the direction Holly and Steve had headed.

Laura gasped and her hand flew to her mouth.

'Hey!' Charlie called out angrily as he witnessed a distressed Holly pushing a drunken Steve away from her.

Holly angrily wiped her mouth, disgusted at Steve's attempt to kiss her. She backed away from him. 'I think you've got the wrong idea here, Steve. Go back to the bar to your *fiancée*.'

Steve wobbled slightly on his feet and slowly turned

408

to face Laura and an angry Charlie who was charging towards them.

'Stevie!' Laura shrieked. 'How could you?' She ran from the hotel with tears streaming down her face, closely followed by a protesting Steve.

'Uuggghh!' Holly said with disgust. 'I did not want to do that *at all*!'

'Don't worry, I believe you,' Charlie said, placing his hand comfortingly on her shoulder. 'I saw what happened through the door.'

'Ah well, thanks very much for coming to my rescue!' Holly complained.

'Got here too late, sorry. But I must admit, I did enjoy her witnessing that,' he laughed, referring to Laura.

Holly smiled as she stared down the corridor at Steve and Laura screaming at each other.

'Oops,' she said.

Holly knocked into everything in the bedroom as she tried to make her way back to her bed in the darkness. 'Ouch!' she yelped, stubbing her toe on the bedpost.

'Sshhh!' Sharon said sleepily.

Holly tapped Denise on the shoulder continuously until she woke up.

'What? What?' Denise moaned sleepily.

'Here,' Holly forced a mobile phone in Denise's face, 'phone your future husband, tell him you love him and don't let the girls know.'

The next day Holly and Sharon went for a long walk on the beach just outside Galway city. Although it was October the air had warmth in it and Holly didn't need her coat. She stood and listened to the water gently lapping. The rest of the girls had decided to go for a liquid lunch but Holly's stomach wasn't quite ready for that today.

'Are you OK, Holly?' Sharon wrapped her arm around her friend's shoulders.

Holly sighed. 'Every time someone asks me that question, Sharon, I say, "I'm fine, thank you," but to be honest I'm not. Do people *really* want to know how you feel when they ask, "How are you?"? Or are they just trying to be polite?' Holly smiled. 'The next time the woman across the road from my house says to me, "How are you?" I'm going to say to her; well, actually, I'm not very well at all, thank you. I'm feeling a bit depressed and lonely. Pissed off at the world. Envious of you and your perfect little family but not particularly envious of your husband at having to live with you. And then I'll tell her about how I started a new job and met lots of new people and how I'm trying hard to pick myself up but that I'm now at a loss about what else to do. Then I'll tell her how it pisses me off when everyone says time is a healer when at the same time they also say absence makes the heart grow fonder, which really confuses me, because that means that the longer he's gone the more I want him. I'll tell her that nothing is healing at all and that every morning I wake up in my empty bed it feels like salt is being rubbed into those unhealing wounds.' Holly took a deep breath. 'And then I'll tell her about how much I miss my husband and about how worthless my life seems without him. How uninterested I am in getting on with things without him and I'll explain how I feel like I'm just waiting for my world to end so that I can join him. She'll probably just say, "Oh that's good," like

410

she always does, kiss her husband goodbye, hop into her car and drop her kids to school, go to work, make the dinner and go to bed with her husband and she'll have done it all while I'm still trying to decide what colour shirt to wear to work. What do you think?' Holly finally finished and turned to Sharon.

'Oooh!' Sharon jumped, and her arm flew away from Holly's shoulders.

'Oooh?' Holly frowned. 'I say all that and all you can say is "Oooh"?'

Sharon placed her hand over her bump and laughed. 'No, silly, the baby kicked!'

Holly's jaw dropped.

'Feel it!' Sharon giggled.

Holly placed her hand over Sharon's swollen belly and felt the tiny little movement. Their eyes filled with tears.

'Oh, Sharon, if only every minute of my life was filled with perfect little moments like this I would never moan again.'

'But, Holly, nobody's life is filled with perfect little moments. And if they were, they wouldn't be perfect little moments. They would just be normal. How would you ever know happiness if you'd never experienced downs?'

'Oooh!' they both shrieked as the baby kicked for a third time.

'I think this little boy is going to be a footballer like his daddy!' Sharon laughed.

'Boy?' Holly gasped. 'You're having a boy?'

Sharon nodded happily and her eyes glistened. 'Holly, meet baby Gerry. Gerry, meet your godmother, Holly.'

411

CHAPTER FORTY-FOUR

'Hi, Alice,' Holly said, hovering in front of her desk. Holly had been standing there for a few minutes now and Alice hadn't said a word yet.

'Hi,' Alice said shortly, refusing to look up at her.

Holly took a deep breath. 'Alice, are you mad at me?'

'No,' she said abruptly again. 'Chris wants to see you in his office again. He wants you to write another article.'

'*Another* article?' Holly gasped.

'That's what I said.'

'Alice, why don't you do it?' Holly said softly. 'You're a fantastic writer. I'm sure if Chris knew you could write he would def—'

'He knows,' she interrupted.

'What?' Holly was confused. 'He knows you can write?'

'Five years ago I applied for a job as a writer but this was the only job going. Chris said if I hung on then maybe something would come up.' Alice sounded so angry and Holly wasn't used to seeing the usually chirpy girl looking so . . . upset wasn't even the word. She was just *angry*.

Holly sighed and made her way into Chris's office. She had a sneaking suspicion she would be writing this one all on her own.

Holly smiled as she flicked through the pages of the November magazine she had worked on. It would be out in the shops tomorrow, the first of November and she felt so excited. Her first magazine would be on the shelves and she could also open Gerry's next letter. Tomorrow would be a good day.

Although she had organised only the advertisements, she felt great pride in being a member of a team that had managed to produce something so professional-looking. It was a far cry from that pathetic leaflet she had printed up years ago and she giggled at the memory of mentioning it at her interview. As if it would have impressed Chris at all. But despite all that she felt she had really proved herself. She had taken her job by the reins and guided it through to success.

'It's nice to see you're looking so happy,' Alice snapped, strolling tartly into Holly's office and throwing two little scraps of paper on to her desk. 'You got two calls while you were out. One from Sharon and one from Denise. Please tell your friends to call you on your lunch break in future.'

'OK, thanks,' Holly said, glancing at the messages. Alice had scrawled something completely illegible, most likely on purpose. 'Hey, Alice!' Holly called after her.

'What?' she asked coldly.

'Did you read the article on the launch? The photos

413

and everything turned out great! I'm really proud,' Holly grinned broadly.

'No I have not!' Alice retorted, looking disgusted, and slammed the door behind her.

Holly chased her out of the office with the magazine in her hand. 'But look at it, Alice! It's so good! Daniel will be so happy!'

'Well, whoopdeedoo for you and Daniel.' Alice busied herself with random bits of paper on her desk.

Holly rolled her eyes. 'Look, stop being such a baby and read the damn thing!'

'No!' Alice huffed.

'Fine then, you won't see the photo of you with that gorgeous half-naked man . . .' Holly turned and walked away slowly.

'Give me that!' Alice grabbed the magazine from Holly's hand and flicked through the pages. Her jaw dropped as she reached the page featuring the Blue Rock launch.

At the top of the page it read 'Alice in Wonderland', with the photograph Holly had taken of her and the muscular model.

'Read it out loud,' Holly ordered.

Alice's voice shook as she began to read. 'A new alcopop has hit the shelves and our *party correspondent* Alice Goodyear went to find out if the hot new drink for winter was as it claimed to be . . .' She trailed off and her hands flew to her mouth in shock. 'Party correspondent?' she squealed.

Holly called Chris out of his office and he came to join them, a broad grin on his face.

'Well done, Alice; that was a fantastic article you wrote.

It was very amusing,' he told her, with a pat on the shoulder. 'So I've created a new page called "Alice in Wonderland", where you will go to all the weird and wonderful things you love to go to and write about them every month.'

Alice gasped at them and then stuttered, 'But Holly—'

'Holly can't spell,' Chris laughed. 'You, on the other hand, are a great writer. One I should have used before now. I'm very sorry, Alice.'

'Oh my God!' she gasped, ignoring him. 'Thank you so much, Holly!' She threw her arms around her and squeezed her so hard Holly couldn't breathe.

Holly tried to pull Alice's arms away from around her neck and gasped for air. 'Alice, this was the hardest secret to keep from anyone ever!'

'It must have been! How on earth did you manage it?' Alice looked at Holly, startled, before turning to Chris. 'Five years, Chris,' she said accusingly.

Chris winced and nodded.

'I waited five years for this,' she continued.

'I know, I know.' Chris looked like a chastised schoolboy and he scratched his eyebrow awkwardly. 'Why don't you step into my office now and we can talk about that.'

'I suppose I could do that,' Alice replied sternly, but she couldn't hide the glint of happiness in her eyes. As Chris headed towards his office, Alice turned to Holly and winked before doing a quickskip behind him.

Holly made her way back to her office. Time to get working on the December edition.

'Oops!' she said, tripping over a pile of handbags lying outside her door. 'What's all this?'

Chris rolled his eyes as he stepped out of his office to make Alice a cup of tea for a change, 'Oh, they're John-Paul's handbags.'

'John-Paul's handbags?' Holly giggled.

'It's for the article he's doing on this season's handbags or something stupid like that,' Chris pretended not to be interested.

'Oh, they're gorgeous,' Holly said, bending down to pick one up.

'Nice, isn't it?' John-Paul said, leaning against the door frame of his office.

'Yeah, I love it,' Holly said, sliding it over her shoulder. 'Does it suit me?'

Chris rolled his eyes again. 'How can a handbag not suit someone – it's a handbag, for Christsake!'

'You'll have to read the article I'm writing for next month, won't you?' John-Paul wagged a finger at his boss. 'Not all handbags suit everyone, you know.' He turned to Holly. 'You can have it if you want.'

'For keeps?' she gasped. 'This must cost hundreds.'

'Yeah, but I've got loads of them. You should see the amount of stuff the designer gave me. Trying to sweeten me up with freebies; the cheek of him!' John-Paul pretended to be outraged.

'I bet it works, though,' Holly suggested.

'Absolutely. The first line of my article will be: "Everybody go out and buy one, they're fab!"' he laughed.

'What else have you got?' Holly tried to peek behind him into the office.

'I'm doing an article on what to wear for all the Christmas parties coming up. A few dresses arrived today. In fact,' he looked her up and down and Holly sucked in

416

her belly, 'there's one that would look fab on you. Come in and try it on.'

'Oh, goody,' Holly giggled. 'I'll just have a look, though, John-Paul. I have no need for a party dress at all this year. I intend to sit home and *relax* in peace and quiet.'

Chris shook his head and yelled from his office, 'Does anybody in this bloody office ever do any work?'

'Yes!' Tracey yelled back. 'Now shut up and don't be distracting us.'

Everyone in the office laughed and Holly could swear she saw Chris smile before he slammed his office door shut for dramatic effect.

After rummaging through John-Paul's collection, Holly returned to work and eventually called Denise back.

'Hello? Disgusting, stuffy and ridiculously expensive clothes shop. Pissed off manager speaking, how can I help you?'

'Denise!' Holly gasped. 'You can't answer the phone like that!'

Denise giggled. 'Oh, don't worry, I have caller ID so I knew it was you.'

'Hmm,' Holly was suspicious; she didn't think Denise *did* have caller ID on her work phone. 'I got a message you called earlier.'

'Oh yeah, I was just ringing you to confirm you were going to the ball. Tom is going to buy a table this year.'

'What ball?'

'The Christmas ball we go to every year, you dope.'

'Oh yeah, the Christmas ball they always hold in the middle of November?' Holly laughed. 'Sorry, but I can't make it this year.'

'But you don't even know what date it's on yet!' Denise protested.

'Well, I assume it's being held on the same date as it has been every other year, which means I can't make it.'

'No, no, it's on the thirtieth of November this year, so you can make it!' Denise said excitedly.

'Oh, the thirtieth . . .' Holly paused and pretended to flick through some pages on her desk very loudly. 'No, Denise, I can't. Sorry. I'm busy on the thirtieth. I have a deadline,' she lied.

'But we don't have to be there till at least eight o'clock,' Denise tried to convince her. 'You could even come at nine if it was easier. You would just miss the drinks reception first.'

'Look, Denise, I'm sorry,' Holly said firmly. 'I'm just far too busy.'

'Well, that makes a change,' she muttered under her breath.

'What did you say?' Holly asked, getting angry.

'Nothing,' Denise replied shortly.

'I heard you; you said that makes a change, didn't you? Well, it just so happens that I take my work seriously, Denise, and I have no plans to lose my job over a stupid ball.'

'Fine then,' Denise huffed. 'Don't go.'

'I won't!'

'Fine!'

'Good. Well, I'm glad that's fine with you, Denise.' Holly couldn't help but smile at the ridiculousness of the conversation.

'I'm glad you're glad,' Denise huffed.

'Oh, don't be so childish, Denise.' Holly rolled her eyes. 'I have to work, simple as that.'

'Well, that's no surprise, that's all you ever do these days,' Denise blurted out. 'You never come out any more. Every time I ask you out you're busy doing something apparently much more important, like *work*. At my hen weekend you looked like you were having the worst time of your life and you didn't even bother coming out the second night. In fact, I don't know why you bothered to come at all. If you have a problem with me, Holly, I wish you would just say it to my face instead of being such a miserable bore!'

Holly sat back in shock and stared at the phone. She couldn't believe Denise had said those things. She couldn't believe Denise could be so stupid and selfish to think that this whole thing was about her. No wonder she felt she was going insane, when one of her best friends couldn't even understand her.

'That is the most selfish thing I have ever heard anyone say.' Holly tried to control her voice but she knew her anger was spilling out into her words.

'I'm selfish?' Denise squealed. 'You're the one who hid in the hotel room on my hen weekend! *My* hen weekend! You're supposed to be my maid of honour!'

'I was in the room with Sharon, you know that!' Holly defended herself.

'Oh, bullshit! Sharon would have been fine on her own. She's pregnant, not bloody dying. You don't need to be by her side twenty-four seven!' Denise went quiet as she realised what she had said.

Holly's blood boiled and as she spoke her voice trembled with rage. 'And you wonder why I don't go out with you – when you say stupid insensitive remarks like that. Did you ever think for one moment that it might be hard for me? The fact that all you talk about are your bloody wedding arrangements and how happy and excited you are and how you can't wait to spend the rest of your life with Tom in wedded bliss. In case you hadn't noticed, Denise, I didn't get that chance because my husband *died*. But I am very happy for you, really I am. I'm delighted you're happy and I'm not asking for any special treatment at all, I'm just asking for a bit of patience and for you to understand that *I will not get over this in a few months*! As for the ball, I have no intention of going to a place that Gerry and I have been going to together for the past ten years. You might not understand this, Denise, but funnily enough I would find it A BIT DIFFICULT. So don't book a ticket for me, I am perfectly happy staying at home,' she yelled and slammed the phone down.

She burst into tears and lay her head down on the desk as she sobbed. She felt lost. Her best friend couldn't even understand her. Maybe she was going mad. Maybe she *should* be over Gerry already. Maybe that's what normal people did when their loved ones died. She should have bought the rule book for widows to see what the recommended time for grieving was so she wouldn't have to keep on inconveniencing her family and friends.

Her weeping eventually died down into little sobs and she listened to the silence around her. She realised that everyone must have heard everything she had said and she felt so embarrassed that she was afraid to go to the bathroom for a tissue. Her face was hot and her eyes felt swollen from all her tears. She wiped them on the sleeve of her shirt.

'Shit!' she swore, swiping some papers off her desk as she realised she had smudged foundation, mascara and lipstick all along the sleeve of her spensive white shirt. She sat up to attention quickly as she heard a light knock on her door.

'Come in.' Her voice shook.

Chris entered her office, clutching two cups of tea.

'Tea?' he offered, raising his eyebrows at her, and she smiled weakly, remembering the joke they had shared on the day of her interview. He placed the mug down in front of her and relaxed in the chair opposite.

'Having a bad day?' he asked as gently as his gruff voice allowed.

She nodded as tears rolled down her face again. 'I'm sorry, Chris.' She tried to compose herself. 'It won't affect my work,' she said shakily.

He waved his hand dismissively. 'Holly, I'm not worried about that. You're a great worker.'

She smiled, grateful for the compliment. At least she was doing something right.

'Would you like to go home early?'

'No, thanks. Work will keep my mind off things.'

He shook his head sadly. 'That's not the way to go about it, Holly. I, of all people, should know that. I've buried myself inside these walls for the last couple of years and it doesn't help things. Not in the long run, anyway.'

'But you seem happy.' Her voice trembled.

'Seeming and being are not one and the same. I *know* you know that.'

She nodded sadly.

'You don't have to put on a brave face all the time, you know.' He handed her a tissue.

'Oh, I'm not brave at all.' She blew her nose.

'Ever hear the saying that you need to be scared to be brave?'

Holly thought about that. 'But I don't feel brave, I just feel scared.'

'Oh, we all feel scared at times – there's nothing wrong with that – but there will come a day when you will stop feeling scared. Look at all you've done!' He held his hands up, indicating her office. 'And look at all this.' He flicked through the pages of the magazine. 'That's the work of a very brave person.'

Holly smiled. 'I love the job.'

'And that's great news! But you need to learn to love more than your job.'

Holly frowned. She hoped this wasn't one of those get-over-one-man-by-sleeping-under-another-type chats.

'I mean learn to love yourself,' Chris continued. 'Learn to love your new life. Don't let your entire life revolve around your job. There's more to it than that.'

Holly raised her eyebrows at him. Talk about the pot calling the kettle black.

'I know I'm not the greatest example of that,' he conceded, 'but I'm learning too . . .' He placed his hand on the table and started to brush away imaginary crumbs while he thought about what to say next. 'I heard you don't want to go to this ball.'

Holly cringed. He had definitely heard all of her phone conversation.

'There were a million places I refused to go to when Maureen died,' he said sadly. 'We used to go for walks in the Botanical Gardens every Sunday and I just couldn't go there any more after I lost her. There were a million little memories contained in every flower and tree that grew in there. The bench we used to sit on, her favourite tree, her favourite rose garden – just everything about it reminded me of her.'

'Did you go back?' Holly asked, sipping the hot tea, feeling it warm her insides.

'A few months ago,' he replied. 'It was a difficult thing to do but I did it and now I go every Sunday again. You have to confront things, Holly, and think of things positively. I say to myself, this is a place we used to laugh in, cry in, fight in, and when you go there and remember all those beautiful times you feel closer to them. You can celebrate the love you had instead of hiding from it.'

He leaned forward in his chair and stared directly into her eyes. 'Some people go through life searching and *never* find their soul mates. They *never* do. You and I did, we just happened to have them for a shorter period of time than we hoped for. It's sad, but it's life! So you go to this ball, Holly, and you embrace the fact that you had someone whom you loved and who loved you back.'

Tears trickled down Holly's face as she realised he was right. She needed to remember Gerry and be happy about the love they shared and the love she still continued to feel; but not to cry about them, not to yearn for the many more years with him that would never come. She thought of the line he had written to her, 'Remember our wonderful memories, but please don't be afraid to make some more.' She needed to put the ghost of Gerry that haunted her to rest but to keep his memory alive.

There was still life for her after his death.

CHAPTER FORTY-FIVE

'I'm so sorry, Denise,' Holly apologised to her friend. They were sitting in the staffroom of Denise's workplace surrounded by boxes of hangers, rails of clothes, bags and accessories untidily strewn around the room. There was a musty smell in the air from the dust that had landed on the rails of clothes that had been sitting out for so long. A security camera attached to the wall stared at them and recorded their conversation.

Holly watched Denise's face for a reaction and saw her friend purse her lips in an attempt to stop them trembling and nod her head as if to let Holly know it was OK.

'No, it's not OK.' Holly sat forward in her chair. 'I didn't mean to lose my temper on the phone. Just because I'm feeling extra sensitive these days, it doesn't give me the right to take it out on you.'

Denise looked brave enough finally to speak. 'No, you were right, Holly . . .'

Holly shook her head and tried to disagree but Denise kept on talking.

'I've been so excited about this wedding that I didn't stop to think about how you might be feeling.' Her eyes rested on her friend, whose face looked so pale against her dark jacket. Holly was doing so well it was easy for them all to forget that she still had ghosts to be rid of.

'But you're right to be excited,' Holly insisted.

'And you're right to be upset,' Denise said firmly. 'I didn't think, I just didn't think.' She held her hands to her cheeks as she shook her head. 'Don't go to the ball if you don't feel comfortable. We will all understand.' She reached out to hold her friend's hands.

Holly felt confused. Chris had succeeded in convincing her to go to the ball but now her best friend was saying it was OK not to go. And she had a headache and headaches scared her. She hugged Denise goodbye in the shop, promising to call her later to give her a decision about the ball.

She headed back to the office, feeling even more unsure than before. Maybe Denise was right: it was only a stupid ball and she didn't have to go if she didn't want to. However, it was a stupid ball that was hugely representative of Holly and Gerry's time together. It was a night they had both enjoyed, a night they shared with their friends and danced to their favourite songs. If she went without him she would be destroying that tradition, replacing old, happy memories with entirely different ones. She didn't want to do that. She wanted to hang on to every single shred of memory of her and Gerry together. It was scaring her that she was forgetting his face. When she dreamed about him he was always somebody else; a person she made up in her mind with a different face and a different voice.

Now and again she rang his mobile phone just to hear his voice on his answering machine. She had even been paying the mobile company every month just to keep his account open. His smell had faded from the house; his clothes long gone under his own orders. He was fading from her mind and so she clung desperately on to every little bit of him that she could. She deliberately thought about him every night just before she went to sleep just so that she would dream about him. She even bought his favourite aftershave and splashed it around the house. Sometimes she would be out and a familiar smell or song would transport her back to another time and another place. A happier time.

She would catch a glimpse of him walking down the street or driving by in a car and would chase that person for miles, only to discover it wasn't him; merely a looka-like. She just couldn't seem to let go.

Just before heading back to the office she poked her head into Hogan's. She was feeling much more at ease with Daniel. Since that dinner where Holly had felt so uncomfortable in his company, she had realised that she was being ridiculous. She understood now why she had felt that way. Before, the only close friendship she had ever had with a man was with Gerry, and that was a romantic relationship. The idea of becoming so close to Daniel seemed strange and unusual. Holly had since convinced herself that there didn't need to be a romantic link for her to share a friendship with a man. Even if he was good-looking.

And the ease she felt had become a feeling of compan-ionship. She had felt that from the moment she met him. They could talk for hours, discussing her feelings, her life, his feelings, his life, and she knew that they shared a common enemy: loneliness. She knew that he was suffering from a different kind of grief but they were helping one another through the difficult days when all they needed was a caring ear or someone to make them laugh. And there were many of those days.

'Well?' he said, walking round from behind the bar. 'Will Cinderella go to the ball?'

Holly smiled and scrunched up her nose about to tell him that she wouldn't be going when she stopped herself. 'Are you going?'

He smiled and scrunched up his nose and she laughed. 'Well, it's definitely going to be a case of Couples-R-Us. I don't think I could cope with another night of Sam and Samantha or Robert and Roberta.' He pulled out a high stool for her at the bar and she sat down.

Holly giggled. 'Well, we could just be terribly rude and ignore them all.'

'Then what would be the point in going?' Daniel sat beside her and rested his leather boot on the foot rest of her chair. 'You don't expect me to talk to you all night, do you? We've talked the ears off each other by now; maybe I'm bored with you.'

'Fine then!' Holly pretended to be insulted. 'I was planning on ignoring you anyway.'

'Phew!' Daniel wiped his brow and pretended to look relieved. 'I'm definitely going then.'

Holly became serious. 'I think I really need to be there.'

Daniel stopped laughing. 'Well then, we shall go.'

Holly smiled at him. 'I think it would be good for you too, Daniel,' she said softly.

His foot dropped from her chair and he turned his

head away from her, pretending to survey the lounge. 'Holly, I'm fine,' he said unconvincingly.

Holly hopped off her chair, grabbed his face and kissed him roughly on the forehead. 'Daniel Connolly, stop trying to be all macho and strong. It doesn't wash with me.'

They hugged each other goodbye, and Holly marched back to her office, determined not to change her mind. She banged loudly up the stairs and marched straight by Alice, who was still staring dreamily at her article. 'John-Paul!' Holly yelled. 'I need a dress, quick!'

Chris smiled to himself in his office as he heard everyone across the hall making a fuss over Holly. He slid open his desk drawer and peeked at the photograph of himself and his wife. He vowed to visit the Botanical Gardens someday. If Holly could do it, then so could he.

CHAPTER FORTY-SIX

Holly was running late as she rushed around her bedroom, trying to get ready for the ball. She had spent the past two hours applying her make-up, crying and smudging it and then reapplying it. She rolled the mascara brush over her eyelashes for the fourth time, praying the tear reservoir had run dry for the night. An unlikely prospect, but a girl could always hope.

'Cinderella, your prince has arrived!' Sharon yelled upstairs to her.

Holly's heart raced; she needed more time. She needed to sit down and rethink the idea of going to the ball all over again as she had completely forgotten her reasons for going. Now she was faced with only the negatives.

Reasons not to go: she didn't want to go at all; she would spend all night crying; she would be stuck at a table full of so-called friends who hadn't talked to her since Gerry had died; she felt like shit; she looked like shit and Gerry wouldn't be there.

Reasons to go: she had an overwhelming feeling that

she needed to go and, most importantly, an overriding reason preventing her from backing out . . . She breathed slowly, trying to prevent a whole new batch of tears from appearing.

'Holly, be strong. You can do this,' she whispered at her reflection in the mirror. 'You need to do this, it will help you, it will make you stronger.' She repeated this over and over again until a creak at the door made her jump.

'Sorry,' Sharon apologised, appearing from round the door. 'Oh, Holly, you look fabulous!' she said excitedly.

'I look like shit,' Holly grumbled.

'Oh, stop saying that,' Sharon said angrily. 'I look like a blimp and do you hear me complaining? Accept the fact that you're a babe!' She smiled at her in the mirror. 'You'll be fine.'

'I just want to stay home tonight, Sharon. I have to open Gerry's last message.' Holly couldn't believe the time had come to open the last one. After tomorrow there would be no more kind words from Gerry and she still felt that she needed them. In all her excitement back in April, she couldn't wait for the months to pass so that she could rip the envelopes open and read his words but she had wished the months away all too quickly and now it was nearly the end. She wanted to stay in that night and savour their last special moment.

'I know,' Sharon said understanding. 'But that can wait for a few hours, can't it?'

Holly was just about to say no when John shouted up the stairs. 'Come on, girls! The taxi's waiting! We have to collect Tom and Denise!'

Before Holly followed Sharon downstairs she slid open the drawer of her dressing table and took out the November letter from Gerry that she had opened weeks ago. She needed his words of encouragement to help her out now. She ran her fingers over the ink and pictured him writing it. She imagined the face he made when he wrote, which she always used to tease him about. He used to have a look of pure concentration and his tongue licked his lips as he moved the pen. She loved that face. She missed that face. She slid the card from the envelope. She needed strength from this letter and she knew she would find it. Everyday, she read:

Cinderella must go to the ball this month. And she will look glamorous and beautiful and have the time of her life just like always . . . But no white dresses this year . . .
    PS. I love you . . .

The day after Holly had rowed with Denise over whether to go to the ball or not, Holly opened her November letter. Despite pep talks from Chris and Daniel, she had tortured herself all day over what her decision would be. She needn't have worried, as Gerry had chosen for her and his words reinforced the idea that she should go to the ball. This was her new task. She took a deep breath and followed Sharon downstairs.

'Wow!' Daniel said, his mouth dropping open. 'You look fabulous, Holly.'

'I look like—,' Holly started to grumble and Sharon shot her a look. 'But thanks,' she quickly added. John-Paul had helped her choose a simple black halter-neck dress, with a split to the thigh up the middle. No white dresses this year.

. They all piled into the taxi and as they approached each set of traffic lights Holly prayed that they would turn red to delay the moment they arrived. No such luck. For once the traffic on the streets of Dublin was nonexistent, and they made it to the hotel in record time. Despite her prayers, a mudslide didn't cascade down the Dublin mountains and no volcano erupted. Hell refused to freeze over too.

They stepped up to the table just inside the door of the function room and Holly looked at the ground as she felt all eyes in their direction from the women eager to see how the newcomers were dressed. When they were satisfied that they were still the most beautiful people there, they looked away and continued their conversations. The woman sitting behind the desk smiled as they approached her. 'Hello, Sharon; hello, John; hi, Denise . . . oh gosh!' Her face might actually have gone whiter under her streaky fake tanned face, but Holly couldn't be sure. 'Oh, hello, Holly. It's so good of you to come considering . . .' she trailed off and quickly flicked through the guest list to tick off their names.

'Let's go to the bar,' Denise said, linking Holly's arm and dragging her away.

As they walked across the room a woman Holly hadn't spoken to for months approached her. 'Holly, I was sorry to hear about Gerry. He was a lovely man.'

'Thank you,' Holly smiled, and was led away again by Denise. They finally reached the bar.

'Hi there, Holly,' a familiar voice behind her said.

'Oh, hello, Patrick,' she said, turning to face the large

businessman who sponsored the charity. He was tall and overweight, with a bright red face, probably due to the stress of running one of Ireland's most successful businesses. That and the fact that he drank too much. He looked like he was choking with the tightness of his bow tie, and he pulled at it, looking uncomfortable. The buttons on his tuxedo looked as if they were about to pop at any moment. Holly didn't know him very well; he was just one of the people she knew from being at the ball every year.

'You're looking as lovely as always.' He gave her a kiss on the cheek. 'Can I get you a drink?' he asked, holding his hand up to attract the barman's attention.

'Oh no, thanks,' she smiled.

'Ah, let me,' he said, taking his bulging wallet out of his pocket. 'What'll you have?'

Holly gave in. 'A white wine then, please, if you insist,' she smiled.

'I might as well get a drink for that miserable husband of yours,' he laughed. 'What's he having?' He searched the room for Gerry.

'Oh, he's not here, Patrick,' Holly said, feeling uncomfortable.

'Why not? The dryshite. That's two years now he's gone missing. What's he up to?' Paul asked loudly, at the same time mouthing his order to the barman.

'Em, he passed away early in the year, Patrick,' Holly said gently, hoping not to embarrass him.

'Oh . . .' Patrick reddened even more and cleared his throat nervously. He stared down at the bar. 'I'm very sorry to hear that,' he stuttered, and looked away. He pulled at his bow tie again.

433

'Thank you,' Holly said, counting the seconds in her head till he made an excuse to leave the conversation. He escaped after three seconds, mumbling that he had to bring his wife her drink. Holly was left standing at the bar alone as Denise had already made her way back to the group with their drinks. She picked up her glass of wine and she headed over.

'Hi, Holly.'

She turned to see who had called her name.

'Oh, hello, Jennifer.' She was faced with another woman she knew only from attending the ball. She was dressed in an over-the-top ball gown, dripping in expensive jewellery and she held a glass of champagne between the thumb and forefinger of her gloved hand. Her blonde hair was almost white and her skin dark and leathery as a result of too much sun.

'How are you? You look fab, the dress is fab!' She sipped on her champagne and looked Holly up and down.

'I'm fine, thank you. You?'

'I'm just fab, thanks. Gerry not with you tonight?' She looked around the room for him.

'No, he passed away in February,' Holly repeated gently.

'Oh gosh, I'm so sorry to hear that.' She placed her glass of champagne down on the table next to them and her hands flew to her face, her forehead creasing with worry. 'I had no idea. How are you keeping, you poor love?' She reached out and placed her hand on Holly's arm.

'I'm fine, thank you,' Holly repeated, smiling to keep the atmosphere light.

'Oh, you poor thing.' Jennifer's voice was hushed and looked at her pityingly. 'You must be devastated.'

'Well, yes, it is hard but I'm dealing with it. Trying to be positive, you know?' she perked up.

'Gosh, I don't know how you can be. That's awful news.' Her eyes continued to bore into Holly. She seemed to look at her differently now. Holly nodded along and wished this woman would stop telling her what she already knew.

'And was he ill?' she probed.

'Yes, he had a brain tumour.'

'Oh dear, that's *awful*. And he was so *young*.' Every word she emphasised became a high-pitched screech.

'Yes, he was . . . but we had a happy life together, Jennifer,' Holly said, trying to be as cheery as she could.

'Yes, you did, but it's such a shame it wasn't a longer life. That's devastating for you. Absolutely *awful* and *so* unfair. You must feel miserable. And how on earth did you come here tonight? With all these couples around?' She looked around at all the couples as though there was suddenly a bad smell in the air.

'Well, you just have to learn to move on,' Holly smiled.

'Of course you do. But it must be so difficult. Oh, how *awful*.' She held her gloved hands up to her face, looking appalled.

Holly smiled and spoke through gritted teeth. 'Yes it's difficult, but like I said you just have to stay positive and move on. Anyway, speaking of moving on, I'd better go and join my friends,' she added politely and dashed off.

'You all right?' Daniel asked as she appeared beside him.

'Yes, I'm fine, thank you,' Holly repeated for the tenth time that night. She glanced over at Jennifer, who was in a huddle with her female friends, talking and staring over at her and Daniel.

'I have arrived!' a loud voice announced at the door. Holly turned round to see the legendary party animal Jamie standing at the door with his arms held high in the air. 'I am once again dressed in my penguin suit and ready to partaaay!' He did a little dance before joining the group, attracting stares from around the room. Just what he wanted. He made his way around their circle, greeting the men with a handshake and a kiss on the cheek for the women, sometimes 'hilariously' switching the gesture. He paused when he got to Holly and glanced back and forth from Holly to Daniel a couple of times. He shook Daniel's hand stiffly, pecked Holly on the cheek quickly as though she was diseased and rushed off. Holly tried to swallow the lump in her throat angrily. That had been very rude.

His wife, Helen, smiled timidly over at Holly from across the other side of their circle but didn't come over. Holly wasn't surprised. It had obviously been too difficult for them to drive ten minutes down the road to visit Holly after Gerry died, so she would hardly expect Helen to take ten steps towards her to say hello. She ignored them and turned to talk to her real friends, the people who had supported her for the past year.

Holly was laughing at one of Sharon's stories when she felt a light tapping on her shoulder. She turned round mid-laughter to face a very sad-looking Helen.

'Hi, Helen,' she said happily.

'How *are* you?' Helen said quietly, touching Holly gently on the arm.

'Oh, I'm fine,' Holly nodded. 'You should listen to this

story, it's very funny,' she smiled, and continued to listen to Sharon.

Helen left her hand on Holly's arm and eventually tapped her again after a few seconds. 'I mean, how are you since Gerry . . .'

Holly gave up listening to Sharon.

'Since Gerry died, you mean?' Holly understood that people sometimes felt awkward about these situations. Holly often did too, but she felt that if someone had brought the subject up themselves they could at least be adult enough to carry the conversation through properly.

Helen appeared to wince at Holly's question. 'Well, yes, but I didn't want to say . . .'

'It's OK, Helen; I've accepted that that's what happened.'

'Have you?'

'Of course I have,' Holly frowned.

'It's just that I haven't seen you for a very long time so I was beginning to get worried . . .'

Holly laughed. 'Helen, I still live round the corner from you in the same house as before, my home phone number is still the same, as is my mobile number. If you were ever that worried about me I was never that difficult for you to find.'

'Oh yes, but I didn't want to intrude . . .' she trailed off.

'Friends don't intrude, Helen,' Holly said politely, but hoped she had got her message across.

Helen blushed slightly and Holly turned away to talk to Sharon.

'Keep me a seat beside you, will you? I just need to run to the ladies again,' Sharon asked, doing a little dance on the spot.

'Again?' Denise blurted out. 'You were just there five minutes ago!'

'Yes, well, this tends to happen when you have a seven-month-old baby pushing down on your bladder,' she explained, before waddling off to the toilet.

'It's not actually seven months old, though, is it?' Denise said, scrunching her face up. 'Technically, it's minus two months because otherwise that would mean that the baby would be nine months old when he was born and then they would be celebrating his first birthday after only three months. And usually babies are walking by the time they're one.'

Holly frowned at her. 'Denise, why do you torment yourself with thoughts like that?'

Denise frowned and turned to Tom, 'I'm right, though, aren't I, Tom?'

'Yes, love.' He smiled sweetly at her.

'Chicken,' Holly teased Tom.

The bell was rung to signal that it was time to take their places for dinner, and the crowds began to swarm in. Holly took her seat and placed her new handbag down on the chair beside her to reserve it for Sharon. Helen wandered over and pulled out the chair to sit down.

'Sorry, Helen, but Sharon asked me to save this seat for her,' Holly explained politely.

Helen waved her hand dismissively. 'Oh, Sharon won't mind,' she said, plonking herself down on the chair and squashing Holly's handbag. Sharon made her way over to the table and stuck out her bottom lip in disappointment. Holly apologised and motioned over to Helen as her excuse. Sharon rolled her eyes and stuck her fingers in her mouth, pretending to gag. Holly giggled.

'Well, you're in high spirits,' Jamie announced to Holly, sounding very unimpressed.

'Is there any reason why I shouldn't be?' Holly replied tartly.

Jamie replied with some smart retort that a few people laughed at because he was 'so funny' and Holly ignored him. She didn't find him funny any more, though she and Gerry had always been amongst those people who had hung on his every word. Now he was just being stupid.

'Are you OK?' Daniel asked quietly from beside her.

'Yes, I'm fine, thank you,' she replied, taking a sip of wine.

'Oh, you don't have to give me that bullshit answer, Holly. It's me,' he laughed.

Holly smiled and groaned. 'People are being very nice and all by offering me their sympathies but I feel like I'm back at his funeral again. Having to pretend to be all strong and Superwoman-like, even though all some of them want is for me to be devastated because it's so *awful.*' She mimicked Jennifer and rolled her eyes. 'And then there's the people who don't know about Gerry and this is *so* not the place to have to tell them.'

Daniel listened to her patiently. He nodded when she finally stopped talking. 'I understand what you're saying. When Laura and I broke up I felt that for months everywhere I went I was always having to tell people that we broke up. But the good thing is that eventually word goes around so you can stop having those awkward conversations with people all the time.'

'Any word on Laura, by the way?' Holly asked. She enjoyed having bitching sessions about Laura, even though she had never met her. She loved to hear stories about her from Daniel, and then the two of them would spend the evening talking about how much they hated her. It passed the time and right now Holly really needed something to avoid having to talk to Helen.

Daniel's eyes lit up. 'Yes, actually, I do have a bit of gossip about her.'

'Oooh good, I love a bit of gossip,' Holly said, rubbing her hands together with delight.

'Well, a friend of mine named Charlie, who works as a barman in Laura's dad's hotel, told me that her fiancé tried to come on to some other woman who was a guest there and Laura caught him so they split up.' He laughed evilly with a twinkle in his eye. He was delighted to hear of her heartbreak.

Holly froze because that story sounded rather familiar. 'Eh . . . Daniel, what hotel does her father own?'

'Oh, the Galway Inn. It's a real kip of a place but it's in a nice area, across the road from the beach.'

'Oh.' Holly didn't know what to say and her eyes widened.

'I know,' Daniel laughed. 'It's brilliant, isn't it? I can tell you, if I ever met the woman who split them up I would buy her the most expensive bottle of champagne.'

Holly smiled weakly. 'Would you now . . . ?' Holly stared at Daniel curiously, interested to know why on earth he had once been interested in Laura. Holly would have bet all her money against those two ever being together. She didn't seem his type, whatever his 'type' was. Daniel was so easy-going and friendly, and Laura was . . . well, Laura was a bitch. Holly couldn't think of any other word to describe her.

440

'Em, Daniel?' Holly nervously tucked her hair behind her ears, preparing herself to question him on his choice of women.

He smiled at her, eyes still twinkling from the news of his ex-girlfriend and ex-best friend's break-up. 'Yes, Holly.'

'Well, I was just wondering. Laura seems to sound like a bit of a . . . em . . . a . . . bitch, to be honest.' She bit her lip and studied his face to see if she had insulted him. His face was blank as he stared at the candlesticks in the centre of the table and listened. 'Well,' she continued, feeling she had to tiptoe carefully around this subject, knowing how badly Laura had broken Daniel's heart, 'well, my question is really, whatever did you see in her? How could you two *ever* have been in love? You're both so different – at least you *sound* like you're so different,' she back-pedalled fast, remembering she wasn't supposed ever to have met Laura.

Daniel was silent for a moment and Holly feared she had stepped in the wrong territory. He dragged his eyes away from the flame dancing around on the candlestick to face Holly. His lips broke into a sad smile. 'Laura isn't really a bitch, Holly. Well, for leaving me for my best friend she is . . . but as a person, when we were together, she was never a bitch. Dramatic, yes. A bitch, no.' He smiled and turned to face Holly properly. 'You see, I loved the drama of our relationship. I found it exciting, she *enthralled* me.' His face became animated as he explained their relationship and his speech quickened with the excitement of the memory of his lost love. 'I loved waking up in the morning and wondering what kind of mood she would be in that day, I loved our fights,

441

I loved the passion of them and I loved how we would make love after them.' His eyes sparkled. 'She would make a song and dance about most things but I suppose that's what I found different and attractive about her. I used to always tell myself that as long as she kept making a fuss about our own relationship then I knew she cared. If she hadn't then it wouldn't have been worth it really. I loved the drama,' he repeated, believing himself even more this time. 'Our temperaments contrasted but we made a good team. You know what they say about opposites attracting . . .' He looked into the face of his new friend and saw her concern. 'She didn't treat me badly, Holly. She wasn't a bitch in that way.' He smiled to himself. 'She was just . . .'

'Dramatic,' Holly finished for him, finally understanding. He nodded. Although she did cheat on him, Holly thought angrily, but decided not to say it aloud.

Holly watched his face as he became lost in another memory. She supposed it was possible for anybody to love anybody. That was the great thing about love: it came in all different shapes, sizes and temperaments.

'You miss her,' Holly said gently, putting her hand on his arm.

Daniel snapped out of his daydream and stared deeply into Holly's eyes. A shiver went down her spine and she felt the hairs on her arms stand up.

He snorted loudly and twisted back round in his chair, 'Wrong again, Holly Kennedy,' he said, and frowned as though she had said the most bizarre thing ever. 'Completely and *utterly* wrong.' He picked up his knife and fork and began to eat his salmon starter.

Holly gulped back some cool water and turned her attention to the plate that was being set before her.

After dinner and a few bottles of wine, Helen stumbled over to Holly, who had escaped over to Sharon and Denise's side of the table. She gave her a big hug and tearily apologised for not keeping in touch.

'That's OK, Helen. Sharon, Denise and John have been very supportive friends so I wasn't alone.'

'Oh, but I feel so awful,' Helen slurred.

'Don't,' Holly said, anxious to continue her enjoyable conversation with the girls.

But Helen insisted on talking about the good old times when Gerry was alive and everything was rosy. She talked about all the times that she and Gerry shared together, which were memories that Holly wasn't particularly interested in. Eventually Holly had had enough of Helen's tearful whinging and realised that all her friends were up having fun on the dance floor.

'Helen, please stop,' Holly interrupted. 'I don't know why you feel you have to discuss this with me tonight when I am trying to enjoy myself, but you obviously feel guilty for not keeping in touch with me. To be honest, I think that if I hadn't come to this ball tonight I still wouldn't have heard from you for another ten months or more. And that's not the kind of friend I need in my life. So please stop crying on my shoulder and let me enjoy myself.'

Holly felt that she had phrased it reasonably, but Helen looked like she had been slapped in the face. A small dose of what Holly had felt like for the past year. Daniel appeared out of nowhere, took Holly by the hand

and led her to the dance floor to join all her friends. As soon as they reached the dance floor the song ended and Eric Clapton's 'Wonderful Tonight' began. The dance floor began to empty out bar a few couples, and Holly was left facing Daniel. She gulped. She hadn't planned on this. She had only ever danced with Gerry to this song.

Daniel placed his hand lightly on her waist and gently took her hand and they began to circle round. Holly was stiff. Dancing with another man felt wrong. A tingle went down her spine and she shuddered. Daniel must have thought she was cold because he pulled her closer as if to keep her warm. She was led round the floor in a trance until the song ended and she made the excuse of having to go to the toilet. She locked herself in the cubicle and leaned against the door, taking deep breaths. She had been doing so well up until now. Even with everyone asking her about Gerry she had remained calm. But the dance had shaken her. Perhaps it was time to go home, while the going was good. She was about to unlock the door when she heard a voice outside say her name. She froze and listened to the women chatting outside.

'Did you see Holly Kennedy dancing with that man tonight?' a voice asked. The unmistakable whine of Jennifer.

'I know!' another voice spoke with a tone of disgust. 'And her husband not yet cold in his grave!'

'Ah, leave her alone,' another woman said light-heartedly. 'They could just be friends.'

Thank you, Holly thought.

'But I doubt it,' she continued, and the women giggled. 'Did you see the way they were wrapped around each other? I don't dance with any of my friends like that,' Jennifer said.

'That's disgraceful,' another woman said. 'Imagine flaunting your new man in a place you used to come to with your husband in front of all his friends. It's disgusting.'

The women tutted and a toilet flushed in the cubicle beside Holly. She stood frozen in her position, shocked by what she was hearing and embarrassed they were saying it where others could hear.

The toilet door opened beside her and the women were silenced. 'Would you bickering old bitches ever go and get yourselves lives?' Sharon's voice yelled. 'It is absolutely no business of yours what *my best friend* does or does not do! Jennifer, if your life was so bloody perfect then what are you doing sneaking around with Pauline's husband?'

Holly heard someone gasp. Probably Pauline. She covered her mouth to stop herself laughing.

'Right, so keep your noses in your own business and piss off the lot of you!' Sharon yelled.

When Holly had heard everyone leave she unlocked the door and stepped outside. Sharon looked up at her from the sink in shock.

'Thanks, Sharon.'

'Oh Holly, I'm sorry you had to hear that,' she said, giving her friend a hug.

'It doesn't matter. I couldn't give a crap what they think,' Holly said bravely. 'But I can't believe Jennifer is having an affair with Pauline's husband!'

Sharon shrugged. 'She's not but it'll give them something to bitch about for the next few months.'

The girls chuckled.

'I reckon I'll go home now, though,' Holly said, glancing at her watch and thinking about the final message from Gerry. Her heart sank.

'Good idea,' Sharon agreed. 'I didn't realise how shite this ball was when you're sober.'

Holly smiled.

'Anyway, you were great tonight, Holly. You came, you conquered, now go home and open Gerry's message. Ring me and let me know what it says.' She hugged her friend again.

'It's the last one,' Holly said sadly.

'I know, so enjoy it,' Sharon smiled. 'Memories last a lifetime, remember that.'

Holly made her way back to the table to say goodbye to everyone, and Daniel stood up to go with her. 'You're not leaving me here on my own,' he laughed. 'We can share a cab.'

Holly was slightly irritated when Daniel hopped out of the taxi and followed her to her house. It was a quarter to twelve, which gave her fifteen minutes. With luck he would have drunk his tea and gone by then. She had even called another taxi to arrive at her house in a half an hour, just to let him know he couldn't stay too long.

'Ah, so this is the famous envelope,' Daniel said, picking it up from the table.

Holly's eyes widened; she felt protective over that envelope and wasn't happy with him touching it, removing Gerry's touch from it.

'December,' he said, reading the outside and running his fingers along the lettering. Holly wanted to tell him to put it down but didn't want to sound psychotic.

Eventually he placed it back on the table and she breathed a sigh of relief and continued to fill the kettle.

'How many more envelopes are left?' Daniel asked, taking his overcoat off and walking over to join her at the kitchen counter.

'That's the last one.' Holly's voice was husky and she cleared her throat.

'So what are you going to do after that?'

'What do you mean?' she asked, feeling confused.

'Well, as far as I can see, that list is like your Bible, your Ten Commandments. What the list says goes, as far as your life is concerned. So what will you do when there aren't any more?'

Holly looked up at his face to see if he was being smart but his blue eyes twinkled kindly back at her.

'I'll just live my life,' she replied, turning her back and flicking the switch on the kettle.

'Will you be able to do that?' He walked closer to her and she could smell his aftershave. It was a real Daniel smell.

'I suppose so,' she replied, uncomfortable with his questions.

'Because you will have to make your own decisions then,' he said softly.

'I know that,' she replied defensively, avoiding eye contact with him.

'And do you think you'll be able to do that?'

Holly rubbed her face tiredly. 'Daniel, what's this about?'

He swallowed hard and adjusted his stance before her, trying to make himself comfortable. 'I'm asking you this because I'm going to say something to you now, and you

447

are going to have to make your own decision.' He looked her straight in the eye and her heart beat wildly. 'There will be no list, no guidelines; you will just have to follow your own heart.'

Holly backed away from him a little. A feeling of dread pulled at her and she hoped he wasn't going to say what she thought he was.

'Em . . . Daniel . . . I d-don't think that this is . . . the right time to . . . um . . . we shouldn't talk about . . .'

'This is a perfect time,' he said seriously. 'You already know what I'm going to say to you Holly and I *know* you already know how I feel about you.'

Holly's jaw dropped as she glanced at the clock.

It was twelve o'clock.

CHAPTER FORTY-SEVEN

Gerry touched Holly's nose and smiled to himself as she wrinkled it up in her sleep. He loved watching her while she was sleeping; she looked like a princess, so beautiful and peaceful.

He tickled her nose again and smiled as her eyes slowly opened. 'Good morning, sleepy-head.'

She smiled at him. 'Good morning, beautiful.' She cuddled closer to him and rested her head on his chest. 'How are you feeling today?'

'Like I could run the London marathon,' he joked.

'Now that's what I call a quick recovery,' she smiled, lifting her head and kissing him on the lips. 'What do you want for breakfast?'

'You,' he said, biting her nose.

Holly giggled. 'I'm not on the menu today, unfortunately. How about a fry?'

'No,' he frowned, 'that's too heavy for me,' and his heart melted as he saw Holly's face fall. He tried to perk himself up. 'But I would love a big, huge bowl of vanilla ice cream!'

'Ice cream!' she laughed. 'For breakfast?'

'Yes,' he grinned, 'I always wanted that for breakfast when I was a kid but my darling mother would never allow me to have it. But now I don't care any more,' he smiled bravely.

'Then ice cream you shall have,' Holly hopped happily out of bed. 'Do you mind if I wear this?' she asked, putting his dressing gown on.

'My dear, you can wear it all you like,' Gerry smiled, watching her modelling the oversized robe up and down the bedroom for him.

'Mmm, it smells of you,' she said, sniffing it. 'I'm never going to take it off. OK, I'll be back in a minute,' and he heard her racing down the stairs and clattering around in the kitchen.

Lately he had noticed her racing around every time she left his side. It was as though she was afraid to leave him for too long on his own, and he knew what that meant. Bad news for him. He had finished his radiation therapy, which they had prayed would target the residual tumour. It had failed, and now all he could do was lie around all day, too weak to get up most of the time. It just seemed so pointless to him to be wasting time like that because it wasn't even as if he was waiting to recover. His heart beat wildly at the thought. He was afraid; afraid of where he was going, afraid of what was happening to him and afraid for Holly. She was the only person who knew exactly what to say to him to calm him down and ease his pain. She was so strong, his rock, and he couldn't imagine his life without her. But he needn't worry about that scenario, because it was her that would be without him. He felt angry, sad, jealous and scared for her. He wanted to stay with her and carry out every wish and promise that they had ever made to one another, and he was fighting for that right. But he knew he was fighting a losing battle. After two operations the tumour had returned, and it was growing rapidly inside him. He wanted to reach into his head and tear out the disease that was destroying his life but that was just another thing he had no control over. He feared that after this month Holly would be alone . . .

They had become even closer over the past few months, which was something he knew was a bad idea, for Holly's sake, but he couldn't bear to distance himself from her. He was living for their chats that carried on till the early hours of the morning and left them giggling, just like when they were teenagers. But that was only on their good days.

They had their bad days too.

He wouldn't think about that now. His therapist kept telling him to 'give your body a positive environment – socially, emotionally, nutritionally and spiritually.'

And his new little project was doing just that. It was keeping him busy and making him feel as if he was doing something other than lie in bed all day. His mind was kept occupied as he mapped out his plan to remain with Holly even when he was gone. He was also fulfilling a promise he had made to her years ago. At least there was one promise he could follow through on for her. Shame it had to be this particular one.

He heard Holly thudding up the stairs and he smiled; his plan was working.

'Babe, there's no ice cream left,' she said sadly. 'Is there anything else you would prefer?'

'Nope,' he shook his head. 'Just the ice cream, please.'

'Oh, but now I have to go to the shop to get it,' she complained.

'Don't worry, hon, I'll be fine for a few minutes,' he assured her.

She looked at him uncertainly. 'I really would rather stay.'

'Don't be silly,' he smiled, and lifted his mobile off the bedside table, placing it on his chest. 'If there's a problem, which there won't be, I'll call you.'

'OK,' Holly bit her lip, 'I'll only be five minutes down the road. Are you sure you'll be all right?'

'Positive,' he smiled.

She slowly took off his robe and threw on a tracksuit. He could see she still wasn't happy about the arrangement.

'Holly, I'll be fine,' he said firmly.

'OK.' She gave him a long kiss and he heard her race down the stairs, rush out to the car, and speed off down the road.

As soon as Gerry knew it was safe, he pulled back the covers and slowly climbed out of bed. He sat on the edge of the mattress for a while, waiting for the dizziness to pass, then slowly made his way to the wardrobe. He took out an old shoebox from the top shelf that contained junk he had collected over the past few years and that now also contained nine sealed envelopes. He took out a tenth empty envelope and neatly wrote 'December' on the front. Today was the first of December and he moved himself forward one year from now when he knew he wouldn't be around. He imagined Holly to be a karaoke genius, relaxed from her holiday in Spain, bruise-free as a result of the bedside lamp and, he hoped, happy in a new job that she loved.

He imagined her on this very day in one year's time, possibly sitting on the bed right where he was now and reading the final instalment to the list. He thought long and hard about what to write for this last message. Tears filled his eyes as he placed the full stop beside the sentence; he kissed the page, wrapped it in the envelope and hid it back in the shoebox. He would post the envelopes to Holly's parents' house in Portmarnock where he knew the package would be in safe hands until she was prepared to open it. He wiped the tears from his eyes and slowly made his way back to bed where his phone was ringing on the mattress.

'Hello?' he said, trying to control his voice, and he smiled when he heard the sweetest voice on the other end. 'I love you too, Holly . . .'

CHAPTER FORTY-EIGHT

'No, Daniel, this isn't right,' Holly said, upset, and pulled her hand away from his grip.

'But why isn't it right?' he pleaded with her.

'It's too soon,' she said, rubbing her face tiredly. Things for her just seemed to get more and more complicated.

'Too soon because that's what people have been telling you, or too soon because that's what your heart's telling you?'

'Oh, Daniel, I don't know,' she said, pacing the kitchen floor. 'I'm so confused. *Please* stop asking me so many questions!'

Her heart beat wildly and her head spun, even her body was telling her this wasn't a good situation to be in. It was panicking on her behalf, indicating that danger was ahead. This felt wrong – it all felt so wrong, 'I can't, Daniel. I'm married! I love Gerry!' she said in a panic.

'Gerry?' he asked, his eyes widening as he went over to the kitchen table and grabbed the envelope roughly. 'This is Gerry! This is what I'm competing with! It's a piece of paper, Holly. It's a *list*. A list you have allowed to run your life for the past year without having to think for yourself or live your own life. Now you have to think for yourself, right now. Gerry's gone,' he said gently, walking back over to her. 'Gerry's gone and I'm here. I'm not saying that I could ever take his place but at least give us a chance to be together.'

She took the envelope from his hand and hugged it close to her heart as tears rolled down her cheeks. 'Gerry's not gone,' she sobbed. 'He's here, every time I open these, he's here.'

There was a silence as Daniel watched her crying. She looked so lost and helpless he just wanted to hold her. 'It's a piece of paper,' he said softly, stepping closer to her again.

'Gerry is *not* a piece of paper,' she said angrily through her tears. 'He was a living breathing human being that I loved. Gerry is a man that consumed my life for fifteen years. He is a million billion happy memories. He is *not* a piece of paper,' she repeated.

'So what am I?' Daniel asked quietly.

Holly prayed that he wouldn't cry. She didn't think she could bear it if he cried.

'You,' she took a deep breath, 'are a kind, caring and incredibly thoughtful friend who I respect and appreciate—'

'But I'm not Gerry,' he interrupted her.

'I *don't want* you to be Gerry,' she insisted. 'I want you to be Daniel.'

'How do you feel about me?' His voice shook slightly.

'I just told you how I feel about you,' she sniffed.

'No, how do you *feel* about me?'

455

She stared at the ground. 'I feel strongly about you, Daniel, but I need time . . .' she paused, '. . . lots and lots of time.'

'Then I will wait.' He smiled sadly and wrapped his strong arms around her.

The doorbell rang and Holly silently breathed a sigh of relief. 'That's your taxi.' Her voice shook.

'I'll call you tomorrow, Holly,' he said softly, kissing her on the top of her head and making his way to the front door. Holly continued to stand in the middle of the kitchen after he'd gone, running over and over in her mind the scene that had just occurred. She stood there for some time, tightly gripping the crumpled envelope close to her heart.

Still in shock she eventually made her way slowly up the stairs to bed. She slipped out of her dress and wrapped herself in Gerry's warm oversized robe. His smell had disappeared. She slowly climbed into bed like a child, tucked herself under the covers and flicked on the bedside lamp. She stared at the envelope for a long time, thinking about what Daniel had said.

The list *had* become some sort of Bible to her. She obeyed the rules, lived by the rules and never broke any of them. When Gerry said jump, she jumped. But the list had helped her. It had helped her get out of bed in the morning and start a new life at a time when all she wanted to do was curl into a ball and die. Gerry had helped her and she didn't regret one thing she had done in the past year. She didn't regret her new job or her new friends or any new thought or feeling she had developed all by herself without Gerry's opinion. But this was the final instalment to the list. This was her tenth

Commandment, as Daniel had phrased it. There would be no more. He was right: she would have to start making decisions for herself, live a life that she felt happy with without holding back and wondering whether or not Gerry would agree with it. Well, she could always wonder, but she needn't let it stop her.

When he was alive she had lived through him, and now he was dead she was still living through him. She could see that now. It made her feel safe, but now she was out on her own and she needed to be brave.

She took the phone off the hook and switched off her mobile. She didn't want to be disturbed. She needed to savour this special and final moment without interruptions. She needed to say goodbye to Gerry. She was alone now and she needed to think for herself.

She slowly tore open the envelope, carefully trying not to rip the paper as she slid the card out.

Don't be afraid to fall in love again. Open your heart and follow where it leads you . . . and remember, shoot for the moon . . .
    PS. I will always love you . . .

'Oh, Gerry,' she sobbed, and her shoulders shook as her body heaved.

She got very little sleep that night and the times she did nod off, her dreams were obscure images of Daniel and Gerry's faces and bodies being mingled together. She awoke in a sweat at 6 a.m. and decided to get up and go for a walk to clear the jumbled thoughts from her head. Her heart felt heavy as she walked along the path of her local park. She had bundled herself up well to protect herself from the stinging cold that whipped at her ears and numbed her face. Yet her head felt hot. Hot from the tears, hot from her headache, hot from her brain working overtime.

The trees were bare and looked like skeletons lining the pathway. Leaves danced in circles around her feet like wicked little elves threatening to trip her up. The park was deserted; people had once again gone into hibernation, too cowardly to brave the winter elements. Holly wasn't brave, nor was she enjoying her stroll. It felt like punishment to be out in the icy cold weather.

How on earth had she found herself in this situation? Just as soon as she was getting round to picking up the pieces of her shattered life, she dropped them all again and sent them scattering. She thought she had found a friend, someone she could confide in. She wasn't looking to become entangled in some ridiculous love triangle. And it was ridiculous because the third person wasn't even around. He wasn't even a possible candidate for the job. Of course she thought of Daniel a lot, but she also thought about Sharon and Denise, and surely she wasn't in love with them? What she felt for Daniel wasn't the love she felt for Gerry, it was an entirely different feeling. So perhaps she wasn't in love with Daniel. And, anyway, if she was, wouldn't she be the first person to realise it, instead of being given a few days to 'think about it'? But then why was she even thinking about it? If she didn't love him, then she should come right out and say it . . . but she was thinking about it. It was a simple yes/no question, wasn't it? How odd life was.

And why was Gerry urging her to find a new love? What had he been *thinking* when he wrote that message?

Had he already let go of her before he died? Had it been *so* easy for him to just give her up and resign himself to the fact that she would meet someone else? Questions, questions, questions. And she would never know the answers.

After hours of tormenting herself with further interrogations and the freezing cold nipping at her skin, she headed back in the direction of her house. As she walked down her road, the sound of laughter caused her to lift her gaze from the ground. Her neighbours were decorating the tree in their garden with tiny Christmas lights.

'Hi, Holly,' her neighbour said, stepping out from behind the tree with bulbs wrapped around her wrists.

'I'm decorating Jessica,' her partner laughed, wrapping the tangled cords around her legs. 'I think she'll make a beautiful garden gnome.'

Holly smiled sadly as she watched them laughing together. 'Christmas already.'

'I know,' Jessica stopped laughing long enough to answer. 'Hasn't the year just flown?'

'Too fast,' Holly said quietly. 'It went far too fast.'

Holly crossed the road and continued on her way to her house. A scream caused her to swirl round and see Jessica lose her balance and collapse onto the grass, wrapped in a pile of lights. Laughter echoed down the street as Holly stepped into her house.

'OK Gerry,' Holly announced as she closed the front door, 'I've been for a walk and I've thought deeply about what you said and I have come to the conclusion that you had lost your mind when you wrote that message. If you really *really* mean it then give me some sort of sign, and if not I'll completely understand that it was all a big mistake and that you have changed your mind,' she said matter-of-factly into the air.

She looked around the living room, waiting to see if anything happened. Nothing happened.

'OK then,' she said happily, 'you made a mistake, I understand. I will just disregard that final message.' She looked around the room again and wandered over towards the window. 'OK, Gerry, this is your last chance . . .'

The lights on the tree across the road flew on and Jessica and Tony danced about their garden, giggling. Suddenly the lights flickered and went out again. They stopped dancing and their faces fell.

Holly rolled her eyes. 'I'll take that as an "I don't know".'

She sat down at the kitchen table and sipped on a hot mug of tea to thaw out her frozen body. Friend tells you he loves you and dead husband tells you to fall in love again so you make a cup of tea.

She had three weeks left at work until she could take her Christmas holidays, which meant that, if she had to, she would only have to avoid Daniel for fifteen working days. That seemed possible. Hopefully by the time of Denise's wedding at the end of December she would have made a decision about what to do. But first she had to get through her first Christmas alone and she was dreading it.

CHAPTER FORTY-NINE

'OK, where do you want me to put it?' Richard panted, dragging the Christmas tree into her living room. A trail of pine needles led all the way out of the living-room door, down the hall, out the front door and into her car. Holly sighed. She would have to vacuum the house again today to get rid of the mess and she stared at the tree with disgust. They smelled so fresh but, damn, were they messy.

'Holly!' Richard repeated, and she jumped from her thoughts to face him.

She giggled. 'You look like a talking tree, Richard.' All she could see were his little brown shoes sticking out from underneath the tree.

'Holly,' he grunted, losing his balance slightly under the weight.

'Oh, sorry,' she said, suddenly realising that he was about to fall over. 'Just by the window.'

She bit her lip and winced as he sent lamps, photo frames and candles from the fireplace crashing around him while he made his way over to the window.

'There now,' he said, wiping his hands and stepping back to take a look at his work.

Holly frowned. 'It looks a little bit bare, don't you think?'

'Well, you will have to decorate it, of course.'

'I know that, Richard, but I was referring to the fact that it only has about five branches left. It's got bald patches,' she moaned.

'I told you to buy a tree earlier, Holly, not leave it until Christmas Eve. Anyway that was the best of a bad lot; I sold the best ones weeks ago.'

'I suppose,' Holly frowned.

She hadn't wanted to get a Christmas tree at all this year. She wasn't in the mood to celebrate and it wasn't as if she had any children in the house to please by putting up decorations. Richard had insisted, though, and Holly felt that she had to help him out with his new Christmas tree selling venture in addition to his flourishing landscaping business. But the tree was awful and no amount of tinsel could hide that. Looking at it made her wish she had just bought one from Richard earlier. At least then maybe it would have looked like a real tree instead of a pole with a few pine needles hanging off.

She couldn't believe it was Christmas Eve already. She had spent the past few weeks working overtime, trying to get the January issue of the magazine ready early before they all took their Christmas break. They had eventually finished the day before, and when Alice had suggested they all go for Christmas drinks at Hogan's, Holly had politely declined. She still hadn't spoken to Daniel; she had ignored all of his calls, had avoided Hogan's like the plague, and had ordered Alice to tell

462

him she was in a meeting if ever he called the office. He called the office nearly every day.

She didn't intend to be rude but she needed more time to think things through. OK, so it wasn't as if he had just proposed to her but it almost felt like it.

Richard's voice snapped her back to reality.

'Sorry, what?'

'I said would you like me to help you decorate it?'

Holly's heart fell. That was her and Gerry's job, nobody else's. Every year without fail they would put the Christmas CD on, open a bottle of wine and decorate the tree . . .

'Eh . . . no, it's OK Richard, I'll do it. I'm sure you've better things to be doing now.'

'Well, actually I would quite like to do it,' he said eagerly. 'Usually myself, Meredith and the children do it together but I missed out on that this year . . .' he trailed off.

'Oh.' Holly hadn't even thought about Richard's Christmas as being difficult as well; she was too selfishly caught up in her own worries.

'OK, then, why not?' she smiled.

Richard beamed and he looked like a child.

'But the only thing is, I'm not too sure where the decorations are. Gerry always used to store them away in the attic somewhere . . .' she murmured.

'No problem,' he smiled encouragingly. 'That used to be my job too. I'll find them.' He bounded up the stairs to the attic.

Holly opened a bottle of red wine and pressed play on the CD player. Bing Crosby's 'White Christmas' played softly in the background. Richard returned with a black sack slung over his shoulder and a dusty Santa hat on. 'Ho ho ho!'

Holly giggled and handed him his glass of wine.

'No no,' he waved his hand, 'I'm driving.'

'You can have one glass, Richard,' she said, feeling disappointed.

'No no,' he repeated, 'I don't drink and drive.'

Holly threw her eyes up to heaven and knocked back his glass of wine before beginning her own. By the time Richard left she had finished the bottle and was opening another. She noticed then the red light flashing on the answering machine. She had switched it on for some peace and quiet that day, and was hoping the message wasn't from who she thought it was. She hit the play button.

'Hi, Sharon, it's Daniel Connolly here. Sorry to bother you but I had your phone number from when you called the club months ago about entering Holly into the karaoke. Em . . . well, I was really just hoping you could pass on a message for me. Denise has been so busy with the wedding arrangements that I knew I couldn't rely on her to remember . . .' He laughed slightly and cleared his throat. 'Anyway, I was wondering if you could just tell Holly that I'm going down to my family in Galway for Christmas. I'm heading down there tomorrow. I haven't been able to get through to her on her mobile, I know she's on holiday from work now, and I don't have her home number . . . so if you . . .'

He got cut off and Holly waited for the next message to be played.

'Eh, sorry, Sharon, it's me again. Eh . . . Daniel, that is. I just got cut off there. Yeah, so anyway, if you could just tell Holly that I'll be in Galway for the next few days and that I'll have my mobile with me if she wants to reach me. I know she has some things to think about so . . .' he paused. 'Anyway, I'd better go before I get cut off again. I'll see you all at the wedding next week. OK thanks . . . bye.'

The next message was from Denise, telling her that Daniel was looking for her, the fourth message was from her brother Declan, also telling her that Daniel was looking for her and the fifth message was from an old school friend whom Holly hadn't seen in years, telling her that she bumped into a friend of hers called Daniel in a pub the previous night, oh yeah, and Daniel was looking for Holly and he wanted her to call him back. The sixth message was from Daniel again.

'Hi, Holly, it's Daniel here. Your brother Declan gave me your number. I can't believe we've been friends so long and you never gave me your home number, yet I have the sneaking suspicion I've had it all along without realising . . .' There was a silence as he exhaled. 'Anyway, I really need to talk to you, Holly. I think it should be in person, and it should be before we see each other at the wedding. Please, Holly, please take my calls. I don't know how else to get to you.' Silence, another deep breath and exhalation. 'OK, well, that's all. Bye.'

Holly pressed play again, lost in thought.

She sat in the living room staring at the tree and listening to Christmas songs. She cried. Cried for her Gerry and for her baldy Christmas tree.

CHAPTER FIFTY

'Happy Christmas, love!' Frank opened the door to a shivering Holly standing on the doorstep.

'Happy Christmas, Dad,' she smiled, and gave him a big bear hug. She inhaled as she walked round the house. The beautiful smell of pine mixed with wine and Christmas dinner cooking in the kitchen filled her nostrils, and she was hit with a pang of loneliness. Christmas reminded her of Gerry. Gerry was Christmas. It was their special time together where they would hide from the stresses of work and just relax in between entertaining their friends and family and enjoy their time alone. She missed him so much it gave her a sick feeling in the pit of her stomach.

She had visited the graveyard that morning to wish him a happy Christmas. It was the first time she had been there since the funeral; she had avoided visiting the grave since then as she found it too painful. It had been an upsetting morning. No parcel under the tree for her, no breakfast in bed, no noise, no nothing. Gerry had wanted to be cremated, which meant that she had to stand in front of a wall that had his name engraved on it. And she really did feel that she was talking to a wall. However, she had told him about her year and what her plans were for the day, had told him Sharon and John were expecting a baby boy and they were planning on calling him Gerry. She told him that she was to be his godmother; that she was to be maid of honour at Denise's wedding. She explained what Tom was like because Gerry had never met him, and she talked about her new job. She didn't mention Daniel. She had felt peculiar standing there talking to herself. She wanted to get some deep spiritual feeling that he was there with her and listening to her voice, but she really just felt like she was talking to a drab grey wall.

Her situation was no extraordinary sight on Christmas day. The graveyard had been packed with visitors, families bringing their aged mothers and fathers to visit their departed spouses, young women like Holly wandering alone, young men . . . She had watched as a young mother broke down over a gravestone while her two startled children watched, not knowing what to do. The younger child could only have been three years old. The woman had quickly dried her eyes to protect her children. Holly was thankful that she could afford to be selfish and only have to worry about herself. How on earth that woman could find the strength to carry on through the day with two infants to worry about had cropped up in Holly's head regularly since then.

All in all it hadn't been a good day.

'Oh, happy Christmas, dear!' Elizabeth announced, walking out of the kitchen with her arms held open to embrace her child. Holly started to cry. She felt like the young child at the graveyard. She still needed her mammy too. Elizabeth's face was flushed from the heat of the kitchen, and the warmth of her body warmed Holly's heart.

'I'm sorry,' she wiped her face, 'I didn't want to do that.'

'Hush,' Elizabeth said soothingly, hugging her even tighter. She didn't even need to say anything more; her just being there was enough.

Holly had called round to visit her mother the previous week in a panic about what to do about the Daniel situation. Elizabeth, not usually the baking kind of mother, was in the middle of making the Christmas cake for the following week. Her face was powdered with patches of flour, the sleeves of her sweater rolled up to her elbows, bits of flour gathered in her hair. The kitchen counter was covered in stray raisins, sultanas and cherries. Flour, pastry, baking trays and tin foil cluttered the surfaces. The kitchen was decorated in colourful glittery decorations and that wonderful festive smell filled the air.

The moment Elizabeth had laid eyes on her daughter, Holly knew that she could sense there was something wrong. They had sat at the kitchen table that was overflowing with red and green Christmas serviettes with picture prints of Santa, reindeers and Christmas trees. There were boxes and boxes of Christmas crackers for the family to get competitive over, chocolate biscuits, beer and wine, the whole lot . . . Holly's parents had stocked up well for the Kennedy family.

'What's on your mind, love?' Holly's mother had asked, pushing a plate of chocolate biscuits towards her.

Holly's stomach had rumbled but she couldn't stomach

468

any food. Once again she had lost her appetite. She had taken a deep breath and explained to her mother what had happened between her and Daniel and the decision she was faced with. Her mother had listened patiently.

'So how do you feel about him?' Elizabeth had asked, studying her daughter's face.

Holly had shrugged helplessly. 'I like him, Mum, I really do, but . . .' She had shrugged again and trailed off.

'Is it because you don't feel ready just yet for another relationship?' her mother had asked gently.

Holly had rubbed her forehead roughly. 'Oh, I don't know, Mum. I don't feel like I know anything any more.' She had thought for a while. 'Daniel is a brilliant friend. He is always there for me, always makes me laugh; he makes me feel good about myself . . .' She had picked up a biscuit and began to pick away at the crumbs. 'But I don't know if I'll *ever* feel ready for another relationship, Mum. Maybe I will, maybe I won't; maybe this is as ready as I'll ever feel. He's not Gerry but I'm not expecting him to be. What I feel now is a different kind of feeling; but a nice one too.' She had paused to think about that feeling. 'I don't know if I'll ever love the same way again, I find it hard to believe that will happen, but it's a nice thought to have that maybe someday I could.' She had smiled sadly at her mother.

'Well, you don't know if you can if you don't try,' Elizabeth had said encouragingly. 'It's important not to rush into things, Holly. I know you know that, but all I want is for you to be happy. You deserve it. Whether being happy is with Daniel, the man on the moon, or alone, I just want you happy.'

'Thanks, Mum,' Holly had smiled weakly and rested her head on her mother's shoulder. 'I just don't know which of those things will do that for me.'

As comforting as her mother had been to her that day, Holly was no closer to making her decision. First she had to get through Christmas Day without Gerry.

The rest of Holly's family – minus Ciara, who was still in Australia – joined them in the living room, and one by one they greeted her with warm hugs and kisses. They gathered around the tree and exchanged gifts, and Holly allowed the tears to flow throughout. She hadn't the energy to hide them; she hadn't the energy to care. But the tears were a strange mixture of happiness and sadness. A peculiar sensation of feeling alone yet loved.

Holly sneaked away from the family so she could have a moment to herself to think, her head was a jumble of thoughts that needed to be sorted and filed. She found herself in her old bedroom, staring out the window into the dark blustery day. The sea was fierce and threatening and Holly shuddered at its power.

'So this is where you were hiding.'

Holly turned to see Jack watching her from the bedroom door. She smiled weakly and turned to face the sea again, uninterested in her brother and his recent lack of support. She listened to the waves and watched the black water swallow the sleet that had begun to fall. She heard Jack sigh loudly and felt his arm round her shoulder.

'Sorry,' he said softly.

Holly raised her eyebrows, unimpressed, and continued to stare ahead.

He nodded to himself slowly. 'You're right to treat me

like this, Holly. I've been acting like a complete idiot lately. And I'm so sorry.'

Holly turned to face him and her eyes glistened. 'You let me down, Jack.'

He closed his eyes slowly as though the very thought of that pained him. 'I know, I'm so sorry,' he said even more softly than before. 'I just didn't handle the whole situation well, Holly. I found it so hard to deal with Gerry . . . you know . . .'

'Dying,' Holly finished for him.

'Yeah.' He clenched and unclenched his jaw and looked as though he had finally accepted it.

'It wasn't exactly easy for me, you know, Jack.' A silence fell between them. 'But you helped me pack away all his things. You went through his belongings with me and made the whole thing so much easier,' Holly said, feeling confused. 'You were there with me for that, why did you just suddenly disappear?'

'God, that was so tough to do.' He shook his head sadly. 'You were so strong, Holly . . . you *are* strong,' he corrected himself. 'Getting rid of his things just tore me up, being in the house and him not being there just . . . *got* to me. And then I noticed you were getting closer to Richard so I just figured it would be OK for me to take a step back because you had him . . .' He blushed at the ridiculousness of finally explaining his feelings.

'You fool, Jack,' Holly said, thumping him playfully in the stomach. 'As if Richard could ever take your place.'

He smiled. 'Oh, I don't know, you two seem very pally-pally these days.'

Holly became serious again. 'Richard has been very supportive over the past year – and, believe me, people

471

haven't failed to surprise me at all during this whole experience,' she added pointedly. 'Give him a chance, Jack.'

He stared out to the sea and nodded slowly, digesting this. 'I'm sorry, Holly.'

Holly wrapped her arms around him and felt the familiar comforting hug of her brother. 'I know. So am I. I'm sorry that all of this had to happen. But I need you, you know.'

'I know,' he said, hugging her even tighter. 'And I'm here for you now. I'm going to stop being so selfish and take care of my little sister.'

'Hey, your little sister is doing just fine on her own, thank you very much,' she said sadly as she watched the sea crash violently against the rocks, its spray kissing the moon.

They sat down for their meal and Holly's mouth watered at the spread of food before her.

'I got an email from Ciara today,' Declan announced.

Everyone oohed and aahed.

'She sent this picture of her.' He passed around the photograph he had printed off.

Holly smiled at the sight of her sister lying on the beach eating barbecued Christmas dinner with Mathew. Her hair was blonde and her skin was tanned, and she and Mathew looked so happy. Holly stared at the picture for a while, feeling proud that her sister had found her place in the world. After travelling around the world searching and searching, she reckoned Ciara had finally found contentment. Holly hoped that would happen to her eventually. She passed the photo on to Jack, and he smiled as he studied it.

'They're saying it might snow today,' Holly announced, taking a second helping of dinner. She had already undone the top button on her trousers, but it was Christmas after all; the time of giving and er . . . eating.

'No, it won't snow,' Richard said, sucking on a bone. 'It's too cold for that.'

Holly frowned. 'Richard, how could it be too cold to snow?'

He licked his fingers and wiped them on his napkin that was tucked into his shirt, and Holly tried not to laugh at his black woolly jumper with a big picture of a Christmas tree emblazoned across the front. 'It needs to get milder before it can snow,' he explained.

'Richard, it's about minus a million in the Antarctic and it snows there. That's hardly mild,' Holly said.

'That's the way it works,' he said matter-of-factly.

'Whatever you say.' Holly rolled her eyes.

'He's right, actually,' Jack added after a while, and everyone stopped chewing to stare at him. That was not a phrase they often heard from Jack. He went on to explain how snow worked and Richard helped him out on the scientific parts. They both smiled at each other and seemed satisfied they were Mr Know-it-alls. Abbey raised her eyebrows at Holly and they shared a look of shock.

'You want some vegetables with your gravy, Dad?' Declan asked seriously, offering him a bowl of broccoli.

Everyone looked at Frank's plate and laughed. Once again it was a sea of gravy.

'Ha-ha,' Frank said, taking the bowl from his son. 'Anyway, we live too close to the sea to get any,' he added.

'To get what? Gravy?' Holly teased, and they all laughed again.

'Snow, silly,' he said, grabbing her nose like he used to do when she was a child.

'Well, I bet you all a million quid that it snows today,' Declan said eagerly, glancing around at his brothers and sister.

'Then you'd better start saving, Declan, because if your brainiac brothers say it ain't so, it ain't so!' Holly joked.

'You better pay up then, boys.' Declan rubbed his hands together greedily, nodding towards the window.

'Oh my God!' Holly exclaimed, excitedly jumping out of her chair. 'It's snowing!'

'So much for that theory, then,' Jack said to Richard, and they both laughed as they watched the white flakes sparkling down from the sky.

Everyone deserted the dinner table and threw on their coats to run outside like excited children. Holly glanced down into the gardens lining the street and spotted the families of every household standing outside staring up into the sky.

Elizabeth wrapped her arms around her daughter and squeezed her tight. 'Well, it looks like Denise will have a white Christmas for her white wedding,' she smiled.

Holly's heart beat wildly at the thought of Denise's wedding. In just a few days she would have to confront Daniel.

As though her mother had been reading her mind she asked Holly quietly so no one else would hear, 'Have you thought about what to say to Daniel yet?'

Holly glanced up at the snowflakes glistening down from the black star-filled sky in the moonlight. The moment felt so magical; there and then she made her final decision.

'Yes I have,' she smiled, and took a deep breath.

'Good.' Elizabeth kissed her on the cheek. 'And remember, God leads you to it and takes you through it.'

Holly smiled at the phrase. 'He'd better because I'm going to need Him a lot over the next while.'

'Sharon, don't carry that case, it's too heavy!' John yelled at his wife, and Sharon dropped the bag angrily.

'John, I am not an invalid. I am *pregnant*!' she shouted back at him.

'I know that, but the doctor said not to lift heavy things!' he said firmly, walking round to her side of the car and grabbing the bag.

'Well, screw the doctor, he's never been bloody pregnant,' Sharon yelled, watching John storm off.

Holly banged down the boot of the car loudly. She had had enough of John and Sharon's tantrums; she had been stuck listening to them bicker all the way down to Wicklow in the car. Now all she wanted to do was to go to the hotel and relax. She was growing quite afraid of Sharon as well. Her voice had risen three octaves in the past two hours and she looked as if she was going to explode. Actually, by the size of her bump, Holly was afraid she really would explode, and she didn't want to be around for that happening.

Holly grabbed her bag and glanced up at the hotel. It was more like a castle. Tom and Denise couldn't have picked a more beautiful place as the venue for their New Year's Eve wedding. The building was covered in dark green ivy, and a huge fountain adorned the front

475

courtyard. Acres and acres of beautifully kept lush green gardens surrounded the hotel. Denise hadn't had her white Christmas wedding after all: the snow had melted minutes after it had arrived. Still, it had been a beautiful moment for Holly to share with her family on Christmas Day, and it had succeeded in lifting her spirits for a short time. Now all she wanted to do was find her room and pamper herself. She wasn't even sure if her bridesmaid dress would still fit her after piling on the pounds over Christmas. It was a fear she wasn't willing to share with Denise, who would probably have a heart attack. Perhaps some minor alterations wouldn't be too difficult . . . She also regretted telling Sharon she was worried about the fit, as Sharon had screamed that she couldn't even fit into the clothes she had worn the day before, never mind a dress she was fitted for months ago.

She dragged her bag behind her over the cobblestones and was suddenly jerked forward and sent flying as someone tripped over her luggage.

'Sorry,' she heard a singsong voice say, and looked back angrily to see who had almost caused her to break her neck. She watched the tall blonde as her hips swung boom, boom, boom, heading towards the hotel. Holly frowned: that walk was familiar. She knew she knew it from somewhere but . . . uh-oh!

Laura.

Oh no, she thought, panicking. Tom and Denise had invited Laura after all! She had to find Daniel quickly so that she could warn him. He would be disgusted to find out his ex had received an invite. And then if the moment was right Holly would finish off that chat with him – if he still wanted to hear from her. After all, it had been almost a month since she had last spoken to him. She crossed her fingers tightly behind her back and rushed towards the reception area.

She was greeted with mayhem.

The place was crowded with angry people and luggage. Denise's voice was instantly recognisable above all the noise.

'Look, I don't *care* if you've made a mistake! *Fix it!* I booked fifty rooms *months* ago for my wedding guests! Did you hear me? *My wedding!* Now I am not sending ten of them to some crappy B&B down the road. Sort it out!'

A very startled-looking receptionist gulped and nodded wildly, trying to explain the situation.

Denise held her hand up in his face. 'I don't want to hear any more excuses! Just get ten more rooms for my guests!'

Holly spotted Tom looking perplexed, and she beat her way through the crowd to him.

'Tom!'

'Hi, Holly,' he said, looking very distracted.

'What room is Daniel in?' she asked quickly.

'Daniel?' He looked confused.

'Yes, Daniel! The best man . . . I mean *your* best man,' she corrected herself.

'Oh, I don't know, Holly,' he said, turning away to grab a member of the hotel staff.

Holly jumped to face him, blocking his view of the staff member. 'Tom, I really need to know!' she panicked.

'Look, Holly, I really don't know. Ask Denise,' he mumbled, and ran off down the corridor, chasing the staff member.

Holly looked at Denise and gulped. Denise seemed like someone possessed, and Holly had no intention of asking her in that mood. She queued in line behind all the other guests, and twenty minutes and a few sneaky moves to skip the queue later, she reached the front.

'Hi, I was wondering if you could tell me what room number Daniel Connolly is in, please?' she asked quickly.

The receptionist shook his head. 'I'm sorry we can't give out guests' room numbers.'

Holly rolled her eyes, 'Look, I'm a friend of his,' she explained, and smiled sweetly.

The man smiled politely and shook his head again, 'I'm sorry, but it's against hotel policy to—'

'Listen!' she yelled, and even Denise, beside her, shut up screaming. 'It's very important that you tell me!'

The man shook his head slowly, apparently too afraid to open his mouth. Finally he said, 'I'm sorry but—'

'Aaaaaggghhh!' Holly screamed with frustration, interrupting him again.

'Holly,' Denise said gently, placing her hand on Holly's arm, 'what's wrong?'

'I need to know what room Daniel is staying in,' she yelled, and Denise looked startled.

'It's room three four two,' she stuttered.

'Thank you!' Holly yelled angrily, not knowing why she was still screaming, and stormed off in the direction of the elevators.

Upstairs, Holly rushed down the corridor, dragging her bag behind her and checking the door numbers. When she reached his room she knocked furiously on the door and as she heard footsteps approaching the door she realised she hadn't even thought about what she was going to say. She took a deep breath as the door was opened.

She stopped breathing.

It was Laura.

'Honey, who is it?' she heard Daniel's voice call, and saw him step out of the bathroom.

'You!' Laura screeched.

CHAPTER FIFTY-ONE

Holly stood outside Daniel's bedroom door and glanced from Laura to Daniel and back again. She gathered from their semi-nakedness that Daniel had already known Laura was coming to the wedding. She also assumed that he hadn't informed Denise and Tom that she was here as they hadn't warned Holly. But even if they had known they wouldn't have considered it important to tell her. Holly hadn't shared what Daniel had told her before Christmas with any of her friends. As Holly stared into the hotel room, she realised this meant that she had absolutely no reason to be standing where she was right then.

Daniel hung on to his tiny towel tightly, glued to the spot, his face a picture of shock. Laura's face was stormy. Holly's jaw had dropped. Nobody spoke for a while. Holly could almost hear everybody's brains ticking. Then eventually someone spoke and Holly wished it hadn't been that particular person.

'What are *you* doing here?' Laura hissed.

Holly's mouth opened and closed like a goldfish's. Daniel's forehead wrinkled in confusion as he stared from one girl to the other. 'Do you two . . .' He stopped as if the idea was totally ridiculous, but then thought about it and decided to ask anyway, 'Do you two know each other?'

Holly gulped.

'Ha!' Laura's face twisted in contempt. 'She is *no* friend of mine! I caught this little bitch kissing my fiancé!' Laura yelled, and then stopped herself as she realised what she had said.

'Your *fiancé*?'

'Sorry . . . ex-fiancé,' Laura mumbled, staring at the floor.

A small smile crept across Holly's face, glad that Laura had dumped herself in it. 'Yeah, Stevie, wasn't it? A good friend of Daniel's, if I remember correctly.'

Daniel's face reddened as he looked at them both. Laura stared back at Daniel, angrily wondering how this woman knew her boyfriend . . . her current boyfriend, that was.

'Daniel's a good friend of mine,' Holly explained, crossing her arms over her chest.

'So have you come to steal him from me too?' Laura said bitterly.

'Oh, please, like you're one to talk,' Holly fired at Laura, and she blushed.

'You kissed Stevie?' Daniel asked Holly, slowly getting the gist of the story. He looked angry.

'No I did *not* kiss Stevie.' Holly rolled her eyes.

'You did too!' Laura yelled childishly.

'Oh, would you ever shut up?' She looked at Laura.

481

'What does it matter to you, anyway? I take it you're back with Daniel, so it looks like everything worked out for you in the end!' Holly then turned to Daniel. 'No, Daniel,' she continued, 'I did not kiss Stevie. We were down in Galway for Denise's hen weekend and Stevie was drunk and tried to kiss me,' she explained calmly.

'Oh, you're such a liar,' Laura said bitterly. 'I saw what happened.'

'And so did Charlie,' Holly continued to face Daniel. 'So ask him if you don't believe me but if you don't believe me I really don't care either,' she added. 'Anyway, I came to have that chat with you but you're obviously busy.' She glanced down at the skimpy towel wrapped around his waist. 'So I'll see you both later at the wedding.' And with that she turned on her heel and marched off down the corridor. She glanced back at Daniel, who was still staring at her from his door, and looked away as she turned the corner. She froze when she realised she had reached a dead end. The elevators were the other way. She kept on walking to the end of the corridor so she wouldn't look completely stupid by going past their door again, then waited at the end of the corridor for a while until she heard the door close. Tiptoeing back up the hall, she rounded the corner, sneaked past Daniel's bedroom door and rushed down to the elevator.

She pressed the button and breathed a sigh of relief, closing her tired eyes. She didn't even feel angry with Daniel; in fact in a really childish way she was glad he had done something to stop them having their little chat. So she had been dumped and not the other way round, like she was expecting. But Daniel can't have been that much in love with Holly if he was able to get over her and go back to Laura so quickly. Ah well, at least she hadn't hurt his feelings . . . but she did think he was a complete fool for taking Laura back . . .

'Are you getting in or what?'

Holly's eyes flew open; she hadn't even heard the elevator doors open. 'Leo!' she smiled, stepping in and hugging him. 'I didn't know you were coming down!'

'I'm doing hair for the queen bee today,' he laughed, referring to Denise.

'Is she that bad?' Holly winced.

'Oh, she was just in a tizzy because Tom saw her on the day of her wedding. She thinks it'll be bad luck.'

'Well, it will only be bad luck if she thinks it's bad luck,' Holly smiled.

'I haven't seen you for ages,' Leo said, glancing at Holly's hair, making it *very* obvious.

'Oh, I know,' Holly moaned, covering her roots with her hand. 'I've been so busy at work this month I just haven't had time.'

Leo raised his eyebrows and looked amused. 'Never did I think I would ever hear you say those words about work. You're a changed woman.'

Holly was thoughtful. 'Yes. Yes, I really think I am.'

'Come on then,' Leo said, stepping out on his floor, 'the wedding isn't for another few hours; I'll tie your hair up so we can cover those awful roots.'

'Oh, are you sure you don't mind?' Holly asked guiltily.

'No, I don't mind at all.' Leo waved his hand dismissively. 'We can't have you ruining Denise's wedding photos with that head on you, can we?'

Holly smiled and dragged her suitcase out of the

elevator after him. That was more like it. For a minute there he was just being too nice.

Denise looked at Holly excitedly at the head table of the hotel's function room as someone rapped a spoon against a glass and the speeches began. Holly fumbled nervously with her hands in her lap, going over and over her speech in her head and not even listening to what the other speakers were saying.

She should have written it down because now she was so nervous she couldn't remember the start of it. Her heart beat wildly as Daniel sat down and everyone applauded. She was next and there was to be no running into the toilets this time. Sharon grabbed her trembling hand and assured her she would be fine. Holly smiled back at her shakily, not feeling at all fine. Denise's father announced that Holly was going to speak and the room turned to face her. All she could see was a sea of faces. She stood up slowly from her chair and glanced over at Daniel, for encouragement. He winked at her. She smiled back at him and her heartbeat slowed. Her friends were all there. She spotted John sitting at a table with his and Gerry's friends. John gave her the thumbs-up and Holly's speech went out the window as a new one formed in her head. She cleared her throat.

'Please forgive me if I get a little emotional while I speak but I am just so happy for Denise today. She is my best friend . . .' She paused and glanced down at Sharon beside her, '. . . well, one of them.'

The room laughed.

'And I am so proud of her today and delighted that she has found love with a wonderful man like Tom.'

Holly smiled as she saw tears fill Denise's eyes. The woman who never cried.

'Finding someone you love and who loves you back is a wonderful, wonderful feeling. But finding a true soul mate is an even *better* feeling. A soul mate is someone who understands you like no other, loves you like no other, will be there for you *for ever,* no matter what. They say that nothing lasts for ever, but I am a firm believer in the fact that for some, love lives on even after they're gone. I know a thing or two about having someone like that and I know that Denise has found a soul mate in Tom. Denise, I'm glad to tell you that a bond like that will never die.' A lump formed in Holly's throat and she took a moment to compose herself before continuing. 'I am both honoured and petrified that Denise asked me to speak today.'

Everyone laughed.

'But I am delighted to have been asked to share this beautiful day with them and here's to them having many more beautiful days like this together.'

Everyone cheered and reached for their glasses.

'However!' Holly raised her voice over the crowd and held her hand up to silence them. The noise died down and once again all eyes were on her.

'However, some guests here today will be aware of the list that a marvellous man thought up,' Holly smiled as John's table, as well as Sharon and Denise, cheered. 'And among one of those rules was to *never ever* wear a spensive white dress.'

Holly giggled as John's table went wild and Denise broke down into hysterics, remembering the fateful night when the new rule was added to the list.

'So on behalf of Gerry,' Holly giggled, 'I will forgive you for breaking that rule only because you look so amazing and I will ask you all to join me in a toast to Tom and Denise and her very, very spensive white dress – and I should know because I was dragged around every bridal shop in Ireland!'

The guests in the room all held up their glasses and repeated, 'To Tom and Denise and her very, very spensive white dress!'

Holly took her seat and Sharon hugged her with tears in her eyes. 'That was perfect, Holly.'

Holly beamed as John's table held their glasses up to her and cheered. And then the party began.

Tears formed in Holly's eyes as she watched Tom and Denise dancing together for the first time as husband and wife, and she remembered that feeling. That feeling of excitement, of hope, of pure happiness and pride, a feeling of not knowing what the future held but being so ready to face it all. And that thought made her happy; she wouldn't cry about it, she would embrace it. She had enjoyed every second of her life with Gerry, but now it was time to move on. Move on to the next chapter of her life, bringing wonderful memories with her, and experiences that would teach her and help mould her future. Sure, it would be difficult; she had learned that nothing was ever easy. But it didn't feel as difficult as it had been a few months ago, and in another few months it would be even less difficult.

She had been given a wonderful gift: life. Sometimes it was cruelly taken away too soon, but it's what you did with it that counted, not how long it lasted.

'Could I have this dance?' A hand appeared before her and she looked up to see Daniel smiling down at her.

'Sure,' she replied happily, and took his hand.

'May I say that you're looking very beautiful tonight?'

'You may,' Holly smiled. She was happy with how she looked. Denise had chosen a beautiful lilac-coloured dress for her with a corset top that hid her Christmas belly, and there was a large slit up the side of the skirt. Leo had done an inspired job with her hair, pinning it up and allowing some curls to tumble down on to her shoulders. She felt beautiful. She felt like Princess Holly, and she giggled to herself at the thought.

'That was a lovely speech you made,' Daniel smiled. 'I realise that what I said to you was selfish of me. You said you weren't ready and I didn't listen,' he apologised.

'That's OK, Daniel; I don't think I'll be ready for a long, long time. But thank you for getting over me so fast.' She raised her eyebrows and nodded over at Laura, who was sitting moodily on her own at the table.

Daniel bit his lip. 'I know it must seem crazy fast to you, but when you didn't return any of my calls, even I got the hint that you weren't ready for a relationship. And when I went home for the holidays and met up with Laura, that old flame just sparked again. You were right, I never got over her. Believe me if I hadn't known with all my heart that you weren't in love with me I never would have brought her to the wedding.'

Holly smiled at Daniel. 'Sorry about not getting back to you, Daniel. I was having a bit of "me" time. But I still think you're a fool.' She shook her head as she watched Laura scowl back at her.

Daniel sighed. 'I know me and her have a lot to discuss over the next while, but, like you said, for some people love just lives on.'

Holly threw her eyes up to heaven. 'Oh, don't start quoting me on that one,' she laughed. 'Ah well, as long as you're happy, I suppose. Although I don't see how you ever will be.' She sighed dramatically and Daniel laughed.

'I am happy, Holly. I guess I just can't live without the drama.' He glanced over at Laura, and his eyes softened. 'I need someone who is passionate about me and, for better or for worse, Laura is passionate. What about you? Are you happy?' He studied Holly's face.

Holly thought about it. 'Tonight I'm happy. I will worry about tomorrow when tomorrow comes. But I'm getting there . . .'

Holly gathered in a huddle with Sharon, John, Denise and Tom, and awaited the countdown.

'Five . . . four . . . three . . . two . . . one! HAPPY NEW YEAR!' Everyone cheered and balloons of all colours of the rainbow fell from the ceiling and bounced around on the heads of the crowd.

Holly hugged her friends, with tears in her eyes.

'Happy new year.' Sharon squeezed her tightly and kissed her on the cheek.

Holly placed her hand over Sharon's bump and held Denise's hand tightly. 'Happy *new* year for all of us!'

EPILOGUE

Holly flicked through the newspapers to see which one contained a photo of Denise and Tom on their wedding day. It wasn't every day that Ireland's top radio DJ and a girl from *Girls and the City* got married. That's what Denise liked to think, anyway.

'Hey!' the grumpy newsagent yelled at her, 'this is not a library. You either buy it or put it down.'

Holly sighed and began to gather every newspaper from the newsstand once again. She had to take two trips to the counter, due to the weight of the papers, and the man didn't even think to help her. Not that she would have wanted his help anyway. Once again a queue had formed behind the till. Holly smiled to herself and took her time. It was his own fault: if he would just let her flick through the papers she wouldn't have to hold him up. She made her way to the top of the queue with the last of the papers and began to add bars of chocolate and packets of sweets to the pile.

'Oh, and can I have a bag too, please?' She batted her eyelashes and smiled sweetly.

The old man stared down at her over the rim of his glasses as though she was a naughty schoolgirl. 'Mark!' he yelled angrily.

The spotty teenager appeared from the shopping aisles with a pricing gun in his hand.

'Open the other till, son,' he was ordered, and Mark dragged his body over to the till.

Half the queue behind Holly moved over to the other side.

'Thank you,' Holly smiled and made her way towards the door. Just as she was about to pull the door open it was pushed from the other side, causing her purchases to spill out all over the floor once again.

'I'm so sorry,' the man said, bending down to help her.

'Oh, it's OK,' Holly replied politely, not wanting to turn round to see the smug look on the old man's face that was burning into her back.

'Ah, it's you! The chocoholic!' the voice said, and Holly looked up startled.

It was the friendly customer with the unusual green eyes, who had helped her before. 'We meet again.'

'Holly, isn't it?' he smiled, handing her, the king-size chocolate bars.

'That's right. Rob, isn't it?' she smiled.

'You've a good memory,' he laughed.

'As do you.' She piled everything back into her bag, lost in thought, and got back onto her feet.

'Well, I'm sure I'll bump into you again soon,' Rob smiled, and made his way over to the queue.

Holly stared after him, still in a daze. Finally she

walked over to him. 'Rob, is there any chance you would like to go for that coffee today? If you can't, that's fine . . .' She bit her lip.

He smiled and glanced down nervously at the ring on her finger.

'Oh, don't worry about that,' she held her hand out, 'it only represents a life-time of happy memories these days.'

He nodded his head understandingly. 'Well, in that case I would love to.'

They crossed the road and headed over to The Greasy Spoon. 'By the way, I'm sorry for running off on you the last time,' he apologised, looking into her eyes.

'Don't worry; I usually escape out the toilet window after the first drink.' Holly teased.

He laughed.

Holly smiled to herself as she sat at the table waiting for him to bring back the drinks. He seemed nice. She relaxed back in her chair and gazed out of the window to the cold January day that caused the trees to dance wildly in the wind. She thought about what she had learned, who she once was and who she had now become. She was a woman who had been given advice from a man she loved, who had taken it and tried her hardest to help heal herself. She now had a job that she loved and felt confident within herself to reach for what she wanted.

She was a woman who made mistakes, who sometimes cried on a Monday morning or at night alone in bed. She was a woman who often became bored with her life and found it hard to get up for work in the morning. She was a woman who more often than not had a bad hair day, who looked in the mirror and wondered why she couldn't just drag herself to the gym more often; she was a woman who sometimes questioned what reason had she to live on this planet. She was a woman who sometimes just got things wrong.

On the other hand, she was a woman with a million happy memories, who knew what it was like to experience true love and who was ready to experience more life, more love and make new memories. Whether it happened in ten months or ten years, Holly would obey Gerry's final message. Whatever lay ahead, she knew she would open her heart and follow where it led her.

In the meantime, she would just live.

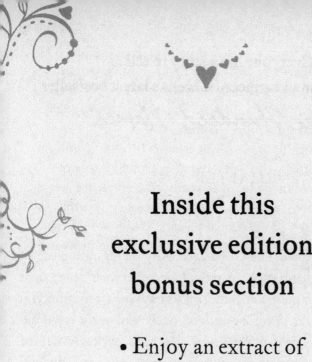

Inside this exclusive edition bonus section

- Enjoy an extract of *One Hundred Names*

- Find out more about the rest of Cecelia's novels

- Stay up to date with news on the latest releases

Everyone has a story to tell....

Read on for an extract of Cecelia's latest bestseller

One Hundred Names

CHAPTER ONE

She was nicknamed The Graveyard. Any secret, any piece of confidential information, personal or otherwise, that went in never, ever came back out. You knew you were safe; you knew you would never be judged or, if you were it would be silently, so you'd never know. She was perfectly named with a birth name that meant consistency and fortitude, and she was appropriately nicknamed; she was solid, permanent and steady, stoic but oddly comforting. Which is why visiting her in this place was all the more agonising. And it *was* agonising, not just mentally challenging; Kitty felt a physical pain in her chest, more specifically in her heart, that began with the thought of having to go, grew with the reality of actually being there, and then worsened with the knowledge that it wasn't a dream, it wasn't a false alarm, this was life in its rawest form. A life that had been challenged, and would subsequently be lost, to death.

Kitty made her way through the private hospital, taking the stairs when she could take elevators, making deliberate wrong turns, graciously allowing others to walk before her at every opportunity, particularly if they were patients moving at a snail's pace with walking frames or wheeling intravenous lines on poles. She was aware of the stares, which were a result of the current crisis she was in, and the fact she had at times walked in circles around the ward. She was attentive to any bit of conversation that any random person wished to have with her, anything and everything that she could do to postpone arriving at Constance's room. Eventually her delaying tactics could continue no longer as she reached a dead end: a semicircle with four doors. Three doors were open, the occupants of the rooms and their visitors visible from where Kitty stood, though she didn't need to look inside. Without even seeing the numbers, she knew which room contained her friend and mentor. She was grateful to the closed door for the final delay she had been granted.

She knocked lightly, not fully committing to it, wanting to make the effort to visit but truly hoping she wouldn't be heard, so she could walk away, so she could always say she'd tried, so she could rest easily, guilt free. The tiny part of her that still clung to rationality knew that this wasn't realistic, that it wasn't right. Her heart was pounding, her shoes were squeaking on the floor as she moved from foot to foot, and she felt weak from the smell. She hated that hospital smell. A wave of nausea rushed through her and she breathed deeply and prayed for composure, for the supposed benefits of adulthood to finally kick in so she could get through this moment.

While Kitty was in the process of looking at her feet and taking deep breaths, the door opened and she was faced, unprepared, with a nurse and a shockingly deteriorated Constance. She blinked once, twice, and knew on the third time that she ought to be pretending, that it would not help Constance to see her visitor's true reaction to her appearance. So she tried to think of something to say and words failed her.

There was nothing funny, nothing mundane, nothing even nothing, that she could think of to say to the friend she'd known for ten years.

'I've never seen her before in my life,' Constance said, her French accent audible despite her living in Ireland for over thirty years. Surprisingly, her voice was still strong and solid, assured and unwavering, as she had always been. 'Call security and have her removed from the premises immediately.'

The nurse smiled, opened the door wider and then returned to Constance's side.

'I can come back,' Kitty finally said. She turned away but found herself faced with more hospital paraphernalia and so turned again, searching for something normal, something ordinary and everyday that she could focus on that would fool her mind into thinking she wasn't there in a hospital, with that smell, with her terminally ill friend.

'I'm almost finished there. I'll just take your temperature,' the nurse said, placing a thermometer in Constance's ear.

'Come. Sit.' Constance motioned to the chair beside her bed.

Kitty couldn't look her in the eye. She knew it was rude, but her eyes kept moving away as though pulled by magnetic force to things that weren't sick and didn't remind her of people that were sick, so she busied herself with the gifts in her arms.

'I brought you flowers.' She looked around for somewhere to put them.

Constance hated flowers. She always left them to die in their vase whenever anybody attempted to bribe her, apologise to her or simply brighten her office. Despite knowing that, buying them had been a part of Kitty's procrastination, particularly as there had been an enticing queue before her.

'Oh dear,' the nurse said. 'Security should have told you that flowers aren't allowed in the ward.'

'Oh. Well, that's not a problem, I'll get rid of them.' Kitty tried to hide her relief as she stood up to make her escape.

'I'll take them,' the nurse said. 'I'll leave them at reception for you so you can take them home. No point in a beautiful bouquet like that going to waste.'

'At least I brought cupcakes.' Kitty took a box from her bag.

The nurse and Constance looked at one another again.

'You're joking. No cupcakes either?'

'The chef prefers patients to eat food which has come only from his kitchen.'

Kitty handed the contraband to the nurse.

'You can take them home too,' she laughed, studying the thermometer. 'You're fine,' she smiled at Constance. They shared a knowing look before she left, as if those two words meant something entirely different – they must have done – because she wasn't fine. She was eaten away by cancer. Her hair had begun to grow back, but sprouted in uneven patterns around her head, her protruding chest bones were visible above the shapeless hospital gown and she had wires and tubes connected to both arms, which were thin and bruised from injections and tube insertions.

'I'm glad I didn't tell her about the cocaine in my bag,' Kitty said just as the door closed behind the nurse, and they heard her laugh heartily from the corridor. 'I know you hate flowers but I panicked. I was going to bring you gold nail varnish, incense and a mirror, because I thought it would be funny.'

'Why didn't you?' Constance's eyes were still a sparkling

blue and if Kitty could concentrate on just them, so full of life, she could almost forget the emaciated frame. Almost, but not quite.

'Because then I realised it wasn't funny.'

'I would have laughed.'

'I'll bring them next time.'

'It won't be so funny then. I've already heard the joke. My dear . . .' She reached for Kitty and they clasped hands tightly on the bed. Kitty couldn't look at Constance's hands, they were so sore and thin. 'It is so good to see you.'

'I'm sorry I'm late.'

'It took you a while.'

'The traffic . . .' Kitty began and then gave up joking. She was over a month late.

There was a silence and Kitty realised it was a pause for her to explain why she hadn't visited.

'I hate hospitals.'

'I know you do. Noscomephobia,' said Constance.

'What's that?'

'Fear of hospitals.'

'I didn't know there was a word for it.'

'There's a word for everything. I haven't been able to poop for two weeks; they call it anismus.'

'I should do a story on that,' Kitty said, her mind drifting.

'You will not. My rectal inertia is between you, me, Bob and the nice woman I allow to look at my bottom.'

'I meant a piece on phobia of hospitals. That would make a good story.'

'Tell me why.'

'Imagine I found somebody who is really sick and they can't get treatment.'

'So they medicate at home. Big deal.'

'Or what about a woman in labour? She's pacing up and down on the street outside but she just can't bring herself to go through the doors of the hospital.'

'So she has the baby in an ambulance or at home or on the street.' Constance shrugged. 'I once did a story on a woman who gave birth whilst in hiding in Kosovo. She was all by herself and it was her first child. They weren't found until two weeks after, perfectly healthy and happy together. Women in Africa have their babies while working the fields, then they go straight back to work. Tribal women dance their babies out. The Western world goes about childbirth the wrong way around,' she said, waving her hand dismissively in the air, despite having no children herself. 'I wrote an article on that before.'

'A doctor who can't go to work . . .' Kitty continued to push her idea.

'That's ridiculous. He should lose his licence.'

Kitty laughed. 'Thanks for your honesty, as usual.' Then her smile faded and she concentrated on Constance's hand wrapped around hers. 'Or how about a selfish woman whose best friend is sick and she wouldn't visit her?'

'But you're here now and I'm happy to see you.'

Kitty swallowed. 'You haven't mentioned anything about it.'

'About what?'

'You know what.'

'I didn't know if you wanted to talk about it.'

'I don't really.'

'Well, then.'

They sat in silence.

'I'm being torn apart in the newspapers, the radio, everywhere,' Kitty said, bringing it up anyway.

'I haven't seen any papers.'

Kitty ignored the pile of papers on the windowsill. 'Everywhere I go, all week, everyone is looking at me, pointing, whispering as if I'm the scarlet woman.'

'That is the price of being in the limelight. You are a TV star now.'

'I'm not a TV star, I'm an idiot who made a fool of herself on TV. There's a distinct difference.'

Constance shrugged again as if it wasn't a big deal.

'You never wanted me to work on the show in the first place. Why don't you just say "I told you so" and get it over with?'

'They are not words that I use. They do nothing productive.'

Kitty removed her hand from Constance's and asked quietly, 'Do I still have a job?'

'Haven't you spoken to Pete?' She looked angry with her duty editor.

'I have. But I need to hear it from you. It's more important that I hear it from you.'

'*Etcetera*'s stance on hiring you as a reporter has not changed,' Constance said firmly.

'Thank you,' Kitty whispered.

'I supported you doing *Thirty Minutes* because I know that you're a good reporter and you have it in you to be a great reporter. We all make mistakes, some bigger than others, but none of us is perfect. We use these times to become better reporters and, more importantly, better people. When you came to be interviewed by me ten years ago do you remember the story you tried to sell to me?'

Kitty laughed and cringed. 'No,' she lied.

'Of course you do. Well, if you won't say it, I will. I asked you if you were to write a story for me then and there about absolutely anything, what would it be?'

'We really don't have to go through this again. I was there, remember?' Kitty blushed.

'And you said,' Constance continued as though Kitty had never spoken, 'that you had heard of a caterpillar that could not turn into a butterfly . . .'

'Yes, yes, I know.'

'And you would like to examine how it would feel to be denied such a beautiful thing. You would like to know how it feels for the caterpillar to watch other caterpillars transform while all the time knowing he would never have that opportunity. Our interview was on the day of a US presidential election, and on the day a cruise liner sank with four thousand five hundred people aboard. Of the twelve interviewees I saw that day, you were the only person who did not mention anything about politics, about the ship, or about wanting to spend a day with Nelson Mandela, for that matter. What concerned you most was this poor little caterpillar.'

Kitty smiled. 'Yeah, well, I was just out of college. I think I still had too much weed in my system.'

'No,' Constance whispered, reaching out for Kitty's hand again. 'You were the only person who truly told me in that interview that you weren't afraid to fly, that in fact you were afraid that you wouldn't.'

Kitty swallowed hard, close to tears. She certainly hadn't flown yet and was, she felt, further from it than ever.

'Some people say that you shouldn't operate from a place of fear,' Constance went on, 'but if there is no fear, how is there a challenge? Often that is when I've done my best work, because I have embraced the fear and challenged myself. I saw this young girl who was afraid she wouldn't fly and I thought – a-ha – she is the girl for us. And that is what *Etcetera* is about. Sure, we cover politics but we cover the people behind the politics. We want them for their emotional journeys, not just so we can hear their policies but so we can hear the reason for their policies. What happened to make them believe in this, what happened to make them feel this way? Yes, we sometimes talk about diets, but not organic this and wholewheat that, but of *why* and *who*. We are all about people, about feeling, about emotions. We may sell fewer but we mean more, though that is merely my opinion, of course. *Etcetera* will continue to publish your stories, Kitty, as long as you are writing what is true to you and definitely *not* what somebody else is telling you will make a good story. Nobody can pretend to know what people want to read or hear or see. People rarely know it themselves; they only know it after the fact. That is what creating something original is all about. Finding the new, not rehashing the old and feeding a market.' She raised her eyebrows.

'It was my story,' Kitty said quietly. 'I can't blame anyone else.'

'There are more people involved in telling a story than the writer, and you know that. If you had come to me with this story, well, I would not have covered it, but hypothetically, if I had, I would have pulled it before it was too late. There were signs and someone above you should have been able to see them, but if you want to take the entire blame, well then, you ask yourself why you wanted to tell that story so badly.'

Kitty wasn't sure if she was meant to answer then and

there but Constance gathered her energy and continued: 'I once interviewed a man who seemed increasingly amused by my questions. When I asked him what he found so entertaining, he told me that he found the questions an interviewer asked revealed much more about the interviewer than any of his answers revealed about himself. During our interview he learned far more about me than I about him. I found that interesting and he was right, on that occasion at least. I think that the story one covers often reveals more about the person writing it than perhaps the story is revealing itself. Journalism classes teach us that one must extract oneself from the story in order to report without bias, but often we need to be in the story in order to understand, to connect, to help the audience identify or else it has no heart; it could be a robot telling the story, for all anyone cares. And that does not mean injecting *opinion* into the pieces, Kitty, for that bothers me too. I don't like it when reporters use a story to tell us how they feel. Who cares what one person thinks? A nation? A genre? A sex? That interests me more. I mean inject understanding in all aspects of the story, show the audience that there is feeling behind the words.'

Kitty didn't want to have to think about what covering that story said about her – she never wanted to have to think or talk about it again – but that was impossible because her network was being sued and she was a day away from going into a libel court. Her head was pounding, she was tired of thinking about it, tired of analysing what on earth had happened, but she suddenly felt the need to repent, to apologise for everything she had ever done wrong just to feel worthy again.

'I have a confession.'

'I love confessions.'

'You know, when you gave me the job, I was so excited, the first story I wanted to write for you was the caterpillar story.'

'Really?'

'Of course I couldn't interview a caterpillar, but I wanted it to form the basis of a story about people who couldn't fly when they really wanted to, what it meant to be held back, to have your wings clipped.' Kitty looked at her friend fading away in the bed, big eyes staring up at her, and she fought the urge to cry. She was sure Constance understood exactly what she meant. 'I started researching the story . . . I'm sorry . . .' She held her hand to her mouth and tried to compose herself but she couldn't, and the tears fell. 'It turned out I was wrong. The caterpillar I told you about, the Oleander, it turns out it does fly after all. It just turns into a moth.' Kitty felt ridiculous for crying at that point but she couldn't help it. It wasn't the caterpillar's predicament that made her sad but the fact her research then as now had been appalling, something that had got her into serious trouble this time. 'The network have suspended me.'

'They've done you a favour. Wait for it to settle and you can resume telling your stories.'

'I don't know what stories to tell any more. I'm afraid I'll get it wrong again.'

'You won't get it wrong, Kitty. You know, telling a story – or, as I like to say, seeking the truth – is not necessarily to go on a mission all guns blazing in order to reveal a lie. Neither is it to be particularly groundbreaking. It is simply to get to the heart of what is real.'

Kitty nodded and sniffed. 'I'm sorry, this visit wasn't

supposed to be about me. I'm so sorry.' She bent over in her chair and placed her head on the bed, embarrassed that Constance was seeing her like this, embarrassed to be behaving this way when her friend was so sick and had more important things to worry about.

'Shush now,' Constance said soothingly, running her hand gently through Kitty's hair. 'That is an even better ending than I originally wished for. Our poor caterpillar got to fly after all.'

When Kitty lifted her head, Constance suddenly appeared exhausted.

'Are you okay? Should I call a nurse?'

'No . . . no. It comes on suddenly,' she said, her eyelids heavy and fluttering. 'I'll have a short nap and I'll be all right again. I don't want you to go. There is so much for us to talk about. Such as Glen,' she smiled weakly.

Kitty faked a smile in return. 'Yes. You sleep,' she whispered. 'I'll be right here.'

Constance could always read her expressions, could dismantle her lies in seconds. 'I didn't like him much anyway.'

Within seconds Constance's eyes fluttered closed.

Kitty sat on the windowsill in Constance's hospital room, looking down at the people passing below, trying to figure out the route home where the fewest people would see her. A flow of French snapped her out of her trance and she turned to Constance in surprise. Apart from when Constance swore, in all the ten years she had known her, Kitty had never heard her speak French.

'What did you say?'

Constance seemed momentarily confused. She cleared her

throat and gathered herself. 'You look far away.'

'I was thinking.'

'I shall alert the authorities at once.'

'I have a question I've always wanted to ask you.' Kitty moved to the chair beside Constance's bed.

'Oh, yes? Why didn't Bob and I have children?' She sat up in the bed and reached for her water. She sucked the tiniest amount from a straw.

'No, know-it-all. You've killed every plant you've ever owned, I can't imagine what you'd have been like with a child. No, I wanted to ask you, is there any story you wish you'd written but for whatever reason never wrote?'

Constance lit up at the question. 'Oh, that *is* a good question. A story in itself perhaps.' She raised her eyebrows at Kitty. 'A piece where you interview retired writers about the story that got away, ha? What do you think? I should talk to Pete about that. Or perhaps we should contact retired writers and ask them to write the story that they never wrote, especially for the magazine. People like Oisín O'Ceallaigh and Olivia Wallace. Give them their opportunity to tell it. It could be a special edition.'

Kitty laughed. 'Do you ever stop?'

There was a light knock on the door and Constance's husband, Bob, entered. He looked tired but as soon as he laid eyes on Constance, he softened.

'Hello, darling. Ah, hello, Kitty. Nice of you to join us.'

'Traffic,' Kitty said, awkwardly.

'I know the feeling,' he smiled, coming around and kissing her on the head. 'It often slows me down too, but better late than never, eh?' He looked at Constance, her face all twisted up in concentration. 'Are you trying to poo, my love?'

Kitty laughed.

'Kitty asked me what story have I always wanted to write but never have.'

'Ah. You're not supposed to make her think, the doctors said so,' he joked. 'But that's a good question. Let me guess. Is it that time during the oil spillage when you had the exclusive interview with the penguin who saw everything?'

'I did not have an exclusive with the penguin,' Constance laughed, then winced with pain.

Kitty became nervous but Bob, used to it, continued.

'Oh, it was the whale then. The whale who saw everything. Told everyone who so much as inched near him about what he saw.'

'It was the captain of the ship,' she threw at Bob, but lovingly.

'Why didn't you interview him?' Kitty asked, arrested by their love for one another.

'My flight got delayed,' she said, fixing her bedcovers.

'She couldn't find her passport,' Bob outed her. 'You know what the flat is like, the Dead Sea Scrolls could be in there, for all we know. The passports have since found their home in the toaster, lest we forget again. Anyway, so she missed her flight and instead of Constance's great exclusive, the captain spoke to someone else who we shall not name.' He turned to Kitty and whispered, 'Dan Cummings.'

'Oh, you've done it, you've killed me now,' Constance said dramatically, pretending to die.

Kitty covered her face in her hands, feeling it wrong to laugh.

'Ah, finally we are rid of her,' Bob teased gently. 'So what is the answer, my love? I'm intrigued.'

'Do you really not know this?' Kitty asked Bob. He shook his head and they watched Constance thinking, which really was an amusing sight.

'Ah,' she said suddenly, eyes lighting up, 'I've got it. It's rather a recent idea, actually, something I thought of last year before . . . well, it was somewhat of an experiment but it has occupied my mind since I've been here.'

Kitty moved in closer to listen.

Constance enjoyed making Bob and Kitty wait.

'Possibly one of my greatest.'

Kitty groaned impatiently.

'I'll tell you what, the file is at home. In my office. Teresa will let you in if she's not too busy watching Jeremy Kyle. It's filed under N. Titled "Names". You get it for me and bring it back and I'll tell you about it.'

'No!' Kitty laughed. 'You know how impatient I am. Please don't make me wait.'

'If I tell you now, you might never come back.'

'I promise I will.'

Constance smiled. 'Okay, you get the file, and I'll tell you the story.'

'It's a deal.'

They shook on it.

One hundred names
One extraordinary story

Everyone has a story to tell

One Hundred Names
Cecelia Ahern

Kitty's is just about to start...

ebook • audio

Have you read the rest of
Cecelia's bestselling novels?

Find out more about them
on the following pages...

All available in paperback,
ebook and audio.

WHERE RAINBOWS END

Rosie and Alex – best friends or soulmates?

Since childhood, Rosie and Alex have stuck by each other through thick and thin. But they're suddenly separated when Alex and his family move from Dublin to America. Rosie is lost without him. Then, just as she is about to join Alex in Boston, she gets life-changing news – news that will keep her at home in Ireland.

Their magical connection remains but can their friendship survive the years and miles – as well as new relationships? And always at the back of Rosie's mind is whether they were meant to be more than just good friends all along. Misunderstandings, circumstances and sheer bad luck have kept them apart – until now. But will they gamble everything – including their friendship – on true love?

'A heart-warming, completely absorbing tale of love and friendship' *Company*

'A winner' *Glamour*

www.cecelia-ahern.com

IF YOU COULD SEE ME NOW

What if love was right there in front of you
– you just couldn't see it?

Elizabeth Egan is too busy for friends. As a reluctant mother to
her sister Saoirse's young son Luke and with her own business to run,
every precious moment is made to count.

But with Saoirse crashing in and out of their lives, leaving them both
reeling, Luke and Elizabeth are desperately in need of some magic.

Enter Ivan. Wild, spontaneous and always looking for adventure,
Ivan changes Elizabeth in ways she could never have imagined.
With her newly open eyes and heart, Elizabeth sees what
she's been missing all along.

As for Ivan, he thought he was there to help Luke,
not Elizabeth – or himself . . .

'Captivating' *Irish Independent*

'Enchanting and unexpected' *You*

www.cecelia-ahern.com

A PLACE CALLED HERE

Ever since the day her classmate Jenny-May Butler vanished, Sandy Shortt has been haunted by what happens when something – or someone – disappears. Finding has become her goal.

Jack Ruttle is desperate to find his younger brother Donal who vanished into thin air a year ago. So when he spots an ad for Sandy's missing persons agency, he's certain that she will answer his prayers and find his missing brother.

But then Sandy disappears too, stumbling upon a place that is a world away from the one she has only ever known. Now all she wants, more than anything, is to find her way home.

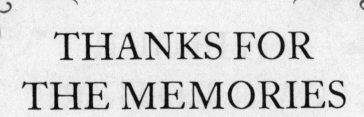

THANKS FOR THE MEMORIES

How can you know someone you've never even met?

Joyce Conway remembers things she shouldn't. She knows about tiny cobbled streets in Paris, which she has never visited. And every night she dreams about an unknown little girl with blonde hair.

Justin Hitchcock is divorced, lonely and restless. He arrives in Dublin to give a lecture on art and meets an attractive doctor, who persuades him to donate blood. It's the first thing to come straight from his heart in a long time.

When Joyce leaves hospital after a terrible accident, with her life and her marriage in pieces, she moves back in with her elderly father. All the while, a strong sense of déjà vu is overwhelming her and she can't figure out why ...

'Cecelia Ahern is queen of the modern fairytale'
Irish Times

'You'll love this sweet and very readable tale'
Heat

www.cecelia-ahern.com

THE GIFT

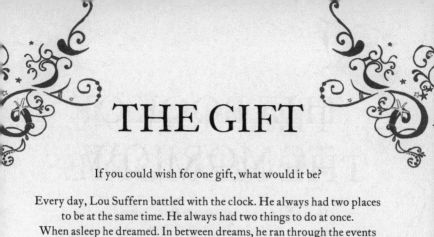

If you could wish for one gift, what would it be?

Every day, Lou Suffern battled with the clock. He always had two places
to be at the same time. He always had two things to do at once.
When asleep he dreamed. In between dreams, he ran through the events
of the day while making plans for the next. When at home with
his wife and family, his mind was always someplace else.

On his way into work one early winter morning, Lou meets Gabe,
a homeless man sitting outside the office building. Intrigued by him,
Lou gets Gabe a job in the post room.

But soon Lou begins to regret helping Gabe. His very presence unsettles
Lou and how does Gabe appear to be in two places at the same time?

As Christmas draws closer, Lou starts to understand the value of time.
He sees what is truly important in life yet at the same time
he learns the harshest lesson of all.

'The key to Ahern's success is her
ability not just to tell a good story, but
sprinkle it with plenty of laughs, tears,
and a little bit of magic'
Mirror

www.cecelia-ahern.com

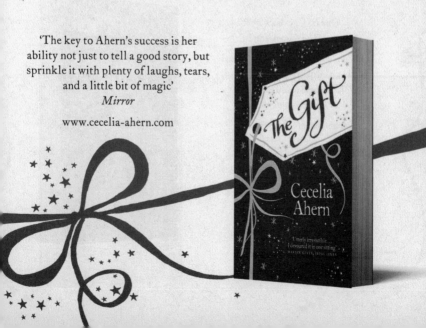

THE BOOK OF TOMORROW

This is a story about how tomorrow can
change what happens today...

Tamara Goodwin has everything she ever wanted and she never has to
think about tomorrow. But suddenly her world is turned upside down
and she has to leave her glamorous city life for a new one in the country.
However, Tamara is soon lonely and longing to return home.

Then a travelling library arrives in the village, bringing with it a
mysterious leather-bound book locked with a gold clasp and padlock.
What Tamara discovers within its pages takes her breath away and
everything starts to change in the most unexpected of ways...

'One of Cecelia's best'
Irish Independent

'Told with a sprinkling of magic,
this is an endearing tale of family,
friendship and secrets'
Woman

www.cecelia-ahern.com

THE TIME
OF MY LIFE

Are you taking your life for granted?

Lucy Silchester is. She's busied herself with other stuff: friends' lives, work issues, her deteriorating car, that kind of thing. But she's stuck in a rut – and deluding everyone. Only Lucy knows the real truth.

Time for a wake-up call – a meeting with life. And life turns out to be a kindly, rather run-down man in an old suit, who is determined to bring about change – and won't let Lucy off the hook.

Sometimes we all need to make time for our life . . .

Keep up to date
with Cecelia!

- BOOKS
- NEWS
- INTERVIEWS
- EVENTS
- PHOTOS
- And much more!

Log on to www.cecelia-ahern.com
for the latest Cecelia news, competitions,
photographs and events.

You'll also find details on all Cecelia's books and short
stories, as well as the film adaptation of *PS, I Love You* and
the hit US comedy *Samantha Who?*, co-created by Cecelia.

And why not join Cecelia on Facebook and sign up for the
exclusive HarperCollins Cecelia Ahern newsletter while
you're there?

  facebook.com/celeliaahernofficial